Empire of Dust

Tempest Rising Book 4

Elliott VanDruff

Belle Rose Press

Books by Elliott VanDruff

TEMPEST RISING SERIES

Beyond the Shroud

The Last Dusk

A Gilded Cage

Empire of Dust

The Tempest Queen

Dedication

To Olivia, our Baba Yaya, and Buttons the cat.

Map of Lyrica

Chapter 1

THE CREAKING OF THE CARRIAGE drifted through the air like a song, lulling me to welcome thoughtlessness. I stared out the window. Surrounding us was a large group of men. Some traveled as protection for Agramon and me. Most were led by Baron Samael, the Butcher of Bruin and Imperial Commander of the Lyrican Army, answering the call of blood and smoke that began to eek its way throughout the empire. I was finally tasked with ending the drought, but the expedition began with a coming war.

"We head south first," Agramon had said, motioning to the map displayed to the Emperor's Council. "First Calla, then we'll spend a month in Solin before moving on to Ardent."

"Why so long in Solin?" Captain Diardo asked. His leg was still bound from the injury he'd sustained escorting the empress's company through the marketplace when I'd first arrived in Somme. He hobbled everywhere with a crutch and an awful temper. Though another guard replaced him as the emperor's protector, Diardo still attended council meetings and often sided with Sam when arguments broke out. "Solin's farmland pales in comparison to those of Calla, Nordow, and

Bruin. Yet you seek to stay in Solin for a full month of the girl's procession? How can you dignify that?"

Agramon's eyes hardened. "There's a bit of business that I wasn't able to sort out while working at the capitol, busy as I was ensuring Rowyn's safe passage to the eastern shore."

He must have meant my kidnapping and imprisonment. Agramon's eyes flicked to me, and I understood perfectly. He needed to be available if I tried to escape. I rolled my eyes. It must be awful to have those pesky victims trying to run off and mucking up everyone's business plans.

"I understand how hard it is to run your allotment when you have so many other obligations to juggle," Sam said, leaning back in his chair. "But the fact remains that the empire needs the lady's rain sooner rather than later. I agree with Diardo; the procession shouldn't be held up for a month on one man's needs alone . . . not when so many are desperate for her." He turned to the emperor. "Agramon can remain in Solin to conduct whatever pressing business he must attend to, and the rest of the procession can carry on. Agramon can meet up with us again, in the Port of Diardo, perhaps, or even Bruin with Elgar the Swift's help."

Agramon's eye twitched. "I bet you would love that, wouldn't you?"

Sam continued without a glance at Agramon. "I don't think it would be beneficial to hold up the drawing of arms either. If I'm to collect men for Lu Shen, we must do it swiftly and without delay."

"Then by all means," Agramon said, sweeping his hand out. "Don't let me keep you from building your precious army. You are free to leave Solin whenever you please, but the girl stays with me."

Sam's eyes flashed. "I will not leave Rowyn to your scheming."

"It is decided then," the emperor said, leaning back in his chair with his hands behind his head. "Everyone will sojourn to Solin for a month's time. Afterward, you all are expected to continue your procession as planned. I don't really care about your route. Just get the procession done with and be back here in time for the quinquennial. I imagine the great army of Lyrica marching in as the start of the celebration, led by our famed sorceress of the age. It will be a brilliant way to begin the parade, don't you think?" The emperor looked around the table for assent. There was a pause, where the other council members glanced at each other, before a number of them nodded in agreement and praised the emperor for his brilliant idea.

That moment was a cruel realization for me. I'd been raised to think that the emperor was outright cruel and unjust. That he worked diligently to keep us downtrodden. But no, the empire was simply run by the most foolish men I'd ever encountered.

Now, Agramon sat across from me in the carriage, his eyes on my markings as I toyed with my gown. He watched me more of late, his gaze dancing from my gems, to my markings, then down, toward my chest, my waist, and back up in a reel. I supposed I gave him something to look at. Something besides the unending sea of dust that choked us as we wound our way across the barren land.

But when he wasn't looking, when his attention was diverted by another, I stared and studied and plotted.

Finally, I was playing a game I knew. I watched every little movement he made.

Each flick of the wrist.

Every twitch of his mouth as he read something that displeased him.

He clutched his staff when he felt threatened. He did it often in my company. Even more in Sam's.

I knew when he commanded others in his mind by the way he tilted his head to the side, as though in conversation.

I'd hunted prey like him before in Espiria. The kind where you had to bide your time. Set all the correct traps. Choose your moment with utter care and precision.

I imagined his death countless times. I'd find a way

to steal his enchanted jewelry that protected him from poisons, blades, and curses. Then I'd stab him in the gut. He would collapse to his knees, reaching toward me, asking for mercy. He would find none.

Or perhaps I could sever a hand. That might work. He would bleed out while I watched.

Poison was another appealing prospect. Some would give a very slow and painful demise. Galena had taught me that before I'd left Solridge.

Except Agramon never took his jewelry off.

Not. Ever.

Since the night of Ena's death, I'd studied his habits. His movements in the day were a practiced waltz. He was awake before dawn, dressed in immaculate robes. The gems adorning his fingers would catch the morning light, taunting me by casting dancing rainbows along the walls. Luc, the boy I'd been betrothed to in another life, now acted as Agramon's bodyguard and puppet. He would be waiting in the receiving room where Luc slept. They would look in on me before disappearing for most of the day and leave behind a guard to keep me caged.

The one respite from my room was the emperor's nightly dinner. Agramon would let me roam the hall, trailing Luc behind me like a dog. I'd watch Agramon as he met with mayors, nobles, and tradesmen. His eyes would crinkle when he genuinely thought something was funny, he would lean in if something intrigued him, and often he would glance at the emperor on his throne.

After dinner, Agramon would sit on the low-lying couch in the receiving room, finishing a glass of the emperor's best wine and scanning the constant stream of letters that came in from around the empire.

When was I coming?

How soon could I bring the rain?

How far could my power reach?

What was my favorite food?

Would gold be a proper gift?

Did I prefer linen sheets or silk?

What was my favorite entertainment? Singing? Dancing?

When Agramon asked, I merely stared at him. My favorite entertainment of late was collecting the heads of those who'd wronged me. It consumed all my thoughts. It was a game that demanded patience.

A shadow swept over the carriage window, and I craned my neck toward the unforgiving eye of Sol. Arden let loose a shrill call before coasting down on a current of wind to land painfully on Luc's arm as he rode next to our carriage. Though he wrapped leather on his forearm to guard against the worst of Arden's talons, they still managed to slice through.

The shadow falcon had followed us from the citadel.

Though Agramon had noticed her presence, he didn't comment on it.

Perhaps he hadn't realized that she roosted outside my window. Perhaps he was ignorant of the fact that she hailed from my homeland.

He might have taken her as a good omen. After all, his sigil from Solin was an eagle, and they were similar birds. Now she was forever riding on Luc's shoulder guard, watching the procession with interest and preening next to his ear.

Luc. The poison of his betrayal leaked into my memories, turning them bitter. How he scoffed at my youth when I tried to follow him and Ferris on guard duty. How Father would turn to Luc to discuss the strategy of a raid and turn his back on me. I saw my old life in Espiria with new eyes. It was as though the shroud of youth was lifted, and I saw things as they truly had been.

Luc had never loved me. He'd loved my father. He'd loved my cousin, Ferris, and loved being fated to take the mantle of chief when Father was ready to give it up. But he'd not really loved me. From the beginning, it was he who revealed me to the Lyricans. He had sold me to the empire we fought against to save his own skin. There was no coming back from that.

Each sentiment he'd murmured seemed practiced now—as though he was saying what was expected of him. A show to get him what he wanted. What he'd always thought he deserved.

Espiria.

It must've been so easy to convince me that he was in love. It was what I'd waited my whole life to hear.

I'd wept and grieved and grown bitter over a figment of my imagination. Still, it was hard to see him following Agramon day in and day out—his dark hair tied up in a knot at the crown of his head, his beard that Agramon had forced him to trim, something that Luc had loudly resisted. But he still had the same mischievous dark eyes. The same markings to show that he was my blood and brethren. No matter what he'd done, he still reminded me of home.

That was another reason I hated seeing him so much.

I stared into the fire, the flames a constant reminder of Destrian. An errant tear coursed down my cheek. At the capitol there was so much to distract me from missing him, but on the road, trapped as I was to Agramon, I seemed to be a prisoner to my own thoughts as well. My mind kept taking me back to the western shore and all I'd left behind.

Across the flames my eyes met Sam's. He was watching me with a furrowed brow, his elbows on his knees, an empty bowl clutched in his hands. Since we'd taken to the road, he kept his tunic sleeves rolled up, his muscles straining the fabric. Flames cast shadows across his features, making him look like a creature belched out of the darkness.

"Eat," Sam ordered.

Agramon glanced down at me and my untouched bowl of stew. "I'll thank you not to give orders to my ward," Agramon said. "There are plenty of fires to enjoy. Why don't you go sit where your presence is desired? With your men. I'm sure they have doubts about this war that you need to quell."

"Are you just going to let her waste away?" Sam asked.

"Mind your business, Butcher. Despite what you might think, the emperor sent you on this exhibition to collect the necessary forces for the campaign against Lu Shen. It was not to play nursemaid, nor constantly badger me about the care of a young woman whom you have no connection to."

Sam's eyes glinted in the firelight as if something occurred to him. "What happened to the girl's nursemaid?"

Luc cleared his throat and shifted behind Agramon.

I set the bowl of stew down and rose. Luc grabbed my arm before I could walk away. I shoved him, hard. "Don't you presume to touch me. I claim no kinship to Morganite traitors."

Luc's eyes narrowed. "Get off your high horse,

Rowyn," he hissed. "I heard about you and the consul's son."

I slapped him as hard as I could. Those words were so near to what his father, Conal, had said to me before leaving me to Agramon, and I had long since not deigned to think of them again.

Luc stepped back, his hands clenched into fists. Agramon rolled his eyes.

"Enough. Rowyn, go get some sleep."

For once I was happy to follow his orders.

Chapter 2

I STARED AT AGRAMON'S TENT, my fists clenched at my sides. Few stirred so late at night, though watchmen lurked at the edges of camp.

Agramon had eluded my power before. He'd used Ena and Luc so I couldn't call lightning. That meant he was afraid of it. Perhaps he didn't know if his little talismans and enchantments could protect him.

It was time for me to find out.

I took a deep breath, feeling the swell and heat of my power. The gems on my hands and between my brow began to glow.

A sharp blade kissed my neck, breaking the skin. I froze.

"Don't," a voice whispered in my ear.

"I'd think you'd rejoice if I managed to deliver us both from this servitude," I said.

Luc stepped in front of me, careful to keep the blade pointed at my throat. I wanted to lean in, to drive the blade deep into my flesh and end my misery once and for all.

The only way out of Agramon's hold was death. Either his or mine. Sometimes I wished for the easiest release.

"He's worked some kind of trigger into my mind," Luc said. "If you try to kill him, I'll have no choice."

"The noble Luc Butler, now playing guard dog to the most evil man in the empire." I wished his father could see him. Perhaps then he wouldn't have judged me so harshly.

"Please," Luc said, his voice breaking. The hand holding the dagger trembled as though he were trying to pull it away. "Don't ask this of me."

His plea threw me off guard. I wanted him to give me every reason to hate him. I wanted to revel in my fury and cast my angry thoughts upon the world. But what was more, I wanted to be righteous in my anger.

I stepped back and drew Iranoct. "I owe you nothing."

"I know you may not think that my life is worth saving," Luc said. "But yours is." He let his blade fall beside him. Lifting his head, he bared his neck. "Make it swift."

I gritted my teeth. My hands trembled around Iranoct's hilt. I could only think of how angry I was with him.

"Why you," I said, almost to myself. "Why did it have to be you?"

"Because he knows what will hurt you most," Luc said. "He knows what we meant to each other."

"You think your death would hurt me?" I scoffed.

"Now?"

Luc dropped to his knees. My blade followed his path and he leaned into it, the point at his flesh. "I didn't have a choice, Rowyn. He plants things in my mind. When I saw you, I was impelled to notify Agramon immediately. I cannot help myself. He had a deal with the owners of the fighting pits. They were to keep me there, alive, until he deemed otherwise. I was meant to die when you came to the eastern shore. I'm sure of it. He had no use for me anymore."

I raised my brows at his unspoken words. He didn't realize what I'd meant to Luc because, in Luc's mind, it would've meant nothing. Destrian's reaction to me leaving probably gave weight to the thought that Luc was no longer dear to me. But then, I'd showed him otherwise, hadn't I? I'd risked everything to set him free. The Lu Shen had just attacked, and the emperor had declared war in retaliation. The court was in an uproar, marching the diplomats back to their ship and sending them on their way. I could've probably escaped that night. There was such chaos that it might've been several hours before anyone noticed me missing.

I could've helped Ena escape.

At the thought of her, I pressed Iranoct's point into Luc's throat, drawing blood as he sucked in a breath. A lazy rivulet drew a path along his neck before disappearing under his black collar.

"If you come at me again, I *will* kill you," I hissed. With one last glance at Agramon's tent, I turned and stepped briskly toward my own, sheathing Iranoct as I went.

In my anger over missing a chance at ending Agramon's hold on me, I ran into something large.

I pulled a knife from my thigh holster and tried to twist away as one hand tangled in my hair and the other gripped the hand holding the knife.

"Rowyn," the body grunted, the grip on my wrist tightening. "Rowyn, it's me."

I froze, recognizing Sam's voice.

"What are you doing out here?" I hissed, trying to elbow my way out of his hold. "Am I not to have a moment's peace?" But Sam refused to release me. Instead, he pried my fingers open until the knife fell to the ground, then he kicked it away. I shoved his chest, but again, Sam refused to release me.

Sam looked down at me, his jaw set. "Where have you been? Why weren't you in your tent?"

"I thought Agramon made it clear that I wasn't your concern," I snapped.

"He's not . . . making you do anything, is he?" Sam growled, his voice low and dangerous.

"Of course he's making me do things. I'm being held here by force!" I said, trying to wrench myself free.

Sam's grip on my hair tightened and he forced me to

look up. I stopped fighting when I noticed his scorching glare. I'd never seen him so angry.

Sam tightened his hold to the point that I felt as though I couldn't breathe. "Is he making you share his bed?"

I nearly choked. "You think I would let that monster touch me? Who do you think I am?"

A muscle in Sam's jaw jumped. "You were meeting the boy then, his other Morganite."

"Why are you here, Sam?" I asked, refusing to dignify his statement with a response.

Sam searched my eyes for the truth. After a moment, his gaze softened along with his grip. I managed to pull away.

"You can't wander around the camp at night," Sam said, studying me in the moonlight. "The seer's words are spreading like poison. She's made people afraid of the empress. Afraid of you."

"Go sleep in your own tent, Sam," I ordered. "The men are gossiping enough as it is."

Sam shook his head. "You place far too much trust in Agramon's abilities to keep you safe. He's not a god, Rowyn, no matter what he thinks."

I stooped to pick up my fallen knife and thrust it back into the holster, feeling Sam watching my movements. "It was I who survived Chassandre's golgeman. I survived those who wished me ill in Helena, and

Ayastaren, and Solridge. By all the gods, I survived the Nightlands. It is all of you who place too much trust in your abilities to keep me shackled."

"I would free you from these chains if I could," Sam said softly. "I would free you and help you get away if it was within my power."

"And why can't you?" I scoffed. "When I lose these shackles, I will bathe in the blood of my enemies."

A flash of pain crossed Sam's face. "I am not your enemy, Rowyn."

"Maybe not yet," I said, standing at the entrance to my tent. "But the road is long."

Though Sam kept insisting on putting himself in my way, I'd be a fool to trust him. I'd trusted Luc and he sold me to the empire. I'd trusted Gillius, and he'd been working under Duke Agramon the entire time. I'd trusted Vianne and she'd wiped my memories. Even Destrian had withheld the fact that I was lost Morganite royalty for a year. My own family had sold me to the empire. The people closest to me had only ever used me to further their own ends.

I'd be a fool to trust anyone.

I strode into my tent where Arden was sleeping on her perch. I pulled off my dress and sat on my pallet to rebraid my hair. Next to me, I felt the presence of an invisible figure, Echo, my shadow of an ancestor who had followed me from the Nightlands.

"Every Morganite I know has betrayed me," I murmured, thinking back to Luc. My voice didn't break. I held no emotion for the others anymore. I was simply matter-of-fact.

"*Not all*," she whispered.

That night, as I dreamed, Echo whisked me back in time, to earlier that day. We'd stopped for our midday meal. I'd spent the time walking around the outskirts of camp, haunted by my thoughts. Agramon and Sam were sitting across from each other, with Luc towering behind them, his eyes on the Butcher of Bruin.

"No," Sam was saying. "You may do as you please and turn the mayor and his family out of their home, but Rowyn will camp with us where we can make sure she is safe."

I wondered about Sam's demand, then remembered we had passed a large town just before we stopped for the night.

Agramon looked up at Luc and smiled. "Quite right you are, Mordog. His thoughts about our dear Rowyn skirt the line of indecency."

Sam's eyebrow twitched as he met Luc's glare. He rose, gripping his sword as he looked down at Agramon. "That wasn't a request. If you wish to remain close to your ward, you will camp outside the town, with us."

"And will she be sharing your tent as well? From

what I heard of your campaign in Yliria, it wouldn't be the first time you forced yourself into a woman's bed."

"Of course not," Sam said, his eyes snapping in fury. "She will sleep in her tent, *alone*." His eyes moved from Agramon to Luc. When neither disputed him, he turned and strode away.

"How can you think that she would give affections to a villain like you?" Luc hissed, following Sam.

Sam stopped. Even though he had to look up to meet Luc's eye, he wasn't cowed by him. Quite the contrary, it seemed he'd perfected the ability to intimidate despite his size. "Everyone's a hero who dies young," he said, his voice gruff. "To survive when so many do not is the ultimate villainy. You will find that in time." He pulled his arm out of Luc's grip. "If you live to see it."

Luc watched Sam disappear behind another row of tents. When Luc turned, Agramon shook his head with a smirk.

A group of soldiers nearby had watched the entire interaction. Echo moved closer to them, hearing the words "Morganite witch" whispered under their breaths, their eyes on Sam's retreating back. They shook their heads, expressions dark.

I recognized the soldier who pitched my tent every evening. He turned to the others. "She's bewitched him, just as the empress bewitched her city scum. I've never seen him behave this way. Not with anyone, and I rode by his side in Yliria."

An older man was leaning against a wagon. "That is the way with women. The girl didn't need witchcraft to ensnare him."

The young soldier scoffed. "And what of Lu Shen? This entire ordeal all started because of her, and now we're off to war again!"

The older man shrugged as though he couldn't help but agree. The young soldier turned back to his comrades and dropped his voice back to a whisper, but Echo had, had enough. She swept through camp until she found Sam standing beside his horse, Hale, absentmindedly stroking his mane and offering a bite of apple. He looked beyond the carriage and horses to where I stood on the edge of camp, my eyes on Arden swooping above us.

"Lord Commander," a voice said. A soldier had appeared next to Sam, his fist over his heart.

"At ease," Sam said, giving the soldier his full attention. "Have you set up the watch schedule?"

The soldier nodded but glanced over at me before clearing his throat.

"What is it?" Sam asked.

"There's a problem with the sorceress. She makes the others uneasy, and what with Agramon so close to her . . . all the posts around camp are filled, but there's no one left to guard her as you requested."

A muscle in Sam's cheek twitched. He turned back, his eyes on me once more. "I'll take care of it."

The soldier bowed. "Yes, Lord Commander," he said as he turned away. Sam's attention went back to me, but Echo was still watching the soldier as he glanced towards me again, his eyes narrowed in enmity.

Chapter 3

I REMEMBERED ARACELI DESCRIBING her city to me at Solridge—how the four main roads spoked out from the great tower of Calla. The single spire rose above the land looking as though it reached the heavens. Swinging from the very top, almost hidden among the clouds, was the great bell.

It began its relentless tolling as soon as the tower came into view. The deep sound rumbled across the countryside, announcing our arrival. Sam rode on one side of the carriage while Luc, with Arden perched on his shoulder, rode on the other, both seemingly annoyed that the count was calling attention to our arrival. The road began to crowd with all manner of spectators: women and children, men from the fields, tradesmen and merchants, and the wealthy all seemed to have flocked to the road to greet us.

"Wave to them," Agramon said, nodding to the window.

I gritted my teeth, willing myself to refuse his order. Thanks to the Girdle of Ephema, a gift from the empress, Agramon couldn't read my mind, nor make me do anything. But he had other ways of forcing my hand, and I wasn't going to needlessly risk another innocent's life again. I'd resolved to choose my battles carefully.

I peeked out the window and saw a little girl on her father's shoulders, calling to the carriage as we passed. I forced a smile, leaned out the window, and waved to her. The girl brightened and waved with both hands, her father laughing as he gripped her legs. The crowd grew louder and I continued waving, feeling like a fool as all manner of people reached toward the carriage, trying to get my attention.

"Now them," Agramon said, motioning to the window on the other side. I took a deep breath and waved until my arm grew tired and my face ached from holding the false smile.

Finally, I pulled myself back into the carriage with a sigh of relief. Agramon studied me. His gem cast a rosy hue in the carriage. He'd done that many times before, and I could feel him testing his reach into my mind.

"Do you remember when we first arrived in Somme? How you called the rain to follow us as we rode to the capitol?" Agramon asked, his eyes back on the crowd.

I nodded.

"Do it again. A wall of water falling behind the carriage as we make our way to the first stop."

"Men are marching behind us," I said, raising my brows. "The soldiers won't appreciate me soaking them to the bone."

Agramon tilted his head to the side. "Do you really think I care what a lowly infantryman thinks?"

"They hate me as it is," I reminded him. "Surely you've seen this in their thoughts."

Agramon sighed deeply. When he fixed his gaze back on me, his muddy eyes were ablaze. "I wasn't asking."

"Fine," I grumbled. I directed my thoughts to my power, calling it up easily. Clouds pooled behind the carriage. The air grew thick with moisture, and the wind whipped the soldiers' banners in the air. The first patter of raindrops fell onto the carriage itself.

I looked up, aware that I'd erred. Agramon was clutching his staff, his eyes on me. "I said behind us," he reminded me.

I gritted my teeth and nodded. Closing my eyes, I concentrated on nudging the clouds back. A shout came from behind us as the rain fell harder.

The people lining the road were impressed. They held their hands to the sky, smiling and dancing in the drops. Children splashed through the mud, and dogs darted between drops, trying to seek cover.

"Very good," Agramon said, looking behind us at the gale that followed the carriage along the road. "An impressive display of control."

I rested my chin in my hands as the people along the road, distracted by the wall of rain clouds, pushed and shoved to get to the water on the other side of the carriage.

A buckskin stallion appeared in the window. Hale. Glancing up, I found Sam's eyes on me before they flicked away. His leather jerkin sparkled with rain. He must've ridden up to be free of the deluge. Something most of his men would've probably wished to do as well.

I sighed.

Let the games begin.

The iron bars of the portcullis were crafted like a series of keys melded together in interlocking pieces. The sigil was present throughout the city: on pennants hanging from the marketplace, painted signs, and the city guards' insignia. Araceli had gifted me a key before I left for the Nightlands as a sign of good luck, and I kept it tied to Iranoct's hilt. I clutched it tight, along with Fin's timepiece and Pedr's chess queen. A gesture that Agramon didn't miss.

We reached the center of the city where the castle of Calla fanned out below the great tower. As soon as the carriage pulled up to the bottom of the steps, Agramon had me call off the rain.

Luc opened the carriage door and offered his hand to Agramon, who used it to steady himself stepping down. Luc then offered his arm to me. I accepted it but ignored the way he squeezed my fingers. Despite what he'd said the night I'd tried to end my tie to Agramon, I still held no quarter with his treachery.

Sam stood nearby, barking orders to his men, most of whom were soaked. I tried to shrug it off. It wasn't the first time I'd wondered if Agramon made others hate me on purpose, but did he actively seek to put my life in danger?

Agramon pulled me with him as he ascended the steps. I kept my gaze trained on the figures of Count Grachan and Countess Violeta at the top of the long marble staircase. Standing next to them was a face I recognized.

I stumbled and Agramon clenched my arm tight. Araceli broke into a smile, her gray eyes bright. She held her hand low so as not to arouse attention and gave me a small wave. She looked like a princess, her chestnut hair woven with gems that matched the jewels sewed into her gown. I smiled at seeing my friend but resisted the urge to rush into her arms. Instead, I followed Agramon and Sam to the count.

"Welcome to Calla, your lordships," Count Grachan said, stepping forward. "The countess has made ready for your stay, taking great effort to honor all of your *requests*." The last word erupted from the count's lips like a spark of fury.

I raised my brows and glanced at Agramon. What requests?

"It is with regret that I accompany Agramon on this journey. I didn't wish to see you again in these circumstances for quite some time," Sam said.

A muscle in the count's jaw jumped. "You know I'll fulfill my debt to the crown, but I intend to make my displeasure known to His Imperial Majesty. This foolish campaign will break the empire."

"I do not come to ease your mind. I come only to claim the men that are due. In Yliria, Calla's forces were some of my best-trained. I hope that has remained the case since they've returned home."

"You know I always keep my men trained and outfitted."

Sam bowed. "I'm grateful to you for it."

The count turned his gaze to me. "We are honored by your visit, Lady Rowyn. My daughter speaks highly of you. If there is anything you need, please do not hesitate to ask."

I curtsied. "Araceli is a great friend to me, your lordship. I am blessed that she is here."

The countess smiled and held her hand out to me. I couldn't help but notice a bracelet dangling from her wrist. I recognized the delicate chain, the clear stones that caught the sunlight. It was a symbol of the empress's favor. I wondered how the Countess of Calla earned it so far from court. It was my understanding that the empress granted the bracelet to those in her inner circle.

The countess caught my curious eye and seemed to instinctively cover the chain with her other hand, as though to hide it from my sight.

I hugged the count's daughter while Agramon stepped behind me, a false smile of fatherly affection on his face. If the count's cool greeting was any indication, he wasn't fooled.

"ARACELI HAS TOLD ME MUCH of your time together at Solridge," the count said at dinner a few hours later, his voice stern. "I wonder why you were not pleased with your studies there that you traveled to the capitol to finish your schooling."

I could feel Agramon tense beside me at the count's question and felt gratified that, for once, I might have the upper hand. "I was called away unexpectedly after I'd gained my gems."

"She said that you struggled in your studies," Count Grachan continued.

Heat pooled in my cheeks, and I looked down at my plate. "Many things did not come as naturally to me as to others."

The count set his knife and fork down and steepled his fingers. "None of what is taught at Solridge comes naturally unless you count the sorcerers' powers. Any meaningful skill is learned and honed through years of study and practice."

"A sentiment that my father shared," I agreed. "But I was not raised to grace the emperor's court."

Count Grachan nodded, mollified by my answer.

Countess Violeta shot her husband a withering look. "Please do not mistake the count's words, lady. We do not mean to be unkind. Araceli spoke at length about how you applied yourself and tried to appease your instructors."

"You forget, Father, how Rowyn spent much of her free time training others in skills that she already excelled in," Araceli said from next to her mother. "I owe her credit for my knowledge of archery and knives."

"An admirable trait," Sam grunted from across the table, his eyes on me.

I expected Duke Agramon to voice his displeasure at such an unladylike declaration from the count's daughter. I glanced at him from the corner of my eye, but he was sitting back in his chair, his eyes darting from the count, to his wife, to his daughter, to Sam. He was measuring and waiting and biding his time.

Count Grachan nodded, studying me as he chewed. He swallowed and motioned for a servant to refill the wine glasses before sitting back and resting his hands over his stomach. "Now to business—"

"Your lordship," Agramon said, leaning forward. "We've been traveling for more than a week, and I imagine that Rowyn and Araceli have much to catch up on." He glanced over at Araceli, whose cheeks flamed.

He was reading her mind.

"Let's say we leave the unpleasant matter of business to the parlor so the ladies can enjoy their own company."

"I must be getting back to my men," Sam said, throwing his linen napkin down onto his plate and rising.

The count and countess rose. Sam took the countess's hand and kissed it. "I trust that Rowyn will be safe within your halls."

I would've thought the count would take offense at the remark, but instead he nodded gravely. "All steps have been taken to ensure that the lady's needs are respected and have been reviewed by my wife to maintain propriety. Rowyn will room next to my daughter, with my guards on watch."

"I requested that Rowyn room beside me. She is my ward, after all," Agramon said, his voice measured.

Everyone turned to look at Agramon, but it was the countess who spoke. "In the halls of Calla, the girl will be under the protection of our guards, who have sworn loyalty to the count. We will not risk any damage to her person, physical or otherwise."

"Very well," Agramon said with a smile. "As always, your hospitality is unmatched."

Sam nodded to the count, then strode out of the hall.

"Ladies," the countess said, motioning us to the door. "That is our cue." She led us after Sam and we split ways.

Araceli looked over her shoulder.

"I've been waiting forever for you to get here," she hissed. "For there is much to say."

Chapter 4

"TELL ME OF SOLRIDGE," I murmured to Araceli. We sat on her four-poster bed, the green silk covers embroidered with flowers. Her windows looked out to the north where she must have watched our procession.

I'd expected Araceli to be in Solridge when I visited Calla. To have her beside me was more than a welcome surprise. Though I couldn't completely trust her against Agramon's prying, she was, at least, a friend.

Arden landed on the windowsill with a squawk.

"Now who's this?" Araceli asked.

"It's a shadow falcon. She appeared in Somme and has stuck with me ever since, for better or worse. I think Imor sent her to watch over me. Ena named her Arden."

Araceli's nostrils flared as she sank down next to me. "Where is Ena? Did she stay at the capitol?"

The tears came instantly. For the first time in a while, I lost control of my resolve and felt everything melt from my eyes. I drew my knees up and wept anew. A hand rested on my shoulder.

Through gasps and hiccups and wiping my incessantly runny nose, I told Araceli everything. From seeing Luc in the fighting pits, to trying to rescue him, to Ena's complaints about Agramon invading her thoughts, and finally to that fateful night that Agramon made me choose.

The only thing I left out was Mellan Lyon's role. I'd developed a friendship with the young man during my time at the capitol, surprised by the fact that I'd murdered one of his brothers and was instrumental in the death of another. Apparently, there was no love lost between the seven sons of Ayastaren.

Agramon was sure to peer into Araceli's mind. Anything I divulged I'd have to understand might be shared unwittingly. I'd thought back over that night over and over, worried that I'd used Mellan's name when I was with Luc. Nobody came after Mellan, though, and he stayed away from me after that. Occasionally, at the emperor's nightly banquets, I would catch Mellan watching me, but I always shook my head and kept my gaze far from his. I couldn't speak to him. Not until I was sure he was in the clear. His friend, Gray, who had helped us try to break Luc free that night, wasn't so lucky. His body was found several days later. A fact that Agramon was gleeful to relay to me, but he didn't know about Mellan . . . not yet.

"At least here you'll have a reprieve from him," Araceli said. "My mother has ensured it. His rooms are all the way up the tower."

I placed my hands on hers. "I'm grateful for it."

Araceli handed me a silk kerchief, and I wiped my sopping face, feeling as though all the emotion from the capitol was finally eking out of me.

"Mother is concerned about you," Araceli confessed. "She says the duke is not someone you should trifle with."

The flesh on the back of my neck prickled. I would have to be careful how much I revealed, lest Agramon use it against me later. "He isn't."

Araceli was watching me closely. She ran her fingers through her hair. "Mother says that the best way to win a man's favor is to listen to them, to show that you understand them. That is all men want from us."

"You think I should seek his favor?" I asked.

Araceli shrugged. "A man's favor can be used for many different things. Once they trust you, any path is open because they feel sure in the path that you will choose. There is freedom in knowing that."

"Agramon is unpredictable though. He knows so many things, it's impossible to know how he will react."

"That's because he doesn't trust you yet," Araceli said.

There had to be another way. I'd tried to use my powers against Agramon, but Luc had foiled that attempt. There was still something else I hadn't tried. What if it was luck? If I could make it appear an accident, Luc wouldn't be triggered. Perhaps his gems wouldn't either. I didn't want to give anything away to Araceli, though, and opted to change the topic.

I looked over to Arden preening herself at the window. "What happened to Fin?" When I was at the capitol, I'd received word from Araceli and Pedr that Fin had disappeared from Solridge, riding away without a backward glance and disappearing into the horizon. Nobody had seen nor heard from her since.

"She left soon after she returned from her quest. I wasn't able to say this in my letter for fear of Duke Agramon reading it, but Lady Vianne and Lord Obi disappeared soon after she did. The other masters at Solridge said they went to look for Fin, but there was a rumor they went to Morgania."

I raised my brows. Lord Obi had appeared to me in Helena when I'd returned from my quest to the Nightlands. It was he who had given me the Girdle of Ephema that protected my mind from Agramon's meddling.

"Have you heard whether or not they returned?"

Araceli nodded. "Lord Obi returned, but Ingrid was certain she saw Lady Vianne near the citadel in Helena."

"Ingrid?" I asked, my heart plummeting as I forgot Lady Vianne entirely. Ingrid had pursued Destrian relentlessly at Solridge. Given that they were together so much, I figured they were betrothed in all but words. Destrian denied that fact, strongly, which was why I allowed myself to get close to him in the Nightlands. "What is Ingrid doing in Morgania?"

"Destrian's sister, Ilisa, is married to Ingrid's brother. Her entire family traveled to Helena to honor the passing of Consul Colman and offer their support."

"What did she say of Destrian? How is he doing?" I hadn't received any word of Destrian since I'd left him on his knees on the road in Morgania, his father's bleeding body next to him. As far as I knew, he'd never tried to contact me, and I'd not had a chance to contact him. I refused to give Agramon fodder to hurt Destrian more than I already had. The only time that I tried to reach out was to warn him about Agramon and the Count of Gryse's plot to unseat him from the consulship. That was foiled when Luc returned to Agramon's hold.

Araceli picked at a thread in her skirt, not meeting my eye. "Apparently, they've been spending a lot of time together. She speaks highly of Helena and mentions that she is prolonging her return to Solridge at Destrian's request. She might stay in Helena indefinitely."

Nerves prickled at my spine. I had no right to Destrian's affections. Not anymore. But it still hurt to hear of me being replaced so quickly, and to so odious a girl as Ingrid Byrne.

"What really happened between you and Destrian in the Nightlands?" Araceli asked slowly.

I couldn't meet her eye. A part of me wondered if she was asking for herself, or for Ingrid. They were cousins after all. How much loyalty did Araceli pay to her mother's side of the family?

When I didn't respond, Araceli tilted her head, trying to get me to face her. She sighed when I avoided her and looked out the window. "He has feelings for you, Rowyn. Everybody at Solridge saw it."

"I know," I croaked, wiping my eyes. "I loved him, too, in the end."

Araceli's brow furrowed. "What happened?"

"Luc, Agramon's new bodyguard, is a kinsman of mine. His father shot the arrow that killed Consul Colman. Then Agramon came to get me, and there was no way for our feelings to continue." I shrugged. "I left him completely broken, Araceli. I ruined his life."

Araceli dipped her head to meet my gaze. "Do you really think it's possible that he does not still love you?"

"Of course it is, and your words from Ingrid seem to confirm it, don't they?"

"But what of the quinquennial? You will see him then, and you will be able to explain everything," Araceli insisted.

I shook my head. Though Araceli was being kind, I

knew it was too late. She hadn't seen the look on his face as I left him. As though his entire world was caving in, and I was the catalyst. "If I hold out hope for Destrian and it turns out he cannot forgive me, it will break me. I wouldn't be able to come back from that."

"But surely he knows why you left. The entire empire knows you were trying to save him."

I shook my head, fiddling with the embroidery on my skirt.

Araceli sighed. "The Butcher of Bruin watched you all throughout our meal."

"He's certainly put himself in my way," I admitted.

"Despite his reputation, he seems to want to protect you," Araceli went on. "Perhaps that's not such a bad thing."

I leveled my gaze at her. "Be serious. You can't possibly suggest I encourage his feelings."

Araceli looked away. "Vianne wrote and asked me to deliver a message to you. I burned the letter as soon as I read it."

I raised my brows. "What did she say?"

"She said to remind you that this journey is an opportunity to gain allies. You don't have to be alone, if you choose not to be."

"What is it you are trying to say?"

Araceli met my glare. "Baron Samael controls the Imperial Army. Maybe getting close to him wouldn't be such a bad thing."

"You can't be serious."

"He listens to you, Rowyn. He hangs on to your every word. That is power. Use it."

"Are you not afraid Duke Agramon will read this from your mind?" I asked. Araceli might have burned the letter that Vianne had sent her, but that wasn't the first place Agramon would look.

"Before you came to Solridge, Lady Vianne had taught all of us about how to avoid the influence of a mind reader. There are a few tricks to keep some secrets hidden from his prying."

"What?" I asked, incredulous. "Why didn't she teach me?"

"It wouldn't have mattered," Araceli said. "Lady Vianne made a point to say that it was impossible to block someone like Agramon out if you had prolonged exposure to them. Eventually they would get inside unless you had a magical block. At some point you would lose track of your thoughts in their presence, and they would know immediately if they kept an ear tuned toward you. She said that for Agramon, it's like hearing someone talk."

I shook my head. "My power keeps me from his grasp," I lied. "Tell me what happened at Solridge."

"There isn't much to tell," Araceli said. "Ingrid is convinced Fin went to prove herself to her father and wants to be taken under his roof since she's able to use his family gift. Lisbet says it's a fool's errand. General Ivar's wife, Delisia, is far too fond of her reputation to allow Fin to claim kinship to them."

"I wonder why I didn't see them at Somme, if she's so fond of courtly airs."

Araceli shrugged. "Like most in the Marendesly line, they stay in Maryse. It's a really popular court, next to Somme and Ardent."

"So, Fin is related to Lord Alexander," I said. In my mind I was tallying up the others who seemed to be related. Tristam the Miraculous, the court healer at Somme, along with the emperor and the empress's friend, Lady Noemi, were Marendeslys, the oldest noble family in Lyrica.

"There are so many cousins, they could fill the arena in Somme. The Marendeslys have spent two centuries marrying sorcerers. There is so much mixed blood that it's almost impossible to guess what talent their children will end up with, if they end up with one at all. Furthermore, they are one of the only families who have seen multiple sorcerer children within a single family. Their blood is steeped in all kinds of magic."

"Even the emperor?" I asked, thinking back to the palace.

"Arthello never had magic, and he was the heir, so . . ." She shrugged.

"I didn't realize Fin and Lord Alexander were related. He never seemed to pay special attention to her."

"Given the other branches of Marendeslys, it's really not surprising. They aren't close to each other."

"I wish we could at least know that she was all right," I admitted, resting my chin on my knees once more. Fin had been my closest friend at Solridge.

"I was thinking about that." Araceli pulled something off her bedside table. She held up a small portrait of Fin. I gasped, recognizing the same work from Sal, the artisan who'd painted my portrait and sent it to the Emperor's Council without me knowing. "I've been asking around Calla if anyone has seen the likes of her. I thought, since you'll be making your way through the Eastern Empire, that you could continue looking for her."

"Araceli," I said, tears pricking at my eyes. I'd failed Fin at the capitol. I'd let myself get distracted by everything else around me, by the empress's commands and the emperor's banquets, and Agramon's demands. I hadn't paid as close attention to her disappearance as I should've. Was it too late for me to make it up to my friend? "This is a wondrous thing you've done."

Araceli patted my hand. "I'm sure she's well enough, Rowyn. Whatever her reasons were for leaving, I'm confident they were good ones."

"And if they weren't?" I sighed, running a finger

over Fin's portrait. "What if she was in trouble? What if something happened in Horan? Could one of the Others have come after her?" I asked, naming the mysterious creatures who dwelled in Horan where Fin had to obtain her gem. They were masters of magic and riddles, and entirely distrustful of human outsiders.

Araceli leaned back against the pillows on her bed, crossing her feet at the ankles. "Then Master Haris would've said something. I assure you that everything was normal when they returned. Fin was excited about her gem, then she met with the masters and after that she disappeared. It could be about her gaining mastery. Isn't that what you are doing now that your quest for your gem is over?"

"I suppose," I said, resting my chin on my knee again. "Though Agramon hasn't even really mentioned mastery. I'm just supposed to follow orders."

"I'm sure she's all right," Araceli said. "Though I want you to find her, in my heart of hearts, I feel as though she is on a path that few could follow."

"I hope you are right." I wanted to trust what Araceli was saying. Fin left on her own terms. Thanks to our time together at Solridge, she knew how to use a bow and dagger, and with her ability to speak to animals, she wouldn't be without friends. By all the gods, she'd had more animal friends at Solridge than human ones. Fin would be able to take care of herself, I hoped.

Still, that didn't mean I couldn't look for her. Just to make sure she was all right and let her know I cared.

Araceli began showing me a set of daggers her father had gotten her over the summer. I admired the engravings and tested the heft, flowering compliments on the blades. Araceli insisted on another dagger lesson, and I welcomed the distraction. Soon Araceli had pulled me from my tormented thoughts, and I began to feel more like the girl I'd been at Solridge. All was not lost. I still had some friends, though I'd have to guard them carefully. Araceli was lucky she was a count's daughter, as Agramon wouldn't be able to use her against me. Despite my misgivings about my journey throughout the empire, I felt safe for the moment, and more like myself than I had in months.

THAT EVENING, A KNOCK SOUNDED at my door. I opened it to Luc.

"You must bring the rain tonight," he said simply.

"All right, I can manage it from my room."

Luc shook his head. "They want you to come."

I sighed and followed him out.

Luc led me up the stairs of the tower as they wound

around and around in a dizzying spiral. I caught glimpses of the city through the windows, the pricks of light getting smaller the higher we walked. "You don't seem pleased with this task," Luc grunted behind me.

"Do you find it pleasant to be under Agramon's thumb, being ordered about and dragged around Lyrica like a new toy?" I snarled.

"Remember that time we helped that caravan of Morganites that were about to be shipped overseas? Remember what you told me then when I asked if the cost would be worth it?"

I scowled, knowing exactly what he was about to say.

Luc noticed and took that as an invitation to go on. "*You* said, if we can save one, the cost is worth it. Whatever happened to that girl?"

"She's been long dead, Luc," I mumbled, turning my attention back to the stairs. But his words needled me. How full of honor I'd been then. How committed to always doing what was right. Of course, that was before the gods seemed determined to beat me into compliance, but still, Luc was right. What happened to the honor I once had?

What happened to the girl I could've become?

"Even then, I knew that you were destined for greater things than me," Luc said, surprising me into looking up.

"What are you talking about?" I asked. "Before your father mentioned that our union could be a gift from the gods, I always felt like I was an annoying little sister to you. It took forever to get you to notice me!"

Luc snorted. "Because the chief's only daughter who controlled the weather with her emotions was so unnoticeable at the time. I was trying to stay away from you, not because you were annoying—which in truth you sometimes were. It was because I knew that you were bound for a greater life beyond Espiria. I knew that, one day, I would fall behind. It was only a matter of time."

"How could you have kept those thoughts from me?" I asked, furrowing my brow. "Why say anything now? Why not then? We were betrothed, Luc. We were almost married! Your father insisted that fate had brought us together, that we were destined!"

"I know," Luc said gruffly. "But how could I have said anything, knowing it was probably too good to be true? I know you wanted me then, but Rowyn, you were fifteen years old! You'd never even imagined a life outside of the shroud. You'd never been anywhere! Done anything! It was like you had no imagination!"

I stopped, angry. "How dare you," I hissed. "I wanted that life behind the shroud. I've wept countless days, grieving what might have been if you'd just stayed home. It was you who left me."

"They would've found you eventually, Rowyn."

"Maybe not," I growled. "Considering they only knew about me through your betrayal!"

I stormed upward, angry that Luc had managed to hurt me once more. He'd never believed in us. Not really.

He'd never thought we would last. Maybe that's why he never tried to come home. Maybe that's why he was so ready to give Agramon the information he needed.

Either way, I realized that my memories of Luc were ghosts of what might've been. I mourned a future that only I had envisioned. Was that why Luc had left? Could that be the reason that he ventured beyond our city after our marriage was announced? Had he been trying to escape from me? If that were the case, then I was ever more the fool.

We finally stopped at an open door that led to a roofed balcony where the count and his family waited for us.

We exchanged no words. I walked to the edge and looked out over the city. I almost felt pity for ruining such a peaceful night. The air had cooled without the relentless sun. The night sky was filled with an abundance of stars.

I felt everyone's eyes on my back. Agramon always insisted my powers be given an audience. I hated being raised up as though I were a trophy, but I reminded myself that the people, not the nobles, had suffered the worst from the droughts. Despite Agramon's under-handed moves for power, I was still doing a good thing. Perhaps he had always counted on me to succumb to that fact. This was the reason I was here. Even though I didn't believe in fate, I couldn't deny that there was suffering before my eyes, and there was something I could do about it.

I gripped the balcony ledge and closed my eyes. A storm roared in the distance. Wind whipped through my skirts and hair. I resolved to braid my hair entirely next time I called the rain, as that would happen often enough on this trip. I was tired of untangling snarls.

When I opened my eyes again, there was a deluge pouring down, masking the view of the city and stars beyond. The smell of rain was thick in the air, and the wind roared around us.

I fed the storm my power to sustain it through the night. The wind calmed, and the rain poured down heavily, the lightning and thunder quieting.

I stepped back and took a deep breath.

"It's amazing how one person could carry the fate of the empire," Count Grachan said, stepping beside me. His eyes shot to me in the darkness. He moved closer. "I admit, I was averse to the friendship between you and my daughter at Solridge. When Violeta got a letter from her sister, it warned of the poor influence you might have over the other girls. Her sister wanted me to join some other noble families from the west in requesting that you be removed from the school and placed in more specialized care." He glanced at Agramon who was talking to Luc. "But Araceli is more cunning than others give her credit for. You carry so much weight with you that you could tip the scales in anyone's favor. The western nobles are fools for not seeing that."

"It is Agramon who holds the strings," I said, looking back at the storm. "I'm merely a puppet."

"Only because you choose to be," Count Grachan said, his gaze following mine. "And when the time comes that you step into your own, remember that Calla is a loyal friend. Unlike other nobility, we do not repay benevolence and friendship with treachery."

I nodded while fighting back tears. I could feel in my bones that Count Grachan was speaking the truth. He reminded me of my father. Like Araceli, he reminded me that I didn't have to do this alone. Not if I chose it.

Chapter 5

"I FIND IT UNBELIEVABLE we are at the eve of war once more, especially with so formidable a foe as Lu Shen," said Count Grachan in the memories Echo played in my dreams. The count ran his hand over his face. "What folly brought about this new development?"

"A mere slight, to be sure," Agramon sighed, slowly turning his staff in his hands as he lounged back in the chair, sipping his goblet of wine. He always fiddled with his staff if he was unsure of someone. I figured the gem affixed to the end gave him an extra store of power, though not nearly so much as the gems on my hands provided me, since they were embedded in my being. He was probably using the power then, trying to read the count's mind. It seemed Araceli's father was not someone he could play so easily. The thought gave me comfort.

"How could the council let this happen?" Count Grachan poured another glass of wine with a glower. "Isn't it all of your job to keep the emperor from making these types of catastrophic mistakes?"

Agramon's eyes flashed. "We are all at the whims of better men, your lordship. You should know this, considering you served on the old Emperor's Council."

Count Grachan huffed. "The old emperor had the countenance to rule."

"There are cooler heads at the capitol, Count," Agramon said with a smile. "Though others prefer to sit aside and feed the emperor's little fancies, many of us take the pains to curb his basest instincts and desires."

"Let us hope he comes to see reason before this disaster takes place. Another war will make dust of us all, either ground under the heel of Lu Shen's army, or by the surge of revolution among the lower classes."

"It will not come to that, Count, I can promise you that," Agramon said, leaning forward in his chair. "The war with Lu Shen will be easily won."

The count raised his brows. "I wonder at your confidence, Your Grace."

Agramon waved his hand. "We have a fair number of spies in Lu Shen. One of my contacts is making good with their emperor to ensure they are complacent. There may not even be need of war in the end."

"Yet the Butcher of Bruin is here asking for me to fulfill my oath and deliver my men."

"You'll have to send your men, but I can ensure that Rowyn is gracing your lands with rain so that you can remain profitable in their, hopefully, short absence. It's quite astonishing when she unleashes all her abilities on the heavens. There is an opportunity here for your people to be satisfied, even with the possibility of a coming war."

The count's eyebrows rose. "What is it you propose?"

"Rowyn will bring enough rain to fill your barrels and replenish the land, but I cannot ask her to do this without the promise of a favor."

His eyes narrowed. Count Grachan seemed to expect Agramon's response. "What is it you want?"

"There is a possibility of a vote coming in the summer to the council of lords. I want your word that you will vote in my favor."

"What will the vote be about?" Count Grachan asked, but Agramon shook his head.

"I can give no more details now, but you will know it when you hear of it. I will need support for an initiative that will keep us all out of endless wars and the tyranny of weaker men. Many others are looking for change in Lyrica, and we must ensure that, for the good of all, those changes take place."

The count was quiet for some time, staring at the fire. There was no way he would agree to it. Everything Araceli had told me about her father pointed to the fact that he was a measured man. It was quite obvious to me, and should be obvious to the Count of Calla, that what Agramon was suggesting stank of treason.

"That is quite a favor you ask of me," said the count,

taking another sip from his glass. "I will require more than just the girl bringing rain. I will require a favor in return."

Agramon's teeth clenched. Clearly that wasn't part of his plan. "Rowyn bringing the rain is a large undertaking and could upend the morale in the empire if she does her job accordingly. What more could you possibly ask for?"

"As I said, another favor, one that is of little consequence to you and wouldn't be too much trouble to see to fruition, especially with so clever a statesman as yourself."

"What is it?"

"As you know, I have no children except for Araceli. She's a smart girl and understands the running and management of Calla far better than I could've hoped for in one so young. I'm loath to go through the process of finding a suitable ruler for these lands through marriage. Considering she is already well-equipped to succeed me when I step down, I want her honored as my successor. I want Calla to pass to her when I'm gone, and no other."

"You are still a young man, Grachan. You shouldn't speak of your own demise so soon."

"When you have children, you find yourself constantly planning for the future, for the inevitable," the count said. "If I can give Calla to my daughter, then it would free Araceli to make her own choice in a husband. She wouldn't choose lightly, but it would give her and her mother peace of mind to know that she will rule here regardless."

"You are far too doting a father. The right to rule has been passed to the male heirs for a thousand years at least. What you claim as a small favor is enough to disrupt the entire empire."

"Araceli has worked her whole life for this. She deserves the honor, and what's more, she would be the best for our people. They love her as they love her mother, and Violeta is quite keen on the idea."

"I'm surprised you are giving in to the whims of your women," Agramon chided. "I thought you to be made of far stronger stuff."

"I will not sway from this," Count Grachan insisted. "I know you seek to bend the other nobles to your will, Agramon. I do not think I fly my own banner in saying that many of the older nobility of the empire defer to each other and move as one, me included. If you wish for my help in swaying others in your mysterious vote, then you will need to fulfill my request. I want Araceli named as heir of Calla."

Agramon glared at the count for a moment, but the count met his eye, stare for stare. Finally, Agramon looked away. "Very well," he said. "I will mention your request to the Emperor's Council. It should be easy enough to bring forth, though I don't know whether or not it will pass."

"Given your influence on the council, you must see that it does. I will not let this vote be swayed by anything other than my conscience unless Araceli is set to succeed me."

I AWOKE EARLY, ECHO'S MEMORIES replaying through my mind. I wished I could write down what I saw in my dreams, but I knew if Agramon saw such a thing, he would lose his mind, and I could lose my head. "He's gaining allies," I said. "He's making deals."

"*He's preparing,*" Echo whispered. "*You know what he covets.*"

"He's gathering a coalition to rise against the emperor," I agreed. "But how will he bring it about? He'd have to get the entire court on his side to unseat him."

"*He has what the rest of the empire wants,*" Echo hissed.

I wished I could look the spirit in the eye. "Me," I said. I didn't even need Echo's response to know that it was true.

I set my teeth. I needed to finish testing the limits of Agramon's protective jewelry. There was still something

I could do to try to defeat him. I resolved to try it that very morning. It was the last thing I could think of. A lifeline that I'd clung to all along the road. It had to work, for I had no other plan.

I WATCHED AGRAMON OUT OF THE corner of my eye as we gathered in front of the castle to inspect the fighting forces of Calla.

The duke frowned at the guard holding his horse's reins. The man was struggling to quiet the fidgety animal. I mounted my horse, Starstruck, a snow-white mare Sam had lent me for the trip, and leaned on the pommel, watching the others. Agramon stepped into the stirrup and mounted, but as soon as his bottom hit the saddle, the horse reared with a cry. Agramon held onto the reins as the horse came back down and twisted its spine, bucking Agramon from the saddle.

I held my breath as Agramon went sailing into the air, but my hopes were dashed when he landed in a large mound of straw. He rose, dusting off his silk robes, with nary a scratch on him.

My heart plummeted as all hope was dashed to the ground. I gritted my teeth to keep from screaming.

"Guards!" Count Grachan shouted. "See to His Grace!"

Agramon stepped away from the straw and grabbed his fallen staff. "No worries, Grachan. I'm unharmed, I assure you."

"I apologize, Your Grace," Count Grachan said, dismounting. "I've trained this horse myself, and he's gentle as a mouse. I've never seen him behave this way."

Luc had also dismounted and was investigating the horse. I froze as he unbuckled the saddle and pulled it off. Next came the saddle blanket. Luc turned it over to investigate.

"There's several burrs here," Luc announced, picking the offending pieces off the woolen blanket. "The poor animal was in pain."

"Burrs?" Count Grachan asked, incredulous. "Where's the stableboy? I'll have his hide for this!"

The blood drained from my face and down to my feet. I should've thought better about my plan. How could I not realize that someone else could be punished for my crime.

"There's no need for that," Agramon said. I belatedly realized his eyes were on me. With the way he glared at me and the sly smile spreading across his face, it was obvious what he meant. He knew. "Though having the boy beaten for a crime he didn't commit would serve as a warning to others, I'd hate to spoil our day with the screams of the innocent. Plus, there are ladies present."

Agramon sort of bowed to me, and the blood came rushing back to my cheeks as quickly as it had left. I'd thought long and hard about what to do with Agramon and his protective jewelry. He couldn't be struck with fists or weapons—I thought that was a golden chain embedded with multicolored stones that I'd caught a glimpse of—he couldn't be poisoned because of the beryl ring on his right finger, and he was immune to magical interference thanks to a quartz earring. I'd hoped that he could be hurt by an accident or misfortune. A tree limb falling on him or getting bucked off a horse. Sadly, I seemed to be mistaken. It couldn't be a coincidence that he landed in the one place on the entire stone drive that could save him from harm.

Agramon couldn't be defeated through death. I'd tried everything I could think of and came too close to another innocent getting harmed in the process. If I didn't stop, someone else would get hurt, and Ena would never have wanted that. The need to avenge her death pulsed through me, but I had to work within my limits. Instead, I would have to take away the one thing he prized most. The tool he was using to gain power. Myself.

Escape was the only way, but I couldn't be stupid about it like the times before. I would have to plan it with careful precision, not allowing for any failure. Looking back on my attempts in the past, when I tried to escape Solridge, then when trying to help Luc get back to Morgania, I was embarrassed about how foolish I'd been. I was working against the likes of Agramon the Divine. He would have always been able to find me. I would need to plan with care. I would need all the help I could get, but finding allies in the venture would prove difficult if they were someone who could not have their mind read by Agramon. I would need to have an infallible plan.

I wracked my brain for options and realized an opportunity was already being presented to me. The quinquennial celebration would bring every noble family, merchant, and tradesman to the capitol of Somme, not to mention the entire Imperial Army. When the celebration ended there would be a mass exodus. It would be easy to slip away among all those people.

Destrian would be at the festival. I would be able to see him again, to apologize, and then I could leave everything and everyone behind to start a new life somewhere else. I'd thought to travel to Horan when I'd first left the shroud over a year ago. If I was unable to find Fin on my journey through the empire, then I was resolved to finish my travels with the Others. They might know where she'd gone. She might've even gone back to join them. There were tales of others doing the same.

The quinquennial was perfect. It would also give me enough time to plan my escape. If I could get Luc away that would be better, though I wouldn't count on it. I didn't feel the same burden of responsibility to Luc as I had before. I didn't want to see him hurt, but he'd also hurt me plenty without a second thought.

In the meantime, I would have to complete my journey. When I'd met the seer, Arda, at the Last Dusk, she'd told me that the only way to be free was to help others. I'd been a burden to my clan and had killed so many I'd been trying to protect in my clumsy attempts at controlling my powers. Though I didn't really believe in fate and portents, I could see now that the gods had been punishing me, and I had to earn penance. Luc was right. I needed to strive to save as many people as I could.

And I would.

I would leave nothing to chance this time.

I would start by helping the empress. Echo could show me all of Agramon's little deals and bargains, and I could relay those to Lesedi the Peerless. She agreed to help me escape, as long as I kept her informed and helped her remain on the throne. I didn't have a choice but to trust that she would keep her word. After all, she'd helped Lady Vianne. It was well within her means to sneak me out of the capitol.

I took a deep breath, already feeling freedom nipping at my fingertips. The quinquennial was months away, and there was much to plan, but I felt as though a weight had been lifted from my shoulders with my new resolve. I would do everything I could to help the people of Lyrica, and then I would escape.

Araceli and I rode behind the others as they inspected the fighting forces of Calla. A field of men swelled before us. They stood in neat rows, with well-oiled uniforms and sharpened steel at their waist.

I glanced at Araceli. "How are you able to keep such a force?" Though Consul Colman had guards to man his cities and castles, he didn't keep a large standing army. Not like what Ayastaren marched on Espiria with, nor like what I was seeing in Calla. When the banners and oaths were called up for Morgania, Consul Colman would empty his prisons and jail cells first, then conscript the rest.

"Because we're a trade city, we collect taxes on many of the goods that travel in and out of our walls. We aren't as rich as Morgania, but we can afford to outfit our men properly."

"You're a credit to your oaths, Count Grachan," Sam was saying in front of us. "I don't see the need for these men to march with us to Bruin for training. Just make sure the host arrives in time for the quinquennial at Somme. We will leave from there."

The count glanced at Agramon before nodding. "It will be done."

WHEN WE ARRIVED AT THE CASTLE later, Agramon and Count Grachan were deep in discussion. I figured Agramon would have plenty of time to punish me for my attempt at murder later. I'd resolved to return to my room to begin planning my escape. Could I slip through with the army when they left the quinquennial? Though Lu Shen was far out of my way, Agramon might not think to look for me among them.

"Rowyn, I would speak with you for a moment," Sam said, grabbing my arm.

Sam led me down the corridor and into another guest room where I recognized his packs discarded unceremoniously on the floor. He began to shut the door, but I stuck my foot out, blocking him from closing it entirely.

"It's like you insist on giving others reason to gossip," I snapped, feeling a swell of anger at his lack of propriety. Echo's dreams were ever-present in my mind. I wondered if Agramon was fueling some of the soldiers' animosity toward me, or if their disdain was due to the fact that I was an outsider, like the empress.

"They talk enough as it is."

Sam grabbed my shoulders, moving me to the back of the door as he slammed it shut.

"I don't give a shit about gossip, and what I wish to speak about doesn't require an audience."

"What do you want?" I asked through clenched teeth.

"Why do you punish me?" Sam asked, leaning closer, his hands pressed against the door, caging me in. "I bear the guilt of a million souls, Rowyn. Why must you lay Ena's fate on my shoulders?"

No, that burden of guilt lay on Agramon and me. But Agramon had been allowed to trap me in his terrible hold by others like the emperor, the Council of Five, and Sam.

"You may not have thrown her from the window, Sam, but you're still complicit. I know of the suspicions everyone has about Agramon. He is using me to gain more power, and yet you and the others on the emperor's precious council have done nothing. He has sought to control every aspect of my life since I left the shroud over a year ago, and the great men of Lyrica have merely bolstered the hold he has until every freedom I've had has been ripped away. How do you expect me to feel toward you, Sam? You, who have allowed him to bully me around, murder my innocent friends, and blackmail me into submission."

"What would you have me do?" Sam growled. "I asked the emperor to allow me to go with Agramon so I can protect you. What more can I do?"

I took a deep breath. "If you really cared about me, then you would help me get away."

Sam's nostril's flared as he studied me. "You know I can't do that."

"Why?" I hissed. "Is it because your precious emperor would be angry with you?"

"That's not the only reason and you know it," Sam whispered.

I glared at Sam, angry at every Lyrican in the capitol who continued to let Agramon hold sway over them. Who continued to let the emperor beggar the people of the kingdom, grinding them under his foot until they were crushed to dust.

"If you aren't going to help me escape, then what use is your protection?"

"I know you feel I've failed you, but what will it take for you to forgive me?" Sam asked.

"If you truly want my forgiveness, I want you to start being honest with me," I insisted. Sam was hiding something. He wanted something from me, something I couldn't quite put my finger on, something that he hadn't shared yet, and I refused to let myself be duped again. "Tell me why you took such an interest in me while I was at Solridge. I don't believe you about the haunted look in my eyes. I want to know the truth about that painting. It's for the same reason as everyone else, isn't it? You're trying to gain control of my powers, aren't you?"

Sam dropped one arm and looked down, his eyes grim. "I fear your reaction if I tell you. Your mind is clouded with grief. Another time, perhaps."

I shoved him away from me, ready to scream. Destrian had said the same thing about that gods-forsaken book, keeping the fact that I was lost royalty to the Morganian throne away from me, using the excuse that it was "for my own good."

"How dare you," I snarled. "How dare you try to lecture me about what I can and cannot handle. I'm so sick of being surrounded by pompous asses, with such a bloated sense of selves that they feel they know me better than I know myself."

Sam gritted his teeth. "Fine." He shook his head as though trying to avoid my eye. "The first hint I had at your existence was a fortune-teller in Yliria."

I raised my brows.

"She'd been captured with some villagers. As I was passing her cage, she caught my attention and requested an audience. Against my better judgment, I had her brought to me for a reading."

"She was sent by Chassandre I bet," I snapped. Sam was a fool.

"No," Sam disagreed, finally meeting my eyes. "This was before Chassandre's prophecy, before the council or Agramon even knew about you."

I quieted as Sam looked down once more.

"The soothsayer said that my redemption would come in the form of a woman, whose rain would wash away the blood and sins of the war. She said that if I take up my sword and shield for you, that I would be free of the ghosts of the past."

I thought my eyes would roll right out of my head. How convenient that amid all the prophecies claiming my soul, Sam heard one bearing him good fortune in my name. "You think we're fated to be together, don't you?" I sneered. Imor save me from ill-fated men. If one more person came courting with words that we were "destined" to be together, I would swear off love altogether.

"I don't take her words as lightly as you do, Rowyn, not with the phantoms who haunt my thoughts."

I scowled. "Did you ever think that it's for the best that the ghosts haunt you? If they didn't, you're liable to repeat the mistakes of the past."

I shoved his arm away and opened the door, striding toward my rooms without a backward glance.

"THIS WASN'T WHAT WE DISCUSSED," Araceli's mother said in my dream, shaking her head at Count Grachan as he sipped from a glass. He watched the sunset out of their window in the tower. "Why couldn't you go to the emperor about Araceli's inheritance?"

"Because, my dear, the emperor doesn't understand the value of favors like Duke Agramon does."

Araceli's mother froze. "What did you promise him, Grachan?"

"Nothing really, just to vote for some initiative of his. He says it won't be for a while."

"But if you went to the emperor about Araceli, he could push for true change. We would help more than our daughter receive an inheritance. It would open the doors for other young girls to stay in the land that is rightfully theirs. Don't you see the importance of—"

"And when do you think the emperor would get to our request, Violeta? In between war meetings about Lu Shen, which is sure to be our downfall? They aren't the scattered tribes of Yliria. Lu Shen is a large power, with a well-trained army and a bevy of their own war mages. This war will be the end of the emperor's reign. Not only that, his obvious foolishness in bringing us to the brink of destruction means the man isn't in his right mind. He would never honor my request."

"The empress could help you, she could—"

"The empress is even more hated than the emperor. She needs to keep her nose out of state business. She's already earned the ire of the seer."

"But—"

"I will brook no more argument from you, Violeta. You've asked me to speak on our daughter's behalf and secure her legacy at Calla. You must let me do this *my* way. Agramon is the surest path to achieving your dream of her inheriting rule here."

Araceli's mother lowered her head and sighed, biting her lip. "Of course, my lord. Thank you for ensuring our daughter's future."

Chapter 6

I T SEEMED TO HAVE BEEN an unspoken rule in Calla that everyone would give Araceli and me space to enjoy each other's company. I felt invigorated with her presence, as though I was returning to my true self, away from the close eye of my guardian. It was also a welcome reprieve from the pomp of the capitol, where I always felt I had to watch over my shoulder.

Araceli used the visit to show me her favorite haunts. We toured the market where she introduced me to hard candy and we watched the puppet farces in the quarter. She showed me some of the secret passageways built into the tower and castle below it, and we frequented the one to the kitchens to steal treats. My favorite times were when we would go riding. Starstruck was a beauty of a mare, snow white with a fiery personality. We rode throughout the land, always accompanied by a contingent of guards. Every evening, I would go to the window in my room and call the rain, blanketing the land in water.

Too soon our week in Calla came to an end, and the dreary road rose before me once more. A knot formed in the pit of my stomach as the distance grew between us and Calla, and it refused to abate on the road to

Solin, Agramon's duchy. An endless day in the carriage, sitting across from the man I hated most in the world, left me time to feel sorry for myself.

I wished I could escape from my own mind. I didn't think there was anything more to grieve from Luc, but it turned out I was wrong. He'd never held out hope for us, so he'd stopped fighting. Even though it might've been for the best, it still hurt. And now that I had time to really think about it, I felt as if all the hope I'd once drawn from those memories were as good as fairy tales.

"I WOULD LIKE TO GO INTO THE CITY—before we move on," I said when we stopped for dinner the first night on the road. I didn't have a plan for when Agramon inevitably refused my request.

"What business would someone like you have in the city?" Agramon frowned.

Sam leaned forward, his hands on his knees, watching me from across the fire.

"My friend Fin went missing at Solridge. She left and never returned. I wanted to search for her here, on the eastern shores."

"General Ivar's daughter?" Agramon asked.

Sam's brows rose. He would've worked with General Ivar himself.

I nodded.

"You realize that it's far more likely for her to be found in the west," Agramon said.

"There was speculation that she made her way east," I insisted. "I know it's a long shot. I know there is little hope I would find anything, but I must do something for her. She was my closest friend at Solridge, and we're already traveling throughout the empire. What extra trouble would it be to let me ask in the towns we pass through?"

Agramon harrumphed. "Extra trouble indeed. Because I don't want to be traipsing through the city conversing with peasants this entire trip."

I glanced at Luc who was feeding Arden a piece of cooked meat. "Couldn't Mordog accompany me?" I asked, using the name that Luc had gained in the fighting pits. I'd been told it was a shortened form of Imor's dog, stemming from the howling wolf's head tattooed across his chest.

Agramon snorted. "And give you a chance to escape? I'm not a fool, Rowyn."

"I'll take her," Sam said, straightening. I met his eyes before looking away.

Agramon's eyes snapped to Sam. "By Sol above, Butcher, it amazes me that you have so much extra time available to you. Do you not have any other responsibilities you must attend to? Training your men? Seeing to their numbers? Sending your precious correspondence alerting the other consuls and nobles as to the exact number of souls they must send to die in the Lu Shen Mountains?"

Sam met Agramon's eye. "I have no trouble sending my correspondence, and I can easily delegate the training and readying of troops to officers. That is what they're for."

Agramon scowled. "Very well. If you must go traipsing off into the city to look for your friend, then go with the Butcher. Let us hope he can keep you from harm."

Sam took me to the city before we left. I held up the little painting to the innkeeper. "Have you seen this girl? She's a sorcerer and will have a gem in her brow now."

The innkeeper glanced down at the image but shook his head. "We don't get any of your ilk in here, my lady." His eyes shot to Sam, standing surly beside me, his hand on his sword. "I cater to common folk and traders mostly."

I nodded, my heart dropping. Sam turned and led us out of the tavern, holding the door for me as we ventured back out into the light.

"Where to next?" Sam asked.

I looked around us, at a loss. Should I ask everyone in town? Surely there was a better way to search. "Where would you go if you were looking for someone?"

Sam shrugged, his eyes on those passing by. "The market would be your best bet. In these small towns, a woman traveling alone would be noticed, especially a sorcerer. It would be the talk of the town for a while."

I nodded and followed Sam to the city's bustling center. We went from stall to stall, but no one had seen hide nor hair of my friend.

I knew it was silly to think I'd make any headway in the first place I looked. The entire trip could prove to be a disappointment. Still, it hurt when no one could identify the girl in the painting. The girl who seemed to have disappeared off the face of the earth.

"Thank you," I said as Sam lifted me onto Starstruck. "I know that despite what Agramon thinks, you are busy. I appreciate you taking the time to help me find my friend."

Sam looked up at me, gripping the horse's reins, his brows furrowed. "If there's something you need, you have only to ask. If it's within my power to grant it, I will."

"I wish you wouldn't say things like that," I admitted. It would be far easier if Sam was the monster everyone painted him to be. It would be simpler if I hated him as I hated Agramon and the others. After all, he was the worst of the Lyricans, wasn't he?

Sam didn't say anything. He just mounted Hale, tsking him forward, and led us back to camp.

He said nothing about the fruitlessness of our endeavors.

When we finally reached the duchy of Solin, I was bone-tired from sleeping on the road, tossing and turning with the nagging fear of being spontaneously knifed by one of Sam's leering soldiers.

I ignored the beauty of Solin as we passed through, merely glancing at the golden temple of Sol that doubled as the empire's largest observatory. The carriage stopped in front of the castle around midday. Agramon stepped out with a flourish, his eyes on the stairs filled with servants and city folk awaiting our arrival. Agramon held out his hand and helped me down.

Everyone on the steps cheered a little too enthusiastically. I looked around, taking in the doorways, windows, ledges, and anything else of note that might come in handy during our month's stay. I would have to keep my wits about me in Solin, where Agramon reigned and there was no one to curb his worst impulses if he overstepped. No one but Sam.

"Where are my men to make camp?" Sam asked, dismounting Hale.

Agramon pointed to a field beyond the castle. "You

will find barracks, a mess hall, and training fields yonder. Everything you will need to keep busy and stay out of my way."

Sam turned and barked orders to the captains who'd ridden behind him. The long line of soldiers moved on, but Sam remained at my side.

"Come," Agramon said, leading me up the steps. An older man was descending them, wearing a black tunic and breeches. He reached his hand out and greeted Agramon with a smile.

"Your Grace," the man said, smiling at Luc and Sam behind us. "I received your instructions, and everything has been readied for your arrival."

Agramon returned his smile. "Excellent, Wilkin. I would like to introduce you to my new student, Rowyn the Morganite, sorceress of the heavens. Rowyn, this is Wilkin, my steward of many years."

I held back the urge to roll my eyes and curtsied. "Pleased to meet you, Wilkin."

"Here we have my new guard, Mordog," Agramon said, motioning to Luc, "as well as the Imperial Commander of the Lyrican Army, Baron Samael of Bruin."

Sam nodded to the man as Wilkin's grin widened. "Commander, I've heard so much about you."

Sam raised his brows, but Wilkin went on without skipping a beat. "We've prepared your rooms to His Grace's wishes. I can take you there now as I'm sure that you're weary from your travels." Wilkin led us up the steps and into the white castle. "Cook has been spending all day preparing a great feast for tomorrow evening, so a smaller dinner will be held in the lower hall tonight. We invited all the important people of Solin for the celebration," Wilkin said, addressing Agramon, who strode next to him while the rest of us followed. "Melbo has requested an audience, and Solston Navar asked to speak to you as soon as you arrived. The mayor also needs you to make judgments on some issues that have risen in your absence. I figured you could deal with them tomorrow."

Wilkin stopped outside a series of doors in a wide marble corridor. "The lady's rooms," Wilkin said with a bow and a flourish.

Agramon grabbed the door handle and led us into a large receiving room, with a couch and two comfortable-looking chairs, as well as a desk and table. Vases of roses were placed on each of the surfaces, gifting the room with a pleasant fragrance. Off the receiving room was a bedchamber with a large bed draped with rose-colored linens and curtains, as well as several cupboards for clothes with a table and looking glass. Next to the bedroom was a bathing chamber, complete with chamber pot and bath.

"I trust this will do for the lady?" Wilkin said, a hint of question in his voice.

Despite my loathing for Agramon, I was pleased with his fulfilled request. "It's lovely. Thank you for your efforts on my behalf, Wilkin. Please thank your staff as well."

Wilkin beamed at the compliment. "His Grace is right next door, so if you need anything, let him know, and I will ensure you receive it."

"And where am I to stay?" Sam asked, his arms crossed.

Agramon raised his brows. "Your room is in the other wing, near the barracks."

"You know that is not what I require," Sam growled.

"As you are a visiting *noble*, I am required to host you in my castle; otherwise I would've put you in the barracks with the other soldiers. As it is, I am *not* required to place your room where you will be underfoot. My patience has run out. Even though

I outrank you, I acquiesced to your little demands at the capitol and on the road here, no matter how troublesome I found them. However, we are now on my lands, in *my* castle, and I am putting an end to your nonsensical little fantasies."

Behind Agramon, Luc stood with a smug look on his face, his eyes sparkling maliciously.

"Are you questioning my honor?" Sam hissed, his voice dangerously low.

"I suppose I would be, if I thought you had any."

A fraught silence descended on our group.

I cleared my throat. "Can this be decided in the hall? I am weary and would like to rest."

"Of course," Wilkin said, stepping out of my room, followed by Agramon and Luc.

Sam pulled me back by my arm. "I will come to check on you, to make sure everything is all right."

I didn't know what to say, so I said nothing. I nodded and pulled my arm free before shutting the door on all of them.

Though Sam kept insisting on putting himself in my way, I knew I'd be a fool to trust him. He would never aid in my escape, not because of the emperor, but because he feared losing me.

Chapter 7

I STAYED AWAKE LONG ENOUGH to help several servants put my belongings away, then collapsed on the bed, falling asleep instantly. I was awoken a few hours later by a knock at the bedchamber door. I stood groggily and found Agramon and Luc waiting in my receiving room, Arden perched on the windowsill, watching both men closely.

"Dinner will be served soon," Agramon said by way of explanation. I supposed, in the end, they were his rooms, and I was now completely at his whims.

"Of course. I can be ready in a moment," I said, intending to rebraid my hair and straighten my clothes.

Agramon followed me into the bedchamber and opened the cupboard doors. He pulled out a rose-colored gown that I'd worn in Somme several weeks ago. "Wear this," he said, draping it over his arm.

I'd learned the hard truth about picking my battles wisely, so I nodded with a sigh. If I were to make my escape at the quinquennial, I would need to bide my time, surviving Agramon's whims. After shutting the bedchamber door, I slipped out of my travel-worn dress, then groaned at the realization that the gown's sleeves sat below my shoulders. I would have to change into a different corset.

After finding the one I needed, I cursed. It tied up the back.

Wearing nothing but my corset, thigh holster, and undershorts, I opened my door and peeked into the receiving room where Luc and Agramon were seated, waiting for me. "I can't get the corset tied correctly on my own," I said crossly. "Please call for a maid."

Luc rose and stepped to the door, but Agramon pushed his staff forward, blocking him. "There's no need for that," Agramon said smoothly, rising from the couch. "I will be happy to assist."

My blood turned to ice. My breath seemed to freeze on my lips.

Luc looked from Agramon to me. "I can assist her if you wish."

Agramon stalked toward me, his staff clunking on the floor with each step. "No need. Guard the door in the hall, like the good dog that you are."

I tried to shut the bedroom door, but Agramon stopped it with his boot. I backed away, clutching the corset to me as though it could protect me.

"This isn't proper," I said firmly.

Agramon kicked the door. It shut with a resounding thud. "Since when have you been concerned about propriety?"

My breath turned shallow. I looked to the window,

realizing that I was several stories up, and there was no way out except through the door Agramon was blocking.

"Turn around," he ordered.

Feeling as though I had no other option, I faced the mirror and watched Agramon study the back of the corset. He draped my braid over my shoulder and began lacing so tightly that it was nearly impossible to breathe.

When he finished tying the knot, his eyes met mine in the reflection. His hand lifted. After hesitating for a moment, he ran his fingers down my shoulder blade, his touch light, leaving a trail of gooseflesh in its wake. My mind unwillingly flashed back to the Nightlands, when I'd lain in Destrian's arms while he traced the shadow falcon tattooed on my back.

"I've had no time to speak to you alone since the capitol," Agramon said, still tracing my tattoos.

I followed his movements in the mirror. His fingers meandered across my skin, over the peaks and valleys where bone softened to muscle. I stood still, fearful that any movement would encourage him to explore further.

"We've been sitting in the same carriage together for days," I said, trying to keep my voice from trembling. "You were free to speak then."

Agramon tutted as he spread his fingers over my shoulders and held them tight, his face resting against mine as he met my gaze in the mirror. "Not with Mordog and the Butcher shadowing us the entire way. If I'd known they would be this much trouble, I would've tried harder to leave them in Somme. Mordog is expendable though. Should I have him killed? Would you count that as punishment for his betrayal?"

"He's not worth the trouble," I said, my gaze sharp. I wanted to hit him, but the blow wouldn't land, and it might provoke him to go further. If I pulled Iranoct, he would surely take away the sword for good. Was that what he was doing? Goading me to act so that he'd have a reason to punish me, to further take away my weapons and freedoms? He expected me to lash out, so instead I stood quiet, docile, and hated every moment in his presence. Agramon was a murderer. Ena's murderer had his hands on me, and there was nothing I could do about it.

Agramon breathed deep. "So you say, but I would give anything to know what you are thinking."

"You've only to ask," I murmured, my hands clenched at my sides. My knives were right there. "What do you want to know?"

I sucked in a breath when Agramon's fingers began running across my breast, following the top of the corset. They lingered, my skin rising to meet his touch. It felt as though lightning was screaming through my being, every hair standing on end, every nerve on alert. He turned toward my ear, his breath caressing me as he whispered, "Has the Butcher ever touched you like this?"

"No," I admitted, paralyzed with fear that he would take that as an invitation. Should I fight? What use would that do? What of my powers?

Agramon smiled into my hair. "He imagines it so much, it's hard to determine what is fantasy and what is memory."

"You're lying," I said, thankful that my voice grew stronger with my conviction. I hated to sound weak when he had so much power over me. "You can't read his mind. He has his sword. It protects him from people like you."

Agramon's fingers dusted over my shoulders. "Ahhh yes, his sword." Agramon chuckled. "It has to make contact with his skin, you know, for it to work." Agramon met my eyes in the mirror, his dancing with mirth. "He sometimes forgets, like all men do, and in those moments I slip in, bearing witness to all of the depraved delusions he has of you."

Agramon's fingers continued their path down my arms. I hoped he would stop there, but he went farther, his hands dropping to my waist. His lips brushed my ear. My stomach churned, and it took every bit of my resolve not to move or draw away.

"I wonder how he would react if I did those things

to you first."

Fear sent my heart racing. I was sure Agramon could hear it. "You said you wouldn't touch me," I reminded him, trying to keep my voice steady.

"I know, but I can't deny the curiosity is there." Agramon pulled me against him. I shoved my elbows into his sides. He gripped my throat while his other hand snaked down to my thigh and pulled one of my knives from their holster. The blade kissed my flesh as he held it to my throat.

I stilled, conscious of the blade on the verge of nicking my skin. Agramon's eyes shuttered closed as he leaned into my hair. "What are you rebelling against? Am I not good to you?"

When fear stalled my answer, the knife dug into my flesh. "Am I not good to you?" he repeated slowly, his voice dangerously low.

"Wasn't Ena enough?" I whispered, tears welling at the corners of my eyes.

"Now, Rowyn," Agramon said, chuckling under his breath. "Don't tell me I've already broken you. I miss our little witty repartee. What happened to the girl in Somme? The one who showed no fear?"

"Why can't you just leave me be? I'm doing as you ask. I'm following orders." I tried to push his hand holding the knife away, but his arm wouldn't budge. "What more do you want from me?"

Agramon turned me toward him, the knife returning to my throat as he backed me into the mirror. He pressed into the blade, his face inches from mine. "You think I'm doing all of this for you? To you? Oh my dear . . ." He shook his head, one hand holding the knife to my throat and the other smoothing my hair back from my face. His eyes closed and he leaned his forehead against mine, our gems touching. "You should see what your Morganite thinks I'm doing to you right now. He imagines himself bursting in here and rescuing you from my arms." Agramon's free hand gripped a handful of hair at the back of my head. He turned my face up to his. "Do you wish to be rescued by him?"

"Of course not," I stammered. "He betrayed me."

"Ah yes." Agramon smirked. "The betrayal. Well, if it's not Mordog you hold out hope for, it must be that fiery consul across the sea. Do you see him riding to your aid? The one whom you undoubtedly still imagine yourself in love with."

When I refused to speak, Agramon's eyes darkened. "He didn't write, you know. I was so looking forward to reading his letters before throwing them in the fire. Imagine my disappointment when not a single one arrived."

I almost choked as tears coursed down my cheeks. I'd wondered if Destrian had tried to write. I'd hoped he would've found some way to reach out, to let me know that he didn't hate me anymore. To know that he didn't even try to cut far deeper than the knife at my neck ever could.

Agramon raised his brows. "So who does that leave but the lovelorn Butcher." Agramon put a hand on my shoulder, tracing the top of the corset again. "What do they all see in you, I wonder?"

"I don't know," I said, my voice breaking.

Agramon lifted his hand and wiped the tears away. He sighed, cupping my cheek and resting his thumb against my lips. "Sometimes I wonder what such wildness tastes like. Perhaps that's what the Butcher is drawn to."

I closed my eyes as his breath drew closer, the knife edge pressing into my skin. His nose brushed mine, and I wished to all the gods that they could sweep me out of his clutches. I held my breath when the knife moved away from my throat.

Suddenly, a sharp pain lanced over my thigh and I cried out. The knife struck again, and again, opening three gashes on my upper thigh, before Agramon stepped back. I crumpled to the ground, my eyes wide as I took in the blood drenching the wounds that formed a grisly *A*.

Agramon crouched in front of me, playing with the bloody knife in his hands. "You don't think I know what goes through your mind when you look at me?"

My hands covered the wound. I rocked slowly in my shock, slipping on blood while I tried not to scream. He was going to kill me.

In a way I was relieved. That would mean the pain was over.

"I know you planted that burr on my horse. I know that you came to my tent at night, trying to use your powers against me. After everything I've taught you, you still haven't *learned*."

My body began shaking uncontrollably. Agramon placed the blade under my chin and forced me to look at him.

"Since your people love to mark their bodies with blessings, I've decided to gift you one of my own. No more attempts on my life, my dear. Tell me you understand."

I nodded, trying to stay conscious. Trying to hold the tears back.

"I want to hear the words, Rowyn," Agramon chided. "Tell me you understand."

"I understand," I whispered, my voice barely audible.

"Good girl," Agramon said, dropping the knife onto my lap and rising. He looked out the window. "Oh, bother. You're going to make me late for my own dinner. Clean yourself up, quick as you can. I expect you in the hall in fifteen minutes."

I closed my eyes and nodded as he stepped out of the bedroom, not even bothering to shut the door. He whistled a tuneless song in the receiving room before opening the door to my chambers. As he exited into the hall, Luc craned to look at me, his eyes filled with concern.

I took a shaky breath, wiped my cheeks, and crawled over to my cupboard to get scraps of linen to clean up the bloody mess.

I REMEMBERED NOTHING ABOUT DINNER that night. My leg throbbed painfully, but I knew better than to ask for a healer. Agramon had been clear. He wanted to scar me.

I couldn't remember how I avoided speaking to Sam, who sat across from me on Agramon's other side, nor how I turned away from Luc's urgent stare, his expression asking if I was all right.

I wasn't all right—far from it—but fighting Agramon was my battle. Even if I didn't have a way to kill him yet or protect the lives he dangled before me, I couldn't let him break me. I couldn't give up. I just needed to make it to the quinquennial.

"Show me something else," I whispered to Echo

that night through my tears. Though I'd locked the door to my room, I knew it was futile. The lord of the castle would have a key. "Show me any place but here."

"*I can only show you what I've seen,*" Echo whispered back. "*I can only show you my life.*"

"Please," I repeated. "If I can't escape with my body, help me escape with my mind."

Echo's dream was hazy, as though she couldn't remember every detail. I recognized a young Morius being pushed in the dirt by older boys. I was rushing toward him and shoved the boys away.

"Leave him be!" I shouted before I shoved one of the boys away. I slapped another who was leering beside him. I could feel the swell of righteous anger within me as I snarled at them like a beast.

"How dare you!" I was saying. "Why don't you pick on someone your own size?"

The boys backed away, their hands raised. Finally, they turned and ran, disappearing into the huts that made up the village by the river. I turned and picked Morius up from the dirt, dusting his pants and setting him on his feet.

"Why didn't you shout for me?" I asked.

Morius looked glum. "They only make fun of me more—say I need my sister to fight my battles for me."

I crossed my arms. "They are a head taller than you, Morius. They need to learn to pick on boys their own size."

Morius kicked a pebble. "Helen says I need to stand up to them, to fight the battles myself. I need to make them fear me."

"Well, Helen doesn't have to make the poultice for your bruises," I said, my voice dripping with frustration. Helen was not my favorite young girl.

"It's no use," Morius said, tears welling in his eyes. "I'll never be able to prove myself to them."

I lowered to his height, brushing hair from his eyes and tweaking his nose.

"Come, I can show you some moves they teach us at the temple. It won't win you battles, but it may help."

"He should train with us," a voice said behind me.

I turned. My dream self recognized the young man looming behind us. I felt a mix of excitement and longing at his appearance. His face was honest, if not plain, and his eyes danced over me with marked appreciation.

"Morius is right. You shouldn't fight his battles for him, Nirah. You should've sent him to the training fields two years ago."

"He's meant for more than fodder for a battlefield," I said. "The Lyricans are amassing to the south. The smell of blood fills the air. There is a war to come. You've seen what he can do. He must train with Sage Giyermu."

"There is nothing that says he can't train with the

sage *and* the soldiers. You don't want him to be defenseless, do you?" the boy asked.

I sighed and shook my head.

The boy stepped closer and rested his hand on my shoulder. "You are doing a good job caring for him. He is grateful to you."

I rubbed my temples. "I just wish I knew what I was doing."

The boy laughed, then placed his hand on my other shoulder and leaned forward, planting a kiss on my cheek. "You are practicing for when we have our own children. They won't be as hard as Morius, I imagine. At least, hopefully not all of them."

I laughed, comforted by the familiarity of his touch. Morius was trudging away. The young man jogged after him, then slowed. He placed his hand on Morius's shoulder and led him to the fields where other warriors of the clan practiced. I crossed my arms, hugging myself as though chilled, even though it was high summer and the air was warm and fragrant.

I stepped through our village, nodding to those I passed. My eyes were drawn to the children running through the paths between the huts. A sense of longing filled me as I watched them laugh and play, chasing each other with sticks.

On the outskirts of the village, I ducked inside a large hut. When my eyes adjusted to the darkness, I nodded to another woman whose shoulders slumped with relief. She almost pushed me out of the way to escape.

"Took you long enough," a voice said from the shadows.

I placed some logs on the fire in the middle of the hut, building it up to the preferred light and heat. Anis, the girl who left, never cared to get it right.

"I bet it was that brother of yours that kept you," the voice snapped.

I glared at the frail woman on the other side of the fire. "I wish the others would leave him be."

The frail woman clicked her tongue. "It's hard to give grace to the one who will doom them to darkness."

I narrowed my eyes. "You said he would become a great sorcerer. That we would sing our thanks for a hundred years."

Arda nodded once, her strange eyes blinking at me over the firelight. "But at great cost to the clan. You are doomed to the shadows, Nirah."

I gritted my teeth and began preparations for the seer's supper, trying to push her portent from my mind.

Chapter 8

"YOU WERE CALLED NIRAH," I said, sitting up in bed. "You were Morius's sister." Arda had said that Morius had doomed them to the shadows. Now Nirah was a shadow-soul, along with a large portion of the Morganite clan that had ventured through the Nightlands to make it to the other side of the sea to present-day Morgania. Morius had shifted the surviving clan to the shadows and returned alone, leaving the others to their fate. They'd lived hundreds of years alone in the lands of night, with nothing but wayward adventurers for company. Until Destrian and I had come along.

"I was," came the reply. Echo's voice was no longer a whisper, liable to be carried away by the nearest breeze before it reached my ears. I could hear her clearly now, as though she was more human than shadow.

"That means we're related," I mused. "You're an aunt from long ago."

"That we are," Echo said. An indentation appeared on the bed, as though Echo was perched on the side, much as Ena would.

"I should call you Nirah from now on, if that's your name."

"No, that was another life. Echo suits me far better now."

I raised my brows. "Are you getting stronger?" When we were in Somme, Echo could only speak with two or three words. Now she was using whole sentences.

"I am," Echo said. "Your presence . . . your blood gives me strength."

"Is there anything you can do to get me away from Agramon?" I asked, swelling with hope. "Can you help me?"

I felt a cool tingling on my hand, almost like fingertips. "I can only watch," she said, dashing my hopes against the rocks.

"You've been more than helpful already," I whispered, resting my chin against my knees. "You're all I have now."

"It is not enough," Echo said, as though agreeing with my unspoken words.

"No, it is enough for now . . . for this," I assured her. She would help me survive. "I am grateful you followed me here. I need your companionship more than you realize." Coolness brushed my hand once more.

It was what I'd needed. Echo gave me the strength to get out of bed. I went to the cupboard to change my bandages.

AGRAMON LED ME TO LUC AND a group of Solin guardsmen gathered on the stone drive. I avoided Luc's gaze as I tried to ignore the throbbing in my leg and walk without a limp, my eyes focused on the waiting carriage.

Someone shouted. I turned and found Sam striding toward us from the barracks. He appeared angry.

"Rowyn, stop! Don't move," Sam said, pointing to me.

I stopped and relieved my injured leg of weight.

"Where do you think you're taking her?" Sam stopped in front of Agramon.

"We need to train," Agramon said simply, resting against his staff. "You wouldn't deprive the girl of an education, would you? The emperor himself directed me to see to it that she explores all her capabilities."

"She needs a guard if she's to leave the castle."

Agramon rolled his eyes. "The Solin guardsmen will suffice."

"That's not good enough," Sam shouted behind him. Soldiers mounted and rode up, saluting Sam when they came to a halt. "Watch over the sorceress and report back to me everything that happens."

"Yes, Commander," the lead soldier said.

Agramon grabbed my elbow and shoved me into the carriage. I was surprised to find a Solston already seated inside. He wore the white robes of the order with a band tied over his eyes. The golden eye of Sol was threaded through the middle.

"Morganite," the Solston said, nodding toward me.

"Solston," I replied, then turned my attention to the window where Agramon and Sam were having a heated discussion. After several minutes, Sam strode away, shouting commands.

Agramon ducked inside and took the seat next to the Solston. "That man is insufferable," he growled, watching Sam's retreating back. "I swear, I can't wait to get away from him. I'm sure you feel the same." Agramon looked at me pointedly.

I figured no response was best.

"Rowyn, this is Solston Navar, head of Solin's temples and the observatory."

I glanced back at the priest. "It's nice to see you, your holiness."

Agramon's grip on his staff tightened. I met his pointed glare. Attempting to flay me wasn't enough to curb my impulses.

"How can you find your way with that scarf over your eyes?"

"I have other ways of sight, princess," the Solston said, turning his head toward me.

I froze at the name *princess*. It was what Sir Bernard called me when he found out my father had been chief of Espiria. It was what Destrian had realized I was when searching for my history—the last surviving descendant of Philemon and Helen, first king and queen of Morgania.

"Solston Navar is also a sorcerer," Agramon said as the carriage lurched forward. "He has come to train with you."

I raised my brows, wondering how a holy man could help Agramon in his cause.

The carriage stopped at a field overlooking the city. I could see for leagues around us.

"You want me to bring the rain?" I asked.

Agramon nodded. "I want to see how far your reach will go. If you have enough power to rein it in, I would like to avoid the city until tonight, but Navar needs daylight in order to be effective."

"Effective how?" I asked, studying the Solston.

"Navar can see over great distances." Agramon leaned against his staff. "He will be able to determine your range."

"Very well," I said, rolling my shoulders back. I rubbed my hands together and began harnessing the force within, closing my eyes for better focus. "You want it to reach Calla as well?"

"You can reach Calla?" Agramon asked, his voice

sharp.

My eyes flew open, but I realized my misstep too late. I should've tried to hide my range from him. It would just be another thing for him to exploit. Then again, I owed it to Araceli to bring life to her land. I couldn't let her down.

"I believe I can," I admitted. "You want me to do it now?"

"Please," Solston Navar said. "Send it as far north as you can." I closed my eyes and pushed my power outward. It streamed up, then clouds formed and rolled across the land. It helped that I knew the direction of Calla, and the distance between us. I pushed more and more until I was nearly spent. Nearly, but not quite. I could've included the capitol in the storm, but I held back. I wouldn't let Agramon see everything I was capable of.

I opened my eyes as the first raindrop fell.

"Did she make it?" Agramon asked, his eyes on the Solston whose hand was on his head as he faced north. A purple glow emanated from the white band over his eyes.

"She did," the Solston said after a moment. "It's raining there now."

Agramon whistled. "Well, now that is pleasing to hear." He smiled as though he hadn't spent the night before maiming me.

I glared at him.

"Since the count was so forthcoming, please make sure rain reaches Calla during your stay in Solin. He holds more sway at court than even he realizes."

"Of course," I said, turning to the carriage. "Can we go now?"

"As you wish," Agramon said. "Though Navar and I are due at the observatory next. I assume you don't wish to join."

I shook my head.

"Very well, I will leave you in the hands of the guards. You may divert yourself at the castle for the rest of the day, and we'll continue tomorrow on some of your other talents."

I felt an immense sense of relief when we pulled in front of the observatory. It was a domed structure that jutted out from the great temple, its roof plated in gold like the roofs of the wealthy in Somme.

Agramon and Navar stepped out, then Agramon turned and held out his hand to me.

"I thought you were going to let me return to the castle," I said.

"I am," Agramon replied. "But I'm keeping the carriage."

I gritted my teeth and gripped his hand. I jarred my bad leg when I stepped out of the carriage. I fought back the tears as Luc rode forward.

"Let her ride with you back to the castle," Agramon was saying. "Since the Butcher was kind enough to send an additional escort, I'll keep the Solin guards with me."

Luc nodded and offered me his hand. I wished he would get off his horse and help me up, but to say that was to admit I had an injury, something I was loath to do. I could read Agramon well enough to know that I wasn't the only person he'd been trying to manipulate the night before. He was trying to get a rise out of Sam and Luc. I couldn't bear to give him the satisfaction. I refused to be used as bait.

I gripped his hand and fought the scream that nearly escaped as Luc hauled me in front of him. I closed my eyes, willing the pain away, sure the wounds had reopened.

I was so focused inwardly that I missed Agramon and Navar's farewell. When I thought to look around, we were well past the temples and riding through the city streets.

A shriek filled the air, and I lifted my arm in response. Arden landed, her claws digging painfully into my flesh. She walked up my arm and rested on my shoulder, her beak burrowing into my hair. I laughed, brushing her feathers lightly with my fingers, a welcome distraction from the pain.

"Rowyn, about last night," Luc said, his arms resting against my waist as he held the reins. "What happened with Agramon?"

He'd been waiting all morning to ask me that question. Too bad it was the last thing I felt like talking about.

"I'm not going to speak of it," I said, starkly aware that the movement of the horse was not helping the state of my leg. The wound felt wet now. I'd have to change my bandages when we returned and find some healing herbs from the kitchens.

Luc didn't press the matter. That rose him in my esteem. As we rode through the city, Arden took off. I enjoyed watching her fly, soaring above the houses and inns, screeching her call to those below. Her presence made me think of home. Sometimes that feeling was welcome.

We passed by a cheese cart; the woman advertised her wares by listing each type of cheese. I wrinkled my nose at the mold-covered wheels emitting a sharp, foul smell.

"Remember when we raided that one caravan?" Luc asked into my ear.

I couldn't help but laugh at the memory that came. "And we found that cache of cheese? You insisted on trying each one to pick your favorite."

I felt his laughter. "One of my great regrets in life is vomiting halfway through and never finishing the task."

"Ferris was sure you would never live down that

embarrassment," I said. "He made fun of you for weeks."

"He was beating a dead horse. It wasn't *that* funny," Luc said, though his voice was still light. "How is he? How is Father?"

"Ferris was well," I said. "The last I saw of your father, he'd murdered Consul Colman and abandoned me to Agramon's will."

Luc didn't say anything for a moment, then his arms tightened. "I'm sorry for that . . . for how we've treated you."

I shrugged. "What's done is done. It just takes some time getting used to . . . being a commodity."

"I know this doesn't mean much," Luc said. "But I can't stand watching him hurt you. It was supposed to be my job to protect you, and I've failed in every possible sense."

I sighed. "I'm sorry that the reality of the situation you've put me in doesn't conform with the vision you had in your head."

"What do you mean?" Luc asked, his voice stiff.

"I know what you thought about me. You saw me in my fancy dresses and heard about me attending the emperor's banquets. You think I'm spoiled."

"I never said—"

"You didn't have to. It was written all over your face."

"I know that I can't help you against him," Luc said, his voice lowering as we rode through the castle gates. "You can't take me into your confidence, nor rely on me to protect you, but for what it's worth, I wish I could do those things. I wish I could redeem myself for the hurt I've caused."

"I wish you could too," I admitted. In some respect, I was tired of hating those I'd once loved. It took too much energy. "If there is one thing I miss about us, it's our friendship."

"We can at least be friends, can't we?" Luc asked. "Just don't tell me any important secrets."

Luc followed the guards to the stables where he helped me dismount. I was grateful for his help, as the pain in my leg had grown considerably during the ride.

"We can be friends," I agreed, looking up to smile at him. Though I would never forgive him, I was tired of being angry. Luc was not my enemy.

Luc's eyes had caught something on my skirts. I looked down, belatedly realizing that blood had seeped through the fabric of my dress.

"Rowyn, what is that?" he asked, his voice hesitant.

"Nothing." I clutched the folds to mask the stain. Sadly, there wasn't much I could do. I'd foolishly chosen a light green dress, which meant there was no way the blood would blend in with the fabric. I was a fool for not choosing black.

Luc grabbed my wrist when I tried to turn away. "Let me see it."

"What are you doing?" a soldier asked from behind us, unsheathing his sword. The others followed suit. "Let the lady go."

Luc released me and raised his hands. "It's not what you think. She's injured."

"No, I'm not," I said, panic setting in. I wished Luc would keep his mouth shut.

The lead guard watched me suspiciously. He turned to the soldier next to him. "Get the commander."

"No, let me pass," I demanded.

The man nodded toward the stable doors, and several soldiers went to block them. "I'm sorry, lady. I have to follow the commander's orders."

"When the duke hears about this, he will be furious," I said, trying a different approach. I didn't want Luc and Sam involved in my squabbles with Agramon. I had to handle him on my own. Araceli was right. I had to show that he could trust me.

The head guard shrugged. "Then he can take it up with the commander."

"What's going on?" Sam asked, stepping into the stable. He glanced around, taking in the soldiers—half of them with swords drawn—Luc with his hands in the air, and finally me. I nearly screamed with frustration.

"I wish to return to my room," I commanded.

"Right this minute. They are keeping me against my will."

Sam's brows rose.

"The dog says she's injured," the head soldier offered.

Sam's green eyes slid to mine as he stalked forward. "Where?"

"It's nothing." I tried to roll the fabric of my gown to conceal the stain.

Sam looked back at Luc.

"She's bleeding, your lordship," Luc said. "Last night—"

"Stop talking!" I shouted as heat rushed to my face. I was ready to pull a knife from my holster and stab Luc to get him to shut up, friendship be damned. Sam and Luc interfering with Agramon would just give him more of a reason to use them against me later.

Sam's eyes darkened. "What happened last night?"

"I'm fine," I repeated. "I can handle him myself. I don't need to drag the rest of you into this."

Sam's voice lowered. "Show me."

"No, Sam, this is what he wants."

Sam's nostrils flared, his jaw stiff. "Do I need to have them hold you down? I will if I must."

I didn't move. Sam nodded to the soldiers, and they stepped toward me.

"Fine!" I said, backing away from them. I met Sam's

eyes, my voice pleading. "Promise you won't do anything. He's trying to get a rise out of you."

Sam merely stared at the blood as though he couldn't hear me. I gritted my teeth and sat on the ground. Carefully, I lifted my skirt, revealing my injured leg, the bandage on my thigh soaked through.

"Rowyn, why didn't you tell me?" Luc said, his brows furrowed.

Sam dropped to his knees beside me. He unrolled the linen bandage carefully.

"Sam." I stopped his hand. A few tears escaped the corners of my eyes and ran down my cheeks. "He means it as a challenge. Don't give in. This isn't the way to defeat him."

Sam brushed my hand away and continued unwrapping. I couldn't bear the weight of all their stares, the fear rising as I imagined Sam confronting Agramon. He wouldn't stand a chance. I'd lose him too. The only person who had pledged to protect me. I'd be that much closer to having nothing.

A soldier hissed.

"By Sol above," said another, peering over Sam's shoulder to get a better look.

Luc ran his hand through his hair, his mouth taut.

I didn't need their pity. "It's not as bad as it looks," I said, brushing away the tears that came as if to make my lie more obvious.

Sam had gone still as a statue, his mouth flattened to a thin line, his eyes on my wounds. I grabbed the linens and began dabbing at the cuts. It only looked worse because they'd opened on the ride.

"If I can get a healer, it won't look half so bad," I went on.

"Get my horse," Sam ordered as he stood.

"No, wait, this is exactly what he wants you to do!" I yelled, trying to grab him.

Sam was already moving to Hale's stall.

I dropped the bloody linens and stumbled after him. "Sam, don't give in to what he wants." I rammed my entire body against the stall door as Sam went to open it.

"You can't ask this of me," Sam snarled, gripping the latch with white knuckles. "You can't ask me to stand by."

I gripped his hand. "Let me do this my way, just this once. Please."

Sam looked down at me. "There's no controlling him, Rowyn. He's going to keep bullying you, and using your powers, and eventually he will drain you dry until you are no longer of use to him."

"Just give me a chance to do it my way, this one time," I whispered so only he could hear.

Sam gripped the door, leaning in with both hands. Finally, he nodded. "Get her a healer."

Chapter 9

"ROWYN, I WOULD LIKE YOU to meet your new handmaid, Gree," Agramon said as I stepped into my receiving room the next morning.

An old woman stood next to the duke, wearing all gray, her hair hidden behind a wimple and veil. Her eyes narrowed as they looked me up and down. Her nose wrinkled.

"Gree has been a member of my household for many years and served as handmaid to a number of young ladies that I've mentored in the past."

"Pleased to meet you," I said, then curtsied.

Gree sniffed. She stepped forward and circled me. One of my braids lifted, then fell back. The old woman tsked quietly to herself. "She's not your usual fare, is she," Gree said to Agramon.

Agramon was leaning against his staff. "She's here because of her powers. I can't help the package she came in."

I gritted my teeth. Already I hated the woman. It was clear she would be more than willing to spy for Agramon.

"Very well, I'll have her ready to present for dinner," Gree said. Agramon nodded and left me to Gree's care. My heart sank. What on earth would she have me do all day?

HOURS LATER I EMERGED from my room ready to throw myself out of the nearest window. Gree had bathed me, taken a razor to almost all of my body hair, and she barely raised an eyebrow to the swollen *A* on my leg that the military healer had closed.

Gree scrubbed and scrubbed and scrubbed until I was sure I'd molted, revealing a new layer of skin. She'd paid special attention to the tattoos, using a paste made of ground stone-fruit seeds, as though she could scrub the ink off.

Arden had landed on the sill of my bathing room about halfway through my bath. She cocked her head to the side as though wondering what Gree was doing, then promptly left when the woman splashed water at her.

"That's my falcon," I snapped. "And since you're my handmaid now, I would like several perches for her. One for my receiving room and one for the bedroom."

Gree clicked her teeth. "If His Grace says it's all

right."

I rolled my eyes. Every word she uttered was preceded by *His Grace this*, or *His Grace that*.

When Gree finished bathing me, she slathered all manner of oils and lotions onto my flesh before combing my wet hair back. Taking a pair of scissors, she trimmed it so that it fell to my waist, then stuffed me into something that couldn't be called a gown but was more like strips of fabric. She then spent a good hour painting my face with all manner of tinctures and colors before heating a poker and beginning the painstaking task of curling my hair.

When I was presented with the looking glass before dinner, a stranger stared back at me. Gree had powdered my eyes and lined them with liquid kohl, the line far longer and darker than Ena had dared to make it. My hair was a mountain of curls. As I studied myself, Gree ruffled through one of the drawers in my vanity.

"Here," she said, pulling my arm out and slipping on a metal armband. She rummaged some more and found two ear cuffs, set with amethysts of the deepest purple that matched the color of the almost-gown. I adjusted my breasts, making sure the strips of fabric covered as much of them as possible.

"These earrings enhance your beauty," Gree said, adjusting them so they wouldn't slip. "You'll need it."

I gritted my teeth, feeling the tendrils of magic from

the gems begin to wrap around me.

"My, my, my," Agramon said when Gree presented me. He smiled. "I knew I could trust her to your care. You've worked miracles, as usual."

Luc merely stared, his mouth half open.

Gree clicked her teeth, something she did when she was displeased, I noticed. She'd been doing it all afternoon. "She's pretty enough, though she's too skinny for most men's taste, with all those sharp edges. Her tongue is even sharper, but I'm sure you will take care of that." Gree shot me her first smile. It was like looking in the face of pure evil.

"Well, I'm pleased you haven't lost your touch. We'll be back late, as dinner is to be a grand affair."

"So I've heard, Your Grace," Gree said with a bow. She turned, shot me a judgmental sneer, and shut the door, leaving me with Agramon and Luc.

Agramon took my hand, and I immediately pulled away.

"Don't touch me."

Agramon grabbed my hand again. "Now, now, my dear. I require that you impress our dinner guests. As you did not practice your skills today like I intended, you will show them tonight."

I clenched my teeth as Agramon placed my hand on his and led me down the hall. I was hyperaware of Luc's eyes on my back, which was bare and showed the falcon tattoo that he'd helped me earn. I was saving all my courage for dinner, so I didn't even try to meet his eye.

The hall quieted when Agramon led me through the doors. I recognized Solston Navar and Sam in the corner with a few of the officers who had joined us from Calla. Sam folded his arms and leaned against the wall. Though the officers talked among themselves, his eyes were on me, his lips drawn into a tight line.

Agramon commanded the entire hall, his hands out in welcome. I ignored his speech. He didn't need my tongue tonight, nor did he want it. I was a symbol to the folks staring at me over their glasses, nothing more.

Clapping filled the room and Agramon led me around, introducing me to a flurry of people whose names I forgot instantly. They were merchants and tradesmen, the city's mayor, and several Solstons who ran the observatory. Many bent to kiss the gem on my hand, trying to feel the power within.

"My lady," a man said, his voice syrupy sweet. I raised my brow at him, marking him as a cad the way his eyes traveled the length of my body. He was bold, considering he stood with the lower merchants of the city. Despite his standing, his coat was embroidered with gold thread, and his hat sported an expensive feather that I'd seen several noblemen wearing at the capitol.

"Rumors of her beauty weren't exaggerated," the

man said, turning to Duke Agramon. "Are they all true?"

I glared at him. "What rumors?"

The man's eyes slid to mine. "Some bards have said you're free with your charms. I myself wouldn't mind having a taste of the wilds of the north, if you would be willing." My eyes widened when the fellow directed his question to Duke Agramon.

Blood rushed to my cheeks. "How dare you. I'm not his property."

"Oh?" the man said, looking surprised. "That's not what I've heard."

"Come now, Melbo, leave the chit alone," Duke Agramon said in an admonishing tone. "Despite her station, she's due all the courtesy of my other students."

I turned my back on the both of them. Dinner hadn't even begun, and already I was disgusted. Sam was chatting with his officers, so I was loath to disturb him. I cast my eyes about the room and noticed Luc standing in a corner, scanning the room while looking perceptively bored.

I grabbed a goblet of wine from one of the servers and made my way to him.

Luc noticed my approach and smirked. "My lady," he said, bowing slightly. "You look appropriately gild-ed."

"You've relinquished your claim, remember?" I

teased.

Luc's eyes sparkled. "Trust me, I'm trying to."

I punched him in the arm, and he emitted a burst of laughter.

"How is your leg?"

I took a sip. "Well enough. There is a scar, but it's mostly healed."

Luc's eyes flitted to Agramon. "I heard you have a maid now."

I nodded. "A great vulture of a thing. She's been in Agramon's household for years and licks his boots every chance she gets."

Luc's voice dropped low. "Remember, he reads my thoughts, picking out any information he can glean about you."

I raised my brows. "Things from my past?"

Luc nodded. "Sometimes I see you do something, and I have a memory of back home. He stays on those the longest."

I'd figured as much, but I wasn't keen on joining the rest of the guests quite yet. I took another sip from my goblet.

"Does he know why you did it?" I asked, leaning against the wall. "Why you really gave me away to the empire? Was it truly just to save your own skin?"

"Maybe it's best if you think of it like that." Luc said, watching the room with his hands clasped behind his back.

"It wasn't like you," I said. The servers continued to mill about. One appeared beside me and filled my cup to the brim.

A muscle flicked in Luc's jaw. His dark eyes found Agramon once more. "I want you to hear this from me, because I don't want the duke to hurt you with it later." Luc took a deep breath. "I never told you this, but the night of our betrothal, your father pulled me to the side."

"Oh?" I said, my heart steadily beating faster. "What fatherly advice did he bestow to his never-to-be son?"

Luc glanced down at me. "He said, 'Rowyn is a fighter, but she isn't capable of ruling. She doesn't have it in her.'"

It was as though I'd been punched in the gut. "What?" I asked, straightening.

Luc met my eyes. "I promise on Imor, on everything that you and I had, I told him that he was wrong, but he still made me promise that you would never rule Espiria. It would always be me, no matter what. Even if you hadn't married me, I would take over because he didn't have enough faith in you."

I couldn't breathe. Tears threatened the corners of my eyes, but I held them at bay. "I knew he didn't have faith in me," I said, refusing to let my voice shake. "You don't think I saw the way his eyes turned down when he thought I couldn't see? Despite everything I did, I could never undo the fact that he thought me a disappointment."

"Rowyn—" Luc said and grabbed my arm. "Even though he didn't believe in you, I do. I always knew you would harness your powers one day and then you would truly be able to lead, but when I was taken from Espiria, I did everything in my power to return because I had a duty to that promise, to our people. I had to honor it."

I gritted my teeth, shaking with anger. "You all speak of duty and honor, but when has Espiria ever actually been home to me? The people there can't stand me, my own father didn't think I was good enough, and you sold your own kin just to ensure that I wouldn't lead our people to ruin."

"No," Luc said, squeezing my arm. "I never thought you could lead Espiria because it was far too small. Your light will shine so bright that Imor will place it among the stars. Morganites will whisper your name for generations. You will be regarded with Queen Helena and King Philemon. But I had a duty to Espiria. I still do. Let me champion them while you champion the rest of the world."

"And where do you suggest I begin?" I took another sip to calm my quaking nerves. "How does one save the world?"

Luc shrugged, his eyes back on the crowd. "You've already begun. You're ending the drought. You're meeting every important person in the empire. Use this time to find out who will always be an enemy and who could be allies."

Luc was right. Araceli was right. I could be doing more. I needed to pay closer attention for the empress. If I could help her gain allies and more power, she could do great things with the empire. That was the price she demanded to help me escape. That was the price the gods demanded.

"Come, let us eat," Agramon announced, waving us all to the tables that were laden with delicacies rivaling the emperor's banquets.

Luc placed his hand on my back, leading me to the seat beside Agramon. I stood in front of the chair, seating myself as he pushed it in. An elderly Solston shuffled to the seat on my other side.

"Your holiness," Sam said, coming beside him. "His Grace requested that you take the seat of honor." Sam motioned to the chair on Agramon's right. As next ranking noble, technically it should've been Sam's seat. A wide smile broke out over the Solston's face. He shuffled around the great table and collapsed into the chair beside Agramon. The duke glared at Sam and clenched his fork. The Solston looked across the table and smiled at me. He was missing some crucial teeth.

"As a daughter of night, you are a long way from home," the Solston said after Agramon signaled that dinner had begun. At the emperor's banquet, there was food present all around so those in attendance could rub shoulders with the elites as they pleased. Agramon had taken a slightly different approach, with a structured meal at a table. Servants walked about with carving tools and platters.

I nodded, taking a deep drink from my goblet. With a sigh, I picked at the food that servers had piled onto my plate.

"Sol's eye has smiled on the empire, bringing you under our wing and showing you the light," the Solston went on, spooning soup into his mouth. I glanced down with distaste as flecks of the soup speckled the front of his snow-white robes. He didn't seem to notice. "What a blessing for you to be under the tutelage of so illustrious a guardian. I see he is spoiling you," the Solston went on, nodding to my gown, his eyes lingering far too long on my breasts.

I glared at him and drank deeply. By all the gods, it would take everything I had just to endure dinner.

Sam leaned forward. "His Grace was just telling me about the storied work you've been doing at the temples, Solston Burgworth. He mentioned that he has missed your sermons at the capitol and would like to be caught up on all the lessons you've shared with the people of Solin. It wouldn't do for the lord of the land to miss hearing Sol's words, wouldn't you agree?"

"Why yes," the Solston said, a smile spreading across his wizened face. "I can share with you all the sermons the people have enjoyed over the past year, if that pleases you, Your Grace."

Agramon was seething as he glared at Sam. The Solston's smile fell, and he looked quizzically at his plate.

"Although, I may not . . . maybe another time, perhaps. My mind seems less organized of late. I can't quite remember . . ."

"Pity." Agramon lifted his goblet to his lips before striking up a conversation with the person on the Solston's other side.

"Is something wrong?" Sam asked me.

I shook my head and took another drink of wine. If I got through dinner without becoming drunk, I would be surprised.

"You look stunning," Sam said, leaning back in his chair. "What did you and Mordog speak of?"

I glanced over at Luc who had taken his place on the wall behind Agramon. He would eat his meal later, with the rest of the servants.

"We spoke of home."

"Yet his words distressed you."

I met Sam's eye. "Home was not always a happy place for me."

Thankfully, Sam dropped his line of questioning when a man came in with a harp.

Agramon stood. "In honor of my ward, I've invited Bard Gilliven to share his rendition of Rowyn's adventure in the wilds of the north." He led everyone in applause, and the man sat on a gilded chair and began to play the harp.

I tuned the song out. I'd heard enough variations of my journey to the Nightlands that I knew what to expect. Instead, my mind went back to Luc's words.

He and Araceli were urging me to act, as was the empress. I needed to look for more opportunities to turn the tides in her favor. I could help the farmers and people who made their living from the land. Though I was hiding my range from Agramon, I could still cover a great swath of land. My time under the empire's thumb didn't have to go to waste. Arda's words kept nagging at me. To escape, I would have to help the downtrodden of the empire.

It was then I realized . . . the war. Nothing hurt the empire more than the foolish war in Yliria, and now the emperor was trying to start another one.

I needed to get the emperor to stop the war.

What everyone was saying—from Luc, to Araceli, to Arda—started to sink in. What better way to save hundreds of thousands of people than to end senseless bloodshed?

I glanced at Sam and frowned at how tense he sat. The man was practically glaring daggers at the musician whose voice filled the room. I tuned back into his song and felt heat rush to my cheeks now that I heard his words.

And the Dragon of Helena,
The evil beast did he slay,
With tempered sword and strength of steel,
The honorable lord did conquer the night,
And vowed his lady to delight.
From across the sea to thrones of gold,
Their nights of passions spanned many sto-
ries told,
In Helena the Dragon remains,
Waiting till his lady is in his arms again.

I hadn't heard such a romanticized version of it before. Sam was gripping his fork with white knuckles. Agramon shot me a devilish grin, and I buried my head in my hands. How utterly humiliating.

It wasn't bad enough to lose the boy I'd loved. No, it had to be played up as entertainment for the rest of the empire, to have them laugh at my pain and listen spellbound as each of my sorrows was outlined for them.

After what felt like a lifetime, the bard stood to

121

clapping from the dinner guests. I stared at my plate, unable to meet anyone's eye, but Agramon wasn't finished making a spectacle of me.

He stood me up and walked me to the window as the climax of the evening.

"You know what to do," Agramon whispered.

I stepped away from him and raised my arms, putting on a show, calling the rain for all the dinner guests. I closed my eyes and wished them all away, letting my mind wander to the fields of Calla where Araceli's people were sure to be toiling. The mass of storms was the same size as the day before, the rain falling in thick sheets. When I opened my eyes and turned, the dinner guests clapped politely. Agramon beamed as he held his hand out to me, motioning me forward. Not knowing what else to do, I curtsied.

Rain drummed on the windowsills outside, while inside the Solstons commanded the conversation, their ridiculous portents and words of Sol causing more than just my eyes to roll. When the affair appeared to be winding down, I grabbed my goblet and made my way to Sam.

"Walk me back to my room?" I asked, conscious that the wine was starting to get to my head. I'd barely eaten, and the act of bringing rain to so large an area had weakened me. I was more into the cups than I'd realized.

Sam glanced at Agramon, who was deep in conversation with a merchant. He nodded and held out his arm. I took it willingly, and we slipped out of the noisy hall to welcome respite.

"I didn't get a chance to thank you before, for the healer," I said.

Sam nodded. "As I've said before, I'm at your service, my lady."

"I don't need you in my service," I said. "I need a friend. Someone I can turn to that I know won't give me away to Agramon, or try to challenge him," I added when Sam seemed about to interrupt. "I am not without my own weapons."

Sam gripped my arm. "You will tell me if he touches you again."

"Perhaps," I said, noncommittedly. Probably not, considering Sam seemed to have problems controlling his anger and seeing reason. I continued down the hall, Sam keeping pace beside me. "But I need to do this on my own or I'll never truly see freedom. I don't always need you to save me."

"Don't forget that I've been at court a long time, Rowyn. Just because I don't engage in the strategies and games the nobles play, doesn't mean I don't know how the game works. It's not dissimilar to a battlefield."

"So how would you play, if you were me?" I asked. "How would you outwit Agramon?"

"The duke has been in enough minds that it's difficult to outmaneuver him. He plans ahead, as I am planning the war. He foretells each person's actions and reactions to his moves. He tries to plan for every possible result. So, simply put, in order to outwit him, you must do what he least expects."

"That's easier said than done," I said with a sigh, staggering a step. Sam's grip on my arm tightened as he steadied me. "I'm sure if I could act differently, as you say, then I would."

Sam raised his brows. "I wouldn't give up just yet. How does Agramon expect you to behave now?"

I thought a moment. "He expects me to rebel," I said. "I've only ever rebelled against every Lyrican I've come across." I glanced up and shot him a wry smile.

Sam's lips twitched. "And you rebel because you hate all Lyricans. You view the empire as your enemy, and all who work for the empire as your enemy. Isn't that so?"

"I suppose that's close, yes," I admitted. "Apart from a few, of course."

Sam nodded. "He also knows that you are unaccustomed to fighting battles of intrigue and reject courtly customs, so he will be expecting you to do that as well. You are fiercely loyal to your people, no matter how poorly they've treated you in the past."

"No," I said, shaking my head as we stopped outside

my door. I leaned against it, unwilling to go in and face Gree, the witch. "I hold no loyalty to the Morganites of my home. They've made it perfectly clear how they feel about me."

Sam tucked an errant curl behind my ear. "Those words fall from your lips so easily, but your actions suggest otherwise. What of saving Mordog's life in the fighting pits? You are loyal to a fault, no matter what you claim. Agramon has seen this and planned accordingly."

I glowered, thinking back to that fateful night. Hadn't I chosen Luc before Ena? It wasn't because I still held feelings for him as I did in the past. It was because he was of my clan. It was because he was an Espirian. Sam was right. I was a fool to think that Agramon hadn't known who I was going to choose before he set me up that night. Just thinking about it made me sick.

Sam was watching me, letting the thoughts play out in my addled mind. "He doesn't expect you to help those in the empire, not really. He knows that you are bringing rain, not out of the goodness of your heart, but because you fear what he will do to those you love."

"So, what can I do?" I repeated.

"Start caring," Sam said simply. "Start caring for more than just the Morganite cause. If the people you are trying to protect are the people he has no power over, he has no power over you either."

I bit my lip. Sam was right, but he was also a hypocrite. "What about your causes?"

Sam shrugged. "As you see, all I do is what I'm told. The emperor calls on me to raise the army, so I raise it. He calls on me to win a war, and I plan accordingly."

"Why don't you fight the emperor on this fool's errand?" I asked, the question having plagued me from the moment the emperor ordered Sam to call up the reserves. "Why don't you just tell him no?"

Sam raised his brows. "How can I expect my men to follow orders if I do not?"

"But you're an adviser," I exclaimed. "So advise him. Tell him it's folly!"

"It's not my place, Rowyn." Sam grunted. "Nor is it the empress's," he added pointedly.

"This war is needless. Thousands will die!"

"I don't have a choice, Rowyn," Sam growled. "This is my duty to my country, to my emperor. How can I refuse him?"

"Easily." I grabbed his arm. "By doing the right thing."

"He would have my head if I refused him," Sam snapped. Ripping his arm from my grip, he ran his hand through his hair. "Don't paint me to be some hero in your fairy stories. I'm just a man who does what he's told."

"Dogs do what they're told," I spat. "Men think for themselves. Your duty is to your country, not the emperor. How does it benefit Lyrica to throw ourselves into another ridiculous war? To rip the young men of our land from their beds and turn them into monsters."

"And there it is." Sam's body tensed as he glared at me. "So you *do* think I'm a monster."

"Of course I don't," I said, but I couldn't deny the waver in my voice.

Sam's green eyes bore into mine. "Do you think I relish leading my men to early graves?" he whispered. "Instilling fear into the hearts of children? I *never* wanted this life."

"Then refuse to do it!" I pleaded. "Be the first person to tell the emperor no! Tell him . . . tell him I will refuse to bring rain if he drags us into this mess."

Sam laughed, but there was no humor to it. He shook his head. "It's so easy for you, isn't it." His voice softened. "Refusing the emperor, withholding the strength of your power from him. But the rest of us are mere mortals, Rowyn. Who am I to resist his command?"

I grabbed the front of his leather jerkin. "You are the Blade of Lyrica, Sam. The men don't hold loyalty to the emperor; they hold loyalty to *you*. Use it to do the right thing. Convince the emperor that this is wrong."

"By Sol above," Sam said, looking down on me. "If anyone were able to defy him, it would be you."

I caught Sam's hand in mine. "It's not hopeless, Sam. Not yet."

Sam didn't speak for a long moment. His fingers cupped my chin, then raised my face to his as he studied my features. "You're so sweet," he murmured. "You really don't believe I'm beyond salvation, do you?" His expression darkened. "It's too late for me, Rowyn. I am the man who plunges their hands into the blood and filth, so the nobles can keep their gloves clean. It is the order of things."

"I don't believe you," I whispered.

Sam looked down at my mouth, his thumb pressed to my lips. "So soft," he whispered. "One wouldn't think you can inflict so much damage." Sam met my eyes. "And you do. You do much damage to me."

My breath caught in my throat.

We stood there for what seemed like forever. Time hung in a balance as Sam struggled with some decision. I stared at him, recognizing the emotions as they flicked past: anger, fear, want, and need.

Then, Sam dropped his hand and turned away. "It's no use, Rowyn. I am what war and men have made me."

Chapter 10

"COME NOW," MELBO SAID, his beady black eyes shooting at Agramon in Echo's dream. "Demand is sky high for a Morganite girl, *especially* one with dark hair like your little sorceress. If you help me locate the way into that hidden world of hers, I'll give you a quarter of the rewards. We'll make a fat profit, you and I."

Agramon leaned back in his chair, studying Melbo with his blank expression. "I'm unable to get the way to Espiria from Rowyn's thoughts," he said, turning his glass and gazing at the torchlight that fractured through the crystal. "I might've been able to glean the location from Mordog, but I've done too much damage for the information to be deemed reliable."

"Damage?" Melbo asked, taking a drink and wiping his mouth with his sleeve. "I just want a location from the man."

"I know," Agramon said, his eyes meeting Melbo's. "But I had to meddle with his loyalties to get the information I needed for Rowyn's capture and containment. If I'm to be completely honest, I'm not sure Mordog could find his way back himself. Sorry, but I'll have to pass on your offer."

Melbo let out a gust of frustration.

Agramon's eyes narrowed. "If your man is to be believed, you will have no need for my information."

Melbo shook his head. "But his fee is exorbitant. Since it's such privileged information, he's charging me nearly five times the going rate to get girls. I've never had such a hard time obtaining them."

Agramon's lip twitched. "There's no need to go behind the shroud to get a Morganite girl. From my understanding, they dwell all over Morgania and bear the imorets you need."

Melbo grunted as he settled further in his chair. "They want the other markings. I've even thought to stamp the girls myself, but it would be too expensive if I botched it. No, it's best to go for the real thing."

"Well," Agramon said, taking another sip from his glass. "Best of luck to you on this new venture. Morganite women are a fearsome lot, and I don't begrudge you the task of breaking one."

"WAKE UP," AN URGENT VOICE said in my ear. It felt as though a frigid finger was touching my brow. I awoke groggily, rubbing the sleep from my eyes.

The first sign that something was off was the darkness. Echo hadn't ever woken me during the night.

"What is it?" I asked.

"The halls are deserted," Echo whispered. "Melbo will be leaving soon."

I sat up, realizing her meaning, my mind going back to the skin-trader's words. He wanted to get into my home and steal young girls like me, to whisk them across the sea and sell their virtues for profit, just like Agramon.

I gritted my teeth, stepped out of bed, and grabbed my knives. I didn't bother changing out of my chemise.

"Lead me to him," I whispered back. "But if we're discovered, it will be my head."

"I know," Echo whispered. "The way is clear for now."

I nodded and slipped out of my rooms, discovering the hall empty, just as Echo had said.

"This way," Echo murmured, directing me down the hall. I slipped along, darting into recesses, my bare feet allowing me to pass silently by.

When we reached a hallway I didn't recognize, Echo told me to hide. I concealed myself behind a curtain and took a deep breath. I would have to be swift and silent. I couldn't let him cry out. There could be no witnesses. Nothing to alert the others who dwelled within the castle's walls that something was amiss. I shut my eyes, willing my heartbeat to slow. Breathe, calm, swift, silent.

Breathe, calm, swift, silent.

Suddenly, a view of the hall appeared in my mind. My eyes flew open, yet I was still hidden away, not able to see the corridor, nor able to be seen.

I shut my eyes again. It took a moment, but the view of the hall appeared once more.

By all the gods, Echo was letting me see through her eyes.

I could dwell on this newfound skill later. I needed to focus on the task at hand.

Breathe.

My heart skipped as a man turned the corner, holding onto the wall for a moment before staggering forward. I recognized the skin-trader from the ridiculous feather in his hat.

Calm.

The man stumbled and fell.

Swift.

He must be drunk.

Silent.

I wondered what passed during the time Echo had sent me the dream and the present.

Breathe.

He staggered to my side of the hall, gripping the wall for support.

Calm.

He was almost to the curtain where I hid.

Swift.

He reached out to the thick fabric, using the curtain to support him as he leaned too far to the side.

Silent.

I grabbed the curtain and spun, rolling him in the heavy folds. Before his addled mind could comprehend what happened, I stabbed him in the neck, over and over, until he sank to the ground and lay still.

Breathe.

I kneeled, careful to avoid the growing puddle of blood, and made sure he was dead.

Calm.

I cleaned my knife and hands on the curtain, sure that Gree would say something if she found any errant blood spatter.

Swift.

"Is the way clear?" I whispered, rising from my crouch.

"Yes," Echo replied. "Hurry!"

Silent.

I willed my heart to slow as I melted back into the shadows and practically danced down the hall on the pads of my feet. I stopped at the corner and closed my eyes. It happened faster that time, Echo revealing her sight to me. The hall was again clear.

Breathe.

I flew around the corner, slipping into the alcoves until I noticed a bobbing light coming from another direction.

"Hide," Echo hissed as a freezing jolt landed on my arm.

Calm.

"What's behind this door?" I sank into the nearest recess. I shut my eyes as the vision of an empty guest room appeared before me.

Swift.

I cracked the door, hurried in, and shut it quietly behind me. Opening a cupboard, I climbed inside but kept the door open barely a crack.

Silent.

I shut my eyes and Echo revealed her vision of the hall. Two guardsmen walked together, one holding a torch while the other ran his hands along the wall.

"—said to be prepared to ride to the capitol at midsummer," the guard holding the torch said.

"I don't see why he would need us there," replied the other guard. "Somme's soldiers were always enough to protect him before."

Their voices faded down the hall. Echo followed them until they turned the corner, then she flitted down and checked the other way. It was clear now, but the body would surely be found soon, and when it was, I would need to be in my bed.

Breathe.

I scrambled from the cupboard and back out into the hall. Panic pushed my heart to beat faster.

Calm.

A shout echoed through the corridors. The guardsmen were raising the alarm. They'd found the body after all.

Swift.

I darted through the halls. Within moments I was slipping through my door.

Silent.

I shut it quietly, then tiptoed across the floor and into my bedchamber. I took off my knife holster and set it on the table beside my bed, where it always lay when I wasn't using it, and sank into my sheets.

Breathe.

Just breathe.

Though I hated every moment of being under Agramon's thumb, I couldn't deny that it had its benefits. What better way to root out the evil men of the empire than to travel with the worst of them?

Luc and Araceli had told me to find allies, but I was far better at rooting out enemies.

I was just about to nod off to sleep when I heard the receiving door open. I forced myself to lie still, my heart to slow, my breathing to remain deep and calm. My eyes shuttered closed, and Echo showed me

Agramon standing at the door to my bedroom, his gem aglow with its rose-colored light. It cast shadows on his face as though he were a demon in the night.

Breathe.

After a moment, the light went out, and Agramon slunk out of my room. The lock turned with a click.

Chapter 11

"HIS GRACE WANTS YOU in breeches today," Gree said by way of greeting.

I arched an eyebrow.

"He says you are to fly."

Nervous energy built up beneath my skin. I pulled on a tunic and breeches. I strapped Iranoct to my waist, along with the knives. My mind teemed with all of the things that could go wrong. What if I flew too high and fell? What if I hit a building? What if I hurt someone?

I supposed none of those concerns were Agramon's.

His Grace watched me closely in the carriage on the way out of the city. I shifted nervously, trying to keep my eyes on the window while Agramon slowly rotated the staff in his hand. He was unsure of me, trying to get a handle on my mind. It was the one sign I had of whether or not he trusted someone.

"You seem tired," Agramon said. "Did you sleep well?"

My eyes flicked to his, but I schooled my face to impassiveness. "As well as I ever do."

Agramon's mouth quirked, but he didn't press me. I refused to let out a sigh of relief but remained on edge the rest of the journey.

We rode out of the city to a bit of high ground. My makeshift guard from Calla, Agramon's Solin guardsmen, and Luc followed us out, making a sort of grand procession for something so simple as my lessons.

"Are you not worried that I will sustain some injury?" I asked.

Agramon smiled. "You didn't injure yourself when you accidentally blew away into the city. Sometimes our power saves us without too much direction. Magic has always desired its conduits to live."

I sighed and stepped out of the carriage, steeling myself for the task to come. Agramon followed, facing the city.

After a moment, I looked up. He watched me expectantly. "Well? What are you waiting for? Get started."

I took a deep breath and felt the familiar sweeps of power, but instead of sending them up, I pushed them down as I'd done in the past. My hair whipped about me, and I rose a few inches before coming back down to the ground.

I looked over my shoulder to where Agramon had stepped behind me to watch. He motioned me to continue.

I looked down. I'd not been using my full power by any means. I couldn't help but worry that my coming out of this training uninjured was foolish thinking.

I pushed more power down and rose a couple feet, then several more. My hands began to shake as I tried to keep myself aloft and in an upright position. The wind threatened to send my legs to the side. I overcorrected and swung the other way until I was floating on my side, the wind roaring in my ears. My heart raced as I moved higher above the land. Growing up in the mountain of Espiria, I'd learned not to be afraid of heights, but flying was something else altogether. A skill that, at the moment, I figured I could do without.

If Agramon was trying to give me directions, I couldn't hear them. I panicked as I flew farther away from my guardian and the safety of the ground.

I tamped my power down.

The ground rose to meet me far too quickly before everything went black.

I AWOKE GROGGY, RUBBING MY feet against each other on something leather. I smiled. My sleep was dreamless for once. When I opened my eyes, I realized then that my arm was wrapped in a thick bandage.

"But see here? The Lu Shen will use their archers to decimate this faction," I heard Luc say. I turned over and saw him point to a board. "They will form a wedge and cut your forces in two."

Sam was standing beside Luc with a furrowed brow. His chin rested on his hand as he studied the board. "So, what would you do?" Sam asked, pointing to the statues. "We're already at a disadvantage with the terrain, so would you have us go through the mountain pass instead?"

Luc shook his head. "And have villagers pick your squadrons through before they even reach the battlefield? I don't think so. You must keep in mind, this isn't like Yliria where you can see for miles; this is more like Espiria. They will be able to hide along the route and pick your forces through before they see battle. No, what you should do is plant archers here. It will bottleneck their troops."

Sam stopped a moment. "What about their sorcerers?"

"You would head them off here and here, while cutting off supplies and reinforcements here," Luc said, moving the pieces around the board.

"You are not wrong," Sam admitted. "You have quite a mind for battle strategy, Mordog. If Agramon weren't such a cold, unfeeling bastard, I would ask him to allow me to hire you as an officer."

Luc shrugged. "Chief Weldon listened to me when it came to planning for raids."

Luc's words rang true enough. We became very efficient at raiding because of his strategies. We captured more horses with fewer deaths and less injury. He would've been a great chief, had our lives worked out the way our families had intended. Sadly, the gods had other plans.

Sam was nodding. "Did they catch the murderer yet?"

Luc shook his head. "Agramon said the man had many enemies. What he's worried about is that it happened in the castle."

"We can increase the guard," Sam offered. "I have men I can spare."

"What happened?" I asked, sitting up on the leather couch.

Sam and Luc both startled, Luc dropping the statue in his hand. "One of the guests from dinner was found stabbed to death in the corridor."

"I meant . . ." I looked down. "What happened to my arm?"

"Oh, you were flying, until you weren't. You broke your arm when you fell."

"Bother," I grumbled, putting my feet on the floor and rubbing my head with my good hand. "Where am I?"

Sam stepped forward. "My receiving room. The military healer felt more comfortable coming here to work on your arm. He didn't think your room would be . . . appropriate."

I pursed my lips, recognizing the lie, then rubbed my injured arm. "It still hurts a great deal," I said. "Did he leave anything for the pain?"

"Agramon has already sent for a better-equipped healer from the city who will be able to heal your arm entirely," Luc said.

"Where is Agramon?" I asked. I knew I should be happy that he was out of my presence, but I couldn't deny I was hurt that he declared me invaluable in one breath, and then dismissed me for other ventures with another.

"He's at the observatory," Luc said.

Sam frowned. "Again? I thought he spent all of yesterday there."

Luc nodded. "For some reason, he doesn't want me to accompany him either. He's been spending most of his time there, meeting with the Solstons, especially that Navar fellow."

Sam's frown deepened. "You realize that Solin has the greatest observatory in the empire. Some of the greatest prophesies in Lyrica were foreseen there."

"You think that's what Agramon is doing?" I asked, not convinced. "He's trying to read the future in the stars?"

"You don't need to make fun of it," Luc admonished. "I hear there is a library, too, but Agramon is not

142

one to read very often."

"Has he said anything about what the stars are saying?" I asked.

"Leave us," Sam ordered, looking sternly at Luc.

Luc looked like he was about to dissent, but Sam straightened, his eyes brooking no argument.

"Very well." Luc strode to the door. "I hope you feel better soon, Rowyn. I'll see you later."

"What are you doing?" Sam asked, stepping toward me. "You and I both know that the duke is using your old lover as a spy."

"He wasn't my lover," I snapped.

Sam's eyes narrowed. "As I understand it, you were in love with him for years and later became his betrothed. That would make him your old lover."

I let out a gust of frustration. "None of that even matters right now. Agramon is up to something, and we need to find out what it is. He's making a bid for the throne. Are you just going to stand there and do nothing? Or does the emperor have to make an explicit command to save his life?"

Sam shook his head. "Everyone has been saying he's making a bid for the throne for almost a decade. Yet we are all still here. The man has been stymied by everyone surrounding the emperor, including me. You have Captain Diardo, Edmund the Bright, not to mention Sage Bromwell. Why do you think now is different?"

"Because now he has me, Sam," I said, hoping that I didn't sound vain.

Sam raised his brows. "I'm more worried about this faction, the Sons of Sol. We got notice from Elgar the Swift that they've been making inroads in every major city to the east. They are speaking out against you and the empress and are being fed all manner of lies by several well-respected Solstons."

"Those religious nuts aren't the true threat. Agramon is," I urged.

Sam kneeled before me and took my hand. "I'm not worried about the emperor. I'm worried about you."

"But what if that's just how he wants it?" I asked.

Sam didn't have an answer. I knew he wouldn't.

THE CITY'S HEALER STAYED AT Solin the entire month, tending to the cuts, bruises, and breaks I sustained while flying under Agramon's tutelage. Nobody spoke of the body found in the corridor, Echo didn't have much to deliver in my dreams, and nobody in Solin tried to get close to me save Sam, and even he was keeping his distance. Whether that was his choice or Agramon's, I didn't know.

My guardian was relentless, not allowing me to stop

for the day until I'd mastered whatever skills he'd assigned. Lifting off, landing, going straight up, going up in a diagonal, and soaring.

Despite my misgivings, I enjoyed the wind in my hair, the feeling of freedom beneath my fingertips. As I rose high, seeing visions of the land that only a fair few were privileged to, I felt powerful, like I could do anything. The flying, coupled with bringing the rain every other evening, was a welcome release that left me exhausted after every day.

Arden was highly attentive during my training sessions. She would fly along beside me, screeching and beckoning me to follow her. We didn't always practice outside of the city either. When Agramon was sure I wouldn't plummet onto the stone road below, he had me jumping from windows or soaring over the rooftops until I could land on a windowsill with ease.

Still, I couldn't help but feel that Agramon's work was counterintuitive. Wouldn't the ability to fly make it easier for me to escape his clutches? What purpose did he have in developing my skill now? In the end, when he had me spinning up in the air, I figured he was going to use it for show, like much of what he asked me to do. Not only could I bring the rain, but I could turn somersaults in the air while I did it, not that I'd want to. The fear of being struck by lightning was ever-present in that thought.

Before long, the month was nearly over, and Agramon's flying lessons ceased so we could prepare for the next leg of our journey. A few days before we were to leave, Agramon ducked into my receiving room as I helped Gree pack.

"I'm taking the Butcher to collect the Solin recruits. We will be back in time for me to escort you to dinner."

"May I go with you?" I asked, dropping the gown I was holding. I'd been anxious to get out of Gree's presence. "I haven't had an opportunity to ask after Fin in Solin. This is a big enough city that someone might have seen her, maybe someone who has traveled elsewhere."

Agramon sighed. "Very well. I was going to stop by the mayor's residence, so you and the Butcher can ask after her in the market."

"Can we ride?" I asked. I was sick of the carriage.

Agramon scowled. He glanced at Arden's perch where the falcon was delicately preening her feathers.

"I suppose we can, if you promise to be on your best behavior."

I grinned while buckling Iranoct around my waist. Agramon barely batted an eye when he saw the sword now. I'd been wearing it every day, and I guessed that Agramon had resigned to the fact that if I flew down to a dangerous area of the city, my sword would prove useful.

Soon enough, Sam and I were walking through the market street, trailing guards.

"I feel I've barely seen you in days," I said by way of conversation. I couldn't voice my concerns over Agramon's drive to gain more power. Not with other ears present.

Sam shrugged. "War is all-encompassing. Agramon is not wrong when he says I have much to do."

"And how are they, the preparations?"

"They are ongoing," Sam said, but he offered nothing more. Instead, he stopped beside a stall selling women's clothing.

I showed the merchant Fin's picture, but he shook his head, as did the woman selling fruit, the man offering roasted nuts, and the little girl hawking butter. We spent a good hour and a half walking through the market, but no one had seen hide nor hair of Fin.

By the end of the venture, I was too downhearted to try to pry into Sam's mind, especially when he wasn't being forthcoming. He could keep his precious war to himself for all I cared.

We rejoined Agramon and Luc outside the mayor's house and rode to a different part of the city that I'd never seen before. A large stone fortress had been built into the wall. Out front were lines of men, their clothes ragged, most wearing chains. There were hundreds of them, their hair and beards grown out, many scratching as though they were all infested with lice.

"Your troops, Butcher," Duke Agramon said, spreading his hand before the rail-thin men.

Sam frowned. "Where did they come from?"

"The prison of course," Agramon said flippantly. "The jails, the poorhouses."

A muscle quivered in Sam's jaw, giving away his irritation. "You've sat with me on the Emperor's Council long enough to know that I take issue with an entire seat's force being made up of criminals. They are undisciplined and shirk their duties. Furthermore, they are always seeking to escape back to their families, which is easy to do on a campaign of this size. I would much rather have willing men."

Agramon rolled his eyes. "Is that your only concern?" He looked back to the men standing before Sam. Raising his hand, the gems on his brow and staff emitted a bright, rose-colored light, brighter than I'd ever seen it. The men before him covered their eyes and shrank away from him. After several minutes, the light faded, and the men lowered their arms and looked around as if confused. "There, now are you happy?"

Sam's eyes shadowed. "What did you do?"

"I've taken their memories. Now these men have no families to run back to, nor sweethearts pining in their absence. At least as far as they know. They will freely follow you to certain death."

Sam glared at Agramon. "You stole all their memories from them? What of their wives? Their children? What happens when the war is ended?"

"You can take them to the Fields of Forgotten Men," Agramon said with a shrug. "I care not how you repurpose the trash of the empire. I'm merely fulfilling my obligation. Now, I don't want to hear any more about how Solin failed in its oath to the crown."

Sam shook his head as he looked back at the lines of men, who were glancing at each other with confusion and studying the chains on their hands.

"Captain!" Sam shouted. A soldier rode up and saluted. "Prepare these men to accompany us to Ardent. From there you are to take them by ship to Bruin to be trained."

"Yes, sir," the captain said, his eyes sliding to Agramon, then to me.

We rode through the city silently as if each of us pondered the horror of what Agramon had just done. Sam was holding Hale's reins with white knuckles, his jaw rigid and eyes downcast. I rode between them, trying to catch Sam's eye. I'd told him so. I'd told him that he could end this horror. He didn't listen to me. He insisted that there was nothing he could do. If such a terrible display didn't urge Sam to act against the war, then I was resigned to try to end the campaign by myself. There had to be another way.

Suddenly, Agramon gripped my arm, forcing me to rein in. "Butcher," he said, his voice tight.

Sam looked from me to Agramon. The duke's eyes were squinted, eying the people wandering the market around us.

"Circle up!" Sam shouted. Hale danced to the side, joining the soldiers in a ring around our group.

Agramon grabbed my hand as I drew my sword. "I forbid you to fight."

"What?" I asked, flabbergasted. "Why?"

"Who do you think we are trying to protect?" Agramon scolded. "If they overrun us, I want you to fly out of here!" He looked over his shoulder. I followed his gaze and saw a man with the eye of Sol tattooed on his brow. The mark of the Sons of Sol who had spoken out against me at the capitol. The man was carrying a bow and arrow, aiming it directly at me. I hadn't even seen him.

I ducked just in time, the arrow flying into the soldier behind me.

"Shields!" Sam shouted, grabbing his own from Hale's saddle.

"Can't you turn them away?" I yelled to Agramon. "Get in their mind and force them to leave!"

More arrows peppered around us.

Another soldier fell.

"I can't," Agramon said. "I used all of my power on

those men in the prison."

Luc rode out into the crowded street, going after two of the men. His horse trampled one, while his blade made quick work of the other.

"Hold the line!" Sam yelled. Several soldiers had drawn their bows and were returning fire, but the street was pandemonium. One woman grabbed her daughter and escaped down a side street, while an elderly man hobbled toward the wall, away from the stamping horses.

"The roof!" Sam shouted to Luc, pointing to a building where several Sons of Sol were shooting at us.

Luc disappeared inside. A moment later, two bodies fell into the street.

Sam was relentless. He'd discarded the shield for a bow and arrow and picked off archers one by one, firing faster than any man I'd ever seen. Every arrow he fired found its target.

Agramon dragged me off the horse, his arms wrapped around my waist. "Hold still!" Agramon yelled as I struggled against him. We both fell to the road.

"Get off me!" I screamed, getting tangled in his cloak.

"I'm trying to protect you!" Agramon grunted in my ear. "The gems that protect me can protect you too! Just. Stay. Still!"

It was a moment later that Sam lifted both of us out

of the dirt and onto our feet.

"The rest have run off," Sam said, tossing me back onto a horse. "Get her to the castle!" he ordered the soldiers before mounting Hale.

"I will go with her," Agramon said.

Sam turned Hale around to block him. "No, we need your help tracking down the other infidels."

Agramon frowned but handed me Iranoct, hilt first. "Take your sword at least. I'll be there shortly."

I nodded. Sam smacked the rump of my horse, and I galloped through the street surrounded by guardsmen.

THE WAITING WAS THE WORST PART. I paced at the front door, anxious about the attack. The barracks had emptied, and men were stationed outside the doors, down by the gate, and all along the walls of the castle. Many more had ridden into the city to join the search for anyone who'd gotten away.

They didn't return until nightfall. I ran down the steps as the line of horses approached. Sam rode in front, with Agramon behind him, his snow-white robes now dirty with droplets of blood and dust from the road. I looked behind them for Luc, but he wasn't there.

Sam and Agramon dismounted in front of me, Sam looking as though he'd bathed in blood. He stepped forward, cupped my face in his hands, and his brows furrowed. "You are unhurt?"

I nodded. "Where is Luc?" I asked, my voice quivering. Unexpected tears sprang to my eyes. Despite what he'd done, despite being angry at him, I still cared for him. Sam had been right. I couldn't help who I was. I would always care about my Morganite brethren, no matter how much they hurt me. "He's not . . ."

Sam's hands fell. His eyes darkened.

"He's on one of the wagons, with the rest of the wounded," Agramon said, his voice weary. "The injuries are not life-threatening. A healer will tend to him soon."

"Thank Imor," I gasped.

Sam looked as though he wished to say something more to me, but instead, he turned around. "The prisoners will be executed tomorrow," he announced.

Chapter 12

WE LEFT THE DAY AFTER the hangings. The prophecies the men spat at me, the down-turned eyes of the townsfolk who were forced to come watch—images flicked through my mind faster than thought.

Agramon had passed the sentence—death to those who would harm the servants of the emperor. Sam stood with the executioner, ensuring orders were carried out smoothly.

When the last prisoner had stepped to the gallows, he'd smiled at me from across the town center. One of his eyes was swollen to the point that he couldn't possibly see out of it. His leg was also bent at an odd angle. They'd all shown evidence of torture. Had Sam done it himself or did he have some lackeys do it?

"Sol is weak!" the man shouted. "We weaken him and ourselves when we worship this spawn of darkness. She has come to turn our hearts away from our true lord!"

Sam kicked the man off the platform, sending him bouncing in the air, his neck snapping instantly. I turned away, sickened by the display. It was too much like Ayastaren, though the Sons of Sol were hardly the

154

innocents that the family claimed to be. Guilt weighed on my mind, a familiar friend whose company was always unwelcome. I didn't force those men to act against Agramon and me, yet it still felt as though I had a hand in their deaths. I wondered, not for the first time, why they hated me so much.

A hand came to rest on my shoulder. I looked up and found Luc, his mouth drawn into a grim line.

"It had to be done," he said, shifting his weight onto his crutch. He'd been stabbed in the leg by one of the religious militants. Apparently, Sam had helped him back to safety. "I know you hate this, but it had to be done."

I nodded. Sam spoke to the executioner before striding down the stairs, then he disappeared into a line of soldiers marching out of the city.

BACK ON THE ROAD MEANT I was trapped in the carriage with Agramon. He seemed more distant of late, his mind on other things as he stared out of the window, always with a frown on his face.

I let my mind wander to the quinquennial. Sam said that, to outwit Agramon, I would have to do what he least suspected. The night of Agramon's warning and subsequent maiming played through my mind. He'd only ever reacted when I'd misbehaved or gone against his wishes. Agramon wanted me to follow orders, but doing so wouldn't be enough to give me an opportunity to escape.

Araceli had said that I should gain Agramon's favor. Agramon was a man who dealt in alliances and bargains. I needed to do more than be a grudging puppet. I had to show him that I could be a true ally, at least on the surface. I had to gain his trust. Araceli said that all men liked to be heard, to be understood. If I made an effort to know Agramon, not as the Divine, but as a man, he might begin to see me in a different light as well. Only then would I be able to sneak away.

I glanced at the shrunken faces and figures of those toiling along the road. A fine layer of dust coated their clothes and skin. "Why didn't Lord Alexander end the drought?" I voiced it innocently enough, but I watched his reaction closely.

Duke Agramon's gaze snapped to mine. I knew mentioning my old instructor from Solridge would cause Agramon great discomfort—after all, it was Lord Alexander who had seduced away Duke Agramon's lover, Lady Vianne. Though, to hear the empress tell it, Lady Vianne was none too willing a partner to Agramon's attentions.

"He can't pull water out of nothing," Agramon said after a moment, his gaze going back to the window. "The wells have been dry for years, and there is no water to be found underground. He merely moves what is already there."

I turned my attention back to the window and watched the graceful arc of Arden swooping down over the procession. She was a beautiful hunter. I looked back at Agramon. The best hunters studied their prey.

I cast about for something else, something to keep Agramon talking. The more men talked, the more likely they were to reveal their weaknesses. "What of your life growing up?" I asked. It seemed silly to think of a man of his stature as a child.

"I was not blessed with a happy childhood," he said, still gazing out the window. "My mother left me to my father when I was a baby. Ran off with one of the men who farmed our land. My father, he didn't take kindly to her leaving. He always thought . . ." The duke paused. I wondered if he'd even continue, but he took a deep breath and went on. "He was suspicious that I wasn't his son, so when he remarried and his wife bore him more children, he cast me aside."

My eyes widened. What could I say to something like that?

My stomach began to twist into a knot. "I'm sorry," I said, hoping I sounded authentic.

"Don't pity me. I got my revenge on them long ago, after I went to work for the old duke, uncle to the late emperor himself. Now it is I who is in charge, with more power than my father ever had." The duke sat up, puffing his chest out as if to prove it to me, or to his father.

Belatedly, I schooled my expression. Why wouldn't I have expected such a story? Del had told me that he'd been rejected from the academy of sorcery at Somme, due to their distrust of mind readers. He'd taught himself how to master his power while working for the old Duke of Solin. People attributed the childless duke naming Agramon as his heir and successor to his ability to read and manipulate minds. Could there have been a chance that the old duke really had loved Agramon, a boy whose own father rejected him? A boy who probably would've given anything for a father's love? If that were the case, was it fair to attribute that love to manipulation? Agramon was the best one to know what others were saying behind his back. He'd never once been trusted at the capitol. Even the academy he now helped preside over once had little faith in him studying there.

"So, your mother abandoned you," I said, leaning back with a sigh. "Then Vianne did the same?"

Agramon's eyes sharpened. He rotated his staff slowly, the gem emitting a glow. I watched the movement. He didn't trust me at all. Not yet anyway. But I held out hope that I could change that. I couldn't be overly gracious or he would suspect something. No. I still had to be myself.

"My father cast me aside for Luc—not in love, but in trust, in faith. My entire clan has renounced me, people whose love I'd been striving to obtain for my entire life. That's the world, I suppose," I said, running my hands over my skirt. "The people whose regard we care about the most, that weighs heaviest, is the hardest to obtain."

Agramon's nostrils flared. He was studying me, and I felt him nudging at the corners of my mind, but he wouldn't get in.

"Perhaps we are just impossible to love, you and I," I added with a bitter smile. I was sitting across from a man who'd faced as much rejection in life as I had. "We seem to be kindred spirits after all." Let him see me as a version of himself.

"You really feel that way about yourself?" Agramon asked, leaning back in his seat, switching his staff to his other hand.

I shrugged. "I instill fear more than love." I was sure he felt the same. There were few at the capitol who actually seemed to like Agramon. Really, the only two I'd met were Princess Willene and Del. Everyone else seemed to fear him.

Agramon pursed his lips. "Yet there are those who love you, as many have proclaimed in this last year alone."

I bit my lip. "Do they though? I ask myself whether many of my suitors love me or the power I may afford them. If I were just an ordinary girl, not able to bring rain, not able to fly, would I have Destrian, or Sam, or even Luc?"

Agramon stopped rotating his staff and rested his chin on his hand. "Do you want me to find out for you?"

My skin began to tingle. The hairs on the back of my neck rose. "Would you be honest with me if you did?"

Agramon chuckled.

Despite myself, I grinned, turning to look out the window, pondering my next step. There was a moment during our conversation that he let himself relax. I needed to find a way to have more of them.

OUR FIRST NIGHT ON THE ROAD I sent rain to Solin and Calla, then sat down to eat at the fire. Though I watched the camp around me, my thoughts were on the war and what I could do to stop it. If Sam refused to speak to the emperor, I needed to find someone who would. Agramon was a possibility, but I wasn't sure about approaching him. He didn't trust me yet, and asking a favor of him so soon after making a chink in his defenses would reveal me as false. No, I needed other lords to see reason, to rise as one and make it known that sending men to die in Lu Shen was the last thing the empire needed.

I absentmindedly stroked the feathers on Arden's head. The sun set behind the fire. A noise caused me to turn. Sam stepped out of a tent with one of the soldiers who held a slatted crate that he placed on a table. Sam handed the soldier a scrap of parchment. The soldier turned, his back to me as he fiddled with the crate. When he turned around again, he held a scarlet jay. I recognized the messenger birds used at the capitol. The servant tossed the jay into the air where it took flight, flapping north. Sam continued handing the soldier pieces of parchment, while the soldier set loose bird after bird in every direction. It was the summoning of arms.

Arden squawked. Sam met my eyes before turning away as though ashamed. I furrowed my brow. I'd seen Sam sending birds out daily, and some had come back bearing messages from the nobles. Nobles we were about to visit.

What was it Luc had said, figure out potential allies? If anyone dissented from the war, the clues would be in their correspondence with Sam.

Sam had guard duty in the evening, right before lights out. I knew because Echo had shown him talking about it in the dream from the night before. It was part of the reason that Sam drew such loyalty from his men. There was no task too small for Sam to tend to, and his men respected him for it.

I rose from the fire. "I'm going on a walk," I said to Agramon. "My legs are jelly from being in the carriage all day."

Agramon nodded. "I will check that you are in your tent by lights out."

I stepped away, Arden riding on my shoulder while I drew up some pieces of gristle that I'd saved for her from the stew meat. She swallowed happily while I wandered through the camp. "Echo," I whispered. "Where is Sam's tent?"

"Follow me," Echo said, her shadow appearing on the ground where torchlight had cast a glow. Her shadow melded into mine until all I could see was Echo's extended hand.

I followed, twisting and turning throughout the camp until I came to Sam's large tent. "Is anyone there?"

"No," Echo hissed. "All is clear."

I sent Arden away and ducked inside. Sam's bed was a pallet in the corner, covered with sheep's skin. Hale's packs sat at the foot of it, both notched closed. At the other end was a small cart that was used to haul tent gear, but the back wall was missing. Sam had fashioned it into a makeshift desk. I walked over to it.

Rifling through the papers, I looked for correspondence from the other nobles to see who was angry about the war and who supported it, but what I found were Sam's lines of defense that he was planning against the Lu Shen. It didn't escape my notice that bands of Morganites and Morganians made up the front lines. We were nothing but cannon fodder to him. Was that what he thought of me as well? Did he find me expendable? Even though I was sure he cared for me, I couldn't help feeling the insult.

"He comes!" Echo hissed, her voice panicked. I looked toward the opening and heard a rustle. I hastily put the papers back and went to sit on the bed.

Sam lifted the flap and came in. His eyes widened when he saw me. "Rowyn," he grunted in his usual way. "What are you doing here?" He glanced at the table of maps and letters.

"I wanted to apologize," I said, rallying my thoughts. "I feel awful for what I said in Solin. I didn't mean those things. You know that, right? I don't think you are a coward."

Sam met my eye. "Then why did you say them?"

"Rage," I admitted. "Sometimes I can't help where it

spills."

Sam unbelted his sword and hung it on one of the tent poles. "Your man, Luc, came to see me. He warned me off, said that your entire clan would be after me if I pursued you."

Luc was an idiot and a liar then. I hoped Luc's injured leg gave him a few sharp twinges of pain, just for me.

Sam glanced again at the table, probably wondering what I was doing in his tent alone. If I disclosed that I was planning to work against the war effort, he would give me away to Agramon or the emperor. Sam might also take issue with my interference.

There was only one other way I could think of to explain my presence. Vianne had taught me that there was no greater distraction to a man than seduction. Though, it would be out of character for me to be so forward, I'd resolved to command every weapon available to me to ensure that I pleased the gods and created a path of escape.

"And what if they did?" I murmured, rising from the bed and stepping toward him. "Would that stop you?"

Sam narrowed his eyes. "No. I don't govern myself on Morganite treachery."

"But what of my treachery?" I whispered, resting my hand on his chest. "They say that Sol will destroy those who pay me heed."

Sam grabbed my wrist, his nostrils flaring. "You've already destroyed me."

My breath caught as he leaned closer. My heart raced so loud, I was sure he could hear it. It was almost too easy. If Vianne could see me, would she be proud? Then a pang of feeling speared through my heart. What would my mother have said? What of my honor? Was it right to seduce so broken a man as the Butcher of Bruin?

"Lord Commander," a soldier said as he stepped into the tent.

I jumped back. The soldier's eyes widened, flitting between his high commander and the sorceress that the entire army held in deep distrust.

"I should go," I said, stepping away from Sam. The soldier's eyes narrowed, trailing me as I moved around him and left the tent.

"You announce yourself *before* entering my quarters," I heard Sam growl as I walked away.

SAM AND I HAD NO LUCK FINDING Fin in the towns leading to Ardent. Every innkeeper and shop owner shook their heads, saying that I was the first sorcerer they'd seen in a dozen years or more. Despite our lack of luck, Sam called the horses each time I signaled him to venture into a city.

I was beginning to lose hope in ever finding Fin. We would never curl up together, sharing stories on our beds, speaking long past the time we were supposed to be asleep, or practicing archery together, or sparring with knives. I found myself missing her blunt reasoning, her fearless approach to the world that dealt her a cruel hand. She was the voice of reason I'd been longing for ever since I'd crossed the sea. What would she have said about Destrian and me? What would she have said about Luc, or Sam, or Agramon? Wherever she was, I hoped she was well and safe, finding happiness in some corner of the world I couldn't reach.

Sam insisted we camp every night on the way to Ardent. He worked to train the new recruits he'd gathered in Solin and the other townships on our journey. Every afternoon, after setting up camp, Sam would direct the men into groups, practicing sword work, archery, wrestling, and outfitting the men with armor.

Agramon had me practice flying during that time. I performed somersaults in the air and rotated among tiny cyclones off the path. From high up I could see the soldiers watching the path I made in the sky. Every other night, right before lights out, Agramon would come to my tent, and I would send a swell of clouds to Calla and Solin and all the fields in between.

The routine was exhausting, but it cleared my mind of terrible thoughts. The weariness meant that I wasn't worried about the growing factions of the Sons of Sol, nor the moves that Agramon was sure to be making, nor how I would be able to face those in Morgania again, should I chance to see them. When I escaped, none of that would matter anyway.

That was, until one afternoon, when Agramon had received some correspondence that seemed to displease him. His eyes darkened as he read, then he strode into his tent. I was already in breeches and a tunic, the clothes that Agramon allowed me to fly in, but I didn't feel like practicing. It had been far too long since I'd trained with my weapons, and I worried that with all the people out to get me, it wouldn't do for my reflexes to slow.

Making up my mind, I strode to the group of men clustered at the edge of the makeshift training grounds. They glared at me as they parted, revealing Sam leaning against the side of a tree. His arms and feet were crossed before him. He laughed at one of the soldier's jokes. I'd not seen him so casual before. He seemed at home surrounded by his officers.

When Sam saw me approach, he straightened, his smile disappearing. The men's faces hardened.

"I don't mean to interrupt," I said, nodding to the others. "I just wanted a couple of dummies to work with."

Sam nodded and ordered one of the men behind him to grab two. Sam tied one to a tree limb away from the soldiers.

My presence had broken the men's banter. They went back to their training under Sam's watchful eye, but I could feel them studying me.

Luc approached and waited beside a tree. His leg was good as new with the help of Sam's military healer. I hadn't yet admonished him for sticking his nose in my business with Sam. I didn't need Luc's protection—far from it—but there was always the possibility that Agramon had put him up to it. Sometimes I thought Agramon did things just because he fed off the drama of it all. I wondered if there was a way to twist that to my favor.

I brought Iranoct up and squared off against the straw man hanging from the line.

It turned out, I'd just wanted to destroy something. I swooped and swung, dismembering the dummy in sweeping motions as I danced around the bouncing figure, throwing all my weight into each blow. When all the limbs had been severed, I grabbed the knives in my thigh holster and flung the blades into the torso.

At my signal, Luc put up the second dummy, but in too short a time, I'd destroyed that one as well. I hadn't used nearly enough energy.

I glanced over at Luc who was inspecting his fingernails.

"Come, it's no fun if there isn't anything to hit you back."

Luc raised his brows. "You've improved since you've left Espiria . . . but so have I."

"Maybe it's time to see which of us is best?"

Luc shrugged. "No magic?"

"None," I agreed. "Dummy swords, and hits are allowed."

A muscle in Luc's jaw twitched. "Are you sure you can handle a hit from me?"

I shot him a crooked grin. "Are you sure you can catch me?"

Luc grabbed a wooden sword. "Just don't cry when you get hurt."

"I won't," I sneered, accepting his offer of another.

Luc strode to one side of the clearing. He whipped the sword in a circle as he turned to face me.

I smiled, mimicking his movements.

Luc swept in. His blows rained hard onto my sword, but I blocked over and over, my arms weakening with every blow.

At the first opening, I kneed him in the groin and punched him across the face with the hand clenched around the wooden hilt. I relished the power that passed through my fist and connected with flesh and bone as Luc's face swung back from the force.

I smiled, drawing my other fist up and slamming a cut into his jaw.

Luc recovered quicker than I anticipated. He slammed his fist against my cheek, sending me reeling to the side.

I jumped up, my free hand on my jaw. There was no denying that it had hurt.

"How dare you, boy," a voice said behind me. Sam was striding over, his face a thundercloud. He pulled his sword from its sheath.

Luc dropped the wooden blade and backed up with his hands raised.

"I wanted to spar!" I shouted. "It's nothing."

"With blades is one thing, but fists?" Sam shouted, though he slowed down.

"We fought like this all the time at home." I grabbed Sam's arm as he tried to pass me. "It was encouraged. You think those defending the caravans we raided would pull their blows just because there were girls fighting?"

Sam stopped beside me and took a deep breath. "I don't care what you did at home. I will not watch you be beaten. Not by anyone, am I understood?"

"Fine," I agreed, rubbing my cheek. "We'll do it out of eyesight next time."

"Rowyn," Sam said, his voice filled with warning.

"Fine!" I grumbled. "No more fighting."

"Good." Sam stood for a moment, glaring at Luc, who made tracks in the other direction. Sam glanced down at me before turning and striding back to his men.

Chapter 13

WE RODE TO THE COAST, where Ardent's port carried all manner of goods to empires beyond the Ballerian. We came upon a palace built into the cliffs, with open corridors that invited in the sea breeze. Beyond, white sails caught the air, billowing out like clouds. All manner of vessels filled the port. I wondered about our presence there, considering the ground grew rockier the farther south we traveled. It couldn't be very good farmland, but the route of our journey had never been up to me.

"Duke Agramon," the Count of Ardent said, limping down the stairs of his castle with a gilded cane. He smiled at our party. He looked to be about Sam's age, with dark skin and striking blue eyes, just like the emperor's son and daughter. Agramon had told me on our journey that those features were common among Adarites and those of Ember Innes, especially in Ardent, an ancient seat that had been taken over when Lyricans invaded.

"Ariz," Sam said, holding out his hand.

The count clasped Sam's hand and drew him in, slapping him on the back good-naturedly. "Baron Samael, well met, my good man, well met!"

The count turned to me, switching the hand his cane was in, and smiled. "And this must be the sorceress whom the entire empire is indebted to."

"Count Ariz." Agramon drew his hand out to me. "May I present my student, Lady Rowyn the Morganite, Bringer of Rain."

The count clasped his hand to his heart. "I can't even begin to tell you what a pleasure this is. How are you liking the eastern shore? Our air is drier, though some prefer it that way." The count smiled at Agramon, but the smile didn't reach his eyes.

"Arty would spend his summers here, you know," he said, sweeping his hand to the port as we ascended the steps. "We spent long hours climbing up and down these cliffs, stealing eagles' eggs, and fishing out on our paddle boats. Some of the best times of my life were spent here with him."

I raised my brows. Was he speaking of Emperor Arthello? From everything I knew of the man, he seemed lazy and vulgar, not like the carefree lad the count was describing.

The count led us through corridors and into a large room fitted with couches, the windows draped with heavy coverings. A table bore a feast of fish, crab, and sea creatures I hadn't ever seen before. To the side was a heaping bowl of fruit, and another with vegetables tossed in some sort of cold sauce. Sam grabbed a plate and handed it to me, then took his own and began filling it. I followed suit, taking a little bit of everything before sitting in a chair, rather than the couch Sam had chosen. It left Agramon no choice but to sit beside Sam. Luc went to stand at the window behind the men. Arden flew through the large window and rested on Luc's shoulder.

"I didn't realize you were close to the emperor," I said when everyone was settled. It seemed that the duke and count were not close in any way. Rather, they seemed to detest each other if their sour looks were any indication.

"I was—I am," the count said, brandishing his cane. "Now the fields are dry, which is why you and Duke Agramon are here."

Agramon was pushing food around his plate. It seemed he didn't care for fish. "So, I am to bring the rain?"

The count smiled and nodded. "That's what I paid for, but it was the emperor who suggested it."

I choked on my bite of peaches. "Paid for?" I repeated, then glared at Agramon. "Why are my services to be paid? I'm not a master sorcerer, and I'm already in the emperor's service as I understand it, so why is the count paying for my presence?"

Agramon rolled his eyes, then selected a sausage roll from a plate a servant had placed on the table before us.

"Rowyn, you of all people should know by now that no services are free. I must take time out of my schedule to run you all over the empire to bring rain to the people. To top that off, there is the issue of your room and board, your transportation and safety, not to mention the price of us staying so well at the palace."

"But what of the people? How will we ensure that the people who need the rain the most get the service? What if they can't afford whatever payment you're asking for?"

The count laughed, then turned to Agramon. "She's not like your other protégés, is she, Duke? This one speaks her mind. I like that." The count smiled at me and then nodded to my gems. "I've rarely seen a sorcerer with more than one gem before, and here you have three. I was astounded when I'd heard. Tell me, has it made you more powerful?"

I shrugged. "I have nothing to compare it to, other than having no gems at all. I can tell you it gives me control—most of the time."

I took a bite of the vegetables in cold sauce. It was delicious. Refreshing in the southern heat even though it was winter.

Count Ariz smiled as he watched me eat, probably reading the enjoyment on my face. "So, three gems. You must be the most powerful sorcerer in the land. More powerful than the duke here."

I bit my lip, turning to Agramon. He was angry, seething in fact. His jaw clenched as he fought to control his temper. I took a larger bite of vegetables so I wouldn't have to answer.

"Rowyn is powerful indeed," Duke Agramon said. "But as she is my student, I still retain control."

The count sat back easily in his chair, picked a grape from the dish of fruit, and tossed it into his mouth. He chewed and swallowed before grinning mischievously. "Still, though, you can't have as much control over her as the others. My guess? You can read her mind—that would be easy enough—but I don't think you can control her actions, not all the time anyway."

The duke leaned forward. "You presume much, given someone who isn't gifted with the art of sorcery."

The count shrugged. "The libraries in Ardent are the best in the land, and I've always enjoyed reading books. I found it important to study everything I could on the art, even though I was not gifted myself."

Duke Agramon glanced at the necklace around the count's throat, then met his eyes once more. "I see you bear trinkets to protect you from enchantments as well. I'm surprised you were able to afford Rowyn and my presence, given the cost of such gems."

I raised my brows. Gems to protect others from mind readers were quite costly. The emperor's family had many. Sam's sword bore a gem that protected him so long as he carried it, and I had the Girdle of Ephema. I didn't know of any others who bore such gems, though I'd heard most of the nobles carried something that could help prevent manipulation. Their minds could still be read, but they could not be forced to do anything they didn't desire to do. No, that pleasure was reserved for lesser folk.

The count tossed another grape into his mouth. "The emperor helped pay to bring you here, Your Grace. You know I've never been a fan of court, what with all the conniving and scheming. There are always those who think that they can do better, if only they could be given the chance. The truth is, the empire is saved through order and tradition. The minute you upset that, all those who live under our law suffer, from the lonely slave and peasant to the great men of the empire. Nothing is to be gained from it, as chaos only breeds more chaos."

He took a swig of wine, placed his glass on the table, then turned back to me.

"Now Rowyn, tell me of your journey to the Nightlands. I've heard it's quite a tale, and I do love a good heroine. Have you met Mem the Fearless?"

When I nodded, the count smiled. "I can see the two of you getting along quite well. And what of the Dragon of Helena? He went with you to the Nightlands, did he not?"

There it was again, the Dragon of Helena. The count had to mean Destrian, though it was I who had slayed the beast . . . with Destrian's help of course. I supposed I was just jealous, for the name was indeed fitting for the boy who could wield fire. It was far preferable to *Lady of the Heavens* and the rest of the poetic nonsense that Agramon came up with for me.

The Count of Ardent propped his feet on a low stool and rotated his goblet. "I invited him to Ardent to meet you, hoping to be a haven to you lovers, but he never replied to my offer. Pity, for I would've enjoyed the company of you both, after your reunion, of course."

I stilled, looking at Sam and Agramon, confused.

"You must excuse Count Ariz," Sam grunted. "He and his wife like to create situations for their own entertainment."

Count Ariz rolled his eyes. "Come now, Baron, what happens when the Dragon asks for his oath's gift at the quinquennial? He's sure to want the girl."

"Then he would be a fool," Agramon said, his eyes narrow. "Though Helena is one of the wealthiest consulships, Rowyn's abilities make her priceless, and if he insults the emperor in such a way, he may lose his oath's gift altogether. Some have even lost holdings after such an insult."

"I look forward to the excitement of it. Some of the

other nobles have taken bets. Then again . . ." Count Ariz's eyes sparkled with mischief as he looked at Sam. "I've heard there have been other suitors vying for the girl's affections."

"The lady grows overtired of your welcome," Sam said, rising across from me. "Perhaps some fresh air will do her good."

Sam held his hand out while Luc scowled behind Agramon.

"No, please," Count Ariz said. "My cook has concocted the most extravagant dessert I've ever seen. It's a miracle that it still stands. Miyu herself couldn't have done it. Here, the countess brings it now."

I ignored Sam's offered hand and twisted to see a giant of a woman saunter into the room. The silk dress wrapped around her revealed every curve, and her hair dripped with gold and gems, more so than even the empress would wear. Following her was a row of servants that she towered over. They carried a massive cake dripping with rose frosting and adorned with sugared creatures along the tiers. I raised my brows. There were only the few of us in the room. Who was supposed to eat this monstrosity?

"My darlings, how dare you arrive early and miss the grand entrance I'd planned," the countess said as the men on the couches rose. "Put it over there," she directed the servants, motioning to the table behind the sitting area.

The count beamed at us. "May I present my wife, Countess Mahira."

"Baron," the countess said, passing Sam and tweaking his nose. "Always a pleasure."

Sam's cheeks reddened, and he ran his hand through his hair. How well did they know each other?

I eyed the count to see if he had caught the gesture, but he was watching his wife with delight.

"Rowyn the Morganite, I presume," Countess Mahira said, pulling me to my feet. She turned me around her, much as Gree had. "Aren't you a picture. She's as striking as they say, is she not?" the countess asked her husband.

"Indeed," the count agreed, taking a drink from his goblet and studying me. "She would be easy to fall in love with, I think. The only trouble is you may not survive it." His eyes slid back to Sam.

"But what delicious fun it would be, would it not, my lords?" The countess held her hand to Agramon. He bowed and kissed it, but she barely paid him a glance. She spotted Luc standing in the corner.

"Ooooh, is this the famous Mordog I've heard of?" She sauntered to Luc, who straightened, his eyes on the countess's hips. "My, my, my, such warriors you all breed. No wonder you hold them in such high regard, Baron. This one seems to be practically carved by the gods." Countess Mahira shot me a wink before turning her attention back to Luc and running her finger up his chest. "You can guard my body any day."

"Please do not distract him," Duke Agramon said, his teeth clenched.

"Oh, why not? You don't think you're in any danger here, do you, Your Grace?" The countess quirked a softly curved eyebrow.

Agramon didn't answer.

"So, what do you have for the army of Lyrica?" Sam asked, swirling his drink as he looked from the count to the countess as she made her way back to us. "Your battalions of thieves that you sent to Yliria have all perished, so will you empty the jails again?"

The count's mouth creased as though he held in a smile. "Yes, I heard about the untimely fate of Ardent's companies. Then again, that's what happens when you send them to the front lines, isn't it? Duke Agramon's new guard would know."

Sam rolled his eyes. "That one used privileged information to escape the war."

"Ooooh, you don't say," Countess Mahira said gleefully, sinking onto a cushion beside me. "I would love to know more." She rested her hand on the arm of my chair. My eyes were immediately drawn to the bracelet hanging on her wrist. A mark of the empress's favor. I'd seen the same on the Countess of Calla, as well as a few noblewomen at the palace. I'd started to wonder if the piece of jewelry meant something more.

Sam grunted. "I would like to know about the men I'm to take to Lu Shen."

"Very well, very well," the count said, his fingers fluttering before him. "Since you've been so kind to us over the years, I thought I'd grant you a boon, just this once."

Sam's lip twitched, the only sign that Count Ariz was throwing him off his guard. "Go on."

"I used some of our excess funds to pay for a battalion of mercenaries from The Crags."

Agramon rotated his staff. Given our hosts' cold greeting to the duke, I imagined distrust ran both ways. "That must've cost you a tidy sum."

The count grinned. "I wouldn't worry about that, considering the war we have on our hands."

Sam glanced from Agramon to the count. "They would certainly be of help in the mountains of Lu Shen."

"Indeed, and they are on strict orders to follow you for three years' time. After that, you must find a way to pay them yourself if you wish to keep them. I figured the plunder to be had in Lu Shen would suffice."

Sam nodded, his eyes on the windows as he ran his hand over his beard. It seemed he was deep in thought, strategizing the use of these new battle-tested men.

"I'm still curious why you would pay such a sum given that your prisons are usually bursting," Agramon prodded.

The count tilted his head to the side. "Well, if you remember, I went on the diplomatic mission to Lu Shen a few years back when they began opening their borders for imports. I found a great dislike for the emperor's brother. That man was such a pompous prick when we were there, I'd give anything to knock him down a peg, or preferably, to a grave."

"That's the one who Miyu was connected to?" I asked, remembering her behavior during the talks. If I remembered correctly that man had the power to bring unrelenting pain to those who displeased him. It was he who had started the war in the first place, provoking the emperor to act by turning his powers on me.

"She's connected to all of them, but they had some prior relationship in Lu Shen, and everything I'd heard about that evil snark was fully realized when I'd met him. Surely you noticed in the talks?"

"I wasn't paying close enough attention to notice," Sam muttered. I fought the heat in my belly as I remembered the day in the rose garden when he'd kissed me. He'd said himself that he only needed to be a presence in the room and nothing more. As a result, he spent most of the time watching me.

"Well, there you have it." The count leaned back in

his chair. "You have a battalion of the empire's greatest mountaineers at your disposal who answer to you and you alone for the next three years."

"And what do you want for this favor?" Sam asked.

"A simple thank you will suffice for now. Later, I'd love to see Huang Bo's head adorn my gates when the war is over."

"Consider it done," Sam agreed, holding his hand out to the count. "You are a true man of the empire."

Count Ariz's eyes moved to Agramon. "Aren't we all?"

Agramon raised his glass to be filled by a servant. "Speaking of honoring agreements. When would you like Rowyn to bring the rain?"

"Whenever is convenient for you," the count said, addressing me. "You could do it now if you wish . . . you don't even have to get up."

"Really?" I asked, looking toward Agramon, who was actively frowning. I grasped my power instantly. After a moment, rain began to patter on the window-sills. It took a few moments more to spread the clouds over a wider swath, but it was far more preferable than being on display.

"Oh, bravo darling, bravo!" the countess said, craning her neck to watch. "Now that the odious talk of business is over, let us have some cake and discuss more entertaining topics."

184

"Very well. I did not receive an itinerary as I'd requested. I would like to prepare for what to expect during our stay," Duke Agramon said. "Normally, our hosts prefer Rowyn to be seen by the people as it can give them hope. They have banquets or outings out to the city."

Everyone turned to him.

The countess rested her chin on her hand. "Do you really require one? I'd hoped to avoid a gathering of the high men of Ardent." Her eyes went to me. "They are unbelievably boring, Rowyn. I can't bring myself to invite them to the castle but once a year, and even *that* is pushing it."

"So then, how are we to amuse ourselves?" Duke Agramon asked impatiently. I couldn't help but notice how markedly different the nobles of Ardent behaved toward Agramon. Everywhere else Agramon was treated with fearful respect, but in Ardent, the count and countess seemed to view Agramon with disdain, or at least with lax indifference.

"In our usual way," the count said over his glass. "I'm sorry you are unused to how we do things here in Ardent, Your Grace. We prefer a slower pace to life. It is far more enjoyable than the intrigues of lesser men that you find at the capitol. Pity you haven't experienced our hospitality sooner. You may learn to enjoy it in time."

"Despite our close distance, you had yet to invite me," Agramon said frostily. "Until I had something you wanted, of course."

"And now you know why," the count offered, lifting his glass to his lips with a smile.

Chapter 14

"**I** LIKE THEM," I SAID TO AGRAMON later as he sat on the chair in front of my looking glass, a letter in his hands. Gree was tending to my hair while I ran my fingers over Arden's feathers. I'd insisted on bringing one of the perches Agramon had given to me in Solin to use on our journey. It made me feel better to have Arden close.

"You would," Agramon muttered, scanning the contents of the missive.

I raised my brows. "Oh? What do you mean?"

Agramon lowered the paper and met my eye. "Count Ariz and Countess Mahira are the very embodiment of everything you've long railed against. They shirk their people and party to excess, living fat off the profits of those below them. Your hypocrisy knows no bounds, my dear."

Luc, skulking in the corner, snorted. It seemed he was still angry with me about Sam's attentions. I didn't see how that was my fault. Besides, he'd said our betrothal was a charade. He had no right to care about who I gave attention to.

I glared at him. "At least they're genuine," I muttered.

"And I am not?" Agramon asked. "When have I ever lied to you?"

It took a minute for me to come up with an answer. "You had Gillius lie to get me to Solridge."

"No." Agramon returned to his paper. "I ordered Gillius to obtain you by any means necessary. I did *not* explicitly tell him to lie to you to do it. How he interprets my orders is not my problem."

"Were you controlling him?" I asked. I'd never really spoken of my old mentor to Agramon since the wound was still fresh, but I couldn't deny that I'd been curious.

Agramon sat back, palming his staff. "Would it make you feel better if I said yes?"

"No, the truth would make me feel better."

"People always say they want the truth, but very rarely do they mean it."

I glared at him.

"Fine, no I was not controlling him. I gave him an order, a few threats on what would happen to him if he failed me, and sent him on his way to do my bidding. Are you happy?"

"Not really," I grumbled. It would have been better if Gillius had been controlled by Agramon. As things stood, Gillius sought to gain my trust by making me think that he was a simple sorcerer trying to do a good deed, and I was a fool to fall for it. Agramon was right. I'd been happier not knowing. There was no way I would tell him that, though.

A knock sounded on the door.

Luc went to answer and let in Countess Mahira. She graced Luc with a sultry smile before her dark eyes fell on me. "My darling, please come be entertained by my husband and me this evening in our salon. We have all sorts of diversions that I'm sure you will enjoy, especially after so long a journey."

Duke Agramon glared at Mahira over his letter. "Am I to understand the invitation does not extend to myself, her guardian?"

Mahira's lips thinned. "Of course, you may join us, Your Grace, though, given the rumors, I didn't think the entertainment that we afford our guests was up to your standards . . . or taste. There are no great men of the city for you to coerce, nor is there a platform for you to show off to the lower class. Since my lord and I are under the protection of gems, well . . . Your Grace, what would be the point?"

Duke Agramon's nostrils flared. He glanced at me, then met Mahira's eyes once again. "You're quite right. I have some items that I need to send through port."

"I can watch Rowyn for you, Your Grace," Luc offered, stepping forward.

Agramon shook his head. "No, I will take you with me as protection, as that is what I've purchased you to do." He turned to the countess. "Can I trust Rowyn's care to you and the count?"

"We won't let her spoil in your absence, Your Grace." Mahira winked at me.

Countess Mahira laughed as she pulled me into a massive sitting room. Ornate rugs covered the marble floor, while overstuffed cushions and low couches littered the space. Lamps filled with oil and lined with red glass hung along the walls, casting a rose-colored glow on the room. In the corner, a couple sat on mats and picked over fruits, meats, and cheeses that covered a low table. The woman was wrapped in the man's arms as he fed her grapes. Behind them Count Ariz propped his legs on the couch as he sucked from an odd straw attached to what appeared to be a large wooden and glass lamp sitting on the table that emitted a scented curling smoke. Count Ariz caught my eye and smiled as he blew smoke rings into the air.

Countess Mahira pulled me to a couch beside her husband.

"Welcome to our true court, Rowyn," Count Ariz said with a lazy smile, his eyes half closed. "Most deals in the south are made in this very room."

I sat stiffly, studying the space. There were people hidden in alcoves of other doors around the room doing gods knew what.

Mahira laughed, draping her head on the back of the couch and waving someone forward. "Stop looking so tense, Rowyn. We don't bite . . . hard." She winked. Ariz chuckled.

I blushed.

"Tell me, dear girl. Now that the other men are out of our way, who is it you truly prefer?" Count Ariz asked, leaning forward.

"Ariz," Countess Mahira scolded, slapping her husband's leg as my cheeks heated. "You haven't even offered the girl a drink, yet you expect her to spill her secrets?"

"My apologies," the count said, blowing another cloud of smoke into the air. "What is your preferred drink? Wine? Ale? Naranj? We get everything through the port, so you've only to ask."

"Wine is fine," I replied. It took but a moment for a goblet to appear in my hand, filled to the brim.

"Now, I want to hear about the Nightlands. The bards like to add their special flavor, but I'm sure it's nothing to the true story," Mahira said, leaning forward.

In truth, I'd told the story so many times that I didn't mind relaying my travels to the count and countess, especially considering they didn't force me on display like the others. They leaned forward, paying rapt attention to every word while the others in the room continued with their own entertainments. I found myself embellishing like Destrian would, pausing at the exciting bits that felt good to share. Although my audience was small, dispelling some of the rumors felt like a small victory.

"You slayed the dragon!" Mahira exclaimed. She turned to Ariz. "By Sol above, I'd even told you I thought they'd gotten that part wrong. Tell her I knew they were wrong!"

"She did say something to that effect," Ariz admitted with a smile as I accepted more wine.

"I couldn't have done it without Destrian's help," I conceded. "He can't be hurt by fire, so if he hadn't been with me, I would've been turned to ash in an instant."

"Still." Mahira leaned back and accepted the wooden pipe from Ariz. "I'm glad you've vindicated my thoughts."

As she took a deep breath of smoke, the bracelet on her wrist caught my eye once again.

"You are wearing a bracelet from the empress, a mark of the favored," I said, pointing at the jewelry.

Countess Mahira chuckled. "I would hope I'm favored. She is my cousin after all."

"I didn't realize you were related," I said, taking another sip of wine. I drew my feet onto the couch and tried to relax.

"Oh yes," Countess Mahira said with a sigh. "We share Obi the Wayfarer as our grandfather. Did you not meet him at Solridge?"

"Lord Obi is grandfather to the empress?" I asked, dumbfounded.

"Why, yes, you didn't know he was from Ember Innes?" Mahira asked. "Everyone who's anyone in Ember Innes is related."

"I knew, I just didn't know you were connected so closely," I said. I wondered why no one had told me that before.

"It's not common knowledge," Count Ariz offered. "Obi the Wayfarer is almost a hundred years old, and he has a prolific number of children, grandchildren, and great-grandchildren."

"So, is that how the emperor and empress met?" I asked, taking another drink. The count and countess were older, probably between Sam's and Agramon's age. "Through you?"

"We had a hand in setting up the match," the countess admitted.

Count Ariz's eyes were sparkling. "Poor Arty thought the empress would be just like Mahira."

The countess rolled her eyes. "Lesedi likes to work too much for my taste. What's the point in having all this wealth if one must spend their days listening to tedious droning?"

"Quite right, my dear." Ariz leaned his head back on the couch and smiled. "If you run your land as efficiently as we do, then you can employ others to fulfill the more demanding tasks."

Mahira snapped her fingers. "Speaking of, Rowyn, you must experience Jak's magical hands. He could render a stone supple."

A young man stepped forward. At some point he'd lost his shirt, revealing a smooth chest with impossibly large arms. "I had to pay a pretty penny to lure him away from an Ylirian prince's court, but I have to say, it was well worth the money. The man is a god when it comes to relieving tension."

Jak bowed before Mahira, who spoke to him in Ylirian, her eyes dancing as she pointed to me.

Jak's black eyes flicked to me, and he stepped around the couch. He lifted my hair off my shoulders, letting it drape behind me. His fingers began kneading at the base of my neck. I clenched my teeth as he tried to work out the knots, unused to someone's hands on me. I didn't move or flinch away though. It really did feel good.

Jak said something to Mahira and Ariz in Ylirian, and Ariz laughed. I sat even straighter, self-conscious about their smiles.

"Here," Ariz said, handing me the wooden mouthpiece. "Jak says you need to relax or you'll damage his hands."

I furrowed my brow. "What is it?" I asked, my nostrils flaring.

"It's just sweet weed," Mahira said, sucking in a breath from another mouthpiece attached to the pipe and blowing it out in a thin stream.

My mouth began to salivate. Though I was never one to divert myself with sweet weed, it was something my cousin, Ferris, enjoyed regularly. I supposed I could use help to relax.

I took the wooden mouthpiece from Count Ariz and sucked in a deep breath. The smoke caught in my throat, and I coughed ridiculously. My eyes watering, I handed the mouthpiece back to Count Ariz and tried not to look like I was gasping for air as warmth spread through my body.

Jak had stopped his massaging but continued once my coughing fit ended. My skin seemed to awaken under his fingertips as he pushed deeper into my flesh, and I felt my muscles finally begin to relax.

The door opened, and a gust of fresh air spilled into the room, sending the smoke to the ceiling. Sam entered, his eyes darting around the room until they found me. He'd discarded his leather jerkin and wore only a white tunic with its sleeves rolled up, showing off his muscular forearms. I noticed a large scar running along his left arm. However he'd gotten the wound, it had been deep.

"Nice of you to join us, Baron," Count Ariz said. "Especially since I went to the trouble of procuring your favored vintage from the Ylirian market."

"I've just come to fetch Rowyn. It's well past the time she should retire," Sam said, his eyes meeting mine. I wondered if Sam had been sent by Agramon.

I glared at him as Countess Mahira twisted her face into a pretty pout. "But the fun's just getting started, Baron. Why don't you grab a seat and stay awhile."

"No," Sam grunted. He seemed to have come in a hurry, for the man didn't even have his sword on him.

"I'm not ready to leave yet," I said, canting my head to the side and encouraging Jak's fingers on a preferred path along my neck. I closed my eyes. Countess Mahira was right; Jak's hands were magical.

"There," Countess Mahira said, her voice lilting with delight. "The girl wants to stay."

Sam cleared his throat. "We have a busy day tomorrow, Rowyn."

I didn't move. I didn't even open my eyes. "No, we don't. There isn't even an itinerary." I was floating on a delicious cloud of my own choosing, and I refused to end my pleasure just because Sam wanted me to go to bed. I'd been playing nice, following everyone's orders so that I could get the information I needed, but the stress of spying and Echo's dreams, paired with constantly being under watch, had worn on my mind. The count and countess were offering me a diversion, and I was loath to give it up so soon.

Count Ariz chuckled. "Come now, Baron, you wouldn't begrudge the most powerful sorceress in the empire—the one who is single-handedly ending the drought—a night of fun, would you?"

"Be that as it may, I have to review your troops—"

"Which won't happen until the afternoon." Count Ariz waved his hand lazily.

"But in the morning, Agramon will want—"

I cracked open my eyes. "I don't care. I wish to stay, and so I will," I challenged. "Go back and tell Agramon I will return to my room when I'm ready."

Sam's jaw flexed. "I'm no one's messenger." He took a seat on the couch directly across from me. I opened an eye at him. Perhaps Agramon hadn't sent him after all. Perhaps he'd just come to try to tell me what to do. May Imor save me from men who loved giving orders.

"Come, have a breath, Baron," Count Ariz said, holding up the wooden mouthpiece. "It's tradition for you to celebrate when you come. Why should now be any different?"

What a hypocrite! Sam tried to guard my behavior, while at the same time he was known to partake, as well, when the mood struck.

I glared at him. "I can take care of myself."

Sam didn't break his gaze as he took the wooden mouthpiece from Count Ariz's hand and took a long breath. He handed it back when he was done and blew the smoke up into the air. He didn't even cough. What he did do was lean back onto the couch, his hands folded in his lap and his boots propped up on the table as though he could stay there the rest of the night.

Countess Mahira clapped her hands, delighted with how the evening was turning out. "Have you met Di-Oona?" she asked Sam. A gorgeous woman with an ample bosom and tiny waist drifted over, her eyes hungry. She carried a decanter of amber liquor to our table. I glared jealously at her curves. "She's been absolutely dying to meet the heroic Imperial Commander," Mahira said with a hint of mischief.

Di-Oona sank down next to Sam and shot him a sultry smile. Mahira watched them, almost gleeful.

"Of course, I've heard of the brave commandant," Di-Oona said with a strange accent. She poured the amber liquor into a glass and offering it to Sam with a smile on her ruby red lips. She put the top on the bottle and sank to the floor, leaning against the seat of the couch, practically draping herself onto Sam's feet.

Sam said something to Di-Oona in a language I didn't recognize. Di-Oona's eyes widened, and she prattled off questions that I didn't understand. Sam responded, and Di-Oona threw her head back and laughed, full-throated and divine.

Countess Mahira nudged my arm and offered the

mouthpiece again. I took another breath, this one more guarded, and managed not to make such a fool of myself, coughing only a bit.

An unwelcome twinge threatened my calm as I watched Sam and Di-Oona talk back and forth. Was I jealous? No, of course not. There was nothing to be jealous of. Though Sam had made his feelings clear, I didn't return them . . . at least, I didn't share the same level of feelings that he did. He'd proven useful in protecting me against the worst of Agramon, and he held a wellspring of information that I could share with the empress. Otherwise, there was nothing more to us.

My foggy mind couldn't help but think of Destrian. I'd loved him, truly, but his silence could no longer be ignored. Even though I knew it would break his heart, I'd told him we were over and to leave me be. The poor boy had actually listened to me, dashing any hopes I may have had for us against the rocks of the Ballerian Sea. In my heart, I wished he'd have ignored me and fought harder to be by my side.

But he hadn't.

Di-Oona's hand rested on Sam's knee as she looked up at him. He was handsome, in a rugged sort of way, unlike the other nobles at Somme who shaved every morning, wore their hair longer, and splashed scented waters on themselves before they left for the day. Sam kept his hair closely cropped, his beard shaved only once every week or so. He worked tirelessly and had the muscles to prove it.

I wondered what they were talking about. Was she Ylirian? She didn't look Ylirian. Though her skin was sun-kissed, her eyes were lighter, similar to the people on the islands to the southwest. Perhaps she was from Shea Innes. Sam took another drink of his favorite liquor and smiled, his response masked by the language they spoke. The woman had actually enticed a genuine smile from the man, and she'd just met him!

My heart caught in my throat. I *was* jealous. There wasn't anything wrong with that. After all, Sam had only ever been kind to me. Even if I did have feelings for him, what did that matter? It would end the same way it ended with Destrian. We would all be left with broken hearts, and Agramon would be provided his favorite entertainment.

I closed my eyes and followed Jak's fingers. He moved my hair over a shoulder and leaned me forward so he could reach my back. I relished the sensation of his impossibly strong hands moving along my flesh, pushing the sleeves of my gown down. I felt so light, so free, I was liable to float away on a cloud, feeling every movement of Jak's fingers threefold. He worked down my shoulder blades, and before I could stop myself, I moaned.

I opened my eyes a bit. Sam was staring daggers at

Jak who was working more vigorously, given the encouragement he'd just received. Di-Oona said something and stroked Sam's sleeve with light fingers. Sam caught her wrist and met her eyes with a cold shake of his head.

Sam said something in Ylirian. Jak patted my shoulders and moved to Mahira. He held her foot and relieved it of its slipper. Mahira lay back on her pillows, a smile on her face as she dozed. I looked at Ariz and found him with his eyes closed as well.

"It's late," Sam said, rising. "They will stay here all night, but that doesn't mean you have to."

Di-Oona asked a question, her voice sultry. Sam gave her a clipped reply, then held his hand out to me.

"Very well," I said, emitting a theatrical sigh. "Will you accompany me back?" I held my breath, hoping he wasn't intending to stay with Di-Oona the beauty.

"How else am I to ensure that you reach your room safely?" Sam asked. His posture was different. A lazy smile stretched over his lips, and he seemed far more relaxed than I'd ever seen him. It was no wonder he enjoyed the company of the count and countess of Ardent. All they wanted was for their guests to be at ease. It would be a welcome hall for the man who carried the burdens of the empire and war on his shoulders.

He pulled me out into the corridor where the sea air whisked away the last remnants of smoke. I breathed deep, relishing the gaze of Imor peering in through the open arched windows, the white gauzy curtains floating in and out of the breeze, the wind's scent a mix of brine and rain.

"I'm surprised you stayed," I said as I floated down the hall ahead of him. Sam hadn't let go of my hand, and when our arms grew taut, Sam pulled me back. "Though it seemed Di-Oona made it worth your while." I released his hand and dragged my finger down his sleeve, pleased when he didn't pull away as he had with her. "Is that where you're going after you leave me?"

Sam's eyebrows rose in surprise. After a beat, his eyes narrowed. "You think Di-Oona is who I desire?"

"Why else would you have stayed?" I prodded, enjoying the lightness of my thoughts and relishing his attention. I couldn't help but tease him.

Sam caught my shoulders. His eyes flitted down to my lips, then back up. "Don't be foolish. I had to make sure that boy . . . he had his hands all over you."

I laughed, ducking under his arms and continuing on my path down the hall. "It was just a massage, Sam. Besides, you're a *frequent* guest of Ardent. Care to elaborate on how you spent your time here? The countess especially seems to know you quite well."

"The count and countess are forgiving of my faults, more so than the other nobles of the realm." I felt his eyes following me as I practically spun around the corner. I held no memory of a time when I felt so good.

"Forgiving?" I laughed. "They practically celebrate them."

Sam smirked. "What else was I to do if you refused to leave?"

We'd reached my door. I leaned against it, a thrill streaming through my veins. I was unwilling to sleep the feeling away, knowing that it would be gone when I woke, and I had no wish to return to my constant state of guilt and dread. "You could've dragged me out," I said honestly. "That's what Luc would have done. Agramon would've just embarrassed me until I left."

Sam didn't seem to be in a hurry to return to his rooms either. He checked both sides of the hall before leaning on his hand against the door. I stilled, looking up at Sam through my lashes, willing him to read my mind. His nearness was electrifying. I wished he would drag his fingers down my skin so every nerve could alight with his touch.

"I couldn't begrudge you the pleasures I've held so dear," Sam was saying.

"It's good you didn't try to do any of those things," I admitted. "Had you tried to drag me out, I would've stabbed you." He was close. So close that I could smell the liquor on his breath. I remembered his kiss in the rose garden at Somme and longed for another taste.

This was new. I'd never really initiated with Sam before, but desire for his hands on me completely absorbed my mind.

"If Mordog tries to take you anywhere against your will, I'll stab him," Sam said.

"I can defend myself."

"I know." Sam's eyes traveled down my dress as though he were able to see the holster strapped to my thigh. "But you shouldn't have to sully your blades unless absolutely necessary. Besides," he said, dragging his eyes back up. "That boy has been asking for it since we left. How can you deprive me of the pleasure I'd feel in putting him in his place?"

I ran my fingers along the front of his tunic. Sam's eyes followed my hand's path before meeting my gaze once more. "And what of the pleasure I would feel in getting my revenge on the boy who broke my heart?"

Sam leaned closer, my hand pressed to his chest.

"I can deny you nothing," Sam murmured. "Not if you truly wanted it."

I smiled softly. "Is that true? I can ask anything of you?"

Sam caged me in with his other arm. "Whatever you desire."

My skin burned, the warmth overwhelming me. "Kiss me."

Sam froze, his eyes on my mouth. He leaned in and

delicately tasted my lips. He was so gentle, tender, and soft. I could feel the restraint tugging on him as he breathed in. But inside my nerves were screaming. I tried to pull him closer and explore his mouth with mine, but something was holding him back.

Sam ran his hands over my bare shoulders, then broke away, his lips next to my ear. "Has Agramon put you up to seducing me?" I could feel the heat of his breath and turned, trying to capture his lips with mine. "Does he send me these dreams?"

"Would it truly matter to you if he did?" I breathed, my cheek against his.

Sam began to trace a path from my ear down to my neck with his lips, leaving a trail of goosebumps in his wake. "Not as much as it should."

I shivered, heat beginning to swell in my belly.

"Tell me you don't want this," Sam whispered, wrapping my hair around his fingers. "I'll only drag you further into the darkness."

"The darkness is all I've ever known."

Sam caught my lips with his. It was electrifying, as if every nerve in my body was singing, beckoning him to touch me. I wrapped my arms around his neck, urging him on.

Sam's restraint shattered. He pushed me against the door, one hand cupping my cheek while the other ran over my bare shoulder, then down the flesh of my back.

He pulled my waist toward him.

I moaned as his mouth moved from my lips to my throat where Jak's hands had made a path. Sam nipped at the flesh before strumming it with his tongue, and I nearly came undone, gasping into his ear. Sam's knee pushed between my legs, his hands drawing me up so that he could get a better taste. The warmth in my belly moved down to my core and my nerves sang a feverish tune.

Someone cleared their throat behind us. "If you insist on ruining Rowyn's reputation, at least have the courtesy of doing it in her chambers where others won't see."

Sam tensed at the voice as I looked over his shoulder.

Luc was standing inside a stone recess that led to Agramon's chambers, gripping his sword.

Sam was frozen, his eyes blazing in fury. The warmth was slowly seeping from my skin.

"Duke Agramon suggests you close your mind so he doesn't have to experience it with you, Butcher," Luc went on, seemingly unaware of the danger he was in.

I held Sam's arms as he started to turn, sure he was about to beat Luc within an inch of his life.

"Go," I whispered, meeting Sam's eye. "You promised he would be mine to punish."

It took a minute, but eventually Sam relaxed. "I'll see

you tomorrow."

"Tomorrow," I agreed, resting my forehead against his. Sam pulled away, rolled his shoulders back, and faced Luc with every ounce of fury within. A muscle in Luc's jaw jumped, but Sam didn't say anything. He just strode down the hall to his room.

I turned to open my door, content to ignore Luc altogether.

"I commend you for your idiocy," Luc said, his voice lilting. "You're a scourge of a Morganite, dishonoring us all with your ill repute."

I slammed the door, feeling once more like I was hurtling toward blood and chaos. It felt like the Nightlands all over again, but even darker than I could imagine.

Chapter 15

"CAN'T YOU GET THE BUTCHER to stay away from Rowyn?" Luc asked Agramon in the dream Echo sent me that night. "It's becoming indecent."

Agramon glanced up from his writing table, the flicker of candlelight dancing across his face. "I'm disinclined to confront him on such a matter. Despite what he chooses to show you and your pretty kinsman, the Butcher of Bruin remains a dangerous man."

"Don't you care about her reputation?" Luc asked.

"You are hurt, aren't you?" Agramon asked, setting his quill down and sitting back in his chair. The gem on his brow emitted a soft glow. "Why is that, when you profess that you feel nothing for her beyond friendship?"

Luc stopped abruptly. His expression grew pained.

Agramon tilted his head to the side. "Ah, I see. You are angry with her for forgiving the Butcher of his many faults, yet she fails to forgive yours." Agramon stared at Luc a moment longer, then his gem dulled. "You really don't understand why that is? I would think it quite obvious."

"What? What have I done that makes me worse than

the Butcher?" Luc shouted, throwing his arm out. "Who am I that she prefers him to me?"

"You are a fool for one," Agramon said, picking up his quill. "Despite all the evil the Butcher has done, he has never betrayed nor rejected her, both things that you have done, and both are things that she values highly among those she cares for. By all the gods, boy, I thought you knew the girl."

"You forced the information out of me, a fact she surely knows," Luc said, turning to the window and leaning on the pane to look out to sea.

"How quickly you forget that you offered the information to save your own skin. You are a coward, something that my lovely ward abhors and something the Butcher most certainly is not."

"Still," Luc said, shaking his head. "I thought you were trying to make a match for her. Someone who would ally with you. Won't her relationship with the Butcher muck it up?"

Agramon scoffed. "How lovely of you to take such interest in my plans. As it stands, I've had many nobles reach out about Rowyn, from Ayastaren to Maryse, and none of them would care a jot about her past relationships given the power and acclaim she would afford them and their families. Let her ruin him. He won't win her in the end, I can assure you of that."

I WOKE UP GROGGY, RUBBING my eyes as Gree tottered about the room making as much noise as humanly possible.

"Can you be quieter please?" I grumbled, wishing I could have a word with Echo.

"His Grace asked that I make you ready for the day," Gree said, sneering at me. "And we are all at his whims."

Since Gree had become my lady's maid, she had insisted we dedicate a full hour and a half to getting dressed. She bathed me every morning, careful to eliminate any hair that she found growing on my body, before slathering me in a cloud of perfume and oils. My hair was always curled now, my face painted with tinctures and powders until I was forced to reimagine myself as the girl I saw in the mirror every morning. When Gree finished, she dragged me across the hall to Agramon's room and knocked.

"She's ready, Your Grace," Gree said, shoving me inside. I glared at Luc, but he avoided my eye.

"You asked for me?" I snapped.

Gree elbowed me sharply in the ribs.

"Your Grace," I added as an afterthought. I knew I should be trying to worm my way into Agramon's trust, but I was in a foul mood.

"Yes, my dear. How was your night with the best Ardent has to offer? I heard it was rather stimulating."

"I enjoyed myself," I admitted. There was no point in lying, and I wanted to show Agramon that I could speak the truth.

Agramon stepped toward me and brushed something off my shoulder before taking my hand. "The count asked us to accompany them on a boat ride around the port. I thought you would like to join us. The Butcher will be there, if that helps."

I raised my brows. "I don't know what his presence has to do with anything," I said innocently.

Agramon smiled down at me, his eyes darkening. "Do me a favor and ask him about his wife."

Agramon turned as my mind lurched. I tried to catch my breath.

Sam had a *wife*?

THE COUNT AND COUNTESS LOUNGED on the deck of the ship as sailors scurried about, letting down sails and shouting orders to each other. I gritted my teeth as my stomach sickened.

The leader of the mercenaries that the count had

purchased spoke to Sam over a pint of ale, despite the early hour of the day. I clenched my stomach, thankful that I was granted a respite to gather my thoughts.

Sam had a wife.

Sam had a *wife*.

How had I never heard that before? Why had Del never said anything? Or Araceli? How did the gossip of the capitol fail me so completely?

It didn't take long for Sam to find his way to my side. He leaned on the railing as I did and looked out toward the other ships at sea.

I took a deep breath, trying to hold in my anger and breakfast.

"You are angry about last night," Sam guessed, reading my face.

I supposed I wasn't doing a very good job of holding in my emotions. I shook my head. "You have a wife?" I asked through clenched teeth.

Sam's brows furrowed. He looked at Agramon and shook his head. "I *had* a wife," he corrected.

I glared at him. "Why have you never told me about her?"

A muscle in his jaw flexed. "I was going to tell you eventually."

"Tell me now."

Sam sighed. "I married just before the start of the Ylirian War."

"So where is she?" I asked, feeling the hair on the back of my neck rise.

Sam's face sank into a glower. "She died five years ago."

The righteous indignation deflated as my anger turned to embarrassment, then sadness. "I'm sorry," I said, admonishing myself. Agramon had done that on purpose just to drive a wedge between us. Despite what he'd said to Luc, he probably didn't wish me to be close to Sam given that he was threatened by him. He just didn't want Luc to know that. I was an idiot for falling into his trap once more. "We don't need to speak of it."

"No, I should tell you," Sam growled. "I wasn't born nobility, you know. I was given my title after being named commander before the start of the war. I was cocky then, full of ambition. Noblewomen were falling over themselves trying to match me with their daughters. I loved the attention. Girls who had always been off-limits were suddenly clamoring to speak to me."

"That would be enough to turn anyone's head," I said, running my finger over the smooth railing.

"It hasn't seemed to have turned yours." Sam looked down at me.

I shrugged. "Yes, but I'm incorrigible and hate attention."

Sam shook his head. "Eventually, I met a girl, Elinor, who seemed to really like me, and I was sweet on her. She had a gentle spirit, and as wild as my life had been, it was calming being around her. Granted, we didn't know each other very well, but I figured I would have plenty of time for that later. Almost immediately after we married, I had to go to Yliria, leaving Elinor at court."

I didn't say anything, dreading the next piece of the story. Had she sickened while he was away? Was there a child? Judging by Sam's demeanor, whatever had happened to his wife had left its scar on Sam, even leagues away.

"You do not ask how she died," Sam said softly.

"You don't have to tell me if you've no wish to."

Sam clenched his hands into fists. "But you see why I have to, don't you?"

I shook my head. "Sam, I don't . . ."

But Sam was determined to go on. "I'm sure I don't need to relay the stories about me during the war. How barbaric I was, a butcher, slaughtering old and young alike, providing no mercy to entire cities and laughing as they burned. Elinor heard those stories too. I found out, later of course, that the entire court had shunned her company. They'd whispered of all the dastardly things I'd done. Soon enough, she wasn't welcome in the women's inner circles. Friends she'd counted on before had turned their backs. She became a pariah, the girl who'd married a monster. She tried to escape to

Bruin, but she hated it there. She made do, for a time, but in the end, it was too much. She took her own life rather than see the monster I'd turned into."

I gasped, my hand on his arm. "Oh Sam, no. How could they spread such lies?"

Sam glanced down at my hand, then up at me. "You haven't been listening. Every word they said about me was true. I did all those things and more because Emperor Arthello asked me to. I needed to win the war for him, and I chose to win at any cost."

"You didn't have to tell me this," I said, trying to wrap my mind around what Vianne would do in this situation. "I know it must've been hard for you to say, but you didn't have to share this with me, especially since it brings you so much pain." I stopped, not knowing what to say next.

Sam's eyes softened. "I think you know why I needed to say it. I would have you know the truth rather than have you hurt by it later. My loyalty is all I've had."

From Sam's painful story to his near declaration, I found myself wholly overwhelmed. He frowned, waiting for me to speak.

"Please, you've given me a lot to think about. I don't think less of you. I promise. Part of me already knew all those horrid stories were true, but I can't . . ."

"Of course," Sam said with a nod. "I knew last night was a mistake."

"I didn't say that," I insisted, my heart falling at the tortured look on his face.

"You don't have to." Before I could answer, Sam left me at the railing and made his way back to the group of men clustered at the other end of the ship.

I stared back at the water. Did his story change things? Everything he said about court held a ring of truth, and I didn't doubt the cruelty of the other nobility. Tears threatened the corners of my eyes. I hadn't thought the kiss had been a mistake. It was a welcome distraction from everything: the war, my ongoing servitude to Agramon, and planning my escape. It hurt to hear Sam say those words. It seemed that, despite his feelings, he didn't truly want to be with me. Whether he thought it was for my own good or his, I didn't know.

"Do you mind if I interrupt your solitude?" a voice asked beside me.

Countess Mahira leaned against the railing, facing the group of men on the other side as they drank and talked. Agramon was speaking to the count while Sam had gone back to the mercenaries' leader. I didn't have the heart, nor will, to join them. In truth, I wished the countess would let me alone. She'd done enough.

"It is your ship," I said, watching the waves crash against the hull.

"The empress wishes for news," the countess said. "Is there anything from your journey that you wish to relay?"

I stopped breathing for a moment. How had the countess known? The empress wasn't foolish enough to send messages to the other noblewomen, was she? Could I trust Mahira? I glanced at the bracelet Mahira was turning on her wrist.

"Is there a safe way to send word?" I asked.

"Turn away from the men when you speak," Mahira muttered, her voice low. "Some know how to read lips."

I turned away, resisting the urge to look over my shoulder at them. "How do I know I can trust you?"

"You can trust anyone who the empress has shown favor to," Mahira replied, brushing her hair out of her eyes as the wind whipped it behind her.

Despite my misgivings, I didn't want to let the empress down. There was nothing to do but trust her. Luc had told me to find allies to my cause, and here was a woman standing beside me, outright claiming that she could help with a cause she couldn't know about otherwise. If I couldn't trust the empress and her allies, then who was left?

"He is planning something," I whispered. "I've told Sam, the baron, that I think he means to challenge the throne in some way, but I've yet to find out how. He's using me to do it."

Mahira nodded. A false smile spread over her face.

She ran her hand down my arm. "We figured as much with his asking for payment for your services. He is gathering funds and making deals."

I nodded, trying to look easy like the countess. "He told the Count of Calla that there would be some vote that the count would recognize, and that he wanted Calla to vote in Agramon's favor, but he gave no indication what it would be about."

The countess laughed. "Did he say when this vote would take place?" she asked through her teeth.

"I've no clue, but there was something else. Something I overheard in Solin."

"Tell me."

"The guards made mention of the count requesting that they come to the capitol in the summer. They said that he's never called them out of Solin before and were wondering why this time would be any different."

"That's during the quinquennial," Countess Mahira said, turning back to look at the men, a sultry smile on her face. "Keep talking."

I leaned on the railing, facing away from them, knowing that the countess was trying to cover for the both of us. "I have a bad feeling about this war. Agramon seems to be feeding the nobles thoughts that it's unnecessary, and it is, but when he was with the emperor, he was almost . . . egging him on. Somehow it benefits him."

Mahira giggled. "It sows doubt," she said, her voice low. "It sows doubt in the emperor's leadership."

"I had a thought, and I tried to convince the baron to help me, but he said it wasn't his place. We need to convince the emperor to stop the war. It's a fool's errand, and it's pushing the empire to the brink. Maybe Agramon is planning to make a move with the army gone over the mountains. Who would remain to protect the emperor? Who would want to after all this?"

Mahira turned back toward me, her face serious. "I believe you are right. With the army gone, and his most vocal opponent with it, he will strike. You are correct in saying that more should be done to stop this folly. 'Tis the morbid dance of men."

"Can you or the count do anything to convince the emperor to stop?" I asked.

Mahira sighed. "We will have to try. I can't give away too much, mind you, even if my husband is one of the loyal ones. What you and I are playing right now, with the empress, is a woman's game. Don't give us away to anyone, understand?" Her eyes bore into mine, her face having dropped all manner of flirtation and mirth. "You *only* trust those who she has deemed loyal. We protect our own."

"I understand."

"Ladies!" the count said, striding toward us. "Come distract us for a time. We've found ourselves quite bereft at your absence."

Mahira turned, and her countenance changed instantly. Her smile was luminous as she reached toward Count Ariz. "Of course, husband. I was just plying Rowyn for information about which of her beaus she plans on pursuing, given that she has so many. What say you, Your Grace? Do any of us stand a chance with her?"

Agramon took a drink from his goblet. His eyes remained on me.

Chapter 16

THE BULK OF THE ARMY sailed from the port of Ardent, bound for Bruin. Relief battled with unease as I watched them go. On the one hand, I wouldn't have to endure their whispers and angry looks. On the other, it meant we were one step closer to war and ruin. My one hope now lay in Countess Mahira's ability to spread the word and stop the war from even happening.

We left soon after the army did with a small contingent of soldiers to guard us on our journey and help train the next round of recruits we acquired on the way. It was with a heavy heart that I waved goodbye to the count and countess. Even Agramon seemed unnaturally quiet, riding beside me as we wound our way north along the coast.

On our second day of travel, we stopped outside a large town to rest for lunch. When I finished eating, Sam met my eyes. "Come, we can see if they've seen your friend," he said, walking toward the horses.

I was grateful to escape Luc's glares and Agramon's brooding silence. Though Agramon was in a foul mood, it gave me hope that his strategies and intrigues weren't going according to plan. If he was distracted by that, it would make planning my escape easier. There was sure to be merchants and tradesmen from other lands, including Shea Innes. I figured I could steal away on a ship bound for the islands at the end of the festivities. If I didn't find Fin, I could make my way to Horan, evading the western shore altogether. I didn't think Agramon would expect that, considering I'd never been to either place, and I had a well-known aversion to ships.

Sam saddled Starstruck and we rode into town. The people turned to mark us as we passed, though none waved. I caught a glimpse of a man with the Sons of Sol mark tattooed on his forehead, and I twisted to watch his path as he disappeared behind a blacksmith's forge.

"They are here," I muttered to Sam, craning my neck in search of others. "The Sons of Sol seem to be following me everywhere."

"Would you like to turn back?" Sam asked warily. His eyes darted around the marketplace. "We could bring some guards if you wish."

"No," I said, pushing my fears down. "The attack in Solin was planned. I doubt they will disturb us."

Sam palmed the hilt of his sword, unhooking it from his sheath and grabbing his shield, just to be safe. "You have your sword?" he asked, his voice low.

"Yes." I dismounted and grabbed Iranoct's hilt. Sam

nodded and followed me through the market.

None of the vendors manning stalls had seen Fin. When we came to an inn, Sam offered to buy me an ale before we headed back. I agreed, keeping my eyes on those around me.

"Have you seen this girl?" I asked the innkeeper as she placed a mug of froth in front of me.

The woman glanced at the painting, then raised her brow, meeting my eye. "Aye, though she had a gem in her brow, same as you."

My heart raced, and Sam shifted beside me.

"When did you see her?" Sam asked.

"A week ago," the woman said. "Came in looking a fright. She ate and drank a bit, then left."

"A week ago," I repeated. My eyes shot to Sam. "Have you heard rumors of a sorcerer staying in town?"

The woman shook her head. "No, it was odd. She wasn't dressed like I expected a sorcerer to be. It was almost like . . ." The woman trailed off.

I leaned forward. "Like what?"

The woman sighed. "I don't want to speak ill of the girl, but she wore peasant clothes, and ill-fitting they were, hanging off her figure like . . . she'd stolen them."

I raised my brow. Fin was stealing clothes. Was she in trouble? Why did she not reach out to any of the sorcerers in the Eastern Empire? She was close. So close I could almost touch her.

"What sort of horse was she on? Which way did she go?"

The woman shrugged. "She didn't have a horse when she came to the inn. You can check at Albred's stable down the way, but she came to the inn on foot. She went north, from what I saw, but it's not like I followed her out of town. I'm busy here, you know, making a living."

"Of course," I said, trying to hide the excitement in my voice. "Of course you're busy. I'm sorry to have troubled you. Thank you so much for your information."

Sam pulled a coin from his pocket and left it on the wooden counter. The coin disappeared quickly, the woman nodding as we drained our drinks and made our way out of the inn and into the sunlight.

I grabbed Sam's arm. "She saw her. She's alive!" I said, unable to keep my voice steady. "We must try to find her."

Sam stayed my hand. "I can send some scouts to see if she appears in the towns to the north, but I urge you to reconsider. I don't claim to know why sorcerers do all that they do, but it could be that she's gone for a reason. You know she's alive and didn't meet the fate that you feared. Who knows what kind of task she is on?"

I nodded. "She would be trying to attain her mastery now. Perhaps the sorcerers at Solridge can't give more information. Maybe they're protecting her task from others."

Sam nodded. "From my time at the capitol, I've learned that most of what the sorcerers do is in secret. Your friend is alive and surviving well enough. It's probably best to leave it be."

I WAS SO FILLED WITH HOPE THAT I decided to fly the next leg of our journey. Sam was beside himself when he saw.

"What if she lands in a hostile place?" he asked hotly.

Agramon raised his brows. "What place is hostile in this area? Besides, Rowyn can take care of herself. She has a sword."

I smiled. We agreed on that point.

"Are you not afraid she will escape?" Sam asked.

"No, because if she did, I would send this one to cut the throat of her lover across the sea," Agramon said calmly, nodding to Luc.

My breath caught in my throat. I hadn't heard that one yet, but nothing he did should surprise me.

"I would make it look like a Morganite assassination, of course," Agramon added when he saw my expression. "Given that your clan and the Consul of Helena remain on poor terms. Then of course Mordog would be executed or killed in the endeavor."

Luc ran his hands through his hair.

I gritted my teeth. "I will not run away," I said. "I promise." It would probably be beneficial to include Luc in my escape, or at least warn Destrian. Surely he'd be able to protect himself.

"What if she falls in the sea?" Sam railed on. "There are monsters there you can't even imagine, Rowyn."

"I won't fly over the sea, then," I said, which admittedly was a lie. I fully intended to enjoy the sea air.

"What if you land hard? What if someone shoots arrows at you?"

"I fly too high for arrows to matter," I said, then turned to Agramon. "I can send rain while I'm up there." I'd gotten over my fear of lightning and was ready to try it.

"Is Calla too far?"

I nodded. It wasn't, but he didn't need to know that.

"Very well, send it to Ardent and Solin but not any farther north, understand?"

I nodded again, my stomach filling with butterflies.

"Rowyn, I beg of you, don't be this foolish," Sam said, grabbing my arm.

"I'll be fine."

Sam was still fuming when I stepped away from the

road and launched myself into a whirl of air, rising high above the land. Arden appeared, gliding beside me. We flew over the sea, watching the ships below us as I gathered a mass of clouds and sent them southeast. Arden screeched again, and I followed her as she swooped in the air currents. I laughed, reaching out as the wind swept my hair back.

Fin was alive.

Fin was alive, and I was sure I would see her again soon.

I wondered what sort of journey she was on. It must've been something very secret for her to stay hidden for so long. Many times, adept sorcerers who trained for mastery assisted another sorcerer in some endeavor, much like Destrian assisting me in the Nightlands. Perhaps Fin was helping Master Haris. He'd been using her ability to speak to animals to create a series of tomes on their habits. Maybe she had to seek out other species to bring information back to him.

I only wished for her success. The sooner she finished with her task, the sooner I would see her again. I somersaulted in the air from elation. I couldn't wait to tell Araceli and Pedr.

By all the gods, Pedr! I should ask if he was coming to the quinquennial. Since all nobility were due to attend the celebration and oaths giving, he was sure to be there. I couldn't wait to see him. I needed to let him know that I would be there as well, and I fully intended to best him in a game of chess during that time. I was growing much better at strategy, far more so than when I was at Solridge.

Things were starting to brighten. I'd been able to tell my worries to Mahira, who had promised to do her best to stymy the war effort brewing at the capitol. The sighting of Fin relieved my mind to know that she was alive and well. I was helping the folk of the realm by bringing rain and easing the famine. I'd made inroads into Agramon trusting me. Though it was slight, he hadn't actively hurt or punished me for weeks. Despite all the awful things that had occurred since I'd reached the eastern shore, I decided to take my blessings when they came.

DUST BILLOWED UP FROM THE ROAD as the line of men rode behind us. All told, about a hundred men remained of the thousand who had followed us into Ardent.

Riding Starstruck, I turned my gaze to the land. We were passing a family, their cheeks sunken in, their eyes dull as they watched us make our way toward Nordow. Beyond them was a field of shriveled stalks burned through by the sun. My heart sank.

"Can I bring rain?" I asked, twisting toward Agramon.

"Not yet." Agramon's jaw tightened. He'd gotten moodier the closer we came to the stone city rising in the distance.

I shook my head but complied. Agramon liked to make a show of it. That was all. He wanted a grand performance for the Earl of Nordow and his family. Given the suffering I'd seen on the road, I would put my all into the effort.

But as we neared Nordow, the hair on the back of my neck prickled. More people gathered along the road, but they weren't waving at us with smiles and kind words. They were staring, their haunted eyes filled with malice and judgment.

As we neared the city, the crowd of starving people grew to the thousands. Sam glanced at me. "I wish you'd ridden in the carriage," he muttered. "I've put down enough revolts to know that these people are on the brink."

"We should ride past the city," Duke Agramon said suddenly. "We are not welcome here."

"Wait," I cried, reining my horse in. "They need the rain. They are suffering, that is all. Once they have rain, they will be better."

"No, Rowyn," Agramon snapped, glaring at those

on the road. "The Sons of Sol have infiltrated these walls. They do not want your help. They blame you for the drought."

"Me?" My eyes remained on the crowd. It was true, there were many a forehead emblazoned with the mark.

Sam cursed. He shouted at the guard behind us who made quick work of enveloping Agramon and me.

Luc pulled his shield onto his arm. "It was foolish to send the entire army north," he said. "These people outnumber us a hundred to one."

Sam seemed to realize that as well.

We continued at a quicker pace as the number of people grew. The city loomed closer. As we approached the gates, they opened, but Agramon shook his head. "We need to get out of here. We can gather more re-cruits in Perth. The lord there is loyal to the crown."

Sam nodded, clutching his reins and sword with white-knuckled hands. He rode closer to me.

I let out a sigh of relief when, up ahead, a host of armed men spanned across the road, riding toward us.

"That's the earl," Sam said, pointing to the man in front. The soldiers behind him bore gray banners with a golden scale stitched into them. Justice.

"Butcher." Duke Agramon eyed the earl. "He does not mean to help us."

"What are you talking about?" Sam asked as he waved his hand in salute to the earl. The man did not return the gesture. He continued his approach, his face stony, only slowing when he reached our company.

The throng of people on the road began to cluster around us, pulsing like an ocean of flesh, a mob of angry men and women.

"We did not expect such a greeting in Nordow," Sam said when the earl reined in. "Will you not call your people off?"

The earl's eyes were on Agramon. "After submitting me to blackmail and extortion, you dare ride by my city without granting me what is due?"

"I told you the price of her service, Earl. It was you who denied your people this gift," Agramon said. Though his voice was clear, he shifted nervously in his seat. The number of people in the crowd was far beyond what his skills could handle. The earl seemed to know it too. I glanced at Sam, true worry written on my face. Sam met my eye and looked behind him, his brows furrowed.

"Fly," he murmured. "If they attack, I want you gone, understand?"

"I can't leave you," I whispered back. "I can help fight them off."

Sam shook his head. "We can't risk losing you. I want you to fly back to the capitol. They will take care of you there."

"Sam!" I hissed as he raised his sword.

The people were beginning to surge forward, their voices rising. "Scourge!" they shouted. "You are the scourge of all, you witch!"

The earl spit into the dirt at our feet. "I will not bend to your rule." He threw his arm wide. "They will not bend to your rule."

I searched the mob for a reasonable face and found none. The people were sinking into madness, brought on by hunger and thirst, fear and rebellion.

"Call the rain," Duke Agramon ordered, grabbing my hand so tight, I thought my fingers would crack. I hated his touch. I hated everything about him, knowing that he had done this to us. He had given the earl no choice but to call a mob.

I used my other hand to pull Iranoct from my belt and sent a blast of lightning into the air. Clouds billowed above us, turning the air an ominous green. My fear tinged the magic. I fought to keep myself under control as wind whipped around us, sending dirt and debris into our eyes and making it hard to see.

The mob flooded us. The knight beside Sam was pulled off his horse, and our guard began to fight back. Sam was in the thick of it, shouting orders that disappeared in the howl of the wind.

I refocused, even as I felt Agramon grab me with his other hand.

Rain began to fall, but it stank of magic. I could feel

Agramon's power moving through me, working its way into my gems. Rain streamed from the heavens, turning the road and fields around us into a muddy wasteland.

I knew the moment the crowd began to still. Lightning streaked across the sky, illuminating a sea of faces. I tried to meet the eyes of a woman, but her pupils had completely taken over her eyes, and they were glassy and still, with no recognition in them as the rain soaked her and the others around her.

The earl kicked his horse forward. "What are you waiting for?" he shouted to his people. "Seek your justice!"

As one, the crowd turned toward their lord.

The hair on my arms rose. I looked down. Agramon still held me. His magic had tainted my own.

"What are you waiting for?" he shouted, though his voice broke.

Suddenly, the crowd surged toward him. He screamed as they pulled him from his horse.

My eyes widened, the hackles on the back of my neck standing on end. The screaming continued as he disappeared into the bodies of the peasants. I looked away when I realized they were tearing him to pieces. My thoughts blurred with overwhelming fear.

"Go!" Sam shouted, urging his horse forward. We rode hard around the crowd, our guard following us, their eyes wary.

We traveled for miles through the rain. The earl's screams echoed in my ears until I thought I was going mad.

Finally, Sam relented to camping after he sent scouts to make sure there were no angry villagers nearby.

"What have you done?" I seethed as I dismounted and stamped toward Agramon through the mud. "I thought you couldn't enchant crowds of that size!" Luc grabbed my arm, but I yanked it from his grip. "You used me to plant your filthy magic, didn't you! I felt you feeding them your horrible wishes through the rain!"

Agramon glared at me, the rain having soaked us all through long ago. "Do I need to remind you that I just saved us?"

"We wouldn't have needed to be saved if it wasn't for you!" I shouted, shoving my finger in his chest. "Those people were starving. We should've helped them!"

"We did help them," Agramon yelled back at me. "We brought them rain and helped free them from a cruel and manipulative overlord."

"I want no part of this cruelty." I sobbed then, rubbing the rain and tears from my eyes. "None of it! You used me! You used those people to commit this evil act!"

Agramon stepped forward. He grabbed my face roughly and forced it up to him. "And yet you listened to me! Whether you like it or not, you are a part of this, Rowyn. When will you trust me to know what is best?"

"How did you become so cruel?" I asked. "What have any of us done to deserve this?"

"You of all people should know," Agramon said. "If you want to have power over your own life, you have to take it."

"It is ruining you," I exclaimed, "and you are dragging us all down with you."

Agramon's eyes blazed into mine. "There is a cost to greatness, Rowyn. There is a cost to freedom. How much are you willing to pay?" He dropped his hands, shaking his head as he turned and strode away.

I fell to the ground, covering my head as I sobbed. I'd helped Agramon sully the hands of a thousand men, and for what? They were the people I'd been fighting for, and I'd failed to protect them. What would happen when they realized that they had mutinied from their overlord? How would the emperor punish such treason?

Someone dropped down beside me, resting their hand on my shoulder as I wiped my eyes with my ruined sleeve.

Luc pulled me in. I continued weeping, but I wished I could do more. The gods demanded that I do more.

Chapter 17

A CROWD GATHERED in the square at Perth where Sam had gone to recruit. The lord had said the peasants were free to enlist themselves, then he would make up the difference from the jails. I could tell by Sam's expression that he was less than pleased with the lord's offer, but everything was turning into a blur after the incident at Nordow, and I'd scarcely spoken to the others since, choosing my own solitude instead.

Sam tried to urge as many willing men as possible. "I know you are weary from war, and I know that your families need you for the harvest, but the emperor calls on you as well. Lu Shen threatened the very sorcerer who will raise us from the drought, and we must do everything we can to protect ourselves."

"How dare you!" shouted a woman from the seething mob. Suddenly, a piece of rotten fruit flew forward and splattered against Sam's tunic, leaving a sticky trail down his front. I expected Sam to lash out. Sol only knew I'd seen how violent he could be, but Sam surprised me. He looked down at his tunic, gritted his teeth, and met the woman's eyes.

"Will you permit these foreigners to insult us?" Sam

shouted as he looked over the men and women of Perth. "Shall we allow them to steal our secrets, threaten our most vulnerable? The eyes of the world are upon us, and if we allow this grievance to pass unchecked, then who will rise against us next? Yliria will terrorize our borders once more, the westernlands will wrench themselves from our hold. Do you not remember your grandparents' stories of the holdings fighting each other for more power, each lord and nobleman pitting brother against brother, father against son, each in their quest for power? The minute the other empires at our borders see that we are weak, the very second the nobles in our realm feel that they can snatch more power than is their due, then we will be at war forever. Is that what you want?"

The crowd fell quiet. Several men were nodding as their wives and partners held them close.

Sam continued. "We meet them at war on their lands to save our children from dying upon ours. The *sorceress* is the key to ending our misfortunes, not the blood of your children!"

Sam met eyes with every man there. Slowly, one man stepped forward.

Then another.

And another.

The crowd emptied of men, their eyes grimly resolute.

Sam looked them over and nodded. He muttered a few words to his captain before turning, his eyes falling on me. A muscle in his jaw twitched.

He approached me cautiously, as though I were liable to bite.

"So, you've come to pass judgment too," Sam said, his gruff voice dripping with bitterness.

I frowned. "Do you even believe anything you just said?"

Sam looked over his shoulder at the dispersing crowd, the men listening to the captain intently before taking their wives' hands, heads bowed. They'd go home one last time to see their families.

"No," he said, turning back to me. "But I must give them something to fight for, even if I keep nothing for myself. Even if it is a figment of their imagination, men will fight to protect those whom they hold dear, so I must drum up terrors in their minds."

"Oh, Sam," I said, pressing my hand against his cheek. "Why do you keep up this farce? Why not just tell the emperor he's foolish and that you won't drag men across the world to die?"

Sam's eyes filled with some emotion I couldn't place. "The same reason you don't give up on the Morganite cause, even though they've forsaken you. We can't help who we are, and we can't give up on who we want to be. We are creatures of habit, you and I."

Sam turned away, my hand brushing against him until it hung suspended in the air. He walked toward his soldiers without looking back.

My heart plummeted. Sam hid so much suffering in himself, I worried what would happen if he was pushed over the edge or given the barest hint of hope.

"I WOULD ASK A FAVOR OF YOU," a wizened old man rasped, looking out of place in silken robes. He leaned forward, his cloudy eyes on Agramon.

Echo's dreams were so clear now that I could recount them as my own memories. The faint smell of salted fish and fresh bread drifted up from the table, mixed with the scent of vanilla that Agramon wore.

"I know you want allies on the council of lords, and I'm willing to back you."

Agramon leaned back, his hand masking his mouth as he studied the old man. I'd seen enough of his encounters with the other nobles to figure out when he disliked those he bargained with. He held no love for the lord of Perth.

"The deal is for the girl to bring the rain," Agramon said. "Her assistance is worth ten of Perth."

"Perhaps," the lord wheezed. He rubbed his bulbous nose with a handkerchief. "But you are not just asking for the money and gold, are you? You require unwavering support, and soon. I could give you that, on one condition."

Agramon didn't speak for a moment. Given his narrowed eyes, it seemed he detested the man. I wondered why. It couldn't just be his age, as I'd seen Agramon defer to elders in the past. I wondered if it was his manner. Echo's distaste was palpable in the dream too. Her eyes seemed to linger on the thick stubble carpeting his jowls.

"What is this favor you require?" Agramon asked with a sigh.

The lord of Perth chuckled. "My only child and heir, Grayson, has taken a shine to a girl in the city whose father is a relatively wealthy merchant. He wishes to marry her, but they are"—the man's hand waved in the air as he thought—"resisting."

Agramon shifted. "How old is the girl?"

The lord of Perth shrugged. "She will start her cycles soon enough. My son, you see, won't hear of anyone else. He's done everything right, sending her toys and sweets, paying his respects to her father, and offering a tidy sum in exchange for her hand, but they will not see reason. It's taking over my son's thoughts, and he struggles to apply himself to anything else. He's gone about it in the proper way, and they just need a little bit more . . . persuading. If you can't help him, he is prepared to force the match."

"Force the match?" Agramon's staff thumped on the ground.

The lord of Perth shrugged. "You know that no one will take a spoiled girl. I don't wish him to go that far, you understand, but he's frustrated. He's done all he could to convince the family, but they still won't budge. They say she is too young, but I have a feeling it's because they are trying to gain more payment from us."

"Be clear," Agramon ordered, his voice tight. "What is it you are asking me to do?"

The lord smiled. "You have the power to change their minds, don't you?"

Agramon breathed deep through his nose. He glared at the gem on his staff as though he were angry with it. "If I do this, then you will back me on the council of lords?"

The lord of Perth's grin widened. "I will not only back you, but I will call on favors from others as well. I know you young bucks at the capitol feel that other lords are uncultured and ill-equipped for strategy, but I do have some favors tucked away from some very powerful nobles."

"Who?" Agramon asked.

"General Ivar," the lord said, watching for

Agramon's reaction. When he didn't get one, the lord went on. "Duke Eldred of Maryse and Princess Willene."

"You will take me to see this girl and her father to-morrow then? Is that the plan?"

The lord of Perth nodded.

Agramon rose. "Very well. I don't agree, not yet. I will decide after I meet her."

I LURCHED AWAKE, CLUTCHING MY chest and gasping for air. I didn't need Echo to wake me this time. I knew what I had to do. I'd known in my dream, when Agramon had asked after the girl's age, that they were evil men. You had to be if even Duke Agramon was reluctant to work with you. The pig of a lord had said she hadn't even had her monthly courses yet. I'd started mine when I was thirteen. Anger burned within as I rose, a new sense of purpose driving me to act.

Even though Agramon detested the lord of Perth, he was still considering manipulating the girl's mind so that she would be a willing subject to the man. After hearing stories of the ladies at Solridge, I knew I couldn't let that happen. I couldn't save them all, but I could try to save this one from that horrible fate. Arda's words sounded in my mind like the tolling of a bell.

The only way to freedom was in service to others.

Though I didn't believe in fate, I refused to take chances with the gods. I had to do everything in my power to make a difference so that when the time came for me to escape, they would see that I'd paid penance.

"How late is it?" I whispered, conscious that Agramon's room was directly next to mine, just as he always requested. Sam, in retaliation, had demanded the room on the other side.

"*Two bells*," Echo whispered back. "*You wish to go after the lord?*"

I shook my head and pulled my chemise off. "Find the son. He's the one who's been harassing the girl. If I kill the son, the lord's line will end."

I pulled on a black tunic and breeches, buckled the knives to my thigh, and belted Iranoct at my waist. I pulled on boots next, the nice supple ones I used for flying. I looked at myself in the mirror. My gems made me stand out far too much. I grabbed a black, silken wrap that Gree had me wear with several dresses. After replaiting my hair, I wrapped it over my head to cover most of my face, save my eyes. Last, I pulled on gloves. I'd need to be careful. The wrap could be pulled over my eyes if we came to blows. I would need to be careful and fast.

I stared at myself in the mirror, almost hidden by

darkness and shadows. By all the gods, what was I doing? It was one thing to go after a skin-trader like Melbo, but the heir of Perth was a nobleman. Agramon
wouldn't be able to protect me if I was found out. Then
again, Agramon had just had the Earl of Nordow killed,
so I figured he didn't have room to lecture.

"I found him," Echo hissed in my ear. I twisted in
the direction of her voice.

"Can I travel through the castle?"

"Fly," Echo insisted.

I stepped toward the window. "Where?" Though I'd
brought the rain earlier that evening, I still had plenty of
magic left to aid me in my venture.

"Fourth one from the end, with the light."

I leaned out the window and saw what she de-
scribed. I ran my hands along the stone ledge. The windows were uniform, with stone outcrops jutting past
where the opening began. If any windows had been
made to be flown out of, these had been.

I stepped onto the ledge to look down below. I
hadn't seen many guards when we entered during the
day. It seemed Perth was far more peaceful than
Nordow. My gems heated, and I launched into the air.
A gust of wind carried me toward the window and I
landed lightly a few feet before the opening.

The light within was dim. There was a faint sound of
rustling. I pressed myself against the outer wall, directly

next to the window opening, and closed my eyes.

Echo revealed a room rich with furnishings. Lord Grayson seemed to have just come in from somewhere. He disrobed, revealing a lanky body covered in hair.

"You will have to be quiet," he murmured, nodding toward the bed. "If my father finds out, he will be angry."

By all the gods. A young girl less than half my age stepped out from the shadows. She wore a wrapped dress that was common in the whorehouses and brothels. Easy to clean, easy to unwrap. On her arm was a scar in the shape of a sun. Her dark hair had been plaited into two braids, and her blue eyes were wide and glistening with tears. She was a slave but far too young to be working as a brothel girl.

I gritted my teeth. It wouldn't be as simple as Melbo had been.

Lord Grayson motioned to a door. "Go wash in there."

The girl nodded and shut the door behind her.

The circumstances were far from ideal. If it were anyone else with him, I would've left, biding my time until I could catch the heir of Perth alone, but there was no leaving the girl now. It would haunt me forever if I abandoned her to whatever fate awaited her in the lord's bedroom. The gods were testing my resolve.

Now was my chance. I waited but a moment for the

lord to turn his back, then slipped noiselessly through the window, a knife in my hand. I tiptoed into the room, shadowing him as he walked to a table and poured himself a drink. As soon as he set the decanter down, I grabbed him from behind and lunged my knife into his throat, covering his mouth with my hand.

His cry of surprise turned into a gurgle. He collapsed against me, and I lowered him to the floor into a pool of blood.

After cleaning and sheathing the knife, I darted to the window, but Echo hissed a warning.

"They will kill the girl!"

I looked over my shoulder. The slave would surely scream and sound the alarm. What would they do when they found the lord of Perth's son dead? With no one else to blame, the girl would hang. The swinging bodies of Ayastaren appeared in my mind. I would never let that happen again.

I gritted my teeth and stepped to the door leading to the bathing chamber. I waited behind it for her to emerge, mentally cursing my stupidity. I was taking far longer than was wise. What if Agramon woke and went to check on me? What if the guard came to check on Lord Grayson?

May Imor help me, what was I supposed to do? If I took her to the city, she would just be returned to the same place that sent her to Lord Grayson. The brand on her arm meant that anyone could claim a reward for her return.

I wished Mellan was with me. He and his network of slave liberators would be especially handy at the moment. Perth might even have its own network, but I wasn't sure how to find them. It's not like they advertised themselves as breaking the emperor's law.

If I brought her back to my room, Agramon was sure to find her. He always waltzed in unannounced. Even if she were hidden, he would hear her thoughts. Then he would give her to the lord of Perth who would kill her.

I couldn't figure out any option that ended with the girl alive, not to mention giving my own involvement away.

Agramon was the biggest hurdle. In Perth, only one person's mind was mostly protected from Agramon's magic. Besides mine.

The girl stepped out and I grabbed her. I closed my hand over her mouth when she tried to scream.

"Shhh," I whispered. "I'm here to help you." The girl stilled. "I'm going to take my hand off your mouth, but you have to promise me that you will not make a sound."

The girl whimpered but nodded.

"Shut your eyes," I ordered. The girl, entirely too trusting of murderous strangers, let me guide her into the room and past Lord Grayson's body. Her safety pressed on my mind, but there was no way we would make it through the corridors. Even with Echo's help, the lord's chamber had been in another wing from mine. That was a long way to travel while staying secret, especially with a slave child in tow. I looked toward the window. I'd never tried to fly with anyone else before. It was risky, but it was the only way.

The girl was small enough that I could pick her up. She wrapped her legs around my waist and rested her head on my shoulder with another whimper. I stepped onto the ledge and jumped off before I could hesitate.

Chapter 18

I T TOOK A MOMENT for me to get my bearings with her added weight, but she didn't weigh all that much, luckily. After a wobbly spin or two, I landed on a ledge and dropped into the dark room.

"Don't make a sound," I whispered to the girl.

I set her in the corner where she sank to the floor, her arms around her knees, then I approached the bed. Sam was lying on his stomach, his flesh illuminated by the moonlight. I gently laid my hand on his back.

Before I could speak, Sam twisted, grabbed my wrist, and pulled me against him, a blade pressed against my throat.

"Sam, it's me!" I cried. "Rowyn!"

He grabbed my hand, his fingers kneading my palms and feeling the hard gem under my glove.

The blade fell away.

"Am I dreaming?" Sam asked, his hands searching my face. I pulled the wrap down so he could feel the gem on my brow.

"No," I assured him. "You told me, before, that if I needed anything, I was to come to you."

Sam raised himself in bed, his body tense. "What has he done now? I swear if he's touched you again . . ."

"It's not him," I whispered, gripping his hand. "It's what I've done."

"You?" Sam asked.

"I need help hiding her." I motioned to the corner where the little girl cowered.

Sam's eyes widened, and he pulled the covers from his body, then pulled them right back. Sam slept bare.

"Shut your eyes, both of you," Sam ordered.

I readily complied as heat flooded my cheeks. I heard the match before a soft glow lit over my eyelids.

"Now, tell me what you need."

I opened my eyes and found Sam with breeches on, but no shirt. I averted my gaze, trying not to marvel. "I need to get her to safety."

Sam's mouth opened, then closed again. He looked back to where the little girl had hunched down. "Who is she?"

"She's a slave, Sam, in the brothel. I can't send her back."

"How did you acquire her?"

"Does it matter?" I rose. "This is an injustice, one that you can help me solve. Must you always delay courage in favor of duty and service?"

Sam frowned. He turned back to the child. "How old are you, girl?"

"Eight years, sir," she said, her voice soft as a mouse.

Sam rubbed the back of his neck. "What would you have me do?"

"Hide her for me. Agramon is sure to find her in my room. If she stays here, we can try to smuggle her out of the city when we leave."

"Why not just let her out into the city?" Sam turned back to the child. "What's your name?"

"Sweetheart," she said, meeting Sam's eye. "The mum at Lady Bella's just called me Sweetheart. The men do too."

"Who are your parents? Were you taken from anywhere?"

"No sir. My ma worked at Lady Bella's too. She died of the plague two years ago."

I glared at Sam, daring him to challenge me.

"Fine," Sam grunted, "but what about when we leave? What are we going to do with her then?"

"I will fix that problem then, but for right now, I need to keep her hidden. People will start looking for her tomorrow, and if they find her, they will kill her."

"No, they will just return her to her owner," Sam sighed.

"No." I fixed my stare, trying to get him to catch the significance of my urging. "They won't."

"What have you done?"

I just looked at him, refusing to answer.

Sam shook his head. "All right. I'll hide her until we get out of the city, then I expect a full explanation."

THE NEXT MORNING WAS PANDEMONIUM. Soldiers and guards stormed through the palace and city in search of the girl named Sweetheart. The bells in Sol's temple began to toll for the death of Perth's one and only heir.

Agramon insisted that we leave after assurances that we would still send the rain. He feared for his party's safety with an assassin loose in the city. All the while, his eyes followed every movement I made.

I helped Gree pack, wishing that I could check on Sweetheart. I had to trust that Sam would do the right thing. I'd gone to him with that hope.

Agramon waited until we stopped to camp that evening to round on me. "Where is she?" he spat, towering over me as I sat before the fire, quietly eating my stew as I always did.

"Where is who, Your Grace?" I asked, taking another bite. I resisted the urge to meet Sam's eyes across the fire.

"I suspected it was you in Solin, but this? A lord? The emperor has every right to hang you for this!"

"Then why are you talking so loudly?" I hissed. "Do

I need to remind you of the earl?" I didn't care if Luc or Sam heard, but the soldiers guarding us were another thing altogether. They already hated me.

Agramon grabbed my arm and forced me to stand. The bowl clattered at my feet. "It's one thing for me to take risks, but you are wholly ill-equipped to deal with the consequences of your actions."

I shoved him off, and very nearly into the fire. "You knew what they were," I seethed. "Even you detested the evil within those men."

"That begs the question then, doesn't it? How did *you* know what they were?"

I froze. Unable to help myself, I looked to Sam, not for help, but for courage. He'd risen with Agramon, but he hadn't yet felt obliged to interfere. I'd told him to let me fight my own battles, and he was letting me.

"Solridge," I said, unable to think of a better lie. "I heard about the lord of Perth from Solridge. There were rumors that he preyed on girls."

"And Melbo?" Agramon asked.

"He said something during that dinner," I said, scrambling. If I were to save the girl, I would need to speak Agramon's language. "I wish to make a deal."

Agramon's brows rose. "We already have one," he shouted. "You're supposed to do what you are told!"

"You said I couldn't try to end your life. You never said anything about the other evil men I encountered."

Agramon shook his head. "I feel like it goes without saying!"

"Give me one task. One task that you want me to enthusiastically pursue for you, and I will do it. Just let the girl live. I want to find her a haven. She was just in the wrong place at the wrong time. It wasn't her fault. It was mine."

Agramon was glaring at me, but I could see the wheels turning in his mind. There *was* something he wanted me to do.

"Please, Your Grace," I repeated. "I've not asked for much from you. I've been playing my part. Give me this."

"Very well," Agramon said. "There is something more that you can do for me."

"What is it?"

"Maryse," Agramon began. He glanced at Sam. "They are proposing a match between you and one of the lords there. They will pursue it ardently, and I want to find out how much they're willing to pay for your hand."

This wasn't good, but I'd resolved to help the girl by any means necessary. "And? What would you like me to do?"

"Just let yourself be wooed by their choice. I've not yet made up my mind on the person I will burden with you next, but it's highly unlikely to be Maryse. Play a willing flirt, and I will let you get away with this."

"Rowyn," Sam began, his voice filled with warning, but I ignored him.

"It's a deal."

"And please," Agramon added, rubbing his eyes. "Stop murdering people."

"DO YOU LIKE THE NAME SWEETHEART?" I asked the girl after Sam had let her out of a chest he used to carry weapons. Duke Agramon had enchanted our guards and soldiers to forget that they should be looking for a young brothel wench. He'd said it was easier than some would think, given the thought was so newly placed in their minds.

"I'd never thought of me having another name," the girl said, eagerly spooning food into her mouth.

"If you could choose another name for yourself, what would it be?"

"I s'pose it would be the name of a brave lady. I heard there were stories of brave girls, but no one ever told them to me, and I don't know any o' their names."

I smiled. "In my clan, one of the bravest girls we share stories of is Helen. She was queen of my people hundreds of years ago."

The girl wrinkled her nose at the name.

"Or there is Nirah," I went on. "She was my aunt. A braver woman couldn't be found."

"Nirah," the girl said, smiling down into her bowl. "That does sound like the name of a brave girl."

I smiled. "May I call you Nirah from now on?"

The girl nodded. "You can call me anything you like, now that I'm out o' Lady Bella's shop."

"You can sleep with me in my tent then, Nirah. We will take care of you and find you a better home, all right?"

Nirah nodded.

Agramon studied her from beside me for a bit before he looked away. "We'll have to get that mark removed," he said, twisting his staff. "No matter how I manipulate the men's minds, she's marked as a slave. Someone will try to collect the bounty on her."

"Do you know how it can be done?" I asked.

"A sorcerer can do it, one who heals," Agramon remarked, smoothing his cloak. "She will need new clothes. Food, lodging. The family that takes her will want to be paid."

"I will honor my end of the deal," I assured him, guessing where his mind lay. "Do you know who it is they are putting forth as a suitor?"

Agramon shrugged. "That's the thing with Maryse. There are so many options that it's impossible to guess whose turn it is. They are the family of the emperor, mind you, and they keep the intrigues of family interests close to heart. The elders decide who gets to claim what honors based on age, acclaim to the family, and whatever other boons they can come up with."

"Don't worry," I said, turning to Nirah and resting my hand on her shoulder. "I won't let any harm come to you."

Agramon shook his head.

"YOU PET HER FEATHERS DOWN, like this," Luc said, demonstrating while Nirah watched with glowing eyes.

She tentatively lifted her hand and ran it down Arden's back. The hawk's wings extended as she tried to find balance, and Nirah shrank away, suddenly afraid.

"It's all right," Luc said, kneeling so the girl could see Arden better. "She's never hurt any of us."

We were about to cross the Gilded Portal and were waiting for our turn to pass on the bridge. Caravans were already heading to the capitol for the quinquennial, even though it was months away. The queue was lengthy, and the wagons were advertising their wares to anyone waiting. One was filled with clothes for children, so we'd stopped to outfit Nirah with some long-sleeved dresses. Even though winter was waning, the farther north we went, the cooler it would be, so we could get away with hiding Nirah's slave brand until we found a sorcerer who could remove it.

Agramon inspected his fingernails while I pored over the gowns. "What does it matter? Any of this would be far better than what she has now."

"She deserves to have something fine, given the life she's had to endure." I unwittingly thought back to Gillius and me walking through the market in Helena, him letting me choose the colors of my dresses. It had made me feel special, as though he was actually willing to take care of me.

Was I like Gillius then? My mouth soured. Best not to think about that.

Agramon grabbed my wrist. I looked up. "You're getting attached."

I wrenched my hand away. "And you will use it to keep me in line or hurt me . . . I know."

"You can't keep her," Agramon murmured. "Gree is your handmaid, so as soon as we can find her someplace to live, you must leave her there."

"I know," I snapped. "It wouldn't be safe for her, and you can't abide children. I understand."

Agramon's brows furrowed. "Who said I hated children?"

I lifted a gown and turned it, inspecting all sides. "I

can just tell. You avoid them at all costs. Others have even remarked on it. Given your ability to read minds, why is this such a revelation for you?"

"I don't hate children," Agramon said with a scowl. He crossed his arms over his chest, his staff between his wrists as he watched Nirah. She giggled as she stroked Arden's head. "I just don't like listening to their thoughts. It brings back memories that I prefer to forget."

I raised my brows. "Of your father?"

Agramon nodded. "It happens especially with children like Nirah." I glanced at the staff dangling idly from his hand. He wasn't twisting it like he normally did around me. He was starting to become comfortable, complacent with the knowledge that I hadn't yet tried to run. That I was listening to him and giving my best. That was all he'd really asked of me. My plan was starting to work, despite the fact that I'd stolen the girl.

Agramon was beginning to trust me.

"If it's worth anything, I'm sorry for how you've been treated in the past," I said, hoping to accelerate the inroads I was making into his favor. "Not just your father. I've heard that mind readers were scorned for a long time. It must've been difficult, paving your way with so much against you."

Agramon looked down at me. "I made the most of it, as you well know."

"But it couldn't have been easy."

Agramon looked at me a moment longer than was necessary. Araceli was right. He just wanted to be understood.

Nirah picked out several dresses. Once Agramon had given the merchant his coin, she ran back to Luc, who was inspecting a leather merchant's stall.

"This doesn't change things," Agramon said as we walked back to our guard. He motioned between us. "This peace won't last forever."

"I know." I laid the folded dresses over my arms. I'd planned on just picking out two, but Agramon had insisted that she be outfitted for all weather. He said it would make it easier when we found a family to take her. It was more considerate than I'd ever expected from him. In beginning to trust me, he was revealing more of himself, and he wasn't entirely evil like I'd originally thought. There was still good in him somewhere. It wouldn't be enough to save him though. "You will continue to use me to further your own ends by gaining power over the empire."

"So long as you know," Agramon murmured.

When Luc and Nirah returned from their adventures among the merchants, Nirah was hiding something behind her back. I sat with Agramon, about to send rain south, while Sam had gone somewhere with his soldiers.

Nirah and Luc were grinning from ear to ear. Agramon quirked an eyebrow but said nothing.

"What are you two up to?" I asked.

"We got you a nameday present," Nirah said, holding out a wrapped package.

I looked up at Luc and accepted the gift. "You remembered."

"His Grace purchased it, of course," Luc said, his eyes on Agramon.

I unwrapped the package and found a falconer's gauntlet, along with a shoulder guard. Roses had been stamped into the leather. When I pulled it onto my arm, it was a perfect fit. Luc and I had been making do by wrapping thick leather thongs around our arms, but Arden's talons would often slip through the wrappings, and we both bore scars from it.

"This is beautiful," I said with a blush. I smiled at Nirah. "Did you pick it out?"

"They match your marking," she said, running her fingers over the rose tattoo on my neck. I could feel my grin grow wider. "Very smart. They are the exact ones I would've chosen for myself. What a thoughtful gift!"

Nirah grinned. "How old are you now, miss?"

Luc answered for me. "Eighteen years."

Nirah grinned and skipped off to Gree who was calling her for a bath.

Luc sank down beside me. "We were supposed to be

wed today."

"I remember," I said. Agramon had turned toward the movement of the soldiers around us, as though he'd known what Luc was going to say. He probably did.

"Do you regret how things have turned out?" Luc asked, his arms resting on his knees, hands clasped in front of him.

"I regret my mother and father," I said. I traced the rose pattern on the gauntlet thoughtfully. "Do I regret that we won't be married? No."

Luc stiffened, but I refused to look up. "This was Imor's way of showing me who you really were and what I needed for my path."

"What do you need?" Luc asked.

"I don't know," I said, finally meeting his eye. "But not this. You're like a brother to me, Luc, but I need more."

Luc nodded, his eyes on his hands. "Enjoy your day." He patted me on the shoulder and stood.

I listened to him walk away, then looked at Agramon. "Thank you for the gift," I murmured.

"It was their idea," Agramon huffed, turning his staff in his hand. "Like I said, it still doesn't change anything."

Chapter 19

NIRAH WAS HIDING IN SAM'S WEAPONS chest when we entered Maryse. There was no other safe place for her, and Sam was known not to let anyone touch his blades. I would retrieve her at night when the halls were clear and everyone else was asleep. She would stay in my room for the entirety of our stay.

I felt as though I'd taken her just to imprison her. She didn't seem to mind though. Instead, the girl seemed to believe she was on some sort of adventure.

Duke Eldred was the famed patriarch of Maryse. Uncle to the emperor himself, he played matchmaker to Lyrica's most prominent family. He was so famed, in fact, that he felt his presence wasn't warranted in our greeting when we arrived at the large citadel. Instead, a young Lord Achille greeted us, his blond hair and sun-kissed skin making him look like a son of Sol himself.

"Greetings," Lord Achille said, coming down the steps. "Welcome to our halls."

Duke Agramon's eyebrows were raised. "Good afternoon, Achille. May I present my student, Rowyn the Morganite."

Lord Achille was already eying me, scaling my body

as though assessing for imperfections. Gree hadn't let me go a day without painting my face or revealing some part of my body that I'd prefer were hidden. His eyes lingered on my chest the most. He seemed disappointed. Shame.

"Very well," Lord Achille said, turning his back on us. "The family will greet you formally at dinner. Grandfather is holding court tonight, and the whole of Maryse will turn out for it."

I looked at Sam. This Lord Achille hadn't even bothered to greet him, though he was a baron with the entire army of Lyrica at his beck and call. Given Sam's stony expression, he was probably fuming.

We followed Lord Achille inside where he promptly deposited us in our rooms. Just like it had been at every other place, save Solin and Calla, my rooms sat right between Agramon and Sam. Despite my irritation at having them both so close, it would help to ensure Nirah slept safely.

Agramon didn't even bother going into his room. While Gree started putting my wardrobe in order, he fumed.

"They were putting me in my place, sending an heir of an heir to greet us. Couldn't even be bothered to welcome us themselves." Agramon glared at me as though everything was my fault. "How do I respond to such an insult."

"Why would they think less of you? You are a duke, same as the lord here," I said, walking to a decanter on the table and pouring a glass of wine. I glanced at Agramon, grabbed the second glass, and poured him one. I refused to let the opportunity to gain Agramon's trust pass me by. He was keeping Nirah safe in exchange for showing my best in Maryse. I was determined that my best mean more than just playing the spectacle of sorcery. My best could be as a confidant, ally, and fellow schemer. I took both glasses and held them out to His Grace. He stopped talking abruptly, eying me.

"I know you have a charm to mitigate poisons, and I made a promise I would stop trying... for now. Choose a glass. Both are safe."

Agramon chose one, and I met his eyes as I took a sip.

"Perhaps Lord Achille is the person they are putting forth as a suitor." I dropped onto the couch and stretched my legs out in front of me. "Maybe they were hoping he would make a good impression."

"If they are, that would just be another insult. He's not even a sorcerer. Tristam the Miraculous would've been the ideal candidate; instead you get the eldest son of a man who will inherit an earldom."

I took a sip of wine. "Do you still wish me to charm him?" I half-hoped he would say no.

"Of course," Duke Agramon said. "You're not getting out of this. The girl will remain safe for as long as you fulfill your side of the deal."

"I fully intend to comply with your wishes," I assured him. "Do they not need the rain like everyone else?"

"Not as much as most. Lord Alexander visits often enough to ensure they receive the water they need by irrigating it," Duke Agramon scoffed. "It has compounded the fact that the areas around them have been far more destitute."

"Then I must give a good performance," I said. "I can put on a dazzling display. They weren't in the capitol for the Rainbow Ball. I'll do a similar act, while flying in the air, and show them my true worth. If they don't want me for practical reasons, then I'll show them I'm an artist. One thing I've learned on the eastern shore is you rich nobles love fancy, pretty things and spectacular diversions."

"You would do that?" Agramon asked, taking another sip and leaning back in his chair. He let his staff rest against the side table. There it was again. He wanted to trust me. "You would give them such a show?"

"Gree," I called, though I was sure she was already looking. "Is there a piece of jewelry that protects your face paint from washing off with water?"

"Aye, girl, there's a pair o' earrings in case a lady decides to cry," she yelled back.

"Will it protect from the rain?" I met Agramon's eye as I took another sip.

"It should," Gree replied.

"There you have it," I said. "I'm sure you've procured me a gown that would be perfect for the occasion."

Agramon's eyebrows arched.

I rose from the couch. "Since this will happen tonight, Gree will need to have as much time as possible. Will you please make your choice of garment and leave so I can prepare?"

A smile tugged at the corners of his lips as he grabbed his staff and rose.

GREE WAS MAGNIFICENT WHEN SHE wanted to be. Not a cruel word was uttered as she bathed and slathered my body with every bottle in her chest of tinctures. I'd directed her to braid my hair since I would be flying, and she plaited the black locks into the most intricate weaving I'd ever seen. After deliberations, we decided to add a pair of hose. I would wear it under my dress since flying would likely reveal more than even Agramon was comfortable with. Over it was a silken, ice-blue gown, with a low neck and even lower back.

I looked beautiful. Every marking on my body could be seen. The earrings Gree had found to save my paint were made with pearls, which matched the dress to perfection.

"His Grace will expect you to fulfill your end of the bargain," Gree said as she made last-minute adjustments to my hair and face.

"I'll be a woman of my word."

Gree nodded. "Well, there you have it. I can't do much more with what I've been given."

Despite her words, I thanked her.

Agramon's nostrils flared when I emerged from my room at his knock. It was just him and me, since Luc would stay in Sam's room and watch Nirah while the rest of us enjoyed the grand party.

"You look ravishing," Duke Agramon said under his breath. "Always before, you looked as though you were a stranger in your own skin, shrinking from notice. Command everyone's attention tonight. It should not be hard for someone like you."

"I will," I assured him, my head straight, my shoulders back. Agramon was starting to play into my hand. An escape at the quinquennial felt like something that I could touch if I raised my fingers. I tried not to let my excitement show.

The herald announced our arrival, and I entered the

hall with my arm around Agramon's, beaming.

The first eyes I saw were Sam's. He had lowered his glass, his mouth open as he stared at me. I felt Agramon's pull and allowed him to lead me to Duke Eldred of Maryse, who stood among his impeccably bred family.

Duke Agramon stopped before them, and I swept into the most graceful curtsy I could conjure, an image of Lady Ingrid burning in my mind, though I still detested the girl. Eyes slightly lowered, skirt fluttering back as though a petal from a flower, a wide smile spread across my face.

I rose without a wobble and took Agramon's arm once more. He squeezed my hand as he faced the other duke, who wore a richly embroidered white overcoat.

"So, this is the girl my nephew's been on about," the duke said, reaching his wizened hands toward me. With a nod from Agramon, I let the man take my hands and inspect my gems. "We welcome you both to Maryse and look forward to your company here," the duke said, smiling down on me. Though his hair had whitened with age, he was still fit, his grip firm.

"Rowyn has been working hard to restore the harvests to the empire," Agramon said. "She is a credit to His Imperial Majesty and looks forward to demonstrating her skills for you this evening."

Duke Eldred nodded and held his hand out to where

large glass doors opened onto a large balcony. Outside the night air was clear and fragrant, with flowers blooming in the gardens below.

Agramon led me through the crowd of nobles and important patrons of the city. On the balcony, Agramon patted my hand and stepped back. I had to show him that I could give him what he wanted. I had to show him that I could make deals too. I was starting to understand how the game was played.

A breeze began to blow, and the gems on my hands grew warm. I faced the skies beyond, my skirt whipping around my legs as the wind picked up. My back to the audience, I ran, leaping onto the balcony ledge and into the air. I couldn't help but smile when someone screamed behind me.

I harnessed the wind and rose above the balcony. I'd memorized the constant of the current and used it like reins.

Clouds gathered in the sky at my whim. Focusing the wind, I turned my body, facing the host. I rose higher, then spun as a bolt of lightning danced behind me. The clouds swirled as I did, growing darker with every passing moment.

At the crescendo, I flung my arms wide, and a torrent of rain streamed down from the clouds in a wave. Closing my hands around myself, I lowered until my feet touched the balcony once more.

I took a breath and opened my eyes.

The hall exploded into noise as everyone began talking at once.

I smiled.

"My lady," Lord Achille said, approaching me with two goblets of wine. "What an astonishing sight that was."

"Thank you, my lord." I dropped into another curtsy, though this one far smaller than my first. Duke Agramon had said that Lord Achille was unimportant nobility, and I was somebody important. It was he who should defer to me.

And he did bow, almost to his knees.

"Might I show you around the room?" Lord Achille asked, motioning to the crowded hall.

"I would adore it, your lordship—though . . ." I let my eyes travel down my dripping body. "After I've changed into a dry gown."

"I can accompany you. I would hate for a lady as beautiful as yourself to get lost in our halls. Not when so many people here desire your company."

"Allow me," Sam said, appearing at my other side. I took his proffered hand.

"I don't want to pester you to have to leave your family's party on such an insignificant errand. I look forward to your company when I return."

Sam pulled me away. I glanced over my shoulder

and saw that Agramon was watching me go. He lifted his glass and saluted.

I turned back around as Sam's pace increased toward the doors. We left, Sam pulling me along the corridors until we came to one empty of servants and guards. Suddenly, I was against the wall, kissing him.

I gasped with surprise at the intensity, his fingers digging into my shoulders, pulling me into him. His soft lips caressed mine, his tongue teasing. He gripped me tighter, the pain lancing through the pleasure.

I put my hands on his chest as he broke away from my mouth and traveled down my neck, his tongue nipping and tasting the rain that had drenched me not moments before.

"Sam," I breathed as a trail of gooseflesh followed his path. "We can't be seen."

"I know," he whispered. He cupped my cheeks and gave me one tender kiss. "I can't tell you how long I've been waiting to do that."

I sank lower with him, kissing his cheek as I went. "You will spoil Duke Agramon's plans for me."

"I have plans of my own," Sam said, meeting my eye.

"I must change gowns." I stepped out of his arms. "I can't disappoint him, not tonight. Nirah's life is at stake, remember?"

"I know," Sam said gruffly, forcing my arm around

his.

He walked me the rest of the way to my rooms and Gree's care.

When I emerged an hour later, my hair had been curled and lay loosely over my shoulders in black waves. The paint lining my face had remained perfectly intact, thanks to the pearl earrings. I wore one of the gowns I'd first noticed at the capitol to be far too revealing. It was made of filmy fabric. The purple V-neck bodice faded to white at the bottom of the skirt. The only sleeves were little cuffs of sheer fabric that lay off my shoulders. I said nothing when Gree laced the small corset around me and slipped the fabric over my head.

Sam opened the door to my knock and just stared, a muscle jumping in his cheek. Finally, he shook his head when a squeal of delight came from behind him.

Sam stepped aside to reveal Nirah seated on the floor with Luc, a whetstone in one hand and a dagger in the other.

"What are you all up to?" I asked, walking into the room.

"They are showing me how to sharpen knives," Nirah said with a smile, holding the blade up for my inspection.

I took it and tested the edge. "Wonderful job," I assured her. I glanced at Luc and Sam. "I thought you didn't let anyone else touch your weapons?"

Sam shrugged. "She might as well be doing something useful in here. One thing I know about children is that if they are not given tasks, they create their own entertainment."

Luc was glaring at Sam and me. "Well, I should take Nirah into Rowyn's rooms now. It's time we get to bed. Is the hall clear?"

I stepped back, checked, and nodded. "Gree's in there. She can tend to her."

I'd half expected Gree to complain about Nirah's presence, given the additional work she caused the old maid. But she didn't, at least not to me. I doubted it was because she liked the girl. She wasn't especially kind to her. I figured Agramon could do no wrong in her eyes, therefore any order he gave would be followed without complaint. The urgency to follow through with my side of the bargain began to weigh on me as Luc and Nirah stepped out, Nirah disappearing into my room and Luc striding down the hall toward his own on the other side of Agramon's.

"I don't like this," Sam said as he wrapped my arm around his and began leading me back to Maryse's great hall. "The Marendeslys are known backstabbers. Agramon thinks too highly of himself to control the situation, and they will outmaneuver him. This Lord Achille that they are presenting is hardly worthy of your attention."

"At least he's young and handsome," I said, a small smile playing on my lips.

Sam's nostrils flared. "Is that something you require? Someone young and handsome at your beck and call? Do I even stand a chance?"

I rolled my eyes and squeezed his arm. "You're not that old."

"Nor that handsome," Sam said, his voice tight.

"I don't believe that to be true." A smile tugged the corner of Sam's lips as we entered the hall, but it disappeared when he saw Lord Achille waiting by the door.

"My lady," the young man said, eying Sam's hold on my arm. "A ravishing sight must be shared by all."

I tried to pull my hand from Sam's, but he was holding it fast. I glared at him, and he finally let go. "I look forward to getting to know your famous family," I said, taking Lord Achille's offered arm. He shot me a winning smile, and again, I felt as though I'd taken the arm of a god.

Lord Achille led me around, introducing me to members of his family. He brought me to Earl Lodwick, an elderly gentleman who was Lord Alexander's father and Lord Achille's grandfather. He stood with Duke Eldred and Duke Agramon, watching the room as a group of magicians played in the corner and couples started to dance.

"That was a wonderful display of control," Earl

Lodwick said, the light-blue gem on his brow reflecting candlelight. It was the first hall we'd come to that held other sorcerers besides ourselves. "We had not heard that you could fly."

"The skill is recently acquired," I said, accepting a goblet of wine from Lord Achille who'd snatched it from a servant's tray. The servant caught my eye and I turned. It was a boy, with pale skin and dark hair, imorets tattooed around his eyes.

A Morganite.

My eyes traveled down to a brand on the back of his forearm. Agramon cleared his throat, and I met his eyes. He gave a small shake of his head. I could say nothing. I'd made a deal to be on my best behavior, to play Agramon's game his way. He wouldn't give me another chance if I messed up now. I would lose all the footing I'd gained in worming my way into his favor.

I focused on the conversation at hand, ignoring when the Morganite boy moved around me to offer refreshments to the Marysian nobility.

"I couldn't have asked for a better teacher," I continued. "Duke Agramon has ensured that I master all of my abilities without fail." Perhaps I was laying it on a bit thick, but Agramon was nodding.

"Word of your charms have reached our ears as well," Duke Eldred said, his eyes narrowed. "First Helena, and now Ayastaren have put forth suits. You seem to be a popular lady on the western shore."

I took another sip, refusing to cow under Duke Eldred's glare. "We westerners know a gift when we see one."

"Has the Butcher put his name in the running?" Lord Achille asked. His gaze had traveled to the far wall, where Sam was watching us, sipping on his own glass of dark liquor. His eyes burned when they met mine. It was as though I could read the thoughts on his face, the memory of his earlier kiss heating my cheeks. I turned back to the nobles and belatedly saw that they were watching me.

"Not yet," Duke Agramon was saying. "Though I expect more to come. By Sol above, I think I'm even falling in love with the girl."

"Is that a threat, Your Grace?" I asked coyly, leaning into Lord Achille's side. His hand slipped to my waist.

Agramon shook his head, unable to conceal his smile—if he were trying.

"Come," Lord Achille said. "Let us leave the scheming to our elders. It's the young people's job to make merry."

Lord Achille deposited our goblets on a nearby table and pulled me to the dance floor. Now was a true test of my bargain, for I'd always been an abominable dancer. I tried my best not to think of my steps and follow Lord Achille's lead as he swept me about. The gown helped. It flowed around me like a cloud, ballooning as I spun and concealing my worst mistakes.

When we stopped to take a break, Lord Achille handed my goblet back and murmured a joke into my ear. I laughed, gazing up at him through my lashes. Each of us played the parts our elders required. During the entire ordeal, I wondered what he truly thought of me. Was he faking admiration when his eyes traveled down the back of my dress? Was his frown genuine when another young Lord of Maryse appeared beside us and asked me to dance?

I watched him out of the corner of my eye as I stepped in time to the music. The other young nobles crowded around him in my absence.

I looked for Sam but to no avail. I twisted, trying to see him through the crowd, but he was gone. I was surprised when my heart fell. My feelings had always been confused about Sam, given his reputation, but I had my own reputation, and most of it was hyperbole. Though Sam insisted he was as bad as they said, I'd never seen it. No, he had only ever been kind to me. He was strict with his soldiers and was a coward when it came to confronting the emperor, but he wasn't evil, despite what he may have done during the war. Not like Agramon anyway. So how could he abandon me after that kiss?

My head was spinning, so after an appropriate

amount of time, I took my leave from the hall, assuring Lord Achille that I could find my own way back to my room. Agramon was sitting among the other nobles, having what appeared to be a heated discussion. I was sure Echo would let me know in my dreams if it was anything important.

When I reached our corridor, I noticed Sam's door was cracked, the light from a candle casting shadows within. When I peeked in, I found Sam seated on a chair facing the hall, a drink in his hand.

"You left," I said, leaning against the doorframe. A chilly wind curled in from his open window, sending the flame on the candle flickering. I wrapped my hands around my arms, trying not to shiver.

"I couldn't watch," Sam said angrily, his voice slurred. I looked back to the glass, realizing he was drunk.

"You need to go to bed." I strode over and took the glass. I downed the rest in one gulp, then immediately regretted it for it burned my throat, sending me into a coughing fit.

Sam rose to his feet. "I was making sure he wasn't going to invite himself into your bed."

"No one is getting into my room in Maryse, especially not with Nirah there, so you don't have to worry," I said, pulling his jerkin, then his tunic over his head. Instead of letting me lead him to bed as I intended, he pulled me to his chest, wrapping his arms around me in a tight hug.

"You will be the ruin of me," he whispered, one hand stroking my curls, the other on my back. He kissed the top of my head. "You will ruin me, and yet, I don't care."

"I'm not here to hurt you, Sam," I said into his chest, wrapping my arms around him as he squeezed me tight.

Sam sighed, resting his cheek on my head.

Chapter 20

"OF COURSE, ALL ROWYN'S WORK has been for the betterment of the empire," Duke Agramon said in my dream that night. He and the Duke of Maryse were seated in a corner of the hall, the other lords and nobles giving their discussion a wide berth.

Duke Eldred nodded. "We are all servants to the crown, though there is a rumor that her journey is cursed. First the Earl of Nordow is killed in an uprising, and then the heir of Perth is slaughtered in his own bed. I even heard that someone was killed in Solin while you were there. Perhaps the Sons of Sol are right, and the girl is fated to be our undoing."

Agramon straightened, bristling at the noble's words. "Rowyn has also done much good. She cannot be blamed for the evils of others."

"Is that so?" Duke Eldred asked, his eyes narrowed. "Many have wondered what role you play in all of these . . . theatrics." He waved his hand in the air, looking back around the hall. "Lord Achille is the suit we will put forth. We will pay handsomely for the girl, but I can't consent to a match with higher Marendesly nobility."

"She's the greatest sorcerer of our age," Agramon hissed, clearly angry with the way the conversation was going. "Have you lost your touch? You should have offered Tristam the Miraculous for her hand."

"She's hardly proper, Agramon," Duke Eldred said. "You expect me to offer a girl from the wild to one of the most eligible bachelors in the empire? To pollute our bloodline with a Morganite? Don't be absurd!"

"So, you care nothing for the power she could bring? The boy you've presented isn't even a sorcerer."

Duke Eldred sat back in his seat. "Having more than one sorcerer parent meant that the magic wouldn't be passed down as predictably. Tristam himself suggested we should change our strategy."

"Why should I consider this suit? Even the Consul of Helena is a better offer!"

"Commoners like yourself could never understand the importance of bloodline," Duke Eldred said, waving his fingers in the air as though to dismiss him. "The Marendesly line is strong, filled to the brim with magic. Our line's power shows up far more frequently as a result. All I have to do to convince the emperor on a match with his kin, is remind him that with us, there is likely to be another weather sorcerer created in the next generation."

"That is not a sure bet," Agramon sneered, "and Emperor Arthello knows that."

"That is what we are prepared to offer," Duke Eldred said. "Try not to overplay your hand, *Your Grace.*"

"YOU DID WELL LAST NIGHT," Agramon said the next
morning, lounging on the couch while I enjoyed a plat-
ter of rolls. "Though I don't think it did any good."

I selected a bun slathered with honey from the tray.
"Well, Lord Achille was diverting company, I'll give
him that."

"Is he handsome?" Nirah asked, cleaning some of
my jewelry with one of Arden's feathers under the
watchful eye of Gree.

"Very," I said. "He looks like Sol's own son."

Agramon wrinkled his nose when I licked my fingers. "They are famous for being handsome, and they
know it."

"Are you jealous?" I handed one of the rolls to Nirah who gobbled it happily.

"Are you implying that I am not handsome?"
Agramon asked.

I shrugged, choosing not to answer. Suddenly, the
air behind Agramon began to shimmer. I almost
choked on the bun as two men materialized. Agramon

twisted and smiled.

"Ah, Elgar, right on time," Agramon said, rising and shaking Elgar the Swift's hand. Beside him stood Tristam the Miraculous.

My eyes widened, and I thought back to Agramon's words before. He thought the Marendeslys should have offered Tristam my hand. What game was Agramon playing now?

"Where's the girl?" Tristam asked, looking at me.

"Right over here," Agramon said, striding over to Nirah who'd shrunk into the corner at the sight of two grown men appearing in our room.

"What are you doing?" I rushed to Nirah's side.

Tristam looked at Agramon, his brows furrowed. "I thought you said she wanted my help."

"The brand, Rowyn," Agramon said, exasperated.

"Oh, right." I looked down at the girl. "You can remove her brand?"

Tristam nodded. "We could be jailed for doing it without a receipt of payment, but given everyone in the room, I'm sure there are far more weighty crimes attached to our names."

Agramon snorted.

I bit my lip.

Elgar merely shrugged.

"May I see your arm?" Tristam asked, kneeling before Nirah.

She looked up at me.

"Go ahead," I urged. "It will help us find you a new home."

Nirah held out her arm. Tristam closed his eyes and ran his fingers over the raised skin of her brand. His gem glowed, her skin healing as he traced the outline. After a moment, he opened his eyes and looked down. The brand was gone.

Nirah's eyes widened and she smiled, holding her arm close to inspect. "My word, that sure is something." She looked up. "Thank you, kind sir."

Tristam smiled as he nodded. "Don't make too much trouble, now that you're free."

A knock sounded on my door.

"Nirah," Agramon hissed. "Go hide."

"What of us?" Elgar asked, his gem beginning to glow.

"I will give you proper thanks in Somme," Agramon said, his voice low.

Elgar grabbed Tristam's arm and the men disappeared. I helped Gree stuff Nirah into my wardrobe as another knock sounded through the room. I leaped back onto the couch, waving at Agramon who stood by the door.

He opened it to Lord Achille, his hand raised as though about to knock again.

"You're awake," he said, glancing from Agramon to

me. Gree made herself known, bustling about with a feather duster. "We are about to go on a hunt, and I thought that you might like to join us."

I rose, smiling widely. "I would be honored, my lord."

Lord Achille seemed to recover himself, and he smiled back.

I glanced at Agramon. "I should be ready shortly. Is His Grace invited?"

Lord Achille chuckled. "It's just us young people. Duke Eldred requested that we make ourselves scarce during their meetings."

"Have fun, Rowyn," Duke Agramon said, motioning Lord Achille to the door. "We can talk more when you get back."

Gree moved quickly, tying me into a velvet green riding dress. Since she didn't have time, she plaited my hair into braids, rolling them onto one another in a large bun.

I stepped out in short order, painted and primped and excited for my first real hunt since the Nightlands. Iranoct was strapped to my waist.

Sam's door was open. "Where are you going?" he asked when he saw me pass.

"Lord Achille invited me to a hunt," I said. "How are you feeling this morning?"

"Better," Sam said. "Don't move. I'm going with

you." He strode to a chair and pulled his leather jerkin over his head and belted several daggers and his sword to his waist. After rinsing his mouth with mint water, he stepped out and shut his door, then offered me his arm.

"Lord Achille said the elders are supposed to make deals today. Are you sure you should be going with us?"

"When I can manage it, my place is by your side," Sam said, guiding me through the corridor. I smiled at the floor and squeezed Sam's hand.

We found the group of hunters in the entry hall. Lord Achille's gaze followed Sam and me as we descended the stairs. He stepped forward. "Butcher, my father mentioned you are supposed to review the Marysian troops today."

"I am," Sam admitted. "I thought that was later."

"It is this very morning!" Lord Achille smiled wide. "He wishes to see you in the great receiving room immediately."

A muscle in Sam's cheek jumped. "Very well." He released my arm and shot me an apologetic look. "Rowyn can take care of herself." He glared at Lord Achille. "Make sure you do the same."

"Very well," Achille said. He clapped his hands together after Sam left, then led me and the other young nobles through a side door.

We entered a weapons room. The others, mostly men, were chatting with each other, lifting the longbows off the wall. Lord Achille placed his hand on my back and led me past the others to another rack of weapons.

"Let us find you a bow," Lord Achille said, grabbing one. He handed it to me with a smile. I took it and tested the weight. It was unbalanced. I met his eye and put it back, chose a better one, and grabbed a quiver of arrows.

Before long we were riding through the forest, enjoying the view of the trees beginning to bud.

"Did you grow up here?" I asked.

Lord Achille nodded. "Many of the family have houses in the city, though most of the time entertainment is to be had here, at the great palace."

"I wonder why I did not see you at the capitol," I said, nodding to the others. "Do you always just stay at home?"

"My uncle, the duke, likes us to stay close. In fact, he insists on it. Normally the emperor and empress summer here, too, though they won't this year due to the quinquennial."

"Are you related to the emperor?" I asked.

Lord Achille laughed. "He's a cousin. Really, if you ask anyone in Maryse, we're all cousins with each other, in some fashion or another. Now enough about me. I want to know about you."

I raised my brows. "What do you know already?"

"Mellan of Ayastaren wrote to me about you coming. I was to show you the utmost respect, and a bit of fun as well. He seemed to think the Duke of Solin was jailing you."

"Mellan is a friend," I admitted. "A surprising one, honestly, given my history with his family."

Lord Achille grinned. "And what of the Butcher? He seems to take an active interest in your welfare."

"He takes the role of protector fairly seriously," I admitted. "There have been many attempts on my life since I've become a pawn of the emperor, and he is diligent in my care. It's nothing more than that."

Lord Achille leaned toward me, his voice low. "I confess, I don't like the way he looks at you."

"I can hardly apologize for it," I snapped, irritated with the turn in conversation. Since he wished to pry into unpleasant topics, I resolved to do the same. "I see you have Morganite slaves. How do they come by such a fate?"

Lord Achille's smile vanished. "They are indentured, of course. Usually, they've committed some crime. If they are unable to pay their fine, an indenture is placed on their head."

"Yet you brand them. What happens when they pay off their indenture? What becomes of the mark?"

"There is a special cost to get it altered to show resolution of the indenture. That's added to the amount that the person owes."

"So, you purchase these indentures in Morgania?"

Lord Achille shook his head. "No, skin-traders bring them to the eastern shore and we bid in the markets."

I gritted my teeth, fire boiling within. "What if they are not criminals? What if they've been kidnapped and forced into an indenture? How would you know?"

Lord Achille shrugged. "I suppose we wouldn't. I've not thought about it, truth be told."

"But it's someone's life," I said. "Have any nobles become indentured?"

"Of course not," Lord Achille scoffed. "My word, what an idea."

Lord Achille glanced at his companions, and I could tell that he was becoming disenchanted with me. I mentally kicked myself. It was too easy to slip into my old routine. Agramon had paid me a great service in getting Nirah's mark removed so quickly. I couldn't repay him by backing out of our deal.

"Let us speak of other things," I offered, biting back my pride. "I do not wish to seem unfriendly, or rude."

"It's all right. I worried about the Morganite slaves' presence when I found out it was me being offered up as suitor, but it's not my home, so . . ." He shrugged.

Movement to our right sent our party galloping after a stag. I hung back, not caring if someone else got the kill. Lord Achille's gaze followed the others.

"Go ahead," I urged. "I don't need you to entertain me if you wish to be elsewhere."

"You sure you don't mind?"

"Not at all," I insisted. "It's been so long since I've enjoyed a ride in the forest alone."

I watched him gallop off and turned to the trees, smiling at the sunlight streaming through the branches just beginning to break forth with new life. I spurred Starstruck forward, my face to the wind. Yet my thoughts returned to Maryse. Removing Nirah's brand was a huge step closer in making her safe. Now all I had to do was find her a safe home. A place where she could live a good life however she chose.

My spirit buoyed. I couldn't get Sam's kiss out of my mind. When he'd done it in the rose garden at Somme, I'd been so surprised that I didn't know how to react. Then the night turned to one of terror, and I refused to think of it.

The intensity of his gaze, the heat from his lips, the way I could feel the strength in his hands as he held it back. I'd not slept well for thinking of it.

Sam was a man with honor, though misplaced. Despite what he thought, he was undeniably handsome and boasted the body of a warrior. I respected him. I felt safe around him, and I could tell that he respected me. What more could I ask for?

But what of Destrian? He hadn't attempted to contact me at all after I left Morgania. I believed Agramon when he said he didn't send a single letter. Our love had been tainted by Agramon and the death of his father, and I doubted there would be any way to repair that. Destrian had told me how he felt through his absence. Yet, here was Baron Samael of Bruin, who refused to leave my side, doing his best to ensure I remain safe during my imprisonment. Why was I fighting him?

"HERE NOW," GREE SAID, TRACING the line along my eyelid with her brush. "His Grace wishes you to look more romantic this evening."

Gree had done well with the directive. It seemed she approved of me wearing green, for she chose a dress of the same color as my velvet riding gown, though made of sheer layers and a tight bodice. The sleeves sat off my shoulders like my dress from the night before, though these were full, the fabric puffing out a bit more before gathering tight around my wrist. She plaited half my hair up, leaving the rest to fall in black curly waves to my waist. Within the intricate plait wrapped around the crown of my head, she'd tucked sprigs of little white flowers.

I sighed. "I fear I lost Lord Achille's attention during

the hunt this afternoon."

"What do you want me to do about it?" Gree snapped, her brows furrowed as she began painting little flower designs in my crescent tattoos, so I would "stand out from the slaves."

"Do you have any advice in that dusty old head of yours?" I asked crossly.

"Don't talk so much," Gree said. "Nobody cares about your opinions anyway."

I was about to snap back but decided against it. She was probably right.

"Ask him what he thinks of things or have him show you something. Men love to talk about themselves," Nirah said, sorting through my jewelry. I was reminded of what Araceli had said.

A frown tugged at the corners of my lips. "I wish you didn't know that." Nirah had filled out a bit since coming into our care. The gowns no longer fell so loosely, and there were apples in her cheeks. Gree kept her clean and her hair braided. She looked like any other well-cared-for child you would see in the market, following their parents. I wondered again how we would find her a place to stay. Who would take the girl in? How would I ensure that she would be safe?

Nirah noticed me studying her and shot me a shy smile. "Which ones?" she asked, holding up two pairs of earrings.

"The pearl ones for tonight, I think." I opened my mouth so that Gree could paint my lips. "I like not worrying that the paintwork will smudge."

Gree nodded to Nirah. "Grab them, girl, they'll go well enough with this gown. Get that ring there too," she said, pointing to a little gold band set with black stones. "This will hold his lordship's attention." Nirah slipped the ring onto my finger. "He won't be able to think of anything but you. It won't do the whole job for you, but it will help with some."

"Thank you." I rose to inspect myself in the mirror. "I just wish I wasn't so nervous. I get into these halls, and I can't think past my own nerves. Then my mouth runs away from me."

"Get a few drinks of something harder than wine in you and you'll relax," Gree said, capping and cleaning up the potions and balms she'd used to get me ready. "But don't do it in front of his lordship. Men think a woman in her cup spells trouble."

I nodded, rubbing my hands together and pacing the room. "Is Lord Agramon going to accompany me?" I asked after several minutes. Usually, he would appear as soon as I was finished, or be sitting in the room waiting. I figured Gree mentally alerted him.

"He never returned from his meetings. He's probably in the hall already. You can go alone, can't you?" she asked, pursing her lips as though I were completely hopeless.

"Of course." I squeezed Nirah's hand. "Have a good evening, and mind Gree." Nirah nodded, pulling me down and kissing my cheek.

I was prepared to venture to the grand hall alone but reconsidered when I passed Sam's door. Checking to make sure the hall was empty, I knocked softly, praying that Gree would linger in my room.

After a moment, the door opened. Sam looked out questioningly. The hem of a white tunic hung out of his breeches and his hair was wet. His cheeks were lathered with soap, as though I'd interrupted him shaving. When he saw it was me, his eyes softened, lingering on my bare shoulders.

"I'm nearly ready if you would like an escort," he said.

"Actually," I said, unsure of how to begin. "I was wondering if you have any of that drink that you like. The fiery one."

"Of course," Sam said, stepping back. He shut the door behind me as I entered his room. I leaned against the wall and gripped my wrist loosely as Sam poured two drinks from the glass decanter of amber liquid on his table.

Sam handed me one of the drinks and went back to his mirror. He lifted a razor to his neck and ran it down his chin.

I took a sip from the glass, trying to hold back a cough as the drink burned down my throat. I sucked in a breath. Warmth spilled through my veins. "How did reviewing the troops go?"

Sam scratched at his chin with the blade. "Well enough." He met my eyes in the mirror. "Maryse keeps their troops in working order."

"That's surprising," I said, taking another sip. I was beginning to enjoy the burn.

"Why do you say that?" He wiped the razor on a linen rag and scratched some more.

"They don't seem to hold you in very high regard." I hoped he wouldn't take offense. "They call you Butcher, though you obviously hate the name. They've barely marked your presence here, and I wouldn't think any of them are keen on this war either."

"General Ivar was in the running to be named high commander, but I took it from him. They take issue with the fact that I wasn't born with a noble title. It was earned." Sam scratched through the last of the soap on his neck. "They think I'm muscle with no mind of my own."

"Doesn't it bother you?" I asked, finishing my glass. "The constant disdain?"

"Not especially." Sam rinsed his neck and face, then toweled them both off. "There, how does it look?" He turned, rubbing the smooth skin along his cheeks. I tilted my head to the side, studying him.

"Honestly?" I asked.

He nodded.

"I liked it better before."

Sam's nostrils flared. He downed his glass and pointed to my empty one. "Would you like another?"

"Sure," I agreed. He poured us both another drink and I took it, careful to take small sips. I needed just enough to make me amenable.

Sam had opened his wardrobe and pulled out an overcoat. It was a deep red velvet, with black embroidery along the seams. "Your suitor seems to have taken a shine to you," he said as he pulled the sleeves over his arms. "How does it feel being courted by the most handsome man in the room?"

"He's hardly the most handsome."

Sam's brows quirked as he strapped his belt to his waist, replete with his sword and daggers. "Oh? He seems to think so."

I laughed. Heat pooled in my cheeks as I admired Sam. Feeling a burst of courage, I stepped forward and plucked a stray thread from the velvet before smoothing it down under my hands. He smelled of soap and leather. I ran my fingers along the black embroidery. "Is this a bear?"

Sam stilled, his eyes on my hand. "It is my sigil."

"Ah, the bear of Bruin," I murmured. "Sounds fearsome." I stepped back, admiring him as I took another sip. "I don't remember ever seeing you in nobleman's clothes before. You always insist on playing the steadfast soldier around me."

"I figure if you can play a part, then so can I." Sam faced the mirror and adjusted his shoulders. I leaned against the table, admiring his movements.

"You're not known to drink before dinner," Sam said when I poured a little more into my glass. "What are you up to?"

"I failed to keep Lord Achille's attention on the hunt today." I sighed. "Gree suggested I relax. I must put on a better show tonight if I'm to appease Agramon."

"She suggested drinking to relax?" Sam asked, a smile tugging at his lips. "There are far better ways, you know."

I fought a smirk, my stomach somersaulting as heat strummed my veins. His tone dared me, and already the fire liquor made my thoughts blur. "You must teach me your tricks then, my lord." I pulled myself up on the table so my feet dangled off.

Sam stepped closer, his hands on either side of me. "Do you mean to torture me?"

"That depends," I whispered, taking another drink and smiling coyly. "Do you want me to?"

Sam hesitated but a moment from my lips, then kissed me ever so softly. He took the glass from my

298

hand and set it on the table, then combed his fingers through my hair, drawing me toward him. The heat from his breath had me trembling. His hands traveled down, curling under the bottom of my skirt and feeling the bare skin there. I grabbed the shoulders of his coat and let my tongue dance with his, wanting more. His hand traveled up, along my shin, the roughness of his calloused fingers electrifying. He stroked along my knee gently until he brushed the belt of knives strapped to my thigh.

He broke away with a groan and a curse. He practically ripped his coat off and threw it on the chair. I wrapped my arms around his neck, nipping at his lip and feeling as though I were being consumed with desire. His hand traveled higher, to the apex of my thighs, and it was my turn to gasp as he tentatively rubbed his fingers against my core.

"By the gods," he whispered, his eyes on mine as he stroked. I moaned, every nerve coming alive under his touch. "You have me undone."

Chapter 21

I WAS FLUSHED WHEN I ENTERED the hall alone, sure that every eye on me knew what Sam and I had just done. I looked toward Agramon, who nodded in the direction of the dance floor, where my quarry was spinning with a lovely young woman. Lord Achille caught my eye and smiled. He held up a finger for me to wait. I stepped away from the door, heat still crawling along my body, reeling from the precipice Sam's fingers had sent me tumbling down.

Sam strode in not long after, looking divine in his velvet coat. I almost went to him before remembering why I was there. He walked to a window and leaned against it. A servant came with a glass of liquor, but Sam shook his head, his eyes finding me.

I couldn't help myself. I smiled. Heat returned to my cheeks, so I looked away, hoping no one noticed.

"Lady Rowyn," Lord Achille said, coming up beside me. "I felt awful for how I just left you on the hunt. I should've taken more care with my guest. I'll not let you out of my sight this evening, understand?"

I took a deep breath to steel myself and smiled. "I had a pleasant time today; you don't need to coddle me."

"That's good to hear," Lord Achille said, grabbing a goblet and thrusting it into my hands. He led me around the room, filtering from one group of nobles to others dominated by sorcerers. Everyone was amenable, though their eyes lingered on my markings. Lord Achille thrust another glass of wine in my hands when I'd emptied the first. I was trying to take it slow and regretted following through with Gree's advice. Sam had been much more effective.

Suddenly, Lord Achille stopped in front of Sam who'd been talking to a nobleman with white hair. Sam's green eyes smoldered when they looked at me, a smile tugging at his lips. I bit my own, unsure how to proceed.

"I don't believe you've met General Ivar," Lord Achille said, motioning to the older man. I was immediately pulled from my thoughts.

I curtsied, trying to rally. I never thought I would encounter Fin's father on my travels, though I knew they were an important family to the empire. So important that he couldn't be bothered to show more than monetary care to his illegitimate daughter. "I knew your daughter at Solridge. She was a great friend to me," I said, trying my best to hide my emotions.

"I did not hear that you were friends," the general said, shifting his feet. "We do not write much, as I am very busy with my duties here, on the eastern shore."

I raised my brows. "When did you last hear from Fin?"

"She wrote when she returned with her gem. I've not heard of her since, but that's not uncommon. She has her own life to live, and I have mine."

"So, you do not know where she is presently?" I watched him closely. Araceli had mentioned that some were sure that she'd gone to join her father.

General Ivar's brow furrowed. "I would assume she is still at Solridge, attending to her studies there. Why?"

"You have not heard that she has disappeared?" I asked, uneasiness shifting within my gut. How was I the first to tell the man his daughter had been missing for the past seven months, save for a sighting between Nordow and Ardent?

General Ivar's brow wrinkled. "What do you mean, she is missing?"

"Araceli of Calla told me that after she returned from Horan, she stayed a bit at Solridge, then rode away, and hasn't returned since."

"We've been away from home for the past several months, traveling. I must've missed the master's notice," General Ivar said, glancing over to where another woman in the room eyed us uneasily.

We stood awkwardly for a moment before General Ivar stepped away.

"I hope she finds her way back," General Ivar said

passively.

"How can you be so unfeeling toward your own daughter?" I asked, my anger ballooning unexpectedly.

"Rowyn," Sam said, straightening. His eyes were urging me silent, but I ignored him. Beside me, Lord Achille was tugging my hand, trying to pull me away.

General Ivar frowned. "She may be my daughter, but I don't view her as kin. She was not raised in Maryse with the rest of her family. I've only met her twice. I fulfill my duties to the girl, but otherwise I have my own life to lead, responsibilities to follow through on, and she has hers. I wonder at your anger toward the girl. She has great freedom with her position."

"She wants her family's love," I said, remembering Fin's flippant remarks about her mother's husband and their children, the fact that she wasn't wanted with her father. Fin had no family that loved her, that treated her as though she were worth knowing.

"This is the way things are done," General Ivar insisted. "I'm sorry if it seems cruel."

"Why didn't you invite her to Maryse? Why didn't you have her meet her brothers and sisters?"

General Ivar straightened, his eyes flashing. "That would've been the utmost cruelty to my wife, who's been loyal to me for many years. The moment with Fin's mother was a time of weakness. I was young and undisciplined. We were reveling after a battle well fought, and I did something that I regretted. I'd hoped to forget it and move on with my life, but Fin is a constant reminder of my infidelity, to both me and my wife. You cannot ask me to bring the girl here, who is more talented than all the children my wife has given me. They already hate her for what she took from them, and you ask me to force them to live in her shadow as well? No, this is the only way. In this Fin can be free to live her own life, and my family can continue our happy existence."

"You're a poor excuse for a man." Tears sprang to my eyes.

"Come, the refreshments here are the pride of Maryse," Lord Achille said, motioning to a table of desserts on the other side of the room.

"Fin deserves far better than you." I strode away, wiping the angry tears from my eyes. I didn't know what I was thinking. That General Ivar would launch a search, or seek out answers himself? Fin had told me that her father didn't care for her, and I was a fool for thinking otherwise. Guilt nestled in my belly. Fin had nobody—nobody but me. I'd let her down in the capitol. I'd heard that she was missing and went back to living my life within those gilded walls. I was all she had left, and not even I had gone to look for her.

When I got to the door, I was pulled back by Lord Achille. "I didn't realize he would upset you so," Lord

Achille said with a frown. "Let us dance and forget the trouble."

I didn't want to dance. I wanted to return to my room and sleep the rest of the night away. It would have been better if I could do that in Sam's arms. But no, Agramon was already glaring at me from across the room. There was work yet still to do.

"Of course, my lord," I said, taking a deep breath and plastering a false smile on my face. "I forgot myself, but your company will surely lighten my mood."

I took his hand and let him lead me to the dancers. We spun around and around, swaying to song after song until I thought I was getting quite good at it. At least, it was becoming more like fun and less like work. I laughed, joked, smiled, and batted my eyelashes and placed my hand on his arm when he was sure to notice.

"Would you like to take a tour of the palace?" Lord Achille asked when it was starting to get late. He thrust another goblet in my hand and wrapped my arm around his.

"I'm quite tired," I said, wishing I were back in my bed.

"Nonsense." He pulled me toward the door. "Maryse's palace is one of the oldest Lyrican strongholds. So much history to be had in one place, it would be a shame if one were to miss it."

I located Sam deep in discussion with General Ivar,

who'd seemed to calm down from my outburst earlier. Agramon was talking to an older woman with a gem in her brow.

I'd promised to play the part. I sighed and let him pull me through the doors and into the corridor. Lord Achille talked about the importance of the stonemasonry of the halls, pointing out the little suns carved into the keystones. But as we walked further into the palace, the corridors darkened, fewer servants passed by, and fewer guards were posted. We walked until I hadn't spotted any other soul for several minutes. The hair on the back of my neck rose on end.

"In here is Sol's chamber," Lord Achille said, opening a set of double doors. Candles flickered, illuminating a room outfitted with pillows and cushions. Along the wall was a series of windows facing the east, where the sun would rise.

"It's beautiful," I said, taking care to remain by the door. "But I'm afraid it truly is getting late. I would like to return to my room."

"Come on," Lord Achille said, stepping toward me and leaning toward my ear. "Stay with me for a bit. If we are to be married, we should take the time to get to know each other."

His fingers brushed the top of my breast. I stepped back. "You are too close, my lord."

"In what way?" Lord Achille asked, his smile never

faltering as he closed the distance between us. "Am I being too gentle? I know how you Morganite girls like it." He grabbed my shoulders and leaned down to kiss me. I ducked and twisted away, but now he was blocking the only exit to the room.

I'd thought Lord Achille was like Mellan Lyon, flirtatious, fun, but good-natured about it. But Mellan never made me feel unsafe in his presence.

Lord Achille continued his advance, his smile never faltering. I knew how I wanted to react, but I'd made a deal with Agramon. I would be a noble lady, gentle and calm, fulfilling every quality the eastern lords desired. How would Ingrid fight him off? When I'd seen her cornered by Elias Lyon, I hadn't noticed she was doing anything but putting up with it.

I gritted my teeth. I wanted to punch him, though stabbing would be infinitely more satisfying.

"His Grace won't like hearing that you've held me against my will," I said loudly. "Let me pass."

"Oh, stop being so dramatic," Lord Achille said. "I'll let you pass if you give me a kiss."

"Fine," I agreed after weighing my options. "But then you must let me go."

"Sure," Lord Achille said. "Just a kiss."

I stepped toward him, intending to plant a small kiss on his cheek. He turned his head at the last moment, grabbing my shoulders and pulling me to him. He kissed me sloppily.

I shoved him away. "Now, let me pass."

Lord Achille grinned. "I didn't say I wanted you to kiss my face."

I tried to wrench the handle of the door open, but Lord Achille leaned against it and tried pulling my skirt up, laughing all the while. I slapped his hands away, but he went to my bodice next. Acting like the other noblewomen wasn't working.

I kneed him in the groin. Lord Achille doubled over.

"Let me pass," I growled in frustration as I tried the door again, but Lord Achille was still against it.

"You should not have done that," he groaned, his hand on the door. "Grandfather was right about you. You're nothing more than Morganite trash. Agramon should've just branded you and been done with it."

I stopped short. Branded? Would he have done that? I didn't see why not. After all, I was an active traitor to the empire. I'd grown up in a renegade clan, outspoken against the yolk of the empire.

Lord Achille staggered toward me. I pulled a knife out of my thigh holster and opened a shallow wound across his leg.

You would've thought I'd tried to gut him. He took his hand off the door and fell to the floor, screaming murder and cursing as blood dripped to the ground. I ran, thankful that I knew the way back to my rooms.

I flew through my door and slammed it behind me. Glancing at every corner of the receiving room, I strode to the door that held the bedchamber and peeked in. Nirah was sound asleep in bed, but she was in such terrible danger. I'd failed Agramon. He was sure to go after her. It wouldn't matter that she'd been in the wrong place at the wrong time. It wouldn't matter that she no longer had a brand. Agramon would hurt her regardless.

I took a deep breath, then quietly shut the door and ripped my dress off. The sleeveless corset and undershorts would suffice. I needed to be able to move. I needed to be able to reach my knives. If Agramon or anyone else wanted to hurt Nirah, they would have to go through me.

I looked to the window. Lord Achille's story was not what they should hear first. The gems burned my hands as lightning danced across the sky in warning. Thunder pealed so loudly that it seemed to rock the corridors. Heavy rain and winds began to sweep through Maryse. If Agramon were to believe them instead of me, I needed my magic ready to employ within a second. This time, when he sent someone I loved out of the window, I would catch them.

I waited, Iranoct in one hand, a knife in the other, and a storm raging behind me.

It was Luc who appeared first.

"What happened?" he asked, taking in my stance

and choice of weaponry. He ignored the fact that I was half-naked, his hand immediately going to his sword.

"I failed," I stammered. Disbelief began to cloud my thoughts. "I should never have bargained her life."

A tear ran down my cheek. I wiped it away.

"What do you need from me?" Luc asked, stepping closer. "What can I do?"

"Get away," I urged. "Don't let him use you against me. I just need him to listen. Stay out of his range until the skies clear."

Luc nodded. "Then there is no time to lose." He ran back out of the hall.

"Echo," I gasped. "Help me any way you can."

"He will believe you," Echo said.

"What if he doesn't?" I asked. "What if it doesn't matter?"

I'd had time to gather my thoughts when the doorknob turned and the door swung open. I shifted from one foot to the next. Ready to spring.

Agramon stepped through. "Why, Rowyn?" he asked, his eyes on my stance. "Whatever has gotten you in such a temper?"

I licked my lips. "I think you know."

"I would like to hear it from you," Agramon said. "We made a bargain, after all."

"I've failed it, though not by choice."

He regarded me thoughtfully, walking, almost leisurely, to the table where he poured himself a glass of wine. "What happened?"

"He wanted more than we bargained for," I said. "He took me to this room and tried to rip my dress off. I tried to behave like a noble girl, but I failed to convince him to let me leave. I stabbed him, but not that deep. He will live, regrettably. You and I both know I could've done far worse."

Agramon raised the glass to his lips and sipped, watching me. "Why did you go with him in the first place? Why did you not just return to your room?"

"Because I thought you would've wanted me to go."

Agramon turned to the window, leaning his staff and hand against the ledge. "Seeing it from his eyes was interesting. Like most, he overexaggerated your responses to him in his mind. He was sure you would be willing."

I bit my lip. "I only did what you asked me to do," I insisted. "Would you rather I just let him do whatever he wanted with me?"

Agramon didn't answer for a moment. He just looked out the window, ignoring the fact that I still held the sword and knife aloft.

"No," he said finally, resting his staff against the wall. "I suppose I wouldn't have wanted that." He turned toward me. "I believe you."

"But I still failed," I said, another tear dripping down my face. "I know you wanted me to romance Lord

Achille so that he would covet me, and stabbing him was literally the only thing I could've done worst next to killing him, but I can't let you touch her, Agramon."

Agramon raised his brows. "The girl may live . . . for now." He took another sip. "His Grace asks that we quit his halls tomorrow and leave Maryse immediately."

"You are not angry with me?" I asked, disbelief creeping into my voice. I glanced at the abandoned staff. My knife and sword began to tremble as relief trickled through my muscles.

Agramon met my eye. "I know you well enough to understand when you've been provoked. You wouldn't take such a step without a valid reason, whether it fits my political intrigues or not."

"So, they are just making us leave?" I asked. "What of their people? What of their crops?"

Agramon shrugged. "They probably would've let us remain the rest of the week if not for the Butcher's response." Agramon sighed. "Lord Achille will need a healer to fix his nose, and a handful of Marysian guardsmen are sporting black eyes. One has a broken arm. It's too bad Tristam had to leave so quickly, but he'll be back at the capitol now. They won't let the Butcher out of their dungeon until we are ready to go. Maryse doesn't really need you anyway."

I slowly lowered my weapons. "So, you will not punish me by hurting Nirah?"

"No," Agramon said. "I won't. Spending an evening with Lord Achille was probably punishment enough."

I sheathed Iranoct. "I know you'll probably not be honest with me," I said. "But I want to hear your answer. Was there discussion of branding me? Were they considering making me a true slave?"

Agramon's nostrils flared. "It was mentioned. At least that was just talk. They killed mind readers for a hundred years. Did you know that? They always believed we were evil. Called us a scourge."

I straightened. "So that gives you leave to take me and do what you like?"

A muscle in Agramon's jaw jumped. "Do you know why the Emperor's Council left you at Solridge instead of bringing you to the capitol?" He took another sip of wine.

"So I would go with Gillius," I said, matter-of-factly. "So I would trust him. He knew I would've never allowed myself to be taken to the capitol."

Agramon snorted. "No, it's because the council decided that it would be too dangerous to have you in Somme. They said that you couldn't be trusted."

"They were probably right," I said. "What does it even matter that I'm not branded; you've enslaved me regardless."

Agramon downed the wine. "My intention was never to enslave you," he yelled, slamming the glass onto the table and shattering it. "My intention was to save you!" He looked down. Blood was pooling in his hand.

I faltered. "Save me from what?" When he just stared at his hand, I stepped toward him and took it in mine. Picking a shard of glass from his flesh, I pulled out a knife and cut a long piece of silk from the table covering.

"I saw in Mordog's mind how people saw you at Espiria," Agramon said, watching me wrap the fabric around his fingers. "How his own worries of your abilities tainted every memory he had of you. Then the seer learned of your existence, and orders were that you should be taken out. It took everything I had to convince the emperor to save your life."

"Why would you do such a thing?" I tied the fabric in place.

"Because you are like me!" Agramon snapped. "Just like Vianne was."

I raised my brows. "Vianne?"

Agramon nodded, running his other hand through his hair. I'd never seen him so off guard. His staff still leaned against the window, and he wasn't even trying to prod at my mind. "Do you think her Lord Alexander would've been by her side if he'd seen where she'd come from? I met her at her worst, where any street vermin able to rub two silvers together could crawl between her legs. Despite what the others will say, Vianne and I understood each other. We understood what it took to live with the ramifications of our power. People like us have always been hated."

"Can you honestly claim you do not seek to wrest power from the empire?" I asked. "How can I trust you when you've proven you will do anything in your quest, including using me."

"You've always accused me of seeking more power yet have never once asked why." Agramon shook his head. He looked back down to his silk hand wrapping. "We leave in the morning."

He left, shutting the door firmly behind him.

That night, I clutched Nirah to me as I lay in bed, unable to sleep. I wanted to believe Agramon. I wanted to trust that he wouldn't hurt the girl, but I couldn't silence my mind. Thinking back on the evening, I wondered about Agramon's confession. Was he simply trying to help me? Had he always thought he was keeping my best interests to heart?

Agramon had bled. I replayed the scene in my mind. He'd done it himself. He'd broken the glass. Agramon could be hurt as long as he was doing it to himself.

I didn't know how I could use that to my advantage, but somehow, I'd figured out a weakness.

Chapter 22

WE LEFT BEFORE DAWN. The Marysian nobility made their contempt known in the lack of farewell. The only people who saw us off were the guards, there to ensure that none of our party lagged. We rode hard until we reached the boundary of Maryse, then slowed to a more leisurely pace.

I refused to let Nirah out of my sight. She rode in front of me on Starstruck, then slept beside me in my tent. Fear of Agramon kept me awake, and I held her to my chest.

Sam stayed by our side as much as he could. He seemed more worried by the day as the dark circles around my eyes grew deeper. Finally, after a week of riding, Sam had enough. He forced Nirah and me into the carriage before climbing in after us.

"I will watch her for you," he whispered. "You need to get some sleep."

I looked at the girl across from us, already curling up into the seat, her eyes closed.

"I know I'm probably being stupid," I said, leaning against the side of the carriage. "But I don't think I'll ever be able to trust him."

"I don't think that's stupid at all," Sam said. "Everything that man says is to manipulate others."

I hadn't yet told Sam about Agramon's confession during our last night in Maryse. How he'd insisted on saving my life. Honestly, I didn't think I'd ever tell him.

"I heard you broke Lord Achille's nose," I said, unable to hide my smile.

Sam grinned. "One of my finer moments. It took ten of their guards to take me down."

I laughed when he puffed his chest out with pride. He'd come away with a bruise or two, but I'd heard the guards fared far worse.

"Sleep," Sam said again, leaning back. "Nobody is going to get her with me here."

I let the rocking lull me. Darkness filled my dreams as my eyes turned to the starlight.

"Stay with me," Destrian murmured. "Helena is where you belong. We'll find a way for you to gain mastery. You can come into your own, have freedom, whatever you want. Just let this be your home. Help me unite Morgania—Lyrican and Morganite, together as one.

"Don't answer now. Just think on it," Destrian said, brushing the tears away.

I felt the warmth of his chest as I lay against him. He'd always held me so close. "Destrian," I murmured, fighting grogginess as I awoke.

The smell of bear grease filled my nose. I shifted my

head.

Realization dawned on me.

My eyes flew open.

My head was resting on Sam's chest. His arm was draped over my shoulders, his body stiff.

I sat up. Sam's green eyes were filled with despair.

"Sam, please understand . . ."

He stuck his hand outside the window and hailed the driver. "I can't do this."

The carriage stopped with a lurch, and he flung open the door.

I grabbed his hand. "Wait."

Sam shook his head, pulled his hand from my grip, and slammed the door.

I sat back and buried my face in my hands. Nirah had stayed asleep during the entire exchange, but I glared at the empty spot beside her. "Why did you do that?" I hissed to Echo. "Why did you have to show him to me now?"

"You wanted to fight for his dream," Echo whispered back. "Why do you give up so quickly?"

I crossed my arms. "You of all people should know that men don't always do as they say. No matter what they dream about."

"I believe you can still save it," Echo whispered.

"You overstep," I insisted. I looked out the window. "Don't ever do that again."

I'D FALLEN ASLEEP AGAIN WHEN I woke up to shouting. I was about to look out the window when someone screamed. I grabbed Nirah and threw us both down to the carriage floor as arrows peppered the side.

Suddenly, an explosion rocked the carriage. The screams of men and horses filled the air. I scrambled to the door, but it was too late. The coach jolted forward, throwing me back to the ground as the horses thundered down the road. I gripped Nirah tightly to my chest as the carriage began bouncing us around. A crack splintered through the air, and we were flung against the seats where a searing pain shot through my head.

SOMETHING JOSTLED ME AWAKE. I could feel the sway of a horse beneath me. That couldn't be right. I'd been in the coach. I tried to raise my arms, but my hands were bound together. I stiffened, feeling the body of someone behind me.

Arms tightened around me, and a foreign voice shouted to others. I opened my eyes and saw a host of men riding around me, wearing simple tunics and breeches. I'd been captured.

I looked around. We were off the road and riding through a barren landscape. The other men rode alone. There didn't appear to be other prisoners. What had they done with Nirah? What of Agramon? Or Sam?

There was nothing to hide me if I ran, but I would not go down without a fight. I slammed my elbow into the body behind me. The man released his grip, and I swung my leg over and slid off the horse.

I lost my balance when I landed, my bound hands hampering my movement. Rising from my knees, I dodged a rearing horse's hooves and darted away, running doggedly, hoping the element of surprise would deter them. I ran, though I had no idea where I was, nor how long I'd been out, or who the raiders even were.

A horse appeared before me, the rider's black eyes dancing as he lowered a crossbow aimed at my heart. The man was young, with high cheekbones and tousled black hair. He looked Ylirian, or at least like he was from the mountains near the border.

I glared at him but didn't move. He spoke again in a language I didn't understand. Others rode up, circling me, their crossbows bolted and ready.

"We do not want to hurt you," the young man said suddenly, his words clipped. "You must come with us."

"Where are you taking me?" I asked.

"Alf Amun-doon requests your presence," the man said. He nodded to someone behind me.

I glowered. "What does Alf Amun-doon want with me?" I was testing my power within. There was plenty there, ready to be commanded. But something was wrong. It kept slipping out of my mental grasp, flowing like water through fingers, back down into the well. What was wrong with me?

The young man handed his crossbow to another and walked his horse toward me.

"No magic," the man said, leaning on the pommel of his saddle with a lopsided grin. He nodded toward me, his eyes on my throat. My hands shot up and discovered a weight there. A collar lined with stones. It must've been blocking me from calling my magic. Iranoct wasn't at my waist, and I couldn't draw my power. I was trapped.

The man dismounted. His hands were up, and the damnable beast was still smiling. "Do not hurt," he said. "Too far to walk."

"Don't you dare touch me," I hissed, stepping away from him. Someone spoke behind me, but the man shook his head, his eyes never leaving my face.

"You must not fuss. We have much to go." He stepped forward again. I stepped back, but that was as far as I could go. I could feel the anger of the horsemen behind me. They wanted to move.

Realization dawned on me. The way their eyes glanced behind them on the road. The nervous grunts they shared.

They wanted to move quickly because they were being followed.

Sam might not be too far behind. If he were still alive.

The man dismounted. "You must ride now," he said. When he reached toward me, I shrank back, raising my bound hands in front of me. The man grabbed my waist and lifted me onto the saddle. I tried to wriggle down the other side, but another rider grabbed my hair, holding me still while the man jumped up behind me.

The raider spoke in his other language and my hair was released. An arm snaked around my waist, gripping the reins in one hand, while the other drew a dagger to my throat.

"No trouble," the man hissed in my ear. "No trouble and you see Alf Amun-doon in one piece."

The other riders had already kicked their mounts forward. They raced over the earth, kicking up clouds of dust behind them. They would be easy to follow.

The man holding me nudged his horse forward. He moved the dagger away from my throat but kept it firmly in his hand. Our horse followed the others.

"Who is this, Alf Amun-doon?" I asked. The dagger's blade went back to my throat.

"A god," the man said. The cold blade dug into my skin, and I quieted.

MY EYES DARTED AROUND THE CAMP. We'd been riding for hours to the east. I hadn't seen Iranoct in the weapons the men had unpacked from their horses, and the sheath of knives I kept at my thigh was gone as well. I prayed that one of my own party had picked my weapons up. A queasy sensation filled me when I thought of the loss. Iranoct was the one thing I had of my time with Destrian in the Nightlands. It was his gift to me. I'd sooner sell my soul before losing it.

When I first came to Somme, I'd used it almost every night to point the way to Destrian. His sword was linked with mine, and they would always be able to find each other. It had been a while since I'd used the sword in that way. Ever since Agramon said that Destrian had never tried to contact me. Ever since Sam began his suit in earnest.

The raiders growled to each other as the sun set beyond the horizon. Sadly, they were wise. They made no fire, though the cold was creeping over me. I hugged my arms over my knees and shivered. The younger man sat behind me, a dagger still in his hand. He tossed me a bag of dried meat, fruit, and nuts before he joined the conversation with the other raiders. I'd initially thought my young captor was the leader, but I'd been wrong. The leader was an older man who seemed to issue a lot of curt commands. When one of the men used a tone he didn't like, the man punched him straight in the face.

I glanced from the leader to the young man. They shared the same dark rounded eyes and high cheekbones. It had to be a father and son. While the other raiders sat in silence when the leader issued a command, my young jailor simply sat back, toying with his dagger.

He flipped it, caught it deftly, then spun it over his fingertips.

Flip.

Catch.

Spin.

Flip.

Quick as a snake, I caught the dagger with my bound hands, then lunged at the young man.

The kidnapper yelled in surprise, but he'd caught my wrist. Using my momentum, he rolled us and trapped me under him.

The men around us were shouting. The young man's face was far too close to mine and his weight was suffocating. He answered the shouts in his language, then used both hands to pry the dagger from my grip.

"You are fast," the young man said, laughing as he rose. Gripping the rope on my wrists, he dragged me up with him. "But not so fast to get me, no?"

I tried to yank my hands away, but the man tightened the rope cruelly. I gasped when it bit into my skin.

"I do not want to hurt. You need to be calm," the young man said before answering the leader in his language. The man pushed me down to the ground before sinking next to me, one knee propped up while he rested against a boulder.

Damn it. He'd hidden his dagger once more. All the men seemed to take stock of their weapons, making sure they were out of my reach. They sat in a circle, talking to each other as the dusk turned to night.

"How long till we reach . . . wherever you are taking me?" I asked, curling into myself to keep warm.

"Eight moons with good riding," the young man said behind me. I hated how his voice seemed to always have a joking lilt to it. "You are cold, no?"

I just curled into a smaller ball, tucking my chin between my knees as I stared ahead. There was no point in listening to the grunts of the conversation from the men around me. I had no idea what they were saying.

Something heavy fell over my shoulders. I shoved the fur cloak off and scooted away.

"Do not be a fool," the young man said. The cloak was draped over my shoulders once more. "It will be trouble if you are sick."

I gritted my teeth but nestled deeper into the cloak, begrudgingly thankful for its warmth. I could feel the young man's eyes on my back.

"What do they call you?" the man asked.

I considered whether to answer. I supposed conversation wouldn't hurt, especially if they questioned whether to keep me alive. Maybe I could get the young man on my side. Maybe I could convince him to release me. At the very least, I could probably figure out what in all the gods these raiders wanted with me.

"Rowyn," I said, glancing toward him but didn't shift under the cloak. "I would think you'd know that, considering you set out to kidnap me."

The young man chuckled. "Alf Amun-doon do not tell us a name. He tell us to get the girl with stones. So, we get girl with stones."

One of the men near us, his face scarred and grizzled, turned to the young man, his voice low as he spoke to him. The young man laughed and gave a clipped response. The grizzled man turned away, shaking his head and mumbling.

The young man turned back to me. "Ro-een? Did I

say correct?"

I shook my head and repeated my name. The young man leaned forward, screwed up his face, and tried again. "I call you Ro," the man said finally. He smiled. "You call me Alim."

"Alim," I repeated. "I hate to tell you this, but you will have the entire empire searching for me."

Alim leaned back against the boulder. "Alf Amundoon said it was risky. He ask for bravest. So, me, my father, our men, we go. We are bravest."

"But they *will* come after me," I said. Sam may be angry with me, but he wouldn't leave me to my fate. It was also safe to say that Agramon would take issue with his investment getting snatched from under his nose. The band of men surrounding me was not enough to defeat the company I'd ridden with. I figured the carriage horses bolting had given them the chance they needed to grab me and make a quick escape.

"We are not afraid of those men," Alim said, shooting me his crooked grin.

I took a breath, trying to be patient. "I don't think you understand. One of those men is the Butcher of Bruin, one of the most dangerous men in the empire."

Alim raised his brows. "I do not believe you. You are with us now, no? They were beaten easily."

"Alim, I promise you, they will come for me, and when they do, they will be merciless."

"We are the bravest, remember? You should pray for these men. They will not catch us. If they do, they will die."

Well, I tried. I shook my head, turning my attention back toward the others. The men were beginning to roll out sleeping pads. To the right, a man stood watch, crossbow in hand as he scanned the darkness from the path we'd just traveled. I heard Alim rise behind me.

"You sleep now," Alim said, sinking next to me. He held a rope.

"What are you doing?" I asked, eying the cord. Alim tilted his head to the side.

"You are quick. You will try to run. We can't let you." Alim began wrapping the cord around my feet. I kicked at him.

"Stop moving. You make this difficult." Alim grunted and tightened the rope quickly. My ankles screamed as the rope burned my flesh. In a matter of minutes, I was lying on my back, thoroughly bound, staring angrily at the sky.

Alim's face popped into view above me. "You feel fine? No hurts?"

I spit on him.

Alim ducked away, laughing. I thought he would at least have the decency to move away from me, now that I was bound and unable to make a bid for freedom, so it was even more infuriating when I felt him lie next to me, pulling the cloak over himself as well.

"What are you doing?" I hissed. "Can't you leave me in peace?"

"We must guard you. You are tricky, I think. Fast and tricky."

At least he was warm.

Another figure sank down on my other side. It was the grizzled man who had chided Alim before. He scooted his body much too close to mine.

I lay on my back, stiff as a board between them. The older man's hand came to rest on my waist.

There was no way I could sleep with them so close. I listened to the men around me begin to snore. Even Alim's breath was soft and even, warm against my ear.

I tried to refuse the tears at the corners of my eyes. *Please hurry, Sam.* What fate awaited me when I reached Alf Amun-doon?

My fate was ruled by who wanted me most, I supposed. It was laughable. I was wishing my new captors return me to my old ones. My life had turned into an incredible joke.

I clenched my eyes shut, praying for dawn.

Chapter 23

I MUST HAVE SLEPT, because I awoke to the sun breaking over the mountains to the east. I tried to sit up but became painfully aware that my bonds were still in place.

Suddenly, Alim was kneeling beside me, his fingers working through the knots binding my feet.

"You are awake," Alim said, stating the obvious.

When he finished with the rope, he angled my chin up and looked at my throat before pulling the jeweled collar down. He grunted to himself, then pulled me upright by my shoulders.

"You eat. We leave soon."

He grabbed a bag of what looked like dried meat and set it on my lap before rising to talk to the men readying the horses. The leader went over to Alim. Whatever he said involved lots of flinging his arms out and glaring at me. I ducked down, trying not to draw attention to myself as I picked over the food, chewing slowly.

Alim's laugh echoed over the camp. I glanced back up. He clapped his hand against the leader's arm and walked toward me, still laughing and shaking his head.

"We leave now." Alim helped me stand. I shoved

the rest of the meat in my mouth, then allowed him to lead me to a horse that stood, stamping, ready to go.

Alim lifted me into the saddle. I gripped the pommel with my bound hands and the horse's sides with my legs. Alim jumped up behind me, his arm firm around my waist. The wind picked up, sending a chill through my bones.

"You have too much hair, Ro," Alim said, pulling the strands off his face.

"If you untie me, I could braid it back." I tried not to make my voice sound too hopeful. His sword was at his waist. A dagger in his belt. If I could grab one, I was sure I could make a bid for freedom. Of course, that was only if Sam and the others were still behind me. Perhaps they'd given up their search. Perhaps everyone finally came to their senses and realized I wasn't worth it.

"I cannot untie you." Alim chuckled. "Tricky Ro." He mussed the top of my head. "I braid for you." I heard him rummaging in a pack, then he began working through my hair with a brush. I watched the other men breaking camp as he worked. He divided my hair into five sections instead of three and weaved the strands together. His fingers worked remarkably fast.

"Where did you learn to braid?"

Alim chuckled. "I have many sisters."

My breath caught. Alim reminded me of Destrian,

who had two sisters himself. "Your wife must be a lucky woman," I said, swallowing back more tears.

Alim sighed as he tied off the braid with a leather thong. "No wife, not yet. I have to earn my home first. It will not be long. Not after you go to Alf Amun-doon. He will give us a big reward. I will get a large home with it. Wife will come soon after, I think." Alim draped the braid over my shoulder. "Your hair is like girls at home, but your eyes are different. I like your eyes."

I glanced over my shoulder. "Are you flirting, Alim?"

He frowned. "I do not know flirting. What is it?"

I pursed my lips. "It's when you're sweet-talking someone. Like you're trying to romance them."

Alim's eyebrows shot up. "Do you like me to romance you? I can try. You are pretty." His arm snaked around my waist, much tighter than before.

"No, I don't want you to romance me. I'm a prisoner, remember? You kidnapped me?"

"Very well," Alim said into my ear. "You say if you change your mind."

I rolled my eyes and bit back a retort. The other men were mounted, and we began moving east again.

We reached the base of a mountain by the next day. I wondered if Alf Amun-doon dwelled within the range or beyond, in Yliria. The men rode single file up the switchback path of the mountains. Great boulders towered over us, and I prayed we weren't trying to summit the peak. I was so sick of the cold and my skirt had torn. My bare legs kept me shivering even though Alim had gripped me from behind, then wrapped his cloak around the both of us.

It was an odd feeling, being stolen from others who held me against my will. I was a piece of property to be owned, with no one caring what my will was, or whether I wanted to spend my life bowing to others. Was that how it would be when I escaped? Would I easily just fall into the hands of others who wished to own me? At least with Agramon and Lyrica, I knew what I was getting.

I sighed. I'd thought to talk to Echo but decided not to draw attention to her presence by speaking. Instead, I pondered what future lay in wait for me. Sam would not abandon me, that much I was sure about. He would take my kidnapping as a personal slight. If he was still alive, which I believed he was, then eventually he would find me again. It was only a question of when.

If I did meet this mysterious Alf Amun-doon, I wouldn't behave the way I had with Agramon when he'd first brought me to the eastern shore. If my mentor had taught me anything, it was that it was easier to make deals then it was to constantly wear myself out by fighting a bridle. There certainly a deal that Alf Amun-doon wanted to make—I was sure of it. The men who'd grabbed me had taken great care in ensuring my safety. No one so much as touched me. The only one who even spoke to me was Alim, and he was friendly and endearing, always ready to crack a joke. I tried to calm myself with the knowledge that for kidnappings, it could've been much worse. If it had been the Sons of Sol, I doubted I would've lasted the first night.

I'd not slept well after two nights stuffed between two men. I had finally begun nodding off at the swaying of the horse when I heard something streak through the air behind us. I sat up, startled, as Alim's arm clenched around my waist, and he pulled me off the horse. Shouts filled the air.

"Alim!" I shouted, trying to pull him out from beneath the horse's stamping hooves. I recognized the shouts of Lyrican soldiers. They had found us. I dragged Alim behind a large boulder to hide us both. Alim hissed in pain, then I realized an arrow was embedded in the back of his shoulder.

"Ro," Alim said, grunting as he adjusted himself. "Come, I cut you free. You get arrow. I fight."

"No, Alim!" I hissed as he pulled a dagger from his waist and began sawing at my binds. "Stay here. Don't let them find you!"

The rope fell away from my hands, and Alim leaned back with a groan.

"Cut arrow, Ro. I fight," Alim said.

"You don't have to die for this stupid cause," I hissed as the sounds of battle and dying men rose around me.

"If you do not cut arrow, I go anyway. It is easier without arrow though." Alim moved to rise.

"Fine!" I grabbed the dagger. I cut at the base of the shaft, leaving enough room for a healer to pull it out.

"Tricky Ro," Alim said, pulling out his sword. "Stay hid. I make sure they do not hurt you."

Alim raised his sword and leaped from behind the boulder with a war cry.

One moment he was there next to me, his eyes bright for the impending battle. The next, a blade appeared through his chest, cutting off the war cry with a strangled sound of surprise.

I jumped in shock.

Alim's eyes widened. The sword dropped from his hand as he swayed. Sam appeared in front of him, his face a mask of fury as he pulled the blade from Alim's chest.

I didn't even have time to scream before Sam beheaded Alim in a torrent of blood.

Alim's body fell. I could feel something dripping down my face, pooling in my hair, into my braid. I trembled, unable to look away.

"Rowyn!" Sam turned to me. He looked like a monster, dark rivers of blood soaking his arms and chest. I shrank away as he grabbed my hand.

Why couldn't I stop shaking?

Sam lifted me as my body quaked. As he carried me away, I couldn't tear my gaze from Alim lying beside the boulder.

Sam carried me to a low rock and set me down gently before kneeling in front of me. "Rowyn," Sam said, brushing a strand of hair behind my ear. "Look at me."

I tried to meet his eyes, but my thoughts were filled with the laughing Alim. The raiders' bodies littered the mountain pass. The scent of blood and death filled the air. The battle was over.

I'd seen death before. I'd watched my loved ones die away. So why was I so shaken by Alim's death? I took a deep breath, remembering Sam stepping into the light, swinging the blade that ended Alim's life. Sam killed him with a ruthlessness befitting his moniker. In that moment, he'd appeared every bit the horror everyone claimed him to be.

"Rowyn," Sam said, his hands on my shoulders. I must've missed what he'd said. I tried to focus on him. "What is this?" His fingers curled under the collar.

My hands flew to the jeweled metal. "It's suppressing my power, my magic."

Sam turned and ordered several soldiers back to the bodies. The men picked over what remained of the raiders until one of them gave a shout of triumph. He held up a golden key, at his feet the bowed body of the leader of the raiding party.

Sam strode to the soldier and grabbed the key, then issued another series of commands. Returning to me, he kneeled once more, fitting the key into the collar and turning it. The metal fell into Sam's hands while I rubbed my throat.

Sam pocketed the collar and key, then looked back up at me, his brow furrowed. "They hurt you." He touched a bruise on my cheek. I hadn't even realized it was there.

His eyes returned to mine, and a muscle in his jaw jumped as he grabbed my hands, nearly crushing my fingers. "Did they . . ." His voice shook.

I waited, but he didn't continue. I caught onto his meaning. "No," I said, remembering the grizzled man's hands on my waist. "I'm fine."

"You would tell me if they did?" Sam's nostrils flared.

I frowned, trying to pull my hands from his vice-like grip. I didn't know why I bristled at the slight to Alim's honor. He was dead; he wouldn't care. Besides, they had *kidnapped* me. Sam's worry had matched my own in the beginning.

"Please," Sam said, releasing my fingers and curling his hands into fists. He looked away. "I have to know . . . how much I've failed you."

"Sam, you didn't fail me." Alim's body collapsed into my vision. I willed it away. Alim had known the risk. "They didn't touch me, I promise. They were taking me to someone. A man named Alf Amun-doon. It was he who sent them after me. I think their orders were that I make it to him unharmed."

Sam frowned. "Are you sure?"

I nodded. "I guess he's several days away."

Sam turned and stared east up the mountain. "Alf Amun-doon is a warlord in Yliria, near the border." Sam rose to his feet. "Wait here. We'll be leaving in a moment." He stepped away to speak to the soldiers who kept shooting awkward glances at me.

I ignored them.

Someone new was after me. What did Alf Amun-doon want with me? Why did he want me brought to him alive?

"Rowyn, come on," Sam said, holding Starstruck's reins.

I rose and walked toward him, embarrassed by how shaky my legs were. "You're not just going to leave them there, are you?" I asked, my eyes on the butchered raiders. Alim deserved more than to have his bones picked apart by scavengers.

"We can't waste time here," Sam said, his face still bloody. "There are several raiding tribes in the area, and we made too much noise as it is. We don't stop till we're within Bruin's borders."

A soldier led Sam's horse to him. Sam flipped the saddle blanket up, revealing Iranoct in its scabbard and my belt of knives.

I gasped. "You found them."

Sam nodded, pulling the sword out and handing it to me. My hands trembled as I belted Iranoct around my waist. I breathed a sigh of relief at its closeness.

"Thank you," I said, meeting Sam's eye. I lifted the remains of my skirt and belted the knives back to my thigh.

Sam looked away with reddened cheeks. "I know how much the sword means to you." He lifted me into the saddle before stepping into Hale's stirrup and mounting.

With a curt command, the soldiers drew in line behind him as Sam led the way out of the mountain pass. As soon as we reached level ground, Sam kicked Hale into a gallop. I clenched the reins as exhaustion crept through my bones.

We rode west. I called a storm to cover our path and deter anyone from following. Sam's pace was relentless. When we finally stopped for the night, I was bone-tired and weak. The rations the raiders shared had been meager, and my entire body felt as though it were ready to collapse.

I tried to dismount, but my legs wouldn't work and I tumbled off the horse.

"I've got you," Sam said when he caught me, setting me gently on the ground.

I clutched his jerkin, unable to keep my knees from shaking. Sam carried me to where they had begun to build a fire. After I sank down, he busied himself with ordering the others around and tending to the horses. I watched the fire dance over the wood. My mind drifted to Destrian in Morgania, as it so often did. I gripped Iranoct's hilt. Without thinking, I drew the blade and laid it across my lap. I closed my eyes and thought of its twin, Phyranox, the golden blade that Destrian had wielded in the Nightlands. Iranoct twitched in my hands, pointing due west, where Morgania lay across the sea.

I opened my eyes, only to find Sam watching me as he brushed Hale's coat. I glanced at the fire and traced the engraving of the shadow falcon on Iranoct's hilt.

I shrank away from the soldiers' chatter as they began roasting several animals they'd shot on the road. When Sam was finished tending to Hale, he sat near me, though still a healthy distance away.

"You overdid it today, with the magic," Sam said, his arms on his knees. "We don't need rain to cover our path tomorrow. I want you to rest."

Relief flooded me. I didn't think I had it in me to

call the rain unless I had a full night of uninterrupted sleep. Given the lack of rest I'd had the past few nights, I wasn't going to count on it.

"That's fine," I said, carefully sheathing Iranoct. "Is Agramon waiting for us on the road? Is Nirah safe?"

"I sent them on to Bruin with the rest of the men. It was easy to convince Agramon that was the safest path."

I opened my mouth to speak, but Sam interrupted me. "Nirah has a personal guard. Agramon knows she must remain unharmed."

I ran my hand over my face wearily. "And Agramon is uninjured?"

"Naturally," Sam grunted. "He assured me that he would have my head on a spike if I didn't bring you back unharmed. As if I needed the encouragement."

I couldn't bring myself to respond.

"He at least told me where they were headed," Sam said after a moment, his eyes back on the fire. "That's how I knew where to set the trap. We captured several of their men, and Agramon was able to see locations in their minds."

"What happened to those men?"

"I killed them myself," Sam said, his eyes back on the fire. It was almost like he was refusing to look at me.

"What's wrong?"

Sam glanced back at me, then his eyes fell to my dress. When I'd been kidnapped, I was wearing one of Agramon's court dresses, made of sheer fabric. Now it was torn and dirty from sleeping on the ground. "We need to get you into some different clothes. You look . . . cold."

In short order, I'd changed into a tunic and breeches, borrowed from a soldier with a lean frame. I'd even gotten most of the blood and grime off with a wet rag.

Still, that night, I didn't sleep.

Nor did I sleep the night after.

Nor the night after that.

It took us four days to reach Bruin. Four sleepless nights, while I lay awake in a makeshift tent, my ears straining for the smallest hint of sound.

Arda's prophecy resounded in my ears.

The daughter of an ancient queen,
aided by Imor,
protected by Sol,
whose fire will rage through broken cities,
whose rain will quench parched earth,
whose coming will unite children of the empire,
she will rise.

Chapter 24

BRUIN. WHAT COULD BE SAID of such a place? Dust filled the air as men worked the Fields of Forgotten Men, their faces dirty, their backs bent toward the barren earth as they dug. Mountains rose to the north and east, making it feel as though we were hemmed in. Without even being asked, I faced the sky, letting the power flow through me in steady streams till the sun was blotted out by a massive cloud mass.

Wary faces tilted to the sky as drops sprinkled over the dusty ground, turning the earth into mud. I saw a smattering of imorets throughout the crowd of men, though there were no faces I recognized.

The castle had been built of black stone, its scraggly towers rising from the earth like blackened tree stumps. The wall was manned by soldiers—not the men of the fields, but men who were strong, with muscle still on their bones and food in their bellies. They watched the rain and me with reservation.

I wondered how long it had been since Sam had been home.

"Rowyn!" Nirah shouted, running toward me. I gripped her in a too-tight hug, whispering thanks to

Imor that the girl was unharmed.

"What happened to you?" I asked, kneeling in front of her.

"I didn't know what to do," Nirah said, her voice rising. "I was so rattled from the crash that it took me a second to figure out what happened. Then a voice told me to run."

Echo. I would need to apologize to her once I found time alone. "That was a smart move, you getting away." I pulled Nirah in for another hug. "I would never forgive myself if something happened to you."

"I'm all to rights, miss," Nirah said, smiling as Gree came up behind her. "And now that you're safe, we can be as we were."

"The lady will require a proper bath and rest," Sam ordered.

"Of course, my lord, of course. I'll tend to it right away." Gree turned and barked an order at a boy who took off running into the tower. I was about to follow them when Sam grabbed my arm.

"I'll check on you later," he said, his brows furrowed. "Try to get some sleep, will you?"

I nodded, then followed Gree and Nirah up the stairs.

"WELL, AT LEAST HE'S BROUGHT you back in one piece," Agramon said. "Though you look more worse for wear than I expected. By Sol above, girl, how long has it been since you've slept?"

I stared at myself in the mirror. Agramon had insisted I wear an amethyst silk dress, but the fanciest dress in the world couldn't diminish the dark circles under my eyes.

"Do your best to cover those up, will you?" Agramon asked Gree, who nodded as she stirred a pot of cosmetics and began plastering it onto my face. I sat patiently while she worked, happy to rid my mind of thoughts.

Luc was lurking next to the door. I could feel his glare in the mirror, urging my eyes to meet his. I refused.

Arden swooped in and landed on the windowsill. She gave a loud squawk of greeting before flapping over to Luc's shoulder. I sighed. I missed it when Arden was just my and Ena's secret. Now it felt as though she was more Luc's bird than mine.

"Not too shabby for a mountain girl, now is it?" Gree asked, dusting pink spots onto my cheek.

I glared at her.

Agramon was standing at the window that looked out to the west. "What a dismal place this is," he mumbled. "No wonder the man is so depressed all the time."

"Must you always be so cruel?" I snapped. Though I wanted to retain Agramon's favor, my patience was stretched far too thin.

Luc's gaze narrowed.

Gree tsked under her breath.

Agramon turned to me, his brows raised. "My dear girl, are you really defending the Butcher? What a terrible Morganite you are." He turned back to the window, his arms crossed. "Don't worry, we won't be here long. I've business in Gryse that I must attend to. The Butcher can wallow in his mud pits all he likes while we enjoy the comforts of one of the richest ports in Lyrica."

My heart collapsed into my stomach. The memory of Count Balthazo's fingers on me was still fresh in my mind. But I was too tired to fight anymore. If I had a stronger will, I'd just throw myself out of the window and be done with my sorry excuse for a life.

"Does Gryse need rain so badly?"

Agramon chuckled. "No, they don't even farm, but there is much entertainment to be had. Count Balthazo enjoys his sordid delights, and they can be found all through the city."

Nothing could appeal to me less than the promise of sordid delights with Count Balthazo. It took everything I had to push the tears back and ignore the fog of weariness in my head.

Agramon and I entered the great hall together, trailing Luc behind us. Sam turned at our entrance. His lip twitched, his eyes on Agramon's hand resting on my lower back. I could feel the soldiers watching me as I passed. I found myself thankful for the thick cream that covered my cheeks, for I was sure my face was red as a beet.

Sam strode forward. "Welcome to Bruin," he said, addressing both Agramon and me. "I hope you've found the quarters to your liking?"

"I suppose they'll do," Agramon said, scanning the hall. He drew me closer to him. "By Sol above, Butcher, when was the last time these men saw a woman? Their minds are bordering on hysteria."

I glared at Agramon.

"Things will be changing in Bruin, now that we're home from war." Sam kept his eyes on me.

Agramon smirked. "Ah, but for how long, I wonder?"

Serving boys burst into the room carrying platters of food. It was nothing fanciful, just vegetables and meat, but it smelled good, and I was near starving.

"Let's not quarrel," I said, "for one evening at least."

Sam's eyes flickered to Agramon, who was nothing short of amused. "Of course, Rowyn."

I took Sam's offered arm, starkly aware of Luc wrinkling his nose from behind Agramon. As was Sam's custom, instead of kissing the gem, he kissed my fingers.

Sam led us up the steps to the great table. Along the way, he introduced us to several of his captains. I didn't listen to their words of welcome. I retreated into myself and went through the motions, nodding and greeting the men as others sat around the simple wooden table in the darkened hall. Candles glowed on the walls, showing rushes that had been recently cleaned, probably in preparation for our arrival. Everything about the hall was simple—no decorations, no ornate workings within the wooden pillars.

Sam pulled out the chair to his left, motioning me into it. He gestured Agramon to the seat at his right, but Agramon pulled out the chair on my other side instead.

"I'd much prefer the company of my ward," Agramon quipped. A muscle in Sam's jaw tensed, but he turned back to the hall, his shoulders stiff, as he watched his men eat.

Decorum mattered little in Bruin. Dogs twisted through the men's legs, waiting to be slipped scraps of meat from the table. Mugs of ale were passed around while everyone talked loudly, shouting and bickering. A knife flashed when one quarrel got out of hand, but Sam rose and silenced them quickly, ordering both men out of the hall to the cheers of the others.

I chewed slowly, starkly aware that if I stuffed my-self as I wished, the meal would come back up all too quickly. The men watched me between jokes. I could feel their gaze crawling the length of my body.

"Tomorrow, if you desire, we can ride the fields, as long as the weather permits," Sam said next to me, cocking a half smile at his own joke.

"If it pleases my lord. I'm at your disposal." And weather would permit.

Sam ran his fingers over mine. "No Rowyn, it is I who is at your disposal," he whispered. "Anything you ask will be granted to you. Anything you desire, and I will get it for you."

I ignored Agramon barely stifling laughter next to me.

"Thank you for your kindness, Sam, but I am well enough. I promise."

Sam nodded, but he left his fingers on mine.

I stared at them for a moment. When he didn't re-move them, I tentatively reached for my goblet of wine with my other hand and downed a long drink. The memory of Sam's fingers plunging into me in Maryse played through my mind as a warm swell sank to my core. Sam was acting like the incident in the carriage had never happened. In truth, maybe he was trying to forget it. Imor knew I was trying to. But he kept watching me out of the corner of his eye, a frown tugging at his lips. He knew there was something wrong. Agramon probably knew too; he just didn't care.

THE DREAM FADED INTO VIEW, the figures fuzzy before growing clearer in the firelight from the hearth. Agramon was looking out the window, his hands clasped behind his back. Sam was lounging in a chair, glaring at his back.

"What business do you have in Gryse that can't wait?" Sam asked, his green eyes almost black in the firelight.

"It's no business of yours," Agramon said, turning to meet Sam, stare for stare. "Rowyn and I leave at dawn. We should be back in a few weeks, and you can accompany us back to the capitol for the quinquennial."

Sam's eyes narrowed. "We just got here. The girl has gone through a harrowing experience. She needs time to rest."

Agramon rolled his eyes. "You do realize we speak of the same girl who braved the Nightlands for months. She's made of stronger stuff than you give her credit for, Butcher. She'll be fine."

"The emperor made it clear that he wants Rowyn in

Bruin so she can bring rain to the fields. He was explicit in stating this. Now that she's finally made it here, you're trying to sweep her away while my farms lay fallow? I don't think so."

"The emperor doesn't give a damn about your fields, and you know it," Agramon sneered. "Given her range, she will be able to send your precious rain from Gryse. Besides, why does it matter whether your fields get rain when the men who work them will be dying half a world away in a year's time?"

"I see I'm not being clear," Sam said, rising from his chair. "You will *not* be taking Rowyn to Gryse."

Agramon tilted his head. "Oh? Pray tell, who will stop me from taking *my ward* with me?"

"Over my dead body will you take her to Gryse without me," Sam said, palming his sword. "And I will certainly not allow her to stay in the company of Count Balthazo, whom you already tried to have seduce her against her will."

"I am unable to put off my journey to Gryse, Baron. I appreciate your concern, and I'll be sure to pass your words to dear Rowyn, just so she knows how much you care, but I can't leave her here unprotected."

"Do you think that I, Imperial Commander of the Lyrican forces, am unable to protect her?" Sam asked, his voice icy.

Agramon chuckled, his eyes piercing as he regarded

Sam with nothing short of disdain. "Yes, trusting her protection to you worked out quite well on the road here, didn't it? But that's not what I'm really worried about, is it, Butcher? I'm more concerned about protecting her from your lascivious thoughts."

A muscle in Sam's cheek quivered. "My intentions are entirely honorable. I . . ."

Agramon laughed outright. "Yes, Butcher, I see you insist on telling yourself that. Whether it bears any truth in reality, I suppose we'll find out."

"I would never hurt her. Can you say the same?" Sam asked, his brows raised.

"Of course I can't, but the difference between the two of us, Butcher, is I make no claims otherwise. You're so desperately grasping at dregs of honor that you're hiding who you really are from the girl. You claim I have no morality, yet I've never *lied* about my intentions. Furthermore, my intentions have nothing to do with me between her legs."

Sam tensed, his lips almost white. Neither spoke for a moment as they glared at each other.

"You may leave for Gryse in the morning," Sam said finally. "I'll send a squadron of men to accompany you. But unless you plan on turning every soldier in Bruin against me, Rowyn will *not* be going with you." He slammed the door behind him.

Agramon turned back to the window. A broad smile

stretched across his face, and he chuckled.

"Oh Butcher, you make it far too easy," he murmured, looking out into the darkness with nothing short of amusement.

I ONLY MANAGED A FEW FITFUL hours of sleep beside Nirah. When gray light peeked through the window, I rose and looked to the land beyond. All I saw was gray. Men were already toiling under the weak sun while foremen and soldiers walked among them. Beyond the fields were rows of tents, as far as the eye could see. The army readied themselves to be sent to their deaths. I lowered my eyes.

"Good morning, lady," Gree said as she entered and busied herself with my wardrobe. "What shall we wear today? The lord asked that you dressed, ready for riding."

My heart fell. I had no wish to be on the road with Agramon again. I had no wish to go to Gryse. I leaned my forehead wearily against the stone sill. I'd been hoping against hope that Sam's will would win out over Agramon, but I'd overestimated him.

"The green velvet one is so pretty," Nirah said, her eyes bright. Gree sent her to grab it while she laced me into a corset.

"You could at least let me paint your eyes," Gree said grumpily, fiddling with the cosmetics she'd laid out on the dressing table.

"What's the point?" I muttered. It was just distrustful soldiers staring at me all day. Sitting back, I let Gree run her fingers through my hair, plaiting it in a series of long braids that wove into each other. If there was one thing I appreciated Gree for, it was her ability to weave hair.

I stared at myself in the mirror. Perhaps I should let her paint my face. The dark circles were worse, and my eyes were bloodshot. I couldn't even remember the last time I'd slept an entire night.

"Gree," I said, fiddling with one of the brushes. "Please do something about my eyes."

Gree smacked her lips in satisfaction and yanked a large lock of hair to the side. Of course, she would rub it in.

I rolled my eyes at Nirah, who giggled.

"ROWYN," AGRAMON SAID when I descended into the ward. He snapped something to the soldiers clustered around him, then strode toward me.

"Are we not even having breakfast before we leave?" I asked.

Agramon smirked. "I've already eaten. Besides, I'm sure if you're hungry, you need only mention it to the Butcher, and he'll get you *whatever* you desire."

"Don't be an ass," I snapped. "How long till we leave?"

Agramon crossed his arms, studying me. "*We* aren't going anywhere. The Butcher has insisted you stay in Bruin while I travel to Gryse alone."

I tried to hide my glee. I was unsuccessful. "Why am I dressed for riding?"

"The Butcher has requested you tour his fields. Though, I'm sure if you insist on going with me to Gryse, he would oblige you."

"I don't want to go to Gryse."

Agramon sighed. "Very well. I would tell you to have fun in this dismal place, but as it stands, I don't see how that's possible."

"I'm sure the count will ensure you don't miss my company too terribly."

"To be sure, my dear, to be sure." Agramon accepted the reins of his horse from Luc and mounted. He glanced over at Sam before leaning down. "Be wary of him, Rowyn. He's a dangerous man."

Agramon had said that before, but Sam had never lifted a finger against me. I knew I should care that

Agramon seemed concerned over my welfare, but I was too exhausted to think about what it could mean. I waved my hand dismissively. "So everyone says."

"Watch your back," Luc said, climbing onto his own horse. "He's just like all the rest. No matter what you think."

Agramon cocked an eyebrow but said nothing more. Shaking his head, he turned his horse toward the gate and rode through without a backward glance, Luc and a stream of soldiers following him.

I let out a breath of relief as I watched them depart. It felt as though a burden had lifted from my shoulders.

They disappeared over the horizon after a while. I was free from Agramon's hold, from trying to give in to his will while maintaining my own. I would be free from Agramon for a blessed two weeks. Though happiness was doing its best to lift my spirits, weariness wouldn't release its hold.

Chapter 25

"YOU DIDN'T SLEEP," Sam accused, his hand on my arm.

I glowered. What was the point of cosmetics if they didn't work? "I've had a lot on my mind, Sam."

His lips turned down, but he didn't press further. "What I told Agramon was a lie."

My eyes widened. "What?"

"I don't want you to tour the fields. I think I have a home for Nirah. Go pack her bag, and we can take her there."

"How do you know it's safe?" I asked, my heart falling. I would miss Nirah when she was gone, though I knew the safest place for her was far from me. It was I who kept putting her life in danger. It was like a curse, having those I loved constantly at risk because they were close to me.

"I have a friend. I would trust him with my life," Sam said, shoving his hands in his pockets. "He and his family live in town. He can protect her and give her a steady family."

"You are sure they will take her?" I asked. "You are sure it's safe?"

Sam nodded. "I will not fail you in this. I promise."

I rushed back up to my room. Gree was still fiddling about while Nirah tried on the different pieces of jewelry that made up my wardrobe. "Nirah," I said. "The baron has found you a home. We must leave at once."

Nirah shed a few tears as Gree and I packed her things. After hugging Gree, she took my hand and followed me out of the castle and into the ward where Sam lifted her onto Starstruck's back in front of me.

Arden swooped down, landing on the gauntlet on my arm. I transferred her to the leather shoulder guard. We followed Sam out of the castle and onto the road. I was surprised when no soldiers followed us. When I voiced my confusion, Sam shrugged.

"I am lord here. What do I have to worry about? Besides, I don't want Agramon to find out where I've put her."

I smiled, grateful that he would've thought of that.

The town of Bruin was large, even though we seemed to be tucked away in a barren wilderness. The mountains in the east framed the stone houses and shops. Ladies lounged in the windows of several buildings, displaying even more skin than I was forced to. I turned away, figuring they were brothels for the soldiers at the castle. I began to question Sam's choice. I wanted Nirah far from that kind of work. She'd born enough trauma as it was.

But Sam rode past the brothels and turned onto a

road where the houses were larger, made of black clay. We stopped outside the largest one.

I lowered Nirah into Sam's arms before dismounting. We handed our horses to a stableboy and went to greet the man standing at the door. He looked to be about Sam's age, in his midthirties. His hair was longer, which meant he wasn't a military man, and he sported a beard, which was a wonder of itself on the eastern shore where men were encouraged to shave.

"Hugh," Sam said, grabbing the man and thumping him on the back.

"Sam," Hugh said. I'd never heard anyone else call Baron Samael that.

"Hugh, let me introduce you to Rowyn the Morganite." Sam motioned me forward while Nirah leaned against my legs. I'd forgotten it had been a while since she'd been forced to meet anyone new, and now it was a family who might take her in. She would have no idea what to expect. No wonder she was scared.

"Charmed," Hugh said, smiling wide. He took my hand and lightly kissed my fingers. "I've heard stories of you, of course."

My smile faltered.

Hugh kneeled, his eyes on Nirah. "So, this is the girl." His eyes softened when she looked at him. She was older than she looked. I worried her stature was permanently altered due to lack of care and nutrition.

"What is your name, sweetheart?"

Nirah shrank into me at the sound of her past name. I shook my head at Hugh. He seemed to realize his mistake because he gaped and seemed at a loss for words.

"Her name is Nirah now," I said, squeezing her hand. "That is the only name we've been calling her."

"A lovely name," Hugh said, holding his hand out to her. Nirah shrank even deeper into my skirts. Hugh rose with a frown, then ran his hand over his neck.

"I thought Winnie and she would get along," Sam said. "She and the babies."

"Babies?" Nirah asked timidly.

Sam nodded. "I've yet to meet the new additions to the mayor's family. Would you care to join me?" He held his arm out to Nirah, just as a gentleman would. Nirah smiled, taking his arm and letting him lead her into the house.

We entered a bright sitting room where a woman about ten years my senior was seated on a couch, a baby in her arms. Another lay on the floor, pushing its head up to look at us. A young boy and girl were playing with wooden toys by the window. A rich ray of sunshine lit the space around them.

"My dear," Hugh said, motioning to us. "Look who has finally returned!"

"Sam," the woman said, rising and slinging the baby onto her hip. She stood on her toes and kissed both of

Sam's cheeks. "You've come home at last."

"Winnie." Sam smiled, chucking the baby under its chin. "You've been busy in my absence."

Winnie laughed as she deposited the baby into her husband's arms and lifted the other one off the floor. "Little Hugh, Lori, come greet our liege lord."

The boy and girl by the window ran over. They leaned into their mother's skirts where they stared at Nirah, who was leaning into mine.

"You must be the sorceress," Winnie said, curtsying to me. Her eyes went to Nirah. "And this is the girl that Sam wrote of."

"Name's Nirah, mum," Nirah said, gazing up at Winnie through her lashes. I hoped she noticed what I saw. Winnie's smile stretched across her wide, sweet face, her light hair wrapped around her head in rows of braids. She had an apron speckled with flour tied to her waist. She reminded me of Ena, had she been able to live out the rest of her life. Had I not failed her.

"Would you like to play with the children, Nirah?" Winnie asked, holding her hand out to the girl.

Nirah looked up at me and I nodded. Nirah took her hand, and Winnie led her to the couch where they both sat.

"I like babies, mum," Nirah said with a smile. She brushed her finger across the child's cheek. "At Lady Bella's, I got to take care of the babies sometimes."

Winnie smiled. "Would you like to hold Alice?" When Nirah nodded, Winnie placed the baby in her arms. Nirah smiled when Alice gripped a lock of Nirah's dark hair and refused to let go.

Winnie turned to me. "I could use all the help I can get with the children," she murmured. "Hugh has his duties to the town, which takes him away from home most days. We were about to look for a nursery maid when we received Sam's letter yesterday."

I tried to smile. "As long as she receives kindness and is kept from the brothels, I think she'll have a fighting chance in this world."

Sam and the mayor conferred by the window. Winnie offered me a cup of lady's tea. I sipped it while Nirah played with the older children, laughing and giggling. Winnie even let me hold one of her babies. The twins were round little things, sitting up and babbling happily, infatuated with the streaks of color within the stones on my hands.

"You don't seem like you've had much practice with little ones," the mayor's wife said as she pulled down the front of her gown and began to nurse Alice.

"Growing up, the women in my clan didn't trust me around the children," I admitted, wiggling my fingers while baby Hans tried to catch them with his fat fists. "There were none at Solridge, and Agramon, my mentor, shuns their company."

Hans leaned into me, and I dipped my head. He smelled delightful. The baby giggled. A line of drool soaked his chin and pooled onto his shirt.

I laughed, enamored with the little boy.

"Is your journey through the empire going well?" Winnie asked.

I didn't know how to answer. I'd brought the rain to the land—that much was true—but I'd been attacked, kidnapped, and forced to romance lecherous lords.

"I foresee a good harvest," I said instead, watching one of the older children hide in the corner. In truth, I couldn't bring myself to meet Winnie's eye.

"His lordship seems to be in a good mood," Winnie prodded.

I glanced up at Sam. He was watching me, the corner of his lip twitching as if he wasn't sure whether he wanted to smile at me. I quickly looked away and swayed, gently rocking the baby on my lap. "Do you know him well enough to judge his moods?"

"Hugh and Sam grew up together," Winnie said. "When their village was raided by Ylirians, they escaped together to Bruin and joined the army here."

"I hadn't realized Sam's family was killed in a raid."

Winnie glanced at the men and pitched her voice low. "They never speak of it. But Hugh and Sam served many years together. Of course, this was before Sam was promoted to high commander and given that horrid name, *Butcher*. After the emperor rewarded Sam with the barony, he convinced Hugh to stay and help here. So, Sam appointed him mayor, and here we are."

Something prickled at the back of my mind. "Do you really think all those stories about Sam are true? The reasons that they call him Butcher?"

Winnie straightened, slipping her breast back into her dress. "I don't know whether those stories are true or not." I noticed a tinge of anger in her voice. "But I do know that war will make villains out of the best of us. Sam has always been good at what he does. I don't know how he stomachs it, but he is an excellent commander. He *won* the war in the desert when others were convinced we would fail."

"But it ended in a treaty." I looked back down at the baby and ran my fingers over his soft hair. "It's not like we gained the Desertlands. All we got was a piece of paper saying that they would try to still the swords of the men on the border."

My mind went to the warlord, Alf Amun-doon. What could he have wanted with me? Did his interference on my journey signal a breach in the treaty?

"It's better than nothing," Winnie was saying. Her eyes turned to Nirah, who was leading the other children in some sort of rhyming game. "I can tell you are protective of your girl here. I will be grateful for her help with the children, and we will try to raise her as though she were our own."

I nodded. "I'm grateful to you. I . . ." I glanced at Sam, unsure if he would want me to reveal the danger. But Winnie had her own children to think of. "Duke Agramon has said that he will not come after her, but there is always a chance he could change his mind."

Winnie sat back, studying me while her daughter nursed on her other breast, her little fist gripping the strings on her mother's bodice. "You think he will even remember her when she is gone?"

I shrugged. "He could use her to hurt me. He's done it in the past."

Winnie patted my hand. "We will do our best, Rowyn. I doubt he'll think to send someone so far. Especially since I've heard there are far more powerful people who care about you that he could manipulate. He'll forget her in time."

"I hope you're right," I said, placing the baby onto the floor and rising as Sam and Hugh drifted to the door.

Nirah came up and wrapped her arms around my legs. "Are you leaving?"

I kneeled and placed my hands on her shoulders so I could meet her eye. "I must, but you will be safe here. Safe and happy, I'm sure of it. Just mind Winnie and help with the children. I will come visit you as much as I can while we're in Bruin."

Nirah nodded and smiled. She ran back to the other children and collapsed on the ground, eager to continue their game.

"I will send gold," Sam was saying to Hugh as I joined him at the door. "It should cover any additional costs you incur while she's in your care."

Hugh was shaking his head. "You don't have to do that. She's a gift from Sol. We'll be able to manage."

"I insist," Sam said, gripping Hugh's hand.

Hugh sighed. "Very well." He turned to me. "It was an honor to meet such a famed sorceress. Please feel free to visit any time and check up on the girl."

I nodded and tried to smile. It wasn't until we were riding again that the tears came.

"It will be the best thing for her," Sam said as we followed the road back to the castle. "She had no place with us, and it only made you weaker."

"I know," I said, wiping the tear from my eye. "But I will miss her all the same."

"Then you will have to come to Bruin often," Sam replied, smiling at me. "I would always welcome you."

"Thank you, Sam." I held my hand out toward him. He took it, rubbing my fingers with his before breaking his hold. We passed fields as men toiled, their backs bare. They led cattle to plow and used spades and hoes to dig into the earth. They straightened as we passed, though they didn't salute. Their eyes merely watched. A foreman cracked a whip, and the men bent back to their work.

"I must attend the soldiers for the rest of the day," Sam said, his tone apologetic. "The army is camped yonder, over the hill, and I need to speak with my officers and inspect the training protocols."

"Do whatever you need to do," I said. "I will be fine."

"You could accompany me," Sam offered, his tone light.

Were it another task, I might, but the soldiers already didn't like me, as they'd made known throughout our journey across the empire. I worried that I was putting Sam's position in question if he paraded me about all the time.

"No, I would like to rest in my room," I assured him. He nodded but watched me out of the corner of his eye the rest of the way to Bruin.

Chapter 26

"YOU SHOULD WEAR THIS TO DINNER," Gree said, holding up a black gown. It was far more conservative than what Agramon usually chose to put me in. I crossed my arms, wondering at her motives. But, since she was my handmaid and her true lord was nowhere to be found, I decided to take advantage of the fact that I could make more choices for myself.

"No, I don't think that will do." I stepped to the wardrobe where Gree and Nirah had hung my gowns. I flipped through them, pulled out a blue satin one, and held it to Gree. It was not as conservative as the one she'd chosen, but it was not as revealing as many in the closet. "I want this one."

Gree pursed her lips but nodded. I sat patiently as she colored my face. I turned my head this way and that, asking for alterations until, finally satisfied, I rose.

A knock sounded on the door, and I opened it to find Sam leaning against the doorframe. He looked down on me and smiled. "Lovely," he whispered, holding out his arm.

I took it with a smile.

"I am grateful to you," I said as we walked, tightening my grip on his arm. "I don't know how I will ever repay your kindness."

"Do not speak of it," Sam said, his cheeks reddening.

"No." I stopped and turned him towards me. "You were my first friend at the capitol. You protected Nirah. You've protected me and I just want to say, thank you."

Sam reached up and brushed his fingers over my cheek. "You know why I do it."

"The seer," I murmured. "The fortune-teller you met in Yliria. She said that protecting me would save you."

A muscle feathered in his jaw. "No," he said, his thumb running over my lip. My brows furrowed. I thought he would say more, but Sam took my hand in his and led me towards the dining hall.

Soldiers had filled the hall when we entered. Sam's table had been lowered, and we sat among more men than I was used to.

Ale was the preferred drink. Flagons were again passed around as talk filled the room, mostly of the soldiers posturing over heroics—whether real or imagined, it was impossible to tell.

"How do you like Bruin so far?" Sam asked after settling next to me.

"It's lovely," I lied, taking a sip of wine. I hated it. There were too many soldiers. On the road they were simply an irritant that gave me pause when they whispered. In Bruin they were everywhere, and Agramon was gone, along with Luc. My only protection was Sam. I'd thought I could protect myself before, but the kidnapping had severely shaken my nerves. They'd managed to take away my sword and my magic, leaving me utterly defenseless, and they were just common raiders with no sorcerer among them. It had been far too easy. Perhaps I should've joined Agramon in Gryse. "If your men are finished planting, I can start bringing the rain for you."

Sam caressed my fingers. "You don't need to overexert yourself. Not when you're feeling poorly."

"It's no bother," I said, my eyes on our hands. I took another nervous sip. My gems grew warm. Sam's fingers brushed over them, and he looked down in surprise at the heat. Rain fell outside. The soldiers didn't even notice. They continued their carousing with more vulgar language than I was accustomed to.

"She was a right sweet peach too," an older man said from the table beside ours. "Ready to be plucked, she was."

I wrinkled my nose, disgusted. Sam was absorbed in the conversation of an officer beside him. I glared at the table.

"What of that girl in Ardent?" another officer shouted. "She was bound to let you roast four quarters on the spit. Thought she was in love, that one did!"

The men around them broke into laughter.

"Morganite whore," someone sneered to my right.

I met the eyes of one of the soldiers. His hair and beard were a colorless blond, his eyes filled with hate as he glared at me. My spine stiffened as I returned the stare.

Always before, the soldiers had kept their remarks hidden behind their hands or whispered amongst themselves. I'd only gained knowledge of their distaste for me through Echo's dreams. Never had they resorted to outright insults in my presence. A cold shiver ran through me. I was safer with the raiders who'd taken me than I would ever be with Sam's soldiers. There was no way I would be able to escape with the army. They would never let me survive.

Outside, lightning flashed over the window, a peal of thunder blasting through the hall, silencing the others as they turned to me. I was momentarily pleased that my anger was felt.

Sam released my hand and rose from his seat. He walked with purpose to the man who'd insulted me. The soldier rose, his eyes sparkling defiantly. He opened his mouth to speak, but before he could utter a word, Sam drew his fist back and slammed it into his face. The soldier crashed into the table, upsetting drinks and plates with his fall.

Silence descended.

"Let no man offend the lady," Sam announced loudly. Some of the soldiers had risen, their hands on their swords. Others watched the scene not with horror or anger, but with an unnerving passivity.

"My lord honors my name," I said when the silence stretched on far too long. It was a blessing my voice didn't sound as shaky as I felt.

I stood, aware of the eyes following my every move. "The hall grows stifling, my lord. I would take my leave."

Sam nodded, his eyes filled with an apology he couldn't voice. I tried to hide the heat from my cheeks as I descended the steps and made my way to the door, feeling the stares follow me as I passed. It wasn't until I reached the empty corridor that I allowed myself to breathe again.

FEAR ATE AWAY AT MY MIND as I listened to the thundering rain outside that night. I was exhausted. Nirah was safe, and yet, I still couldn't bear to shut my eyes. What of the Sons of Sol? What of Yliria? What of the soldiers' enmity?

Footsteps echoed in the corridor. They stopped outside my door, and whispered voices drifted in. Nerves prickled at my senses.

I held my breath.

After a moment, the footsteps continued down the hall.

I let my breath out.

I couldn't do it anymore. I couldn't lie awake in bed, waiting for someone to kill me. If I didn't sleep soon, I was more liable to kill myself.

I rose and buckled my weapons over my white chemise. Shivering, I stepped to the door and listened.

The hall was silent.

I cracked open the door and peered out.

Empty.

I quietly shut the door behind me. "Echo," I whispered to the darkness.

"*I'm here*," Echo murmured back.

I gritted my teeth. Maybe I could ask Sam for a room without windows. I pushed back the embarrassment. If there was anyone who would understand my fear, it would be Sam. He always seemed to understand me.

"Can you take me to Sam's room?" I asked.

The long pause filled with Echo's disapproval.

"*Follow*," Echo replied finally. A soft tapping filled the corridor ahead. I followed the sound, tiptoeing through the darkness, a knife clutched in my hand. I couldn't believe I was about to do this. I hated myself more than I could stand.

The tapping stopped in a nearby passage. There was a light under one of the doors. I let out a low sigh of relief, then second-guessed myself.

I should go back to my room and try to sleep. I didn't need to inconvenience everyone around me just because I was suffering from a bit of insomnia. I should stop being so selfish.

But the fear was crushing. I looked over my shoulder. By all the gods, how had I become so *weak*? Rowyn the Morganite, the most powerful sorcerer in the empire, conqueror of the *Nightlands*, afraid of the dark.

Before I could stop myself, I knocked. The door was flung open. "Rowyn," Sam said, silhouetted in the doorway. He was shirtless, his skin glistening in the firelight as he held a towel to his damp hair. By all the gods, he'd just finished bathing.

I couldn't help the heat rushing to my cheeks. "I'm so sorry," I stammered. "I shouldn't be here."

I turned, the hand holding the knife trembling uncontrollably, but Sam grabbed my wrist.

"Something's wrong," he said, pulling me into his room. It wasn't a question.

I let myself be pulled, and Sam slammed the door behind me.

"What is it?" He threw the towel to the side.

"It's stupid," I mumbled finally, biting my lip in embarrassment. What must he think of me?

"Tell me." His green eyes darted to the door, then the windows, as if an intruder would come barreling in at any moment. His constant wariness was the most comforting thing about him, and I craved comfort.

"I was . . ." I hung my head, unable to look him in the eye. "I was frightened." He must think me an idiot.

"You? Frightened?" Sam asked. He stepped forward, drawing the bolt on the door. "Agramon isn't here to hurt you."

I ran my foot along the stone floor, refusing to meet his eye. "I've not been able to sleep, for fear . . ." I couldn't bring myself to go on. Everything. Now I was afraid of everything. It felt as though the world was out to get me, and I was powerless to stop it.

Sam frowned. "Did something else happen that makes you think you are in danger?"

I shook my head. "I just can't shake the feeling that the gods are seeking to destroy me. Now Yliria wants me . . . the way the noblemen whisper about me . . . the stares from the villagers . . ."

"I can post men outside your door. Whatever you need, just tell me," Sam said, the crease in his brow deepening.

"Even your soldiers glare at me as though they'd love to slit my throat," I whispered. If he posted guards outside my door, I'd be even more frantic. Still, I hated how *whiny* I sounded. I sighed. "I shouldn't have come. I realize that now. I'll let you get some sleep."

"You're afraid to be alone." He grunted. "Sleep here if you must. Take my bed. *I* will guard you."

"I can't take up your bed," I whispered. "If there is another room, one without windows . . ."

"It would be an honor if you stayed here." Sam gripped my shoulders and turned me away from the door. "I can sleep on the floor."

I opened my mouth to argue, but Sam put his finger on my lips. "I've spent ages sleeping on the ground in the middle of a battlefield. And there are many nights I prefer the floor. You're not inconveniencing me in the least."

"Do you promise?" I asked, hating how meek my voice sounded.

Sam's eyes sparkled, his finger drifting down to my chin, pinching it lightly. "I promise."

Relief made my knees wobble. I couldn't help it.

"Come," was all Sam said. His quarters were made up of a receiving room that held a large wooden desk and chair, along with several skins flung across the floor. Through an arched opening in the wall were his bed, a large tub, and several wooden bureaus. It reminded me of home. There was no splendor, no velvet nor silks, only simple linen sheets piled high with skins and furs of all colors. Though I'd doubted Sam's words, I saw a makeshift mat of furs beside the bed, under the window, with a small pillow tossed in the corner. It meant he wasn't lying about sometimes preferring the floor. That made me feel a bit better.

Sam pulled back the covers. "Do you need anything?"

I unbelted Iranoct and set it on the furs, well within reach. The knife I slid under the pillow, but there was already one there. I lifted it out and glanced at Sam. He cleared his throat, running his hand over the back of his neck, but didn't say anything. We were so alike, he and I. More so than Destrian, if I'd a mind to give it more thought, which I didn't.

"I still don't like turning you out of your bed," I said as he doused the candles with his fingertips.

"I insist on being turned out of the bed." The warm fire in the hearth lit up his smile. "I've been worried about you for days."

Sam kneeled onto his makeshift pallet while I nestled down in the linen sheets. The bed smelled of leather and sweat and man. It smelled like Sam.

"Thank you," I whispered to the darkness, then buried myself in the pillow, immediately at ease knowing he was there.

I'd felt alone for too long. Out of everyone at the capitol, I knew I was the safest with Sam. I thought

back to what Araceli had said in Calla, that men let their
guard down when they thought they could trust you.
That went for everyone. I felt safest with Sam because I
could trust him. I knew what his reactions would be. I
knew that he would put my protection above everything else. Although I'd long railed against the notion
that I needed to be under someone's protection, I realized that I would never be able to make it alone.

It was disturbing how easy sleep came.

WE WERE BACK AT THE MAYOR'S HOUSE. Echo was listening to Sam and Hugh's conversation as they watched
Winnie and me.

"You have feelings for her," Hugh was saying, his
voice hushed. "Is that not a bad idea?"

"You suggest I do not deserve her?" Sam asked,
watching me bounce the baby on my lap. I met his eyes
and immediately looked away.

"No, I wonder what will happen with the lord of
Helena. There are also whispers of her and Agramon. I
know you," Hugh said, his finger on Sam's chest. "You
would not go into anything like this if you were not in
love with the girl. But it is known that she is in love

with someone else. She is sure to choose the young lord in the end."

Sam took a drink. "There is no war won without a fight. I risk everything if I do nothing."

"And if it ruins you?"

"I can't stand by," Sam said softly. "I won't let her slip through my fingers."

Hugh shook his head. "You risk too much." He took a drink. "But you will not be dissuaded. I hope, in the end, she sees you for who you really are."

"That's what I'm afraid of," Sam said.

I GROANED WHEN I WOKE, stretching my arm over my head as I turned over. The fire in the hearth was newly stocked, and Sam sat at his table, a quill in his hand, fully dressed in a black tunic and a leather jerkin.

When he saw me, he set the quill down and sat back in the chair, stretching his fingers in front of him. "How did you sleep?" he asked, his face serious.

"Like the dead." I pulled the furs to my chest as I sat up. The leather tie holding my braid had untied in the night, and my hair hung loosely at my shoulders.

Sam went to the door and peered out. He said something to a person in the hall before shutting the door once more. "You already look much better," he said, turning to me. "I wish you'd come to me sooner."

I bit my cheek. "How could I come to you when it's so . . . embarrassing."

Sam's brow furrowed. "What can I do to show you that you can trust me?"

I ran my hand over one of the furs. It was deliciously soft. "I do trust you."

"But you do not trust my men?"

I glanced up at him through my hair. A hand rested on the sword at his waist. Sam was always ready for battle.

"No," I said finally. "I don't. There were already whispers that our friendship was bad for you at the capitol. They have loyalty to you, not me. They could view it as doing you a favor."

Now Sam was actively gripping the pommel. "Who? Who said this?"

I shook my head. "No one said it," I admitted. "It's just . . . a feeling. Besides, I don't believe anyone should die just because of a thought or a whisper."

Sam's jaw tensed. "I wish you would tell me."

"I most certainly won't."

"Fine," Sam said, turning back to the fire. "What would you like to do today?"

I glanced out the window and noticed Sol's position in the sky. "By all the gods! How long have I been sleeping?"

"It's midday."

"Gree will have my ear when she finds out I slept here." I groaned, my head in my hands.

"She's already been in to check on you," Sam said, returning to his desk. "I assured her that you were well and safe, and that you had come to me."

"I have to go back to my room." I flung back the covers and jumped up. "Before anyone else sees."

Sam straightened. "No, if they see you in the halls in *that*, they will definitely be whispering about you." He pointed to my thin chemise.

A knock sounded on the door.

"Wait!" I shouted as Sam opened it.

In bustled Gree, a gown draped over her arm and a scowl across her face.

Sam glanced over his shoulder. "I'll be out in the hall. Knock when you're ready to come out, and I'll make sure the coast is clear." He shut the door behind him, leaving me to Gree's lectures.

Gree left me in a huff after she'd thoroughly talked my ear off about decorum and reputation and His Grace's wishes. Sam wasn't in the hall, so I stayed where I was, absentmindedly exploring his room. I went to his desk. Looking over the papers, I realized they were summons for other lords to send men. I read that each lord was required to supply a certain number of soldiers based on the amount of land they held. By all the gods, some of the sums were enormous. No wonder they resorted to use of doghunters to steal men away.

"Tsk, tsk, tsk," Sam said behind me. The man moved with disturbing stealth. "Did you find what you were looking for?"

"By all the gods," I gasped, dropping the papers and clutching at my racing heart. "Don't *do* that."

Sam straightened and shut the door behind him before walking slowly toward me and lifting the papers I'd dropped. He glanced over them, then his eyes went back to my face.

"And just who are you spying for, Rowyn?"

He was standing far too close.

"I'm not spying for anyone," I stammered.

Sam chuckled darkly. "I'm surprised Agramon trusted you with a task this important. Usually, he resorts to finding out information himself."

I tried to ignore the ice crawling through my veins. "I'm not a spy for Agramon. You of all people should know that."

Sam stepped closer.

I backed into the desk.

Sam gripped my arms. "Was last night all a ploy? Sneaking into my room to get information?"

"Sam, I . . . I shouldn't have looked. I'm sorry." I

pushed against his chest. "I didn't come here last night to sneak into your room."

"Why should I believe you?"

"You know I'm not lying," I said.

"You're betraying me to the empress."

"Why do you care what I tell her?" I asked. "Your allegiance to the emperor is unquestioned. Everything you do is out in the open for all to see. She's not even concerned about you!"

Samael released my arms. "Call it professional curiosity." He ran a hand over the back of his neck. A muscle in his jaw tensed as he glared at me. "Whatever am I going to do with you?"

Chapter 27

S AM ENDED UP WALKING ME TO my room and leaving me to my own devices. I could tell I'd hurt him, though I hadn't meant to. How could he think I was a spy for Agramon, of all people? I thought he knew me better than that.

I paced my room, wishing I could see how Nirah was doing.

Finally, I could stand the walls no longer. I opened the door and stepped out. There were no guards. Agramon wasn't there to tell me what to do. I'd been so used to the others filling my days that I found myself at quite a loss now that the time was my own. I decided to go on a ride to visit Nirah. Weapons belted to me, Arden on my shoulder, I headed out of my room and down the stairs, leaving the castle and heading to the stables.

A boy was napping in a pile of hay. Instead of waking him, I went to Starstruck's stall and saddled her myself before leading her out and mounting. Arden called above me, and I smiled, shading my eyes with my hand as she soared on the air currents above.

I nudged Starstruck into a canter along the road to town.

"Rowyn," Winnie said with a smile when she opened the door to me. "Please come in. Are you alone?"

Her brows knit together as she looked behind me for a guard. Belatedly, I realized I probably should've brought one. Or at least asked if I could go. Then again, Sam had said I could do as I liked.

"I came to visit Nirah," I said, peeking into the room. It was filled with women. My eyes widened. Their faces turned to me, and their conversation halted.

"We were just having our tea and doing mending for the soldiers," Winnie said, pulling out a chair. "Ladies," she announced, "have you met Rowyn the Morganite?"

I nodded through the introductions, then sat between two older women. Nirah and a host of other children were sitting in front of the fireplace, playing an imaginary game of fairies and giants.

"Does the mighty sorceress know how to hold a needle?" the woman beside me asked, lifting a tunic from a hamper.

"I can mend," I said. "Though embroidery has always been beyond me."

"Well, lucky for us that the soldiers don't need anything fancy." The woman tossed the shirt in my lap. I accepted a needle and thread from another, and they all watched while I threaded it and began to sew along a ripped seam.

Winnie placed a cup of tea beside me, and I recognized the scent of lady's tea. I took a sip, though I'd already had a cup when Gree had come in. Whether on orders from Agramon or not, Gree made sure to serve me the tea every morning.

"They say General Ivar has made it known he disapproves of the whole thing," a young woman was saying as she stitched the knee of torn breeches. "I don't see why the emperor gives cause to care what the nobility of Lu Shen think of us."

"It's not up to us to decide," the old woman beside me barked. "Who knows why men do the things they do."

"What do you make of this business?" the young woman asked me. "You putting on airs that this whole thing was your conjuring?"

"Audra," Winnie said in a disapproving tone. "Be kind to my guest."

"No." Audra's knuckles whitened around her needle. "It is known that this whole thing is her fault. You like it when our menfolk die to uphold your name?"

I wanted to leave. I was so tired of posturing and conjuring conversation with those who hated me. Yet, it felt like my mother was in my mind. I should have courage and stay. That was what the empress would've done. What Vianne would have done.

I lowered the tunic. "I did not start this," I insisted. "One of the representatives used his power against me, but I did not insist upon a war. This entire journey I've been actively trying to stop the cursed thing."

Audra rolled her eyes, but the other women seemed intrigued by my answer.

"The empress has been outspoken against it," Winnie said, her eyes on her work.

The older woman scoffed. "Don't call that foreigner an empress. If she had more mind about her, she could stop the entire thing herself."

"Well, which is it?" I asked, taking a sip of tea. "Are we women supposed to let the menfolk handle it, or are we supposed to take matters into our own hands?"

Winnie snorted.

The old woman glared at me. "We are to know when to engage in battles that we can win."

"I saw the commander ride through town the other day," a younger woman said, breaking the mood. "Is he as handsome up close as he is from afar?"

"I heard he came to visit Sir Hugh."

Winnie smiled down at her work. "He remains as good-looking as ever."

"Now there's one I wouldn't mind catching myself alone with in the hayloft," the old woman said, stabbing a needle into a tunic.

The other women giggled.

Talk continued. Most of it was about the impending war, the scramble to sow crops, and the new children born to the town. Too soon I looked up and saw that Sol was nearly on the horizon.

"I must go," I said, rising and placing the pair of socks I'd been working on in the neat little pile of other garments I'd mended.

Winnie rose with me. "Nirah, come say farewell to your guest."

Nirah bounced up and followed us to the door. Winnie took my hand. "Thank you for staying as long as you did. You honor me with your company."

I returned the smile. "Thank you for letting me join you. Please send me notice when you all meet again for mending. I appreciated the opportunity to help."

"But you do so much," Winnie said, pulling her hand from mine. "We are indebted to you, really." She looked down at Nirah. "Make sure to wash up when you come in. Dinner will be soon."

Nirah nodded, and Winnie left us on her steps. "How was your first day?"

"It was lovely," Nirah said. "Winnie let me hold the babies. They are such funny little things, with their chubby cheeks. I made Alice giggle. Winnie said it was the first time she'd heard them laugh."

I smiled. "I will check on you again soon, all right?"

Nirah nodded and kissed me on the cheek.

I rode back, unable to keep the smile from my face as I replayed the afternoon. I'd missed other women's company. Gree hardly counted, as she was always trying to escape my presence, and I hers.

I heard Arden's cry above me and held out my arm. She landed and hopped onto my shoulder. I let Starstruck amble along so I could enjoy the cool spring breeze. The rains from the night before made the land smell of dirt and life.

Up ahead, a host of soldiers rode toward me. I figured they were probably heading to town to visit the brothels until one pointed in my direction, and their pace quickened. I unsheathed Iranoct. The sky behind me darkened.

"Your ladyship," the one in front said as they reined in around me. "We've been looking everywhere for you."

Oops. "I've been at the mayor's home," I said, lowering my blade.

"Hurry along then. The commander will want to know you've been found." I looked up, realizing my mistake. I shouldn't have called my magic. Sam would think something was wrong.

I cleared the sky, sheathed Iranoct, and galloped behind the soldiers as we raced back to the black castle. I followed the captain through the halls until we came to a wooden door. He opened it, revealing Sam seated in a chair, leaning onto his knees with his hands on his head.

"Commander," the soldier said. "The sorceress."

Sam looked up and his eyes locked onto me. He rose.

"Where were you?" His nostrils flared. The captain nodded to me, then turned on his heel and sped from the room, shutting the door behind him.

"I was in town," I said. "I was checking on Nirah."

"And you didn't think to tell anyone that fact?"

"I didn't know who to tell." I stepped closer. "I'm not going to run away, Sam."

Sam threw his cup against the wall. "I wasn't worried that you'd run away. I was frantic that you'd been taken!"

Right. I really should've thought better about how it appeared. The truth was that I wasn't worried about my safety when I was awake, especially with Agramon gone. But I was vulnerable when I slept. I didn't know how to create a ward.

"I'm sorry," I whispered.

"How was she?" Sam asked, palming the hilt of his sword.

"Who?"

"Nirah," he said, exasperated.

"She was quite well. You were right, it's the perfect place for her."

"I'm glad." By his tone I could tell he truly meant it. "Gree is in your room waiting to bite your head off and ready you for dinner."

I sighed, then turned and disappeared out of the door.

GREE WAS BESIDE HERSELF. I half expected the old woman to have a heart attack during my care, since she was given to such strong emotions in my presence. I'd chosen a black dress for dinner. Deep blue roses were embroidered along the skirt using silk thread that shimmered in the light. After Gree curled my hair, I asked that she leave it down.

"At least let me do a small plait," Gree said, grabbing the hair at my temple. She braided it around the top of my head and left the rest. I supposed I could compromise.

Sam was already at my door when I was ready. He offered me his arm and led me in the opposite direction from the great hall.

"I thought we were going to dinner," I said, recognizing the corridor we were in.

"We are." Sam held open the door to his study. I looked up at Sam, then looked within. A table had been cleared off and set with small platters of food. Lit candles were placed throughout the room, and a vase of flowers adorned the windowsill.

"What is this?" I asked, standing stupidly at the door.

"I know you don't like to be put on display." Sam placed his hand gently on my back and guided me to a chair. He pulled it out for me and pushed it in as I sat. After he took the chair across from me, he poured us each a goblet of wine.

All sorts of thoughts ran through my mind. The setting was so intimate. We were alone, no guards in sight, no Agramon shooting snide comments our way, nor Luc scowling in the corner.

Sam took a sip. Candlelight flickered over his features as he regarded me thoughtfully.

"You were at Hugh's for quite some time," he said, turning the glass slowly. "What did you do there?"

I picked at my plate. "The ladies in town were mending clothes. I stayed to help."

"You?" A smile stretched across his face.

"Yes," I said, taking a bite. "Why should that surprise you?"

Sam shook his head, looking out of the window at the indigo sky. "It shouldn't."

He ignored his plate and seemed content to watch me eat. Several times he drew in a sharp breath. His mouth opened as if to speak, then he seemed to change his mind, looking back out of the window instead.

Finally, I decided to be blunt. "What is it?"

Sam took another sip of wine. "Why are you so scared of Agramon?"

Anger needled through my veins. My eyes narrowed. "What are you doing, Sam?" I asked, looking to the fire in the hearth, to the flowers.

"I'm afraid that the moment I have you to myself, all I've wanted to do was ask you questions." Sam's voice was low as he took another sip. "Everyone can see how you cower in Duke Agramon's presence. It is noted at dinners. Much is said about how well he has you in hand."

I gritted my teeth. Echo had never showed me that. Was Sam lying, or was Echo just not showing something that would only hurt me? "I do not *cower* in his presence," I spat.

"Oh yes you do." The hand holding Sam's glass pointed at me. "I've seen you stand up for yourself with others, and yet with Agramon, it's as though he's the embodiment of your greatest fear."

"He has killed those I've cared about before," I said. "He engages in a type of manipulation that I don't have the stomach for."

"Yes," Sam acknowledged. "I see myself in him sometimes . . . on my worst days."

"You are nothing like him." I leaned back in my chair.

Sam met my eye. "I had to end a war. You can bet I did things that would ensure it went in our favor. We *had* to be feared."

"Warfare is different," I said, thinking of Alim. "We all expect cruelty during such times."

"And what is this to Agramon but warfare?" Sam shook his head. "He is fighting, just in a different way. You should have figured that out already, given how you bow to his every whim."

"How do I listen to him?" I asked. "Since you're such an expert."

"Look at me," Sam said. "You've been shrinking away from the only man who has proven he is out here to protect you. Whyever would you do such a thing, if he's not behind it?"

"There are others who seek to protect me," I said, thinking of the empress and Lady Vianne. Sam was being too honest for my comfort. He was holding the mirror up, forcing me to see all my faults.

"And where is this . . . Lord Destrian?" Sam asked softly.

I bit my lip. I wished Sam hadn't said his name.

"Where is Mellan Lyon?" Sam shook his head. "And Mordog or Luc or whoever he is. That boy that you deign to lower yourself in his presence, to be *ashamed*?"

"What are you talking about?"

Sam's nostrils flared. "I've seen how you avoid him

because he doesn't approve of you. Why do you care so much about what he thinks?"

I gritted my teeth. "Because he is the embodiment of the home I left behind. He's a constant reminder of how I've failed those I've loved."

"There you go again." Sam set his glass on the table. "It was they who failed you!"

"You don't know what you're talking about," I said. "I fear Agramon because I don't know what I'm doing or how to beat him at his game. I am still young, your lordship. Things were not done this way where I grew up. I know nothing about these games, and every misstep I make, someone I love gets hurt."

"And yet, you make an excellent student," Sam said. "Who are you spying for if not Agramon?"

I said nothing.

"The empress then?"

I glared at him, angry that he so easily saw through me. "I thought you didn't care."

"I don't," Sam said. "I am a loyal man. It's the only constant I've had in my life."

"Then why do you continue this ridiculous conversation?"

"Because I want to know."

But I couldn't give anything away. Mahira was right, this was a woman's game. If I revealed anything, it could implicate the empress, Mahira, the Countess of

Calla, and by the gods, Araceli! I wasn't going to admit to anything.

I'd had enough. I rose, tossed my linen napkin onto my plate, and walked to the door. I didn't know what I hated more, Sam pointing out my insecurities or seeing myself through his eyes. "I think it's time for me to retire, your lordship."

Sam's hand appeared in front of me, and he shoved the door shut. "Has Agramon been working his power through you?"

I glared at him. "You know that in Nordow—"

"I'm not talking about Nordow," Sam said, his face close to mine. "You invade my thoughts in the worst way." His eyes flicked down to my lips. "Do you mean to tempt me? Is this all part of the empress's plan? Is she using you to get me on her side against the emperor?"

"Sam, there is no plan."

He lifted his hand to my shoulder, hesitating, perhaps looking for any hint of rejection. When he received none, he lowered his lips to mine.

A tide of warmth pulsed through me, pooling in my gut. My knees began to shake as my nerves were brought to life. I gripped his jerkin and pulled him into me. He rotated until my back was against the door.

"Tell me you don't want this," Sam whispered, his voice raw. His arms caged me in. "Tell me to stop. I beg of you. Tell me that my feelings are false, a distraction, anything."

But I craved his touch with such insatiable greed, emboldened with each breath that swept over my skin. I wrapped my arms around his neck and met his eyes. His hands drifted down to my waist and stilled. I could see it in his gaze. He was preparing for the worst. He was afraid.

I planted a light kiss on his lips, then his cheek, until finally I reached his ear. "If you stop," I said softly, "I don't think I could ever forgive you."

I gasped when Sam pulled my head to the side to nip at the sensitive flesh on my neck. He moved down to my shoulder. Drawing the sleeve of my dress down, his tongue traced the rose marking. His beard brushed over my skin, whipping my nerves into a frenzy.

Sam's lips found mine again. I moaned and his reservations fell away, his hands moving with an earnestness that my mind couldn't track.

I tugged at the laces of his leather jerkin, and he let me pull it over his head, shortly followed by his tunic. Before I could continue disrobing him, he forced my hands against the wall. His mouth explored mine, my neck, then he kissed down to my shoulders. He pulled the sleeves of my gown and lifted my leg to his. He moaned into me as he went as far as he could go, to the apex of my thighs, prodding me, testing, working me to a fever pitch until I was gasping for air.

Sam's fingers slowed, his other hand cupping my face while he kissed my lips, then my cheek, then down my neck again.

"Please," I gasped into his ear. He wrapped his fingers in my hair, gripping it as he pulled my face up. His fingers still worked, almost leisurely, drawing me along, playing each nerve with painful precision. "Don't stop," I whined, feeling as though I was close to something. As though I were on a ship, riding up a wave, nearly at its peak. I closed my eyes with a whimper.

"No." Sam gripped my hair tighter. "Look at me," he commanded.

My eyes flew open to meet his. He held me in his grip, his fingers far too clever to be allowed.

The wave of feeling crashed down. My whole body tensed in Sam's arms before a tempest surged through me and I shuddered. I'd never felt that way before. With Destrian we were both fumbling, neither one of us having any idea what we were doing but safe to know we could learn together. Sam was entirely different. He knew exactly what he was doing. I breathed his name as my nerves tucked back into my body.

Sam turned me to face the wall. I leaned against it for support as he scrabbled at the laces of my gown. He cursed, drawing a blade from his boot and running it along the knots of the stays. The gown he pushed off my shoulders, leaving it to pool at my feet. His lips went back to my neck, his hands now working on the corset. It seemed Gree's knots were too hard to maneuver. The knife made quick work of the garment. It, too, fell away as Sam turned me back toward him and lifted me in his arms, then walked over to his desk where all manner of papers and quills were flung to the floor and I was placed atop it.

"I will map every inch of you," Sam murmured in my ear. He ran his hands up my chemise, lifting it over my shoulders until I was left bare before him. I began working at the laces on his breeches when he grabbed my wrist, stilling my hand.

"You are sure?" he asked. "I don't want to pressure you."

"Stop acting like I will break," I growled, wrenching my hand away and going back to the laces. I wanted to chase that feeling that he'd awoken in me. Where I forgot everything that was wrong with my life, all my worries washing away with the wave of pleasure.

Finally, his pants were undone. I shoved them down. Sam twined my hair around his fingers and gripped my waist with the other hand, dragging me forward. I wrapped my legs around him, my hands around his neck, and I kissed him fiercely. He thrust into me, and I cried out, shattering into a million pieces.

Chapter 28

I SANK BACK INTO THE TUB, checking to make sure my hair was still piled on my head, free of the water. Sam was writing correspondence in his receiving room. The only separation was the partial stone wall, with its arched opening into the bedchamber, but his desk was positioned so that he had a full view of the tub. He'd moved it that very morning.

I splashed lightly, feeling like a new woman. It had been ages since I'd slept so well, since before I'd gone on my journey to the Nightlands at least. I had no dreams, no fits, just a deep, silent sleep. It was amazing how changed I felt.

"How would you like to occupy yourself today?" Sam asked, his eyes on the paper in front of him. By all the gods, the man had to write more correspondence than anyone I'd ever known. No wonder his hands were so strong.

Draping a leg over the side of the tub, I let out a long-suffering sigh. "Is there anything to do in Bruin besides watching broken men and inspecting lines of soldiers?" I hated seeing their faces. The shadows of Morganites and Adarites and wayward Lyricans that had once been men with lives and families and loved ones.

But I had no more pity within. They'd abandoned me. They'd abandoned *me*. I knew I was turning into a monster, but I couldn't bring myself to care.

Sam sat back in his seat, interlocking his fingers and stretching his hands out with a grunt, his eyes on my bare leg. "Today is weapons inspection."

I brought my leg back into the tub and leaned forward onto my arms. "What's that?"

"I mainly test blades," Sam said, rising to answer a knock at the door. Gree came in bearing a pile of my clothes and garments. A soldier was behind her, his arms filled with more bags. Sam grabbed the bags before the soldier could step in and slammed the door in his face.

"What's all this?" I asked, watching Sam direct Gree to a wooden wardrobe against the wall. She began hanging my gowns, her eyes darting steely glances in my direction. Ugh, that woman was the worst.

"I thought it would be easier to move your things into my room," Sam said, dumping the bags onto the bed before going back to the arch and leaning against it with his arms crossed. "Besides, it would be more work for your maid to constantly run clothes back and forth."

I glowered. "You could've asked me. Maybe I was planning to return."

"Maybe I won't let you."

"Maybe it's not your decision."

Sam straightened. "This is Bruin, where *I* am lord. Your safety, whether you like it or not, is my responsibility. Now, get dressed. I need to go speak with our blacksmith's guild, and I don't want to leave you alone."

"Fine," I mumbled, rolling my eyes as Gree pulled out a screen that had been leaning against the wall. She placed it to cover the tub and wardrobe as Sam went back to the receiving room to finish up his business.

"What are you doing?" snarled Gree as she held out a drying cloth.

I stood and glared at her. "I'm minding my own business. What are *you* doing?"

"Hateful child," Gree spat as she drew the cloth roughly over my skin. "His Grace won't like this. Not one bit."

"Good," I whispered back. "He's the one who left me here."

"The Butcher forced his hand," Gree hissed. "You needn't have played right into it. You're putting yourself under the baron's control, and I don't think you'll like where that leads."

"I'd much rather tie myself to Sam than Agramon," I insisted. "Maybe now he won't be able to whore out my powers to all his rich friends, or even worse, whore *me* out."

"You seem to be doing a perfectly good job of that on your own."

I slapped Gree across the face. The sound reverberated through the room. The shuffling of papers ceased.

Gree clutched her face, a red mark coloring her cheek. Sam appeared behind her.

"Leave us," he ordered.

Gree's eyes blazed with anger, but Sam stepped aside and pointed to the door.

After a moment, she hung her head and practically ran to escape. I watched her go, my shoulders sagging in regret, the cloth wrapped tight around my body.

"What was that about?" Sam asked gruffly as I turned away and grabbed the chemise Gree had draped over a chair. Dropping the cloth, I pulled the chemise on.

"She was warning of Agramon's anger," I said, refusing to meet his eye. "And she called me a whore."

Sam didn't say anything as I grabbed my gown. Gree had chosen a red one. Knowing her, she'd done it on purpose.

Hateful woman.

Standing in front of Sam's large mirror, I pulled the gown on, then cursed, realizing it laced behind me.

Sam's hand came to rest on my shoulder. He leaned down, kissing me on a sensitive spot he'd discovered, right where my shoulder met my neck. Gooseflesh blossomed over my skin.

"I'm sorry I moved your things without asking,"

Sam said. He grabbed the silken cords of my gown and yanked them tight.

"You're too used to giving commands," I said, adjusting the gown so that it tightened in the correct places.

Sam began to fiddle with the tie binding my hair up. "Is it so wrong to want you close to me?"

"The others will talk," I said, watching Sam in the mirror. The tie came loose and my curls went tumbling over my shoulders.

Sam ran his fingers through the black strands. "Do you care so deeply what they think?"

"No, of course not. The only one I really worry about is Agramon."

"You shouldn't." Sam kissed the top of my head. He made his way down to my ear, nuzzling his face against mine and breathing deep. "Marry me," he whispered, wrapping his arm around my waist. My spine stiffened and a chill shot through my bones. "Marry me, and you'll never have to return to him."

"Don't joke about that." I leaned away from him. I detached myself from his arms and strode to get my sword belt, refusing to meet his eye. By all the gods, marry Sam? He couldn't be serious.

I was done thinking of marriage. I'd thought to marry Destrian. I'd dreamed of it even. If I had been able to stay in Helena, I was sure it would've come to pass.

My brethren had always dreamed of Morgania falling under Morganite control. In a way that dream could've been realized if Destrian and I had been able to continue our romance, but my tribe saw to that. Cutting off their noses to spite their hateful faces.

Of course, I'd been betrothed to my childhood love, Luc. Most of my life I'd planned on having him as a husband. But Sam? The Butcher of Bruin? Though I was wallowing in darkness, I didn't think I'd ever venture that far. There was no way I could marry Sam. Not even to escape Agramon.

"I'm not joking."

"Well, Agramon would never allow it."

"Why does everyone seem to forget that Agramon is not your true master; it's the emperor? I need only to commission him. Just say the word."

I belted the sword to my side and raised my skirt, clasping the knives around my thigh. When I finished, I finally met Sam's gaze. He was frowning.

"What?"

"I just asked you to marry me, and this is your response?"

I gritted my teeth. "You asked me to marry you to protect me, not because you *want* to marry me. Don't feel obligated to take such a step merely to 'keep me safe.'"

"I don't want to marry you to protect you. I want to

marry you because I'm mad about you."

I rolled my eyes. "The madness will fade, I promise. You've already bedded me, so what's the point?"

"Rowyn, I . . ." Sam rubbed the back of his neck. "I do not ask you this lightly."

I crossed my arms over my chest. "How else am I supposed to take it? You asked like it was a passing fancy that flitted into your mind and out of your mouth. As a solution to a problem. There was no thought at all. If I'm to marry someone, I want them to ask me because they love me. Because they can't live without me." Destrian's face filled my mind, but I pushed the thought away. "Not because it's a convenient solution to a worry that will pass."

Sam's cheeks reddened. "I . . . I suppose that wasn't the right way to go about it, when you explain it like that."

"No, it absolutely was not," I agreed and strode toward the door.

Sam caught my arm as I passed, forcing me to face him as he cupped my cheek. "When I ask you again, I'll do it properly, I promise."

"I'd rather you didn't." I tried to keep my voice steady. "I don't want to discuss marriage with anyone right now."

"Then let me assure you, I will be doing my best to change your mind," Sam whispered, undeterred. He leaned in and kissed me.

"Agramon will make it difficult for us." I pulled back. "He has plans for me."

"I have plans for you, too, my little fiend," Sam said, burying his face in my hair. "More immediate plans that require your utmost concentration." Sam gripped my hip and pulled it into him.

"I thought you had to be somewhere," I murmured.

"We don't have to leave just yet." Sam leaned into me.

He was right. Agramon was away in Gryse. I could worry about him later. I could worry about Somme later.

I sucked in a breath when he found a particularly sensitive spot. Sam leaned his forehead against mine.

"This is how I imagined it," Sam whispered. "I'll keep you here forever, doing my best to take your breath away."

MY DAYS IN BRUIN PASSED EAGERLY from one to the next. I spent my time wandering the castle or venturing to town for Winnie's mending circles and visits with Nirah. I even took Fin's picture with me on a couple of occasions, just to see if she'd been spotted, which she hadn't. At night, after I brought the rain, Sam and I would fall into bed. I would wake up with his arms wrapped around me, his face buried in my hair, and begin the day all over again. It was as though an enchantment had been placed around the land. I forgot about Agramon. I forgot about the empress's directive. I forgot about the Morganites and the war and all my other fears.

One day, Sam offered to take me riding into the forest to the west. I enjoyed how the trees towered as if to shelter me from the world. Starstruck and Hale picked their own path through the woods as Sam told me about the progress of his troops.

We dismounted and walked through the underbrush, which thickened with the nightly promise of rain. Sam took my hand.

"I don't mean to burden you with my worries," he said, squeezing my fingers. "Let us talk of more pleasant things. How have you liked Bruin?"

I smiled. "I think you know that I've enjoyed my time here." In truth, Sam had gone out of his way to shelter me from the army. We now only had dinner in his rooms, away from the soldiers and officers that Sam spent his days with.

Sam's hand moved to my cheek. "What happens when Agramon returns? What happens in Somme?"

I bit my lip. "I don't know," I answered honestly.

"You are about to go to war, and I've not attained mastery, nor fulfilled my obligation to the crown or Agramon. I suppose I will simply do more of that."

"That can't be your answer," Sam whispered, his thumb on my lips. "Everything has changed."

"Everything and nothing. Agramon is still in charge of my care."

Sam kneeled on the forest floor, my hand in his. I would've marked the gesture if I hadn't been distracted by two sets of eyes peering at me through the trees.

I gasped.

The men were dirty, wearing threadbare tunics. Faded imorets outlined the outside of one man's eyes.

He was a Morganite.

They were running away from the fields.

"Did you hear me?" Sam asked, his voice cutting through my thoughts.

"What?" I asked.

"Marry me. Let's announce it to the emperor when we return."

"Sam . . . I . . ." My eyes shot back to the men who were trying to avoid being seen.

Sam rose. "Is something wrong?"

"Not at all," I insisted. I had to move Sam away from the spot. "Shouldn't we head back?" I glanced at the sun. It would be fine if I could get Sam away before others noticed the men were gone. At the moment, I hadn't seen nor heard any signs of alarm regarding escapees. That was, until the bells began tolling, the clanging rolling through the trees.

A muscle twitched in Sam's jaw as he rose and pulled the sword from his side. He looked over his shoulder.

"Wait!" I shouted, grabbing his arm, but Sam ignored me. He strode right into the brush. The escaped prisoners cried out as he pulled them from their hiding place.

"Sam! Have mercy, please!" I ran to block Sam. "Why does the empire insist on keeping the forgotten men anyway?"

"Rowyn," Sam rumbled, "you shouldn't speak of things that you don't understand. These men are abandoning their post, which carries a death sentence. They are property to the crown, and as such, they are responsible for following orders."

No, I had to make him see reason. Dogs barked from the east, the sounds getting closer.

"Sam, you don't have to be the cruel master that everyone views you to be."

"Turn away," Sam said, his voice hard.

"Sam!" But I could tell he was resolved. I turned toward Starstruck and buried my face in her mane, trying to block out the cries of the men as Sam ran his sword through them.

"Rowyn, wait." Sam followed me into the castle. Tears flowed freely down my face. "I must follow laws. My men must follow orders!"

"Have you no mercy in you?" I yelled. "Must everything fall to duty? Where is your conscience?" I twisted back around, wishing I still had my old room. I started toward that hallway, Sam hot on my heels.

"I know life was hard for you in Morgania. You had to have seen your father perform duties and make choices that he didn't entirely agree with. That is the nature of being a leader!"

"What of their choices?" I asked, flinging my hand out. "What choice did they have in this life? They were taken, conscripted, and forced to live out their days as slaves to the empire. You are just as bad as the rest of them!"

I turned the corner.

"Well, well, well," Agramon said, leaning against the wall with his staff in hand. "Trouble in paradise?"

Chapter 29

AGRAMON SUPERVISED AS GREE cleared my things out of Sam's room and moved them back into mine. Gree insisted on being insufferable, shooting me smug grins as though I cared what she or Agramon thought. When everything had been put away, I slammed the door in all their faces and didn't emerge again until two days later when the entire party, along with the army, departed for the capitol.

I refused the carriage, so Agramon rode next to me. He'd been watching me constantly, practically gleeful that Sam and I were in the middle of a fight. I hated him for it.

I resolved to think of my impending escape. The quinquennial was approaching, and I'd decided to find a merchant's ship to bear me west. I would need to ensure it left before I was found missing. If the navy caught up with it, I'd have to fly from there. As long as I escaped the capitol, I could handle any small band sent to collect me.

"Now that your romance with the Butcher has waned, I wonder what other lover you might take," Agramon said, his voice light.

"Leave me be," I growled. Luc's eyes bore into the

back of my head. Sam had been right. I always felt ashamed when I was around Luc. It was as though my parents and grandmother and the entire clan were glaring at me, seeing the men I loved and the choices I made and cursing my name for everything I'd done to them. I resolved to leave him to rot with Agramon when I left.

"I must admit," Agramon went on, "it is certainly entertaining to see what happened in my absence." His voice was low, as though he were testing me.

"You're disgusting."

"And you," Agramon said, one brow raised, "are more talented than I gave you credit for."

I nudged Starstruck forward, trying to ignore his laughter as it followed me along the line. I let Starstruck gallop ahead of the marching men. There was nowhere to go where I could be alone with my thoughts.

Arden soared above the company. I wished I could join her. I missed the solitude of being in the air. Even Echo seemed to be mad at me. She hadn't spoken to me once in the two weeks I'd been wrapped in Sam's sheets. Had I truly ruined everything? Was the way Sam made me feel worth it?

At the time it had been. He'd comforted me and made me feel loved and worth fighting for. All I felt in Agramon and Luc and everyone else's presence was judgment. Sam had only ever celebrated me.

That evening, I took my bowl to my tent and ate alone. When I finished, I sharpened my blades. I processed the knives quickly, then went to my sword. I ran my fingers along the engravings in my blade. I closed my eyes, and the sword began to quiver.

"Rowyn," Sam said, striding into my tent.

I dropped Iranoct, startled.

Sam looked from the blade to the tears in my eyes. "I'll not let it end this way."

"Sam." I rose, backing away. "You shouldn't be in here."

"Don't say that." Sam stepped toward me. "I beg of you, marry me. I will give you anything, whatever you want, just say yes."

I took a deep breath. "Sam, you told me you couldn't help who you are. Well neither can I. I can't forgive you your faults. I'm sorry." I'd thought I could ignore the way I felt about the Morganites, about my homeland. It was no use. Duty to my kinsmen had fed me in the cradle, been my playmate as I aged, and haunted my thoughts into adulthood. The way Sam had cut down the Morganite, seeing them enslaved to the empire, cut me to the quick.

Sam's face fell. He turned and ran his hand over his neck. "No, I don't accept that." He shook his head. "You are young. You have these romantic views about how much power we nobles hold, how much power I hold, but—"

"Sam," I said sharply, tears welling in my eyes. "I only ask that you do the right thing . . . the noble thing."

"I will find a way." Sam grabbed my shoulders, his fingers digging deep into my flesh. "I will show you that you can love me."

I shook my head. "You shouldn't," I whispered. "You should stay away from me. The gods have ensured that everyone I've ever loved is ripped from me. Despite the rain that I bring, it's as though everything I touch turns to ash and dust."

Sam pulled me to him. "I don't fear the gods."

I didn't know why I let Sam stay that night. Perhaps it was because I wanted to return to how we'd been, before the ride to the forest, where I'd been blissfully ignoring every reason why I should hold the Baron of Bruin at arm's length. It was easy to lose myself in the heat of his passion. Sam had an uncanny way of ensuring I let my guard down, but the dream was fading back to reality.

That night, wrapped in Sam's arms, I realized that I couldn't be reckless any longer.

I was still in Agramon's hold.

The Sons of Sol and Yliria were still trying to get to me.

The empire was still a disaster.

With all of those challenges ahead, I couldn't help but worry about whether I'd done enough to please the gods. The quinquennial was fast approaching with every step south, and my time to plan my escape was beginning to run out. I'd brought the rain. I'd ended the drought. I'd tried to end the war, though it seemed to have been a fruitless endeavor. Surely the gods could see I'd done my best.

When we reached the capitol, I needed to shore up my allies. I had every deal that Agramon made tucked into the back of my mind thanks to Echo. As soon as I could find time, I would need to meet with the empress and tell her everything I knew. She'd promised to help me escape if I spied for her. A ship was still my best bet since I was sure that Agramon would expect me to fly. I couldn't return to Morgania. That would be the first place that he would look. No, I would have to say my farewell to Destrian in Somme. I could apologize for what happened with his father and let him know that I wished things had ended differently between us. I didn't know what else to say after that. Enjoy Ingrid's company? Good luck ruling the land that should rightfully be mine yet I do not want? I always knew you could do better and now you do too?

Sam's grip on my waist tightened and he drew me closer, his breathing soft and steady against my hair. I wished Sam could be an ally in my escape, but I knew that was a fool's thought. I believed him when he said he loved me, but Sam would not want me to be away from him, nor would he give up his post as imperial commander on the eve of war. He would find a way to make me stay, either talking me out of leaving or forcing me to remain for my own good.

No. I couldn't rely on Sam's help, which was why I needed to end things with him for good. Though we were alike in many ways, we still held loyalties to opposite entities—he to the emperor, and me, despite my grumblings, to my clan and homeland. I couldn't look past his unflinching loyalty to laws and decisions I disagreed with. I would've been unhappy at Bruin, seeing my clansmen used as slaves daily, watching the broken men of the empire toil under Sam's heavy hand. During Agramon's absence, Sam had hidden me away, careful not to let me see anything that made me unhappy. That never could've lasted. There would be more escapees, more wars, more conscripted men sold for a cause they didn't care about. I liked Sam, a lot, but I would grow to hate him in the end. Him and myself.

The next morning, I sipped the lady's tea that Gree handed to me, my eyes on the trees bordering the road. I could feel Luc glaring at me. Agramon was studying me across from the fire, a smile tugging at his lips. I'd tried to be quiet when Sam and I fell into bed, but you never knew with Agramon. It wasn't like Sam was wearing his sword the entire time. Could Agramon see everything through Sam's eyes? The thought about made me lose my breakfast.

"Did you sleep well?" he asked, his voice light. Innocent. Full of lies and deception.

"Well enough." I stared at the embers.

Agramon nodded. "That's good. I was worried you would be tossing and turning all night."

I gritted my teeth but refused to take the bait.

Luc cursed, then got up and strode away, Arden on his shoulder. I watched him go, then looked back to Agramon. "What is the point of this cruelty?"

Agramon leaned back, smiling as he studied me. "You have your entertainment, and I have mine."

I took a deep breath to control my anger.

The next night, I sent Sam away. And the night after that. And the night after that.

Until he stopped coming to my tent.

He just stared at me, waiting for any signal that I was ready to rekindle our romance.

But I gave none.

Chapter 30

THE ROAD TO SOMME was packed for the quinquennial. White banners bearing the golden sunburst of the emperor danced in the breeze, regaling us from windows and storefronts. The streets were crowded with peasants watching the nobles of the land make their way to the golden citadel in long trains of horses and carriages.

Our party took up the entire road. To the right they raised the banner of Solin, argent white and emblazoned with a golden eagle. To the left, the flags of Bruin were blood red, with a rearing bear stitched in black, its mouth open in a roar.

I looked down at the outlandish gown Gree had poured me into. It was done entirely in gold, with silk feathers sewn around my waist and up my chest, giving the appearance of folded wings. They reached my throat, attached to a choker that held the bodice up. The support was sorely needed considering the tailor had left a considerable gap between where the two wings met, revealing the crests of my breasts and navel. The feathers continued down into the skirt making me look like a ridiculous golden bird. Starstruck's snow-white coat and mane seemed like part of the costume.

I was a walking flag of Agramon's, a trophy he'd brought to present to the emperor he was plotting to overthrow.

I worried that I would grind my teeth to nubs.

We were the last nobles of note to arrive for the quinquennial. Agramon had undoubtedly planned it that way. I couldn't even bear to look at the people anymore, so I stared straight ahead, hating everything about the display we were putting on—as though we'd already won the war in Lu Shen, as though the drought ended, as though the era of suffering were over.

We were not saviors. We were using the people to gain what man wanted most, power. It was all a lie cloaked in white silk and golden thread. That was the promise of the empire. Lies and spectacles and pain.

When we reached the base of the citadel, Luc helped Agramon dismount, while Sam came to my side and held his hand out. I practically fell into his arms. He held me a moment longer than necessary before setting me down to find my way through yards of silk.

We shuffled quickly through the golden corridors. When a herald saw us approach the doors to the great hall, he motioned them open in a hurry. I held my breath as the doors swung inward, revealing the packed throne room beyond.

Silk banners hung from the ceiling, displaying the golden sun of the emperor. The gilded room was almost blinding to behold. It was as though I were standing in Sol's throne room.

Miyu was in her element. I found her on a high balcony, observing the crowd and sending orders to the cooks, serving men, and entertainers.

The crowd parted, allowing a path for us to present ourselves before the emperor's family. Agramon led the way, with Sam and me walking behind him. Most of the faces in the crowd were a blur. The only reason I recognized Del was that she was waving frantically as though she'd counted down the days till she'd see me again. Mellan stood farther on, next to a young noblewoman who seemed to be trying to catch his eye. His curly hair was pulled back into a knot. His eyes darted to Agramon as he took a deep drink from his goblet.

I was turning my gaze from Mellan when I saw him.

A flash of red.

A dark blue overcoat covered in a sea of gilded stars.

The golden sword at his waist.

I sucked in my breath and froze. It felt as though the entire court melted away at the vision of Destrian standing before me.

His dark eyes bore into mine, and I was shocked by the emptiness within. He saw me. I know he did. But within his gaze there was no emotion. No feeling. He'd closed himself off completely.

It was as if seeing me again didn't affect him in the

least.

Nothing to show that my fears for the past several months were unfounded. Destrian had moved on, just as I'd begged him to do in the Nightlands. He held no love for me anymore, his eyes now like darts to my heart.

Someone appeared at his side. Ingrid could've been standing next to him the entire time and I wouldn't have noticed, but she leaned into Destrian's chest as if she would never leave his side.

"The emperor is waiting," said a gruff voice beside me.

I tore my eyes away from Destrian and registered Sam's hand on my arm. The noise in the hall came back with a roar. I stood stupidly, forgetting where I was, until Sam placed his hand on my lower back and nudged me forward. I looked back at Destrian, his emotionless eyes now on Sam.

I willed the tears away and faced forward, the cacophony of the hall filling my ears. I tried to catch my breath. I knew I would see him. He had to come to the quinquennial. So why was I so caught off guard?

The emperor smiled as we approached. Empress Lesedi sat solemnly beside him, acknowledging each of us in turn. On her lap sat the little prince, his ocher skin dark in the sunlight, his blue eyes sparkling as he played with his mother's golden necklace. On the steps to the dais sat the princesses. Little Ledi gave me a wave, while Eladia continued playing with a set of gilded stones.

"Our most honored guests, here at last!" Emperor Arthello said, holding out his arms. "We can finally begin the celebration."

Duke Agramon swept into a deep bow. "Your Eminence was all kindness in waiting on our return. I am happy to report that Rowyn the Morganite has been working her sorcery all through the empire. We can celebrate the end of the drought in Lyrica!"

A cheer went up among the nobles. My cheeks flamed, and I bowed my head. End of the drought indeed. Maybe for those who could spare coin to line Agramon's pockets.

"Well met, then, well met!" the emperor said, stepping down from the dais and resting his hands on my shoulders. "I am proud of the work you have done, dear girl. Very proud."

"Thank you, Your Eminence," I muttered.

"And High Commander, how does Bruin fare? Can we expect a rich harvest this year? I was told the Morganite spent some extended time there."

Sam glanced down at me. "I think the harvest will be better than it has been, though we had to cut our planting short to make it here in time. The army marches now, and I've already called up the reserves. We await your orders."

"The army?" the emperor asked, his brows raised. "Why is the army marching on Somme?"

Sam stiffened.

I couldn't help but stare.

"You ordered me to bring Lu Shen to heel," Sam said slowly.

The emperor's eyes widened. "You can't mean . . . Commander, did no one send word? I decided against an attack on Lu Shen months ago. Count Ariz was right, we had the quinquennial approaching and were too busy with all the preparations to prepare for war as well. It was a mere slight of honor. There was no need to get out of hand with it."

Sam didn't speak. I could feel anger humming within him, as though at any moment he would burst. Agramon, the devil of a man, was near shaking with suppressed laughter.

"So . . . I am to understand that we are not to go to war," Sam forced out each word. The tone almost made me shudder.

"No, man, no, the army just returned from Yliria," the emperor said with a smile, obviously thinking Sam would be pleased by the news.

"What am I to do with my men when they get here?"

"Well, why should they not join in the celebration!"

The emperor spread his hands wide. "After all, they are part of the reason for it, the end of the conflict in Lyrica."

A muscle in Sam's jaw twitched, and he nodded slowly. "As you wish, Your Eminence. Though, I will let those who desire to skip the festivities and return home the choice, given they left right in the middle of spring planting."

"Of course, of course," the emperor said, clapping Sam on the arm. "Today begins the real festivities." He looked at me. "I wish you to enjoy yourselves because when the quinquennial is over, I want you on the road again, dear girl, making sure that our thirsty fields are quenched."

Duke Agramon swept into another bow. "As you wish."

I met the eyes of the empress. She raised her brows but gave no other indication that we'd had an agreement. Given the emperor's pronouncement, Countess Mahira had been as good as her word. I'd helped stop the war. My plan had worked. Arda had said that I would need to help others if I hoped to escape, and ending the drought *and* war meant that millions would be spared. Relief swelled within. It had to be enough for the gods. What more could they want?

I needed to speak with the empress immediately. I would need her help in breaking free, especially if I was to do it by the end of the quinquennial. I could practically taste freedom on my tongue. The possibilities would be endless.

Agramon motioned me to follow him as he strolled through the parting crowd.

Sam followed beside me, though his eyes were elsewhere. Although I'd ended things with Sam, I didn't enjoy seeing him hurt. I stepped closer. "Are you all right?"

Sam glanced down at me, his face stony. "I'm fine," he growled. "It was just a tremendous waste of everyone's time." He shook his head, the muscle in his jaw jumping furiously. "All those men, leaving their homes to do Sol's work. He's made me look like a complete fool."

"It's not you who is the fool," I whispered, grabbing his hand. "You give the emperor more honor than he deserves. I wish your loyalty was bestowed upon a better man."

Sam glared at me. "Those words are treason."

I raised my brows. "I'm Morganite, Sam. My whole life has been treason, and it's far too late to break those habits."

"Still, we're in the capitol now. The emperor could hang you for your words."

"Oh, and risk the drought returning?" I scoffed. "Just worry about sending your men home so they can enjoy their families until the emperor decides to start another war on a whim."

Sam grunted. Agramon led us to a row of chairs lining the wall. Agramon swept the panels of his coat out and found an empty seat. He motioned for me to sit on his left.

"Don't you have a dark corner to return to?" Agramon asked Sam, his eyes on the crowd. "An army to disband? Children to slaughter? I would like some time with my ward without your burdensome presence."

I doubted Agramon's desire to see me alone had anything to do with my sparkling personality. I'd gotten the man to trust me, but that in itself was a double-edged sword. With all the high-ranking nobles in one room, Agramon was sure to be planning something underhanded. The entire journey, I'd made it all the easier on him by being willing and complicit to a point. Now, at the quinquennial, he would surely test the limits of my resolve. I just had to hold out till the end of the festivities, then I would be rid of him for good.

"The most powerful men in the realm are here. If you think I'm going to leave Rowyn's welfare to whatever machinations you conjure up in that scheming head of yours, you're an idiot," Sam said as though reading my mind.

"She's not yours," Agramon sneered. "In fact, she

quite determinedly denied you the pleasure when you asked. So why do you still shadow her heels like a dog?"

I ignored their bickering and turned my gaze to the milling courtiers. A group of richly dressed nobles moved toward the banquet tables. A flash of auburn caught my eyes, and my skin tingled.

Destrian looked like a different person—older I supposed. He'd reclaimed the weight lost on our journey, and though he'd trimmed his beard, he'd left it longer than when he was at Solridge.

My mind was awash with the nights I spent pointing Iranoct toward Morgania, knowing I would give anything for Destrian to be by my side. Even still, I felt thankful that he was safe, if nothing else.

Sam's hand clasped around mine like a steel claw. I tried to tug it away but he wouldn't release me. What was he doing? Had he taken my concern for his feelings as an invitation to rekindle what we had in Bruin? I thought back to the procession when Sam had grabbed my arm. Was he trying to assert a claim over me? Why was he so insistent to show that we were more than we were? Araceli of Calla was standing on Destrian's other side with Ellora of Korballis. Even Ellora's brother, Marc, and Idris of Juno were there. I craned my neck, looking for Fin or Pedr, but I found neither.

"Well, well, well," Agramon said beside me. "Your old schoolmates, I presume?"

I ripped my eyes from the group. "Yes, we attended Solridge together."

"This should be interesting, eh, Butcher?" Agramon went on. "The young, virile lords from the western wilds come to the eastern shore to pledge their loyalty. A strapping lot they are too."

Sam's grip on my hand tightened until he was crushing my fingers. Even when I hissed in pain, he wouldn't loosen. "Let go," I murmured, again trying to pull away.

Sam ignored me.

Agramon refused to be silent. "I remember Lord Destrian from when I retrieved you. He was so in love with you then, wasn't he, my dear?" Agramon leaned toward me. "I suppose you have that effect on people. Though it seems his self-proclaimed misery at your absence has been stemmed by his lovely young friend there. Do you know her?"

I gritted my teeth and nodded as the group began to approach. I stopped struggling against Sam's hand, unwilling to make a scene with so many eyes upon us. I would share my displeasure with him later.

Agramon rose from his chair, his arms open, his eyes sparkling darkly. "The youth of the west!" Agramon spoke as though he couldn't be more delighted to see my schoolmates, something I knew was far from the truth. Anything that could change my temperament, or give me hope, would be seen as a thorn in his side.

"Your Grace," Araceli said, lowering into a curtsy, "it gives us pleasure to be here for the emperor's festivities."

"He has planned quite a celebration, to be sure," Duke Agramon said with a smile. "No doubt you will all find yourselves wonderfully diverted with all the wonders the city has to offer."

There was no mistaking the hint of a threat to his words, nor the way his eyes challenged Destrian, who dared to meet his gaze. Agramon wanted them to stay away.

"I am here to fulfill my duty to the crown and nothing more," Destrian said. "I plan to return to my land as soon as the emperor has released us."

"Ahhh yes, the new consul of Morgania is making his first vows. How could I forget?" Agramon said with a sly smile. "Which means you are granted your oath's gift. I hope that you've thought carefully about what it is you're going to ask for."

Destrian's eyes flashed. "I plan to ask for nothing more than the worth of my domain."

Agramon was studying Destrian carefully. The more he studied, the more his brow furrowed. "Men have lost rights to rule over asking too big a favor from the crown. Be sure you choose carefully, so as not to incur the anger of the emperor."

"Wise advice," Destrian said. He looked at me and bowed his head. "Rowyn."

So much hung in the way he uttered my name. It fell heavily from his tongue, filling the void between us. My mind went back to all the times he'd said my name when we'd been alone in the darkness. How it would wrap around me like a caress, keeping me safe from the horrors. Now it was cold. Unfeeling. A weight of vows broken and a future lost to time.

It was as if my doubts and fears had finally become a reality.

Now seeing him, I felt as though the world were closing in, and I still clung to the promises we'd made to each other in the Nightlands.

No matter what I told Sam. No matter how I tried to convince myself to move on. Destrian was who I dreamed of when I thought of a future without the empire's hold.

It was still Destrian who held the promise of tomorrow.

I looked at Sam. It felt like I was about to fall into a yawning abyss, and he was pulling me down with him.

My voice choked in my throat.

I could think of nothing to say that I wanted Agramon or Sam to hear. Even if they were gone, I wouldn't know how to begin. At the very least I should apologize.

For his father.

For leaving him, broken, on the road.

For trusting in only myself.

I never gave Destrian the chance to save me.

Someone grasped my hand. "Rowyn, it's so good to see you," Ellora said. I shifted my gaze to my short-term roommate. She'd followed her brother's orders and requested to change rooms at Solridge due to me being a bad influence, what with all my thoughts and ideas.

Ellora's smile stayed, but a crease appeared on her brow as her eyes swept over me. If I were Agramon, I would know what she was thinking. As it was, I didn't care.

"Thank you, Ellora," I managed. "It brings me comfort to see familiar faces. I hope to see much of you during your stay."

"Well," Agramon cut in. "We'll be very busy meeting with the other nobles on the councils and planning your second tour of the empire."

"We've missed you on the western shores," Ingrid said, her false smile bright. "But I bet you're enjoying your time in the capitol. It seems you're richly looked after . . . and adored." Her eyes shot to the slip of a gown that made me look like a gilded statue.

"Thank you," I muttered. If looks could kill, the glare I shot her would've left her bloodied at my feet.

Araceli stepped up next, her face guarded under Agramon's watchful eye. "Rowyn," she murmured, taking my hand and kissing the gem that lay there. "You're much changed since I last saw you."

"I am," I said simply. Agramon was studying my every move. I knew he couldn't read my mind, but it was obvious he read theirs clear as day. Warning bells were ringing.

My eyes went back to Destrian. He was so close I could touch him. I just needed to reach out my hand. Ingrid placed her fingers on Destrian's arm, standing on her toes to whisper in his ear.

I'd waited so long to see him. In the awfulness of the moment, I was reminded of everything that had happened since we'd parted. I'd tried to warn Destrian of the threat of Gryse on his consulship, and I hoped the empress's warning reached him, yet he had never tried to contact me. I'd told him to move on and he had. There was nothing for me to be angry about. Though it hurt, I knew it was for the best. He was safer away from me. Morgania was safer without us attached.

I blinked the tears away. The young nobles drifted back into the crowd.

"Are you all right?" Sam asked when they moved on.

"They looked well. I'm glad to see them, I suppose," I said, but it seemed Sam was distracted.

"That is your Lord Destrian?" A heaviness carried

his voice.

"Yes."

"He looked better than when I last saw him," Agramon said, twisting his staff in his hands as he watched the western nobles mill through the hall. "It seems your absence has been good to him."

I clenched my teeth.

Sam released my hand. "You think there may still be a chance?"

My memory shot to the way Destrian's soft mouth felt over mine, how comforting it was to be in his embrace. "No," I said with finality. "He has no doubt cursed my name and tried to burn me from his mind."

"But what about you?" Sam watched me closely.

I couldn't meet his gaze. "What about me?"

"Do you have feelings for him?"

"Of course she does," Agramon said under his breath, though Sam made it clear he heard him by the way a muscle in his jaw flexed.

I let out an exasperated sigh. "Must we speak of this here? Let me have peace."

Sam's brows furrowed. "It was a simple question, Rowyn."

"Yes, but why do you feel you are owed an answer?"

Agramon leaned toward me. "You know the emperor would never allow you two to wed, don't you? The east has always been the emperor's priority. The nobles here are far more powerful and influential than those of the west, and he'll want to keep your talent close to the capitol. You may never see the western shore again."

My temper sparked and I rose from my seat. "I know, Agramon. I don't need you two pointing out how trapped I am. How few choices I have in my life!"

Sam rose and grabbed my arm. "We're trying to help you see reason."

I pulled my arm from his grip. "No, you're trying to drag me closer to you. All anyone does is try to entrap me, and I'm sick of it!"

"Rowyn, come out to the balcony. We can speak freely there," Sam said, his eyes on the courtiers who shot curious glances in our direction.

"No, I want a moment's peace to myself, please!" I said, turning away.

Mellan was standing right behind me, his hand outstretched. "Come," he said. "They've had you all to themselves for months."

I let him pull me away but looked over my shoulder. Sam's eyes were on me. Just a little bit longer. I only had to hold out a little bit longer, and then I would be free from them all.

Chapter 31

"I KNOW THIS IS A LOT." Mellan leaned toward me. "Just breathe."

I sucked in my breath and nodded. Mellan grabbed a goblet from a nearby server and handed it to me. He thrust his hand into his pocket and said nothing so I could collect my thoughts.

When I looked up at him, Mellan took that as his cue.

"How was your journey?" he asked, taking a sip from his glass.

"Exhausting," I said honestly, searching the room for Destrian. "There is so much to tell you, I don't even know where to begin."

"Rumors have been echoing through the halls since you've left," Mellan said, leaning against the wall.

I furrowed my brow. "What rumors?"

"Can we start with the delicious ones first?" A sly smile crept across his face.

"I suppose."

"Are you betrothed?"

"No," I said, taking another drink. "Not to my knowledge at least." Who knows what Agramon had conjured up without my knowing. I had a moment's misgiving about not accompanying him to Gryse. What deal had he made with the lord there?

Mellan nodded. "Did Sam take down a battalion of Marysian guards in response to Lord Achille besmirching your honor?"

I rolled my eyes. "It was not a *battalion*."

Mellan laughed. "All right, did Agramon force himself into your bed?"

"No," I said. "Not yet anyway."

"What of the baron?"

I sighed.

"He didn't." Mellan's eyes widened. Clearly, he'd thought the rumors were wrong.

"He didn't force himself," I amended.

"Well, you've done quite a number on the commander. I'm surprised he hasn't pissed down your leg to mark his territory."

"Stop," I snorted. "What if someone overhears?"

"And now Lord Destrian is here. My word, Rowyn, this promises to be the most diverting quinquennial yet!"

"Have you seen your father?" I asked, trying to distract him from my problems. He had plenty of his own. There was no need for me to share.

"I have," Mellan said. "From afar. We nodded to each other in passing. It was about as best a meeting as I could hope for, given the circumstances."

"And your brothers?" Mellan was by far the most honorable Lyon. Given my reputation with the family, I figured I should keep an eye over my shoulder now that there were more in the city.

"At home, seeing to business there. Aureliana stayed behind also. It seems she caught the shivers right before they were set to leave. Though, Seith sent word he was somewhere in the city. I've not seen him at the palace."

I raised my brows. Seith Lyon had disappeared after the defeat of the Ayastaren army in Morgania. I wondered what he'd been doing that entire time.

"What did he say?" I asked.

"He told me that, despite what our father says about our marriage suit, I should stay away from you. He says that Sol will rain fire down on those who harbor the traitor from the night, and other such nonsense. It seems he's grown to be quite the fanatic on his journey."

"He sounds like the Sons of Sol," I said.

Mellan frowned. "We heard there was trouble in Solin. Did anything else happen?"

"A warlord from Yliria tried to kidnap me," I said. I glanced at Sam, surrounded by some other men. "They were going to take me to some man named Alf Amundoon before Sam rescued me. I wondered if he was tied to the Sons of Sol in some way."

Mellan shook his head. "I still can't get over that you

call the Lord Commander of the Imperial Army, Baron Samael of Bruin, Sword of Lyrica, Sam."

I shrugged. "He was Sam before he was those other things."

"That man has been watching you this entire time," Mellan said, pointing to a cluster of sorcerers from the academy at Somme. I saw Master Gillius standing with them. When I met his eye, he set his plate down and began walking toward me.

"Do you want me to stay?" Mellan asked under his breath.

I shook my head. "No, I would speak with him alone."

Mellan nodded and disappeared into the crowd as Gillius came to my side.

"Rowyn," Gillius said, his voice cautious. "We've been trying to follow all your successes on the western shore. They've proven too numerous to count."

"Spare me your false compliments. Was it hard?" I asked with a scowl. "Duping me into trusting you?"

Gillius looked appropriately taken aback. After a moment, he shook his head. "You know the answer to that, Rowyn. You refused to trust me."

"No, I didn't. I wanted nothing more than to trust you. I didn't want to be a burden on my clan any longer, and you promised me that you would help me."

"How did I not help?" Gillius asked. "Have you ever

given any thought to what would've happened if I hadn't found you? If you hadn't come to Solridge?"

"I would've been free," I said. "I could've chosen for myself."

"No, you would've continued to be a slave to a power you couldn't control. If the golgeman hadn't gotten you, your magic would've finished you off."

"You didn't have to lie to me," I snapped. "Agramon has never hidden who he is or what he wants me for."

"Would you have come with me if I was honest?" Gillius asked.

I opened my mouth to speak, but Gillius held up his hand. "No, I want you to really think about it. Where would you have gone? What would you have done if I hadn't pulled you from that forest?"

"You enslaved me to him," I said. "You hid that you were his servant. Would you have branded me if Agramon demanded it?"

Gillius straightened. "I would *never* have branded you. I am not a servant of Agramon. I'm a servant to the empire. His Grace has much greater means than myself to ensure that your powers are used appropriately and have the farthest reach possible."

"I hate you," I seethed. "You had so many opportunities to tell me the truth and you chose deceit every time. I wish to never speak to you again."

"Very well," Gillius said, looking down at his feet. "I just wanted to come over and say how proud we all are of you."

He left me standing alone as a tear made tracks down my cheek. I brushed it away, annoyed that Gillius had caused such a reaction. I shouldn't care what he thought.

I looked up. Destrian was watching me, a small crease between his brows as Ingrid and the other students from Solridge talked around him. He turned and stepped toward me.

"Rowyn!" a voice shouted. My heart swelled. I brushed another tear from my cheek and turned to find Pedr Tore standing there, beaming.

"Pedr!" I gasped, throwing my arms around him. "Oh Pedr," I murmured in his ear, relishing his nearness. "I've missed you so much."

"Have you heard from Fin?" Pedr asked, breaking away. "What of your travels? Tell me everything!"

I launched in, taking care not to reveal anything that Agramon could glean from his mind and use against me. Pedr told me about Solridge. Lisbet Byrne was now engaged to one of the knights who had been attending. Pedr kept Lord Obi company in the library in the evenings, though he mentioned that the old lord's mind was so lost that they couldn't play chess anymore. Pedr even introduced me to his family.

I curtsied, then bowed my head low as his father took my hand in his.

"I confess, lady, I thought my son was telling tales when he spoke of your friendship," the lord of Livian said, glancing at Pedr whose ears had turned pink.

"Whatever do you mean, your lordship?" I asked, pulling my hand back.

"I just find him to be a bit ridiculous is all," Pedr's father said, his tone light.

"I see nothing ridiculous in a man as talented as he," I said hotly. "As someone who does not take friendship lightly, your son is very dear to me."

The lord of Livian bowed, looking properly admonished.

Pedr and I continued talking well into the night. I ignored Sam's pointed looks and Destrian's glances. I would figure out my problems tomorrow. Tonight was for rekindling friendships that I'd worried I'd lost.

I EVADED SAM AND SNUCK out of the hall, heading back to Agramon and my rooms in the palace. Gree had been sent to prepare them for us, and I was bone-tired, ready to collapse into bed after a long time on the road. It felt as though I'd returned home, though I had misgivings about the thought. It would only be home a short while longer.

I opened the door to the chambers I shared with Agramon. The duke sat on the couch, a blue bottle in his hands. Luc and Gree were nowhere to be found.

"I wondered if you would return," Agramon said slowly, his eyes crawling up and down my body. "I asked Mordog if he wanted to take a bet on whose room you'd end up in this evening."

"What are you talking about?" I shut the door behind me. "I'm going to my own room and sleeping in my own bed." I started for the door.

"I would speak with you before you retire," Agramon said in a sing-song voice, pointing to the seat beside him.

I wanted nothing more than to sink into my sheets and will the world away, but I'd finally gained a semblance of trust with Agramon. I would be a fool if I chose to battle him when I was so close to gaining what I wanted.

"How was your evening? Did Lord Destrian try to speak with you again?"

"No," I said, taking a peach Agramon was offering from the dish on the table. He'd noticed they were my favorite. I glanced at the window where Arden was perched, fast asleep. At least I wasn't entirely alone.

"Now that we have a reprieve from the Butcher, I

wonder what you thought about your time in Bruin. I've gleaned so much from his mind." Agramon leaned back. "He imagines you in quite vivid detail."

I wrinkled my nose in distaste. "And I suppose you couldn't help but read his thoughts?"

Agramon cocked an eyebrow. "It's ghastly stuff, to be sure, but no, I couldn't help myself. Not with the heir of Helena here, plaguing his mind."

"What does Destrian have to do with anything?" I propped my feet onto the table and took a bite of the fruit.

"Oh, my dear, it's too delicious. The baron can't stop himself from thinking of the two of you together. The same goes for Lord Destrian. I swear, I've seen enough of you naked in the minds of men this past day that I'm half convinced that *I've* slept with you."

"You should be so lucky," I said. "Besides, maybe that will keep you out of men's minds."

"I'd give anything to delve into your mind," Agramon said, his eyes sharp, watchful. "Steel trap that it is. What are you playing at?"

"Despite what you may think, not everyone is playing a game, Agramon."

Agramon rolled his eyes and took a swig from his blue bottle. I'd never seen him drink much before. I wondered why he was letting his guard down the first night of the quinquennial. He must be nervous. There was so much at stake, for everyone. I was counting on it being easier to slip away with the rest of the court distracted by each others' intrigues.

"Stop pretending to be naive. *Everyone* is playing some game or other here. Either *you* play very badly, or you're more cunning than I give you credit for. I've yet to figure out which it is, and it's caught me off guard a bit."

"I think it's the second one," I said, taking another bite of the peach.

Agramon tossed his head back and laughed. "Well, the Butcher has asked for you to have rooms outside my quarters. I think he will be demanding a marriage proposal next. I've half a mind to say no, just to see what he would say."

"You should say no. I've no wish to marry him," I quipped, licking the juice from my fingers. I was trying to appear far more sure of myself than I truly felt. Though I cared for Sam, I dreaded a future in Bruin. It was better for Agramon to think I was engaging in heartless intrigue than for him to know my fears.

"You are playing a very dangerous game, my dear," Agramon said, his nostrils flaring. "The Butcher of Bruin is not a man to be trifled with."

"It was either let me be controlled by him, or by you," I said. "At least Sam likes me. At least he wouldn't hurt me."

Agramon leaned his staff against the table and stretched his arm over the back of the couch. "You believe that? That he wouldn't hurt you?"

I scooted farther away. "Yes, I do."

Agramon laughed outright. "Oh, my girl, you really are a fool. You don't know the Butcher like the rest of us. The man has . . . tendencies."

I frowned. "You've always tried to keep me from Sam. You're just worried that he'll hold more sway over me than you. As always, you think only of yourself."

"You're a stupid girl," Agramon said, taking another swig from his bottle. "Can't you see what is happening here? He's obsessed with you. I've seen it happen with him before. His wife took her life because he isolated her from all she held dear, her friends, her family, everyone she knew, then left her to fend for herself, trapped in the tower of Bruin. The poor girl went mad! Then the news broke of the baron's moral repugnance, and she snapped."

"Let me worry about Sam," I said. "What of your own intrigues? How was your evening?"

Agramon shrugged. "Uneventful until your Lord Destrian cornered me."

My heart stopped. "You spoke with Destrian alone?"

"Well, not alone." Agramon smiled at me. "There were plenty of people around."

"What did he want?"

"To know what it would take for you to be returned to Morgania."

I tried to mask the excitement creeping into my voice. "What did you say?"

"The truth," Agramon replied, taking another swig from his bottle. "I will never allow the lost heir of the Morganite throne to return. Who knows what havoc you would wreak if your clan found out. Right now, the land of Morgania is secure within the empire. I intend to see it remain that way."

It felt as though my blood had turned to ice. I swallowed, trying to collect my thoughts. "How long have you known?"

"From the beginning," Agramon said. "When I knew your quest was going to begin, I'd called Solston Navar to the palace and had him check on the progress of your journey through the Nightlands to make sure you were safe. I also needed to know when to leave in order to retrieve you, especially after we received word from Ayastaren that they meant to make an example of you. He'd found out when he saw your Lord Destrian studying the book in his rooms at night. Navar drew the same conclusions that Everett did and informed me immediately."

"Why did you not say anything?" I asked, biting my lip. I supposed I wasn't in danger. Agramon had known the entire time and hadn't spoken a word to the emperor. "Why say nothing until now?"

"It didn't benefit me to reveal it." Agramon shrugged. "It took an entire month to convince the emperor not to kill you like the seer wished. If he found out you were Morganite royalty, not even I could save you." I wondered that he did not use that knowledge to ensure my compliance. It had to have crossed his mind. Or perhaps he didn't make threats if he didn't intend to follow through. He didn't throw away valuable things.

"Does it not anger you that Destrian, your former lover, holds the seat that should be yours by familial rights?"

I looked away. "I'd just found out about my history when Ayastaren . . . when everything happened. I haven't really had cause to think of it since."

"Interesting," Duke Agramon murmured, stroking the back of the couch. "Are you really without any sense of ambition? What would your people say, if they knew?"

I glared at Duke Agramon, but he met my gaze. "Why should I care? My clan abandoned me."

Duke Agramon chuckled softly. "If you truly didn't care, you wouldn't show such strong emotion, either toward or against it. They would want you to seize the throne back, to take it from Consul Destrian and reclaim it as your own. You *know* this is what they would want, yet you're unwilling to capture it."

I shrugged. "I don't know how to rule as a consul. Luc was right, my father and clan were right—I'd be a terrible leader."

Duke Agramon raised his brows. "That hasn't stopped anyone before. Just because heirs train over time to lead, doesn't mean that others can't learn."

My nostrils flared. "I have no wish to gain power in such an underhanded way."

"I never said you had to steal it," Duke Agramon said softly. "What if it was gifted to you, as a favor, for . . . services rendered."

"What kind of services?" I asked, narrowing my eyes. "Bringing the rain? If that's the case, then every lord and lady east of the Ballerian should be offering me their seats."

Duke Agramon glanced at the door before his eyes came back to rest on me. "Maybe for bringing the rain, maybe for loyalty."

I raised a brow. "Loyalty to whom?"

"To those who have clothed you, fed you, who have brought you into your power and showed you every comfort."

But I was done with the conversation. "I wouldn't steal Destrian's seat from him."

"As his family stole it from you?"

"Stop trying to twist my mind for your whims. Stop

trying to sow discord between Destrian and me. He's a good man. He will be a good consul to the people of Morgania."

"It still amazes me that you have such little faith in yourself. After all you've been through, after all you've accomplished, you still think that you are some low street wretch about to have your throat slit by the empire."

"I will not betray Destrian in such a way, no matter what you say."

"As he betrayed you? He kept this information from you for a year, biding his time to figure out what to do with you. Do you really think he would've stooped to court you if your ancestry was as menial as you imagined? Do you honestly believe he would've let his feelings grow into what they became were you not of royal blood?"

Agramon chuckled, then took another swig. "He may be a good man, but he's not without ambition, as you so clearly are. He thought only of solidifying his claim to Morgania. The fact that he was attracted to your . . ." Agramon drew his eyes over my body. "Assets . . . was simply a bonus. Trust me, my dear, I see where his thoughts truly lie, and duty to his people is what drew him to you, nothing more."

His words were barbs in my armor. He meant to wound me, and he had. I tried not to show Agramon how his words affected me. He could be lying. He would say anything to keep me close at hand. But what if he wasn't? What if Destrian's love for me was a lie easily tainted, not because I'd told him to move on but because his power over me was stripped from him?

Agramon sat up, the bottle dangling from one hand. His fingers moved from the back of the couch to my shoulder. He scooted closer, his fingertip stroking my skin.

"Your Lord Destrian, the Butcher, Lord Achille. It strikes me that none of them are worthy of you. Now you say you have no wish to return home, to reclaim your throne. Honestly, I can't think of one good reason why I shouldn't just keep you myself."

I wanted to throw Agramon's hands off me. I wanted to rage around the room or fly out of the window, far from the palace and all the evils within, but I could tell that Agramon was waiting for me to respond that way. He was waiting to see what I would do.

What was it Sam had said? Agramon planned for every eventuality. I had to do what he never expected. I let Agramon's fingers continue on their path toward my throat. My breath was shallow as I tried to gauge a response. He was letting his guard down. If I wanted to act, I should act soon.

My mind went back to Ena. A skilled hunter would let their prey close to them so that when they struck, they wouldn't have time to react.

Agramon leaned forward and kissed the corner of my mouth softly.

I fought the revulsion I felt at his touch. Freedom was so close, I could taste it. I needed Agramon to remain comfortable. If that meant letting him kiss me or put his hands on me, I would endure it. Freedom was worth far more than a moment's discomfort. "What would the emperor say to such a union?"

"Perhaps the emperor won't have a say in it for long," Agramon murmured into my ear.

I threw caution to the wind. "What are you planning?"

Agramon gripped my chin and turned my face to his. "Wouldn't you love to know," he whispered. His thumb pressed into my lips. "Don't worry about anything, my pet. I will take care of all of it."

Agramon rose, leaving me on the couch while he walked to his room and shut the door behind him.

I sat on the couch for a long time, staring at the door, fear needling through my veins. The blue bottle sat next to me. I lifted it to my lips and took a long swig. I was getting in too deep. So deep that I wondered if the empress would be able to get me out.

Chapter 32

"THEY'VE TAKEN TO THE CITY," Elgar the Swift said in my dream, his voice low as he watched those around them. He ran a hand through his stark-white hair. "A large faction of the Sons of Sol are protesting in the temple district as we speak. They are claiming the attack in Solin, and there are rumors that they will make a show sometime during the celebrations."

Agramon shrugged. "The army is in the city now. Perhaps the Butcher can be convinced to send them to round up the leaders."

"Bald Walden's been trying to keep them in line, but it's difficult when most of his men believe the Sons of Sol speak the truth. Nobody trusts that little sorceress."

"What of Berinon?" Agramon murmured.

"He's had a breakthrough with the powder."

"He's certainly taken his time with it," Agramon hissed. "None too soon."

Suddenly, the room turned. I almost cried out in my sleep for Echo to stop. When she looked over her shoulder, I realized what had her spooked.

Pythia Golden-Eyes, the necromancer who could see and speak to the dead, had joined Agramon and

Elgar.

Echo floated through the crowd until she came up-on Sam standing with Captain Diardo, General Ivar, and a towering man with light hair I didn't recognize.

"I can't believe no one thought to notify us," Sam was saying to Captain Diardo. "We look like idiots to all the nobles here!"

"He made the decision while I was bedridden," Captain Diardo said, leaning on his cane.

I had a pang of regret when I saw how much he'd changed since we'd been gone. When I'd first met the captain, he'd been devastatingly handsome, his gray eyes filled with mischief. Since his injury, he'd seemed to age a decade. I wondered what type of poison they'd used that would evade the skills of Tristam the Miraculous. He was the best healer in the empire.

"By the time I'd found out about it, the others on the council were acting like it was old news. I assumed they'd told you about it. We received no word that you were still amassing forces."

General Ivar took a drink from his glass and shook his head. "I'll be sending the Marysian forces home immediately. No sense in paying for them to trample the fields around the capitol. What about the fleet, Admiral Abelard?"

The man I didn't recognize shrugged. "We'll remain docked for now. Who knows when the man might change his mind again? I'm going to continue having them scout and patrol the coasts, just in case Lu Shen decides to strike despite the peace offering."

Sam was nodding. I felt like I recognized the name Abelard. It was fleeting, but I was sure I'd heard it somewhere.

"There are battalions of mercenaries that I will keep," Sam said. "Of those who fight professionally, I'll have them stay, but the farmers and workmen who have only come because they were convinced to, I will send back."

"What of the conscripted?" Admiral Abelard asked.

"They will go to the fields of Bruin," Sam said. "The harvest promises to be fruitful now that we've had steady rain."

"But how long will that last?" Captain Diardo muttered as General Ivar and Admiral Abelard turned away, talking to each other in low voices. Diardo scanned the room. Echo followed his gaze and saw me standing with Pedr, talking animatedly.

"I'm trying to get her to see reason," Sam said, watching me. "If I can convince her to accept my proposal, I'll commission the emperor immediately. We were fools to trust her care to the duke. He's used her our entire trip and worked diligently to turn her against me."

Diardo took a drink. "The council might insist on

having a say in who she weds, if Agramon decides to make a fuss."

"I know," Sam said. "You will back me, won't you?"

Diardo's nostrils flared. "I've told you how I feel about the girl. Who's to say Agramon hasn't put her up to drawing you in?"

"She's not like that," Sam said. "He can't enchant her, and she trusts him less than I do."

"The soldiers are restless about her," Diardo said. "Are you prepared to give up your command for her hand?"

Sam took another drink. "I would, if it came to that."

Diardo nodded. "Then I will back you, though it means you would be off the council too."

Sam shrugged. "I'm prepared to give up more."

Diardo sighed.

Sam looked at him. "You of all people should know what love does to a man."

"I do," Diardo said, his voice guarded. "It makes fools of us all."

I ROLLED OVER IN BED, RUBBING the sleep from my eyes. I'd collapsed in my golden gown, and now it was crushed. If I liked Gree I would've felt bad that I'd given her more work to do to care for the gown. As it was . . .

"Echo?" I whispered after listening for sounds in the other room. Though the shadow-soul had given me the silent treatment while we were in Bruin, Echo returned to her usual self after I'd broken things off with Sam. I wondered why she would approve of Destrian while showing such marked distaste for Sam, but she was never really clear on why she disliked him so much.

Arden opened her eyes and swiveled her head around on her perch.

"I am here," Echo whispered. "His Grace is awake."

I gritted my teeth. I'd hoped Agramon was still asleep or, even better, gone for the day. I didn't know what to make of his kiss from the night before. Would he remember? Was Agramon serious about marrying me?

I got out of bed and went to the door. Opening it, I found Agramon speaking low with Gree. They both looked up as I entered. Gree scowled at my wrinkled gown.

"What is on the schedule for today?" I asked.

"I must go to a council meeting," Agramon said, his brows raised. "There is a women's luncheon today, a grand one given all the visiting nobles. The masquerade is tonight. It will be a very grand ball. I figured that you would appreciate your rest, seeing as we've only just gotten back."

He meant he wanted to keep me hidden, away from my friends. I saw right through his little "I care about you" charade. "I would like to see Del," I lied. I didn't care about Del, but Agramon did.

Agramon sighed. "Very well. If you must go be with the ladies, then so be it. Gree will attend you. I need to leave for the council immediately."

He gave away nothing as he strode from the room. None of his words the night before were uttered, but still, it felt as though something had changed between us. I couldn't waste my advantage. I needed to speak with the empress. I needed her help in finding a safe way out of the city. There was no way for me to master this alone.

"Get me ready," I ordered Gree, trying to wrestle myself out of the dress. "Where did you disappear off to last night?"

"His Grace ordered me to retrieve the rest of your quinquennial gowns," Gree snapped, unlacing the back of my gown and helping me step out of it. "He said that when I returned, the rest of the evening was my own." Had he been planning on seducing me? I'd wondered if his words the night before had been delivered in the moment due to his drinking. Had he planned it all along? What could that mean?

458

In short order, Gree had me bathed and dressed in a morning gown. The light blue brought out the color of my eyes. My hair she half plaited, letting the rest fall to my waist in a straight river of ebony. After some light paint on my face, I was practically running out of the door and down to the gardens.

I slowed when I reached the mob of women laughing and dining on light delicacies. The empress stood among them, Mem at her back, ensuring that each woman was welcomed. There was still a mob around her, so I scanned the room for another face, but someone else found me first.

"Rowyn!" Del screeched, practically skipping to me. "I was trying to catch your attention last night, but you were never without a companion!"

"Del," I said, my bright voice ringing all too false to my ears. "How has it been at the capitol? How is the Crystal Temple?"

Del wrapped her arm around mine. "It is finished, just in time for the celebrations too. Emperor Arthello has insisted that we reveal it as part of the quinquennial. He asked Solston Gowther to deliver a sermon and make quite a thing of it. It will be toward the end of the celebrations though. You know how Miyu is. She prefers to have her hand in everything and can't abide having her plans altered."

Del went on and on about Miyu's preparations for

the quinquennial and how put out Del had been at being asked to alter the columns within the throne room to accommodate the influx of guests that were scheduled to arrive. Never once did she ask about my journey with Agramon. Never once did she even draw breath from talking of her own needs and emotions.

As Del prattled on, I searched the garden for familiar faces. Ingrid was there. I was happy to see her tucked away in a corner with Ellora, looking nervous when it came to meeting the noblewomen of the eastern shore.

There, I'd found Araceli standing with her mother, the bracelet glinting from her mother's arm showing that she was a favored friend of the empress. Beside them was Countess Mahira, the lady of Ardent who'd helped me end the war.

"Excuse me," I murmured to Del. She was mid-sentence in describing the light fixtures her lover, Sparks, had assisted her in making for the temple. Del looked perturbed but released my arm and let me make my way to the other group of women.

All of them curtsied when I arrived.

I furrowed my brow. "What is this formality?"

Araceli glanced at her mother. "We are just trying to give credit where it is due, Rowyn. We are grateful to you."

"Thank you," I murmured, my eyes on the ground.

"It means a lot to hear you say that."

Countess Mahira grinned, grabbing a candle from the table and lighting a pipe hanging from her mouth with it. "Are you not pleased with how things have progressed since we parted last?" she asked, blowing smoke into the air. "I told you I would help, and now there is no war. A promise made, a promise fulfilled."

"Hush," Araceli's mother, Violeta of Calla, hissed. "What if someone were to hear you?"

"Is there anything wrong with celebrating a victory?" Mahira asked, her hands wide. "I challenge any of these women to correct me."

"You mustn't be so obvious." Violeta eyed the others who seemed to be engaged in their own conversations. "There is still much to be done."

"I need to speak to the empress," I said, realizing that both Mahira and Violeta would be able to relay the message. "Things are happening quickly.

"What is it, Rowyn?" Araceli asked.

I shook my head, pitching my voice low. "Agramon is acting . . . not himself." It was far too risky to reveal the real reason that I wished to speak to Empress Lesedi. I couldn't give away my plans of escape to Araceli or anyone else. The empress was protected from Agramon through stones of her own. Requesting assistance from anyone else would be a liability.

Mahira lowered her arms and took the pipe from her

mouth. "What has he said?"

"He wonders why he should not marry me himself," I said, meeting each of their eyes.

Araceli and her mother exchanged pointed glances.

"It was only a matter of time," Violeta said. "Why should he sell you as a bride if he can take you freely? The eastern lords aren't interested in you, and Agramon cares nothing for anything the lords of the west can offer him."

"He said he turned Destrian away last night," I whispered, refusing to let tears fall. "I would've thought the wealth of Morgania would've at least given him pause."

Araceli put her hand on my arm. "Morgania is wealthy now as the only land that escaped the drought, but since you're here, and the drought is over, that wealth will be shared by others. Morgania will not be so great a prospect when that happens."

I sniffed. "Ingrid . . . Are she and him . . . ?"

Araceli shook her head as Violeta and Mahira began murmuring together. I should've probably been listening to them, but I had to know.

"Tell me," I ordered, gripping Araceli's hand.

"When they all came to the capitol for the celebrations, I wondered the same thing, but she was exaggerating what was happening in Helena. Her entire family stayed to help Destrian, even when he asked that they leave, numerous times. She's been trying to recapture his interest."

"I don't know why I care so much," I admitted. "It's not like there's hope for us anyway."

"Don't say that," Araceli whispered. "There is still his oath's gift. Perhaps the emperor will be in a giving mood."

I raised my brows. "Do you know what he will ask for?"

Araceli shook her head. "It's his most closely guarded secret. Ingrid told me that Destrian and Vianne would meet almost every morning—"

"Vianne?" I asked. "Why did she remain?"

Araceli looked over her shoulder, as though checking for eavesdroppers. "I asked Destrian that very thing. He said that Vianne was training him to go against Agramon. He can't keep everything from his sight, but he can keep the important things hidden. Like his next move."

"Araceli," I whispered. "Is there hope for us?"

Araceli bit her lip. "I don't know, but he thinks so. Talk to him tonight, at the mask. Ask him yourself."

I nodded. If anything else, I could finally apologize for how I'd left him.

"Rowyn," Violeta said, resting her hand on my arm. "The empress is about to retire. Perhaps you should make your way back to your rooms?" she said pointedly. I squeezed Araceli's hand and walked hurriedly before the empress. I waited inside the doors, shifting from one foot to the next, until Ledi appeared beside me.

"Come," she said, taking my hand. "I'm to escort you."

"How has it been since I've been gone?" I asked, following the girl. "How are Princess Willene's lessons?"

Ledi rolled her eyes. "She's become more insufferable since the approach of the quinquennial. She finds fault with everything I do, and each of her sermons always seems to end with, I'm a girl and a foreigner, so what I do will change no one's mind anyway."

"I'm sorry you have to put up with her," I said sincerely. "Have you tried to speak with your father about getting a new instructor?"

Ledi shrugged. "What's the point? He doesn't ever listen to any of us. I barely see him anymore."

"Ledi," I began, feeling as though I'd abandoned her. "I'm so sorry you have to do this."

"It's not your fault," Ledi said, stopping outside her mother's chambers. I opened the door for her. "It's just the way of things."

I entered and found the little prince asleep on the couch. Princess Eladia was helping her nurse water the plants near the arched windows. Ledi skipped over to help, and I took a seat on the couch, my leg bouncing up and down. I was anxious to finally speak to the empress after so long. If anyone could help me, she could.

When the doors opened, I stood. Mem peered in, nodding to me before widening the doors for the empress to stride through.

"Rowyn," the empress said, holding her hand out to me.

I was taken aback, but I took it and kissed her fingers. "Empress Lesedi, there is much to say." I took a seat as she did.

"Indeed," Empress Lesedi agreed. "We've been greatly interested in the stories of your travels. Some of us more than others."

I wondered about her meaning, but then I saw that Mem was standing behind her with the biggest grin I'd ever seen on her face.

"I really looked forward to the reports of your latest kill," Mem said, her eyes sparkling.

The empress rolled her eyes. It seemed that she did not agree with my behavior.

"My favorite one was the skin-trader." Mem began to laugh. "A dagger to the nuts . . . classic work, that is."

"I did not stab him in the nuts." I shook my head. "But I'm glad someone is pleased with me," I added, trying to hide my smile when the empress shot me a glare. "I can assure you that Agramon was . . . less than pleased."

"And the other one?" Mem said. "I knew you had the grit to go after a lord. I wonder why you did not stop in Nordow and Perth. I half expected a trail of dead nobles across the empire!"

"Enough," Empress Lesedi said, waving her hands toward the children. She turned to me. "You know I would've found a way to meet soon enough for a report, but what is so urgent that it couldn't have waited until after the quinquennial? There are more eyes and ears than normal."

"You have to help me," I said under my breath. "It's urgent."

"What is it?" Lesedi asked as the princesses filed into the next room. All except the young prince, who was still asleep on the cushions.

"You promised if I helped, you would aid my escape," I said. "The war is no longer an issue, nor is the drought. I learned almost every deal that Agramon made. I want to leave during the quinquennial. It's the perfect time, what with the city overfull and unknown people coming and going."

Lesedi frowned. "Why so soon? You ended the drought for this year, but what about next? You ended the war with Lu Shen, but what happens if Yliria breaks their treaty?"

"Agramon spoke of marrying me himself," I said. "You know if that happens, I will never get away."

The empress sighed. "I will need time."

"We don't have time!" I hissed, rising to pace the room. "It's as though the walls are closing in. He's spurned Destrian's suit, and now the Baron of Bruin is trying to appeal to the emperor to wed me. Agramon already sees that there are no better options than to marry me himself, and he will do it quickly! The emperor will probably have to choose between Agramon's suit and Sam's by the end of the month, and I would prefer to marry neither!"

"You made your bed with the Baron of Bruin," Empress Lesedi said, her voice icy. "Now you have to lie in it."

"What's that supposed to mean?" I asked as Mem cleared her throat, standing at attention behind Lesedi, trying to look impassive.

"You chose to stay in Bruin with him instead of going with Agramon to Gryse. What did you expect but for him to become attached? The entire empire knows what went on there!"

"You think I should've gone to Gryse?" I asked, my brows furrowed. "What was there for me? I would've been in Agramon's hold with no protection! It was Sam who kept me safe!"

The empress stood, her voice tinged with anger.

"The Count of Gryse has a mercenary's fleet two hundred masts strong. I needed to know what kind of deal Agramon was making with him! Did your shadow, Echo, find *anything* out about it?"

"No," I said, "it's too far for her to reach."

Empress Lesedi balled her hand into a fist. "That was the one piece of information I needed to pin Agramon with treason, and the chance has slipped from our grasp. What made you stay in Bruin?"

"I'd just been kidnapped," I exclaimed, flinging my hand out. "I had no wish to go to some lecher's port. You never told me that you were focused primarily on Gryse."

"I didn't think I had to," the empress said, shaking her head. "I told you I needed information. I thought you would've known that you needed to go."

I'd never felt so . . . deflated. I'd failed the empress. I didn't even know what to say. Thinking back now, she was right. I should've known to go. I should've been stronger. I'd let her and everyone else in the empire down. My plan was beginning to unravel. "I'm sorry," I said. "I didn't realize—"

"Of course, you didn't," Lesedi snapped, her eyes flashing. "This entire time you've only thought to save your own skin. Others are counting on us, you know. My children's lives are at stake!"

"There have been other deals!" I exclaimed. "I can

give you Perth, and Calla, and—"

"I already know about them," Lesedi said. "Your shadow passed them to me in dreams last night. She gave me quite a bit of information."

I eyed the empress. "Did she show you Agramon? Did she show what he said to me?"

Empress Lesedi refused to meet my eye. "Please, Empress," I pleaded, "an opportunity like this won't come again. I've secured Agramon's regard. He won't expect me to run away again, I know it. We could even plant evidence that Yliria took me like they tried to do in Bruin, or Lu Shen, or even the Sons of Sol. The gods only know they've been wanting to get their hands on me for months! While Agramon looks for me there, I could make my escape. It wouldn't even have to be that hard!"

Empress Lesedi merely shook her head. "The quinquennial means that more people are watching me. I cannot chance it, not with Agramon and the commander already suspecting my interference."

I thought back to Sam accusing me of spying for the empress. "Echo showed that to you?"

Empress Lesedi finally met my eye, but her expression offered little comfort. I couldn't breathe for a moment. Empress Lesedi wouldn't help me. I didn't know why I ever thought she would. She used me, just like everyone else. I just stood there like an idiot, shaking my head, warring with the feeling that I should just throw myself out of the window and hope my powers didn't catch me.

"You knew he was going to do this, didn't you? You knew that he would try to marry me in the end."

"I suspected it," Lesedi admitted. "That's not the same as knowing."

"So, what now?" I asked. "You'll just abandon me to him?"

Lesedi glared at me. "I don't know if I would call it that," she said. "You now wield infinitely more power and influence than me. Are you really telling me that you can't take care of yourself?"

"I trusted you," I said, unable to keep the disbelief from my voice. "We had a deal."

Lesedi tipped her head to the side. "That's the thing about deals. Each side has to hold up their end of the bargain. Ask Your Grace. He'll tell you."

Suddenly, the air at Lesedi's side shimmered and Prince Artian appeared. I stepped back, my brows furrowed, trying to understand what I'd just seen. He hadn't been hiding behind his mother's skirts, nor did I notice him crawling across the floor. He was just suddenly there, where before there was nothing.

I looked from Prince Artian, clinging to his mother's skirts, to the empress, whose wide eyes were begging me, no pleading, to ignore what I'd just seen.

I understood. Mahira had said that Lord Obi was both her and the empress's grandfather. "Is he?" I asked, pointing at the prince.

"Forget what you just saw," Mem said, her voice deadly as she stepped toward me. "Nobody knows of this, not even his father."

I raised my hands, turned on my heel, and strode from the room, my mind roiling and my heart torn.

Only a few moments had passed, and so much had come to light. The empress and I had failed each other, I was on my own against Agramon, and the young heir of Lyrica was a league leaper.

Chapter 33

I SAT AND PONDERED in the large tub while Gree scrubbed my first layer of skin off. How had I never heard that the heir of Lyrica was a league leaper? Agramon never mentioned such a thing, nor Del, nor anyone else. Could it be possible that the empress had been able to keep it a secret for so long? Why? Wouldn't that put the boy in danger?

I sighed, thinking back to my meeting with the empress. It stung to hear that she'd been less than impressed with the efforts I'd made on her behalf during my journey across the empire. Escaping was something I'd have to manage on my own. It was even more imperative now that Agramon was talking about marrying me.

Gree toweled me off and rubbed scented oils into my skin before tugging me into my bedchamber where she pulled a chemise over my head and tightened a corset behind me. When she finished, she stood to the side, her head bowed.

I looked to the bedroom door when Agramon strode in. "When was the last time you spoke to Vianne?" he asked, his staff clenched in his fist.

I stared at him in shock. "Why do you ask, Your

Grace?"

Agramon stepped forward, a muscle in his jaw jumping. "Do not push me on this. When was the last time you spoke with her?" He raised his staff under my chin, tilting it up. The gem at the end was glowing furiously, though Agramon still could not read my mind. "Has she written you? Have you seen her?"

"I've not spoken to Vianne since I left Solridge for the Last Dusk."

"You don't know what she is up to with the Dragon of Morgania?"

I raised my brows. Araceli had told me of Vianne's involvement with Destrian. "I've not spoken to Destrian apart from our meeting that you witnessed," I said honestly.

Agramon studied me a moment longer before releasing my chin and nodding to Gree, who sat me down in front of the mirror and began plaiting my hair around the crown of my head in an intricate weave. Agramon sat and watched, absentmindedly running his fingers along the back of Arden's head. Every once in a while, Gree would turn, looking to Agramon for approval. Agramon's directives to my maid were silent as he fed Arden scraps of bacon I'd saved from breakfast.

"It wasn't enough to abandon me," Agramon said, almost to himself as he looked to the city below. "Now she has to actively seek to undermine me."

His mind seemed to be plagued with Vianne's inter-ference. I glanced at the staff leaning against the wall. It was too soon to tell if putting Agramon on edge would help or hinder my escape. "Undermine you with what?" I asked innocently. Gree met my eyes in the mirror and I looked away. I had no allies in the room, save Arden, but now she was nuzzling Agramon's hand.

Traitor.

"I want you to be honest with me," Agramon said, crossing his ankle over his knee. "Why am I so hard to love?"

My nostrils flared. I'd never seen Agramon so vul-nerable. I didn't think he was capable of worrying about love. Perhaps I'd been wrong.

Agramon seemed to mark my feelings. "I saw the way you looked at me last night. The Butcher and I are so similar, yet you hold nothing but disgust for me and him in high regard. It's had me baffled ever since you arrived."

I turned to Gree. "Leave us."

Gree glanced to Agramon, who nodded, then she hurried from my bedroom, shutting the door quietly behind her. When I was sure that she was gone, I rose from the looking glass. "You asked me once, why I never questioned why you sought more power." I was attempting to be diplomatic. I figured accusing him of overthrowing the emperor wouldn't go over too well. "I want to know now, what is it you seek?"

Agramon stood, sweeping his robes behind him. "You surprise me that you do not already know the answer."

"I want to hear it from you."

"They didn't merely turn me away from the academy at Somme. They spoke of killing me."

I sucked in a breath. "Killing you?"

Agramon nodded. "The man who headed the academy at the time, Theobald Earth-Shaker, thought I would be too much of a liability. He put a price on my head, and only through the intervention of the old Duke of Solin did the price get lifted." He met my eyes. "I learned young that it is better to be feared than be afraid. I vowed then to never allow myself to be put in that position again."

I finally felt as though I understood Agramon. He was constantly seeking power so that nobody else could have power over him. There was sorrow in his life to pity, but no matter how tragic his history, no matter how alike we were, I could never forgive him for Ena. She'd been innocent. To conquer villains, Agramon had become one. I refused to let myself follow in his footsteps.

No. I could never side with Agramon. I only had a few more days before I could be rid of him altogether. I had to wait it out. I thought back to Maryse, how pleased Agramon had been when I allowed us to work together. That was when he'd trusted me the most. All he'd ever asked of me was to play into his hand. He may not reveal the cards altogether, but if he felt we were allies again, he would lower his guard.

"What do you need from me?" I asked, stepping toward him.

Agramon's breath slowed as we stared at each other. "Now? During the quinquennial?"

"Now . . . in the future . . . What is it you desire from me?"

Agramon stepped closer. "Trust that I will take care of you."

"What would you have me do about the others?" I asked. "What of Sam? Destrian?"

"If they stop playing games, maybe I will let you choose."

"And if they don't?" I held my breath.

"Then I would have you marry me."

"You've gone about this the wrong way, you know," I said, closing the distance between us. "For someone who claims to understand others so well, I wonder that you did not see why I preferred Sam to you. I know what he could offer me. I know what Luc and Destrian and Mellan Lyon could offer, but what of you? What is it you can give me that the others can't?"

Agramon clenched his hands at his sides. "Stop playing coy, Rowyn. I can give you the empire, and you know that."

I tilted my head to the side. "I have demands."

"What are they?"

"I don't want to fear you anymore."

Agramon searched my eyes. "Very well," he said softly. "You do not need to fear me."

"No more threats on those I care about?" I asked. I'd grown more uneasy with Destrian at Somme. I wouldn't have put it past Agramon to unseat or assassinate him if he became too much of a problem. I had only to think of the Earl of Nordow to foresee that.

Agramon shook his head.

"Then perhaps we can make a deal," I said, arching an eyebrow.

"Be careful," Agramon whispered, running a finger along my chin. "If you betray me, I will hold nothing back."

It was what Vianne had done. It was what I had every intention of doing. I couldn't let myself become bound to him . . . but if we were allies, I might be able to persuade him to my cause.

What cause? All I'd ever wanted was freedom. I'd never given thought to beyond that. If survival was my only prerogative, then maybe escape *wasn't* the answer. Agramon spoke of an end to my fear.

So far, out of all my suitors, he'd given me the best offer.

AGRAMON HELD UP MY HAND as we descended the stairs into the grand ballroom. I heard gasps as courtiers craned their necks. Next to me, Agramon was draped in robes of white and gold. His mask covered everything but his mouth. Large sunrays, layered one over the other, framed his sinister eyes.

My dress was the color of the night sky. The bodice was the deepest black but faded to indigo at my waist, before fading to a deep blue at my feet. The skirt was so voluminous, the weight of it was sure to mark my hips. Sewn over the skirt in a swirl to look like the night sky were the tiniest silver beads that sparkled in the light of the ballroom. My mask covered my eyes and half my face in a silver crescent, the face of Imor.

I scanned the crowd. Miyu caught my eye and winked in approval. Del shot me a wide smile, her eyes sparkling in delight, but I moved past her, looking for that flash of red I knew so well. My heart fell. Perhaps he knew that to be here would be folly for both of us.

I ignored the emperor and empress who were mingling with the crowd. Though they'd both donned masks, Mem and the emperor's bodyguard had not. They wouldn't risk their sight being compromised. The emperor was already in his cups by the time I'd arrived and was singing a raucous song with some young courtiers in the corner, while the musicians tried to keep up the beat. The empress looked toward me, along with Mem, whose eyes were filled with warning. I ignored them. I was on my own now. It was up to me to rescue myself. In the end, I'd known it would come to this. It was foolish to look for hope in anyone else.

We joined the crowd. I tried to disguise the nervous energy that seemed to pulse through me. Agramon had taken my bait. He thought we were allied and that I would willingly bow to his commands. I shuddered to think about what he would do when he found out I betrayed him. I was beginning to second-guess myself. Should I betray him? Would it be wise to run away? Could I ever mold my own happiness under his yoke?

Agramon seemed to bask in the admiration the courtiers had for our costumes. Despite the rose-colored gem on Agramon's brow and the silken robes cut in the finest styles of the empire, Agramon had always made himself utterly forgettable. Had he not had his power, you wouldn't have given him a second glance. Now he was all sparkling eyes and white-teethed smiles.

When a dance began, Agramon pulled me onto the ballroom floor, sweeping me around to show off the volume of the skirt he'd spent a significant amount of gold on. "This came together better than I expected," he said, smiling as we spun around the room.

I looked up at him and smiled. "We'll be the talk of the court."

Agramon's nostrils flared. "You look divine. I'm impressed with your improvement, my dear."

"Of course, all of my improvements are due to you." I hoped I wasn't laying it on too thick.

Agramon's eyes flicked to my mouth, then back up to me. "The game is not yet won." He dropped his hand to my waist. "I want you to find Lyon. You two should dance at some point tonight. His father has mentioned increasing pursuit of you. I want to know what he thinks he can offer."

"I would be delighted, my lord," I said automatically. I looked over the crowd and realized Agramon had given me an impossible task. How was I to know Mellan from a guard? Everyone was masked.

"Rowyn," Agramon began, but the song was ending. I waited, my eyebrows raised, but Agramon shook his head. "Find Mellan," was all he said before he disappeared into the crowd.

I glanced around, but Mellan was probably three drinks into the night already. It was a halfhearted effort. Instead, I meandered over to the refreshment table.

A figure in a black overcoat was watching me, leaning against one of the marble pillars, his arms crossed over his chest. Their mask bore a dragon with black scales and a mouth twisted into a snarl. A few locks of red hair peeked from around it.

Heat burned up my throat. I was sure he could hear the hammering of my heart that deafened my ears as the music swelled around us.

Destrian straightened and stepped toward me. I was frozen to the spot, my heart caught in a tight grip.

He stopped and took my hand. Bending, he kissed my fingers. "My lady," he murmured, glancing up at me through the mask.

It was then that I remembered to breathe.

"My lord," was all I could choke out.

Destrian's fingers lingered on mine, brushing them gently. "You're trembling," he whispered. "What is it you're afraid of?"

"Destrian, I can't be seen talking to you," I hissed. I glanced at the side where I'd marked Sam, sitting in a bear mask, deep in conversation with General Ivar, then to Agramon who held a goblet as he watched me from his seat beside Elgar the Swift.

"Then by all means, let us not be caught talking," Destrian said, his voice dripping with defiance. He wouldn't release my hand. Instead, he pulled me with him through the crowd until we reached the dancers.

Heat burned my cheeks as Destrian seized my waist,

leading me in with a spin. I'd waited so long for a moment with him that I couldn't tear myself away.

I had so many questions but only some that I wasn't afraid to ask. "How is Morgania? How has the beginning of your consulship gone?" I should've known nothing was safe to talk about when it came to Destrian and me.

"When you left, I burned half the forest of Morgania, then stayed in my room for a time," Destrian said, his voice husky.

"Then what?" I asked, curious what he had to say about his father's death, about Ingrid, about Vianne, but all Destrian gave me was the barest shrug.

"Then, I waited for you to send word," he said, his eyes flitting over my face as though trying to memorize it. "I waited for months for you to let me know you were all right, that you missed me, that you wanted me to come get you. Yet, there was nothing."

"It was too dangerous," I whispered, trying to guard my words, aware that it wasn't just Agramon and Sam's eyes upon us. Sam's regard for me was a bit of a joke at the capitol, and all who gathered had heard of my travels with Lord Destrian in the Nightlands. Many watched behind their masks, eager to see them come to throes. I was their next entertainment, simply a game for their amusement. "They will never let you have me."

"I know," he breathed into my ear. "But no matter how many times you break me, I know I'm destined to run back. I'll never forgive myself for not following you on the road that day."

I looked up at him. "There's nothing to be done. I'm Agramon's property now."

"Don't say that. I've thought of you every day since. Every day, Rowyn."

"Don't make this harder than it has to be, my lord," I murmured. I'd give anything to go back in time, but it was too late. Agramon would never let me go to Destrian unscathed. It was best if I left everything and everyone behind. They would all be better off without me anyway. Agramon wouldn't have a pawn to use to take over court, Sam wouldn't have a pariah turning the soldiers against him, and Destrian wouldn't have a threat to his consulship. I was cursed, and the kindest thing I could do for everyone involved was run away.

"My love," Destrian whispered in my ear.

"Don't call me that," I said, thinking back to Bruin. "I don't deserve it."

"You're shaking." Destrian pulled me tighter. "Rowyn, what's the matter?"

"I waited for you, Destrian. Every night I would watch the bay with Iranoct, hoping it would change direction, hoping you would find me. Save me. But now I fear I'm lost to you forever."

"I know," Destrian said gruffly. "I dreamed about it last night."

I stiffened.

"How many of them followed you?"

"Just one," I said. I wished Echo would stop interfering. She was bound to get someone hurt with her meddling.

"What have they done to you?" Destrian asked, watching my eyes dart around the room. "What are you so afraid of?"

"Don't mistake my fear," I said, trying to keep my voice formal. I thought back to Agramon's words. It was better to be feared than to be afraid. "I'm not scared for myself."

"So, it's true," Destrian said. "You were trying to save me."

I looked away, but Destrian gripped my hand tighter. "Don't do that," he growled. "You could at least do me the courtesy of not hiding. I think I deserve the truth."

He lifted his arm, expertly spinning me. The colors of my gown and the silver thread of the stars caught the light from the chandeliers in a burst of color. Destrian spun me back in and clutched me to him as the music swelled faster.

"I waited for you to write," Destrian said, searching for emotions behind my mask. "I waited for an explanation ... an apology ... anything. When it didn't come, I began to despair. By the time I received my summoning for the quinquennial, word had reached Morgania of the Butcher of Bruin's partiality to a certain young Morganite girl. A sorceress, whose fate bound the land to her."

I glanced at Sam. He and General Ivar had ended their discussion, and Sam was slouched in his chair, the bear mask discarded at his side, his mouth resting on one hand while the other gripped the arm of his chair with white knuckles. His green eyes narrowed when he saw me looking. I wished I could read the emotion in his eyes, but he closed them to me before glancing toward the other dancers.

"Why didn't you give me a chance?" Destrian demanded.

"What could you have done?" I asked, a tear threatening the corner of my eye. "They would've tried you for rising against your overlord. You would've lost Morgania! Everything you've worked for! How can I claim to love you and let you give up everything for me?"

Destrian's voice caught in his throat. "So, you do love me," he whispered as the song ended. I tried to pull away, but he merely tightened his grip and continued stepping through the ring as the music started again, moving me away from Sam, from Agramon, and everything tethering me to the empire.

"Please," I whispered. "Please don't make it harder than it needs to be." Though Agramon had promised not to threaten those I loved, I had no cause to believe him. When he'd spoken to the Count of Gryse of Destrian, Agramon had mentioned taking the consulship from him. I didn't want to be the reason Agramon succeeded in that venture.

"I'll figure out how to get you out of here," Destrian said, his eyes boring into mine. "I'll do whatever it takes."

"Agramon will never just hand me over, Destrian. We'd have to steal away. Who would replace you if Helena was taken from your family? A Lyon? What would that do to your sisters? To my clan?"

"So, what now?" Destrian asked, choking on his words. "You ask me to simply let you go?"

"Remember your dreams for what Morgania could be?" I whispered. "If you love me, make it a reality."

"You know I would do anything for you," Destrian said, "but you can't ask me to abandon you to this fate."

I gave him a glimmer of a smile. "You know I don't believe in fate, Destrian. I'm trapped here because I have something Agramon wants. It's as simple as that."

Even though I was going to escape, I would never drag Destrian down with me. He was best for Morgania. He always had been. It was too much to ask for the both of us, to have him relinquish his duties in the name of love. There were countless lives at stake.

"If you don't believe in fate, what do you believe?"

A tear rolled down my cheek. I prayed the mask hid it from view as I smiled shakily at him. "I believe in you. I believe that you will be the best for Morgania and our people."

The song ended with a flourish.

Destrian gripped my hand when I began to step away. "Wait, just one more moment."

Sam stepped out of the crowd, and I pulled my hand from Destrian's as if scalded.

"You will overtire the lady," Sam said, his eyes on Destrian.

"You seem awfully invested in her welfare," Destrian replied, his voice tight. "Aren't there more *appropriate* companions you could be giving your attention to? Someone closer to your own age, perhaps?"

Sam straightened, but he was nowhere near the height of Destrian. Still, that didn't make him any less formidable. "I have the power of the Lyrican Army behind me, a force one hundred thousand strong."

I sucked in a breath. My heart sank at the realization that Sam had sounded exactly like Agramon.

"Meaning?" Destrian asked.

Sam's eyes sharpened. "Meaning I can do what I like." Sam held his arm to me. I glanced at Destrian, the need to protect him tugging at my heart. I took the offered arm, letting Sam lead me through the crowd. When we got to the doors of the balcony, he held it open and pushed me through. When we were clear of other courtiers, Sam turned on me with a scowl, backing me against the marble wall.

The hair on the back of my neck rose. He'd never been so forceful with me before.

"What did the boy want?" Sam asked, his hand above my head.

I gripped my skirt to control my shaking fingers. I'd never been afraid of Sam, until now. "He's not a boy, and he just wanted to talk."

Sam huffed. "A likely story."

"I was sending him away."

Sam glowered. "I'm a jealous man, Rowyn." He carefully pulled the strings from my ears and lifted the mask from my face. He dropped it unceremoniously to the ground and ran a finger along my chin.

"It's been over with us since Bruin," I whispered, hating the tremble in my voice.

Sam met my eye. "I'm not going to just step aside and let you fall in love with him again."

I clenched my teeth, hating the fear that began to well up. "I'm here with you, aren't I? What do you have to be jealous of? What *more* do you want from me?"

Sam leaned forward. "I want you in *my* arms," he

said, his lips brushing my neck. "I want to kiss you until you can think of no one else." He pressed his body against mine. "I want to make you shiver as you're moaning my name." Lifting his head, he ran his cheek along mine, his lips at my ear, his hot breath sending an involuntary shudder through my body. "But most of all, I want you to look at me the way you look at him."

My stomach coiled as he looked into my eyes, a fire burning in their depths. "Why do you insist on the one thing I could never give you?"

Sam's lips crashed into mine, insistent. I prayed that Destrian would stay away. I didn't want him set further in Sam's sights. Who knew the danger it would put him in regarding his standing with the emperor and army.

"Please," I whispered, trying to push him away.

Sam ran his fingers gently along my jaw and down my neck to my collarbone. "You know that I understand you better than he ever could."

My blood turned to ice. "I know."

Chapter 34

ECHO'S FOOTSTEPS WERE SILENT as she ventured down a familiar path, one I'd once treaded every morning. Dread coiled in my gut. She reached the familiar doors and melted through them, eying the dark empty room beyond. Toward the back was a door I'd never been through.

Echo melted through the door and into a bedroom. A fire was lit on the hearth, and Echo scurried to a dark corner, obviously afraid her shadow would give her away to the occupants. The lady with familiar flaxen hair and sharp blue eyes lounged on the bed in her chemise, her hair down instead of being held up in her usual cluster of curls. The man was seated at the side of the bed and was in the process of pulling on his boots. If I hadn't been dreaming, I was sure I would have gasped as Agramon rose, his chest bare.

The smell of sweat was evident in the room, and Princess Willene had a satisfied smile on her face as she rolled over, running her hand down Agramon's back.

"Must you leave so soon, Your Grace?" Princess Willene asked in a sultry voice. I thought I would vomit in my sleep.

"I'm due for the council meeting," Agramon said.

Though his voice dripped with regret, I could see the face he hid from Willene. He was impatient, ready to escape her presence.

"You prefer the presence of my fool of a brother to me?" Princess Willene asked, running her finger along his shoulder. "If I ran this empire, I'd force you to stay in bed." She rose, kissing his shoulder.

"You would make a beautiful empress," Agramon said, turning to Willene, his face a mask of seduction. "Just give me time," he murmured. "I'll see you on that throne yet."

"I'd do far better than that foreigner," Princess Willene said, pushing herself up in bed. "I've yet to see what my brother ever saw in her."

"Indeed." Agramon rolled his eyes as he pulled his silk tunic on. "But alas, till then, there is work to be done."

"You will not stay away?" Princess Willene asked, her brow arched. "There are rumors of you and that little sorceress. Impudent, ugly little thing that she is. I can't imagine what you all see in her."

"Rowyn has a great power, you know that. It's my job to see that this empire rises with her."

"So, the little chit means nothing to you?" Willene asked. "I saw you watching her last night. You were practically broiling in your breeches, Your Grace." She fingered his side, as though trying to be playful, but there was a sinister note to her tone that was impossible to miss.

Agramon sneered. "The Butcher of Bruin has been making things . . . difficult."

Willene rolled her eyes. "I don't see why he's still here. If the army is to be disbanded, shouldn't he return to Bruin?"

"He has to renew his vows, same as the rest of us." Agramon pulled on his outer robes. "Have faith, my sweet. Your patience will be rewarded tenfold."

"Promise?" Princess Willene asked, smiling up at Agramon.

He bent down to kiss her, then rose and adjusted his robes before striding out of the door.

Echo followed him to the council rooms. He strode in and sat next to the emperor's chair. The emperor himself hadn't arrived yet, but Sam had. He was watching Agramon angrily.

Before long, the emperor came, his smile wide. "Our council has returned!" he said lightly. "Agramon, Samael, what news of your travels? How are the lords of the land taking to our young protégé?"

"Very well," Agramon said, weaving his fingers together over his propped knee. "She's shown a great range of her abilities and can send a storm from quite a long distance."

"I heard she can fly now," Captain Diardo said. His

chin rested on his hand.

Agramon glanced at him. "Yes, after that unfortunate incident here in the city, I figured it would be best to take that ability in hand."

"Eldred of Maryse has brought forth a formal complaint against her attack on Lord Achille," Captain Diardo went on. "The heir of Perth was murdered in his room. The Earl of Nordow was killed by rebellion. It seems you brought more than rain on this journey of yours. The stain of these attacks will mar the crown for years. I don't believe there is a need for a second tour because I don't think anyone wants you back."

"Come now, Diardo," the emperor said, looking uncharacteristically put out. "Everyone has been saying what a success this has been. The farmers and laborers are happy, are they not?"

"Regrettably," the wizened Solston Gowther said, leaning forward, "they are not. The Sons of Sol have been preaching in the streets. They are saying the girl is cursed."

"My word," the emperor snapped, taking a swig of water. "This empire is filled with the most ungrateful people I've ever seen. No, I will not let any of you dampen my celebrations. I have finally ended the drought in Lyrica, and if any nobleman or countryman says otherwise, they can hang!"

Agramon was nodding while Captain Diardo's frown

deepened. Sam merely watched, his thoughts and emotions hidden behind a mask of impassivity.

"Might I speak?" Agramon asked the emperor, who nodded. "Since we're already in session and the vows will be tomorrow, I wanted to put forth an interesting request the Count of Calla raised."

Something in Sam's face flickered. It seemed he hadn't known about Agramon and the Count of Calla's secret meeting. The emperor leaned forward and nodded.

"He wishes to name his only child, a daughter, as heir."

"That is dangerous," one of the men said. "What kind of precedent does that set?"

Sage Bromwell frowned. "It is tradition to leave holdings to a male heir, if one is to be found. Why does he not seek to marry her to a worthy lord?"

Agramon shrugged. "It's his only child, and he doesn't wish to take on the mentorship of someone new. He stated, quite clearly, that the girl is up for the challenge, and wants to commission the crown to grant him this boon."

"What did the Count of Calla receive for his oath's gift?" Emperor Arthello asked, looking to Sage Bromwell. The sage motioned to a clerk standing by and sent him to the library.

The men talked further. Sam made no mention of

the foiled campaign to Lu Shen. It was impossible to tell whether he was still angry about not being informed of the peace accord sent to Lu Shen in his absence. Though his men were spared death, it seemed that Sam had lost face in front of the council.

The clerk returned with a tome. Sage Bromwell opened it, studying each page he turned with his knobby fingers. "Ah," Sage Bromwell said, pointing to the text. "It says here that when the Count of Calla made his first oath to your father, he requested nothing more than five hundred pounds of seed. Calla is now known for a robust apothecary trade, if I'm not mistaken." Sage Bromwell's eyes rose from the page and met each council member in turn.

"Well, that's not all that much," Emperor Arthello muttered, his chin on his hand as though deep in thought. "Calla is worth far more than five hundred pounds of seed."

"Calla is also very loyal," Agramon said, his eyes narrowed.

"Indeed," Sage Bromwell said. "Though it may set a dangerous precedent. What if a widow seeks to establish her daughter as heir instead of her son? Will wives now be able to rule in their husband's stead?"

"Come now, man," the emperor scoffed. "Surely we can add language to the decree to make it known that this is a one-time occurrence. If someone would like to pass their title and lands onto a female relation, they must declare their intention directly to the crown. That will stop most of them, I think."

"Wise words," Sam grunted. He traced a circle on the table.

Emperor Arthello smiled at Sam.

Agramon studied his fingernails. "There is more. The lord of Perth is now without heir and issue. That holding will need to be decided. I feel the lord himself might be too distraught to make an adequate choice."

"Did you have someone in mind?" Captain Diardo asked.

Agramon shrugged. "Elgar the Swift has been loyal to you for many years. He's been instrumental in assisting Bald Walden take the gangs into hand. Perhaps it's time he had a holding of his own."

Emperor Arthello nodded. "Does anyone else have any ideas?"

"Forgive me, Your Excellency," one of the men said, his finger raised. "Might I make a suggestion?"

It went on like that. Each man requesting the name of some friend of his, someone that they probably owed a favor to. I wondered who the holdings of Perth would go to. It seemed silly that Emperor Arthello alone made the choice. He didn't know most of the men spoken of. Were they even fit to rule?

"MIGHT I JOIN YOU TODAY?" I asked Agramon the next morning, after Gree had helped me dress.

"I would've thought you'd attend the ladies' luncheon," Agramon said, his brows raised as he lifted his staff, about to head out of the door.

"There were too many people there," I lied. In truth, I had no wish to see the empress. I could feel her judging me every time I saw her. She figured that since I had so much power, I could do well without friends. It angered me to find out that I'd meant nothing to her. That her words of friendship rang false.

"I need to visit Berinon's laboratory," Agramon said, glancing at Luc who'd stepped in, then shrugged. "I bet Del would accompany us."

Agramon led me to the hall and out to the circle drive where Elgar the Swift waited. Del came running out after a few moments, her smile bright. "I just got your summons!" she gasped, out of breath. "I would love to come."

We mounted our horses and rode through the city. Elgar and Agramon rode in front, followed by Luc. He was deep in a conversation that I could not hear. Beside me, Del went on about the masked ball. It seemed that she'd been surrounded by suitors all night. I wondered at her meaning, since we were on our way to see her lover.

While she talked, I stroked Arden's feathers atop my shoulder and watched Luc's back. If I were to escape, I would need to go alone. I wouldn't take anyone with me. Luc had sold me to the empire and gotten us into this mess in the first place. He would need to rescue himself, just as I was doing.

Berinon's laboratory was housed in its own nondescript stone building on an abandoned street in the middle of the city, past the market center and near the temple district. The sorcerer met us at the door, shoving spectacles higher up on his nose as he greeted us.

"Well met, Your Grace, well met," Berinon said, sweat dripping down his face. He looked just as he did at the palace, with his plain robes stained with all manner of substances and glasses that seemed to be too small for his face.

Elgar handed him a blue jar stoppered with a cork. "Tristam asked me to bring you the blood of a virgin you asked for. He says to conserve this, as you ran out of the last batch so quickly."

"Oh, very good, man, very good," Berinon said, disappearing inside. We followed into the large room. Despite the heat, a fire burned in the stone fireplace beneath a large pewter cauldron that bubbled lazily with some murky green liquid. The concoction emitted a foul odor.

A slim figure bent over a pile of small metal parts on a table across the room. Nearer to us was another table set against a wall of bookcases filled with moldy books, some appearing to be badly scorched. The table was covered with a maze of glass jars, some stoppered, others with long necks that curved across the table and dripped into a series of steaming vials.

Berinon, lifting his apron and patting his sopping head, placed the jar that Elgar had handed to him on a large storage shelf containing all manner of substances. Several bottles looked to hold creatures, their body suspended in liquid, while others were made of dark glass to keep the contents within hidden from the light.

"Come now, Sparks, His Grace is here for the demonstration," Berinon said to the bent figure across the room. The figure straightened, then turned, revealing a young woman wearing simple breeches and a tunic. Bright orange hair stuck out from her head like the flames of a candle. Over one eye she had strapped a sort of device made of metal and glass that caused one eye to appear far larger than the other. On her brow was a glowing gold stone.

"We're sorry for the mess," Sparks said, lifting the eyeglass and setting it atop her fiery hair. "But the demonstration is set and ready over here if you would like to watch."

Agramon placed his hand on my shoulder and steered me to the wall next to Del. Luc began exploring the shelf of potions and liquids behind us, lifting some of them to read the labels or tip them to the side, inspecting the substance within. Elgar merely stood with his feet spread, hands clasped behind his back. He watched all of us with a steely gaze.

Berinon and Sparks stood behind a table at the center of the room holding a miniature castle made of stones. At the other end of the table stood a small catapult, quite like the ones that Teilo Lyon had brought with him from Ayastaren on his ill-fated campaign to bring the Espirians to heel in the Morganian forest.

Berinon took out a metal rod and measured the distance between the catapult and the castle wall. He adjusted the distance by minute amounts and murmured softly to Sparks as she took a long match and lit it on the underside of her boot.

Berinon straightened and adjusted his spectacles. "We obtained a sizable quantity of this black powder when a merchant group returned from Lu Shen last spring. Originally, its capabilities were limited to alchemy, but since then, there have been rumors of it being used by the Lu Shen army for some rather remarkable weapons that don't require the presence of a sorcerer. I took those reports and have fashioned some prototypes of weapons that could possibly be developed, with help from Sparks and Del, of course, into remarkable siege weapons if we ever find ourselves at war again."

He nodded to Sparks, who held the match to the catapult's basket, then released the catapult's arm, sending a small cylinder soaring into the air before crashing into the tiny castle's wall. The ball exploded, sending rocks and stones pinging around the room while all the sorcerers ducked, our hands in front of our faces as we shielded our eyes from the onslaught.

There was silence for a moment as we brushed ourselves off. Berinon looked to be near bursting with anticipation as he bounced on his toes. An odd movement for a man.

Luc was the first to speak. "Let us hope the time for war is passed."

Agramon stepped forward. "Though I'm sure we all agree, the question of another war is not if it will happen, but when. If the Lu Shen are advancing their armaments to include black powder, then that means other nations probably are as well. It's been my experience that weapons decide a battle, not men."

"Best not to let Sam hear you say that," I muttered under my breath.

Berinon was nodding. "If I can create a steady supply, we can continue to experiment with weapon alterations while I make adjustments to our recipe."

Elgar straightened and began investigating the effects on the castle. He flicked loose stones off the wall and measured the hole with his fingers. "It's certainly effective, and won't tire like a sorcerer, nor is it so easily defeated. You could train a hundred men to use these weapons and raze a building in hours, if not minutes."

I stood back, somewhat shaken by what I'd just seen. If Teilo Lyon had been lucky enough to have black powder in his possession during the Battle of Espiria, the casualties would've been great indeed. While the other sorcerers imagined the uses and devastation of black powder against other armies and nations, my imagination curled inward. The emperor and consuls would surely expand the use of black powder to use against dissidence to their rule. It was lucky that Teilo Lyon had no blast sorcerers in employ at Ayastaren, as sorcery in all forms was still somewhat of a rarity. Black powder was sure to change all that. The emperor and consuls would only become more powerful, more feared. What did that mean for the rest of us?

"It's a frightening thing to behold, isn't it," said a voice to my side.

I turned. Sparks held her hand out to me and I shook it.

"Del told me you're Agramon's new ward?" she asked, nodding to the sorcerer.

"Yes, Agramon has taken me under his wing." I glanced to where Del and Luc were discussing the options for siege weapons. Del was pulling prototypes off the shelf. I wondered what Destrian would make of all this.

"His Grace has been quite keen that the recipe be perfected in a short amount of time. I figure he wants to present the breakthrough during the quinquennial."

"Is it safe enough to present a large amount to a crowd?" I wondered about the safety of the gathered nobles and city folk. If there was one thing I knew about Agramon, it was that he enjoyed creating a spectacle.

"Safe if we don't use too much," Sparks said. "I've not yet heard what he's planning, but now that the recipe is perfected, it won't take any time at all to come up with something."

I nodded. Black powder had been Lu Shen's closely guarded secret in the past. It allowed the users to blast through materials without the use of blaster sorcerers. Part of the reason the talks failed with the visiting empire was because the ambassador wanted to greatly limit their shipments of Lu Shen black powder. Now it didn't matter anymore.

We left soon after the demonstration, Agramon speaking low to Elgar. As we passed through the temple district, a low murmur reverberated from the buildings beside us.

We turned a corner, and a swell of people filled the

road before us. Agramon and Elgar had stopped and eyed the people with frowns. The eye of Sol had been painted on tunics and flags, the mark carved into the brows of many of the men standing there.

I craned, trying to look ahead. "How are we to get out?" I shouted to Del. Worry etched Luc's brow.

"We could go back," Del shouted, "but it will take us an extra two hours to get around the city."

Suddenly, the crowd hushed. Their attention caught on a figure on the steps of a temple, someone cloaked in white with a golden emblem, a sunburst, embroidered on their chest. I squinted to get a better look. I'd seen that face before, though now it was markedly different. The ash-brown hair had been shaved off, but the gray eyes gave him away.

Seith Lyon was on the steps of a golden temple. What in all the gods was he doing, and why was the crowd so keen to hear him speak?

"Friends, true followers of Sol, and believers of the light, we welcome you to commune with us in Sol's greatest city! Our greatest seer, the Matron Chassandre, has bid me speak with you, to call you to arms against a growing threat of darkness upon our empire."

Murmurs swept through the crowd in waves. I was too busy staring at Seith, my mouth hanging open, to pay attention to what the people were saying.

"There is a darkness in your midst that must be

brought to the light. I have born witness to the evils of the black sorceress, whom you all believe to be blessed by the gods, and I have come to tell you, I've seen the evil magic that she summons at night. I have seen the shadows whispering into your ears, telling you to believe that she alone can save you, but only Sol can save your souls. Only Sol can bring you out of the darkness and into the light. The maiden of darkness, Rowyn the Morganite, lures you in and promises to feed your bellies, but she is merely sating a temporary hunger. Who will feed your soul when Sol has turned his back on you? Are you so easily swayed by this shadowy usurper?"

The crowd screamed. Men's faces screwed up in anger as they raised their fists. Seith's eyes were bright, looking over the mass of men.

"She has spoken of the fall of Lyrica time and again. I've heard it from her own traitorous lips. She denies my father's divine right to lead the Western Empire. She's even turned her black magic onto the nobility! The lord of Helena, merely a dog begging at her feet. Agramon the Divine, once a man of great stature among us, is now reduced to trailing behind her as she turns one noble after another into groveling peons, a ploy in her own game to take down our empire. We are just, we are good, we are a strong people who won't be undone by some foolish girl's whims. Who is with me?"

The crowd began to shout angrily, their fists waving in the air. I glanced around, suddenly conscious of how close I was knitted in. We had lingered too long.

As if he'd heard my concerns, Seith met my eyes. My heart raced.

Something akin to triumph flickered over his face. He raised his hands and the crowd calmed enough for him to speak. "Loyal followers of Sol, you are blessed with a clear road. Sol has let his divine light shine down, revealing the traitor among us, the shadowy usurper, Rowyn the Morganite herself!" Seith pointed at me, his sneer triumphant as those around me began to back away. "Sol demands her sacrifice! Send her back to the dark god she loves so dearly!"

I tried to pull Iranoct from its sheath, but the crowd began to crush us. Without thinking, I called my power, lifting off the horse in a great swell of wind and flying above the mob. An arrow flew nearby, but the wind swept it away. I looked down, trying to find the others. The sorcerers were nowhere to be found, but Luc was shouting, his sword raised, cutting through men who tried to pull him off his horse. Of course, Agramon would've left him. I gritted my teeth.

I'd never tried to fly under such tricky circumstances, but I couldn't leave Luc to his fate. I took a deep breath and flew down, pulling him from the horse and into the air.

Unused to the added weight, we barreled right into the crowd, smashing and rolling into people.

Damn. Damn! *Damnit!*

I fought the hands grabbing me until I realized it was Luc who was holding onto me.

I sent a gust of wind around us. It pushed those nearest away. Luc wrapped his arms around me, and I directed the wind back in and down, lifting us both from the ground in a burst of power. We flew high into the air and away from the rabid crowd.

Chapter 35

"WHAT IN ALL THE GODS' NAMES is Seith Lyon doing with the Sons of Sol!" I yelled in our room after landing safely within the castle walls and finding Agramon waiting for me. Elgar and Del were nowhere to be found.

"He's a servant of Chassandre now," Agramon said, running his finger thoughtfully along the couch. "She's been quite outspoken about our need to cast you out. She has the ear of the common people, but the nobles have yet to heed her warnings. She's hoping to change that through one of them."

"You gleaned all of that from his mind?" I asked, stopping short at the window and looking out over the city. Arden landed on the sill. I moved her to the perch. "What's the point of me even being here? Nobody wants my help."

Agramon rolled his eyes. "You're going to let a vocal minority decide your next actions?" he asked, his voice icy. "I know, deep down, that you want to help."

"Why should she help them?" Luc asked, throwing his hand out. "The girl has bent over backward to help Lyrica, and all anyone seems to want to do is throw it up in her face! I don't see how you put up with it,

508

Rowyn."

"What would you suggest I do?" Agramon asked.

"Speak to the emperor!" Luc said angrily. "Have him voice her favor once and for all. Demand a price on whoever's head threatens or seeks to endanger her! I thought you were supposed to protect her!"

A muscle in Agramon's jaw clenched. "Leave us," he ordered.

I shook my head. Luc had gone too far. I sighed, stroking Arden's feathers, avoiding Agramon's eye.

"You know the best way I can protect you, don't you?" Agramon asked, coming up behind me.

"Let me guess . . ."

"If you married me, nobody would dare lay a hand on you."

"Sam could just as easily say the same thing. So could Destrian."

"Morgania is out of the question, and the Butcher? He will demand more of you than you're willing to give. For the most part I would let you be. You can even keep Mordog. Take him as a lover for all I care."

"Until you decide to use him to teach me a lesson," I snapped.

"I'm sorry about Ena," Agramon said, resting his hands on my shoulders. "I lost my temper. Don't let our past decide your future. We could be great, you and I."

I tilted my head to the side. "Is that what you tell Princess Willene?"

Agramon stiffened. Perhaps I'd overplayed my hand. "That woman's a fool," he whispered. "What has she told you?"

I raised my brows. "She's told me nothing. I'm curious what you are planning, Your Grace. Tell me, will the emperor even survive the year?"

Agramon released my shoulders and stepped back. He shook his head, a smile playing at the corner of his lips. "You will not back me into a corner, Rowyn."

Gree strode in as though Agramon had just summoned her. "The oaths ceremony is set to begin soon. We must all be ready, dressed in our finest."

I followed Gree into my room and went over each deal Agramon had made on our journey of the east. What was his next move? Before, I'd thought that Agramon would wait to make his claim after the quinquennial, when the army left for Lu Shen. I was starting to get uneasy that he was planning something sooner. Things were escalating quickly, and I could feel myself getting dragged into it. What was Agramon's plan? How could I find freedom before he made me part of it?

THE MOOD WAS SOMBER in the ballroom as nobles clustered with their families for the oaths ceremony. Solstons from the temple district flanked the dais where the emperor and empress sat, blessing each oath before Sol.

Duke Eldred of Maryse went first. He bowed, several members of his family behind him, all wearing white. He spoke his oaths with solemnity, to both Emperor Arthello and his son, Artian, who was seated on the empress's lap.

I could feel Mem and the empress watching me. They probably wondered if I'd told anyone about the heir to the empire being a league leaper. I wondered how no one had found out before. Shaking my head, I directed my gaze back to the scarlet carpet that had been unfurled for the event. Agramon was striding forward, his robes snow white, his shoulders and neck covered in gold. He went down on one knee, his head bowed low.

"I vow to fulfill my oaths to the empire and follow our emperor's command, in poverty and prosperity, as he is our true lord in the eyes of Sol."

Emperor Arthello smiled as Duke Agramon rose.

"Do you think Sol will strike him dead for those lies?" a voice murmured in my ear.

I stiffened, turning to find Sam beside me. The lines

of Solstons made some hand motion, repeating their blessing for Agramon's domain.

Pedr Tore caught my eye as he stood with his family. I waved, trying to smile, but I was wary of Sam.

When I didn't respond, Sam stepped closer, his fingers brushing mine. "My emotions got the better of me last night. I'm sorry if my behavior was untoward."

"It's fine," I said, not able to think of anything else.

I bit my lip when I found Destrian in the crowd. He was standing with Mellan Lyon, whispering something to him. Mellan's eyes were bright as he listened and asked something further. After a moment, they both turned to me and I looked away, hoping they hadn't seen me staring.

The Duke of Ayastaren was next. I glared at the man as he made his vows. He looked unchanged, despite the deaths of two of his sons and the cult-like defection of a third.

After him was a count who was giving his oath for the first time. I held my breath as Solston Gowther spoke about the importance of give and take. After his little speech, the emperor stood.

"As this is your first oath, I will grant you a gift, up to the value of your domain. What is it you request as payment for your vow?"

"Your Eminence," the older man said, bowing his head. "I request the men and supplies to build a great road connecting my domain to Somme, so I may be honored with further trade with the empire."

The emperor frowned, turning to Sage Bromwell, who was recording the vows. He conferred with him for a moment. The emperor turned back to the lord and smiled.

"Your request is granted," the emperor announced, standing and joining the applause.

More lords kneeled, including Sam, though no others were due an oath's gift, save Destrian. When it came to be his turn, the hall silenced. Agramon had told me that the nobles had taken bets on what Destrian would ask for, and everyone was leaning toward the emperor, waiting on tenterhooks to hear.

Destrian strode forward after he gestured to Mellan, who held something long wrapped in a white Lyrican flag.

Destrian kneeled and repeated the vows that everyone else had given. The emperor nodded, leaning forward in his seat. He looked as though he wished the Solstons would speed up their speech. Finally, the emperor stood.

"Now to your gift," the emperor announced.

"Before I ask for my gift," Destrian said, motioning Mellan to his side. "I would like to bestow one upon you."

A crease appeared on the emperor's brow.

"Your gift is your oath, your lordship," Sage Bromwell said over his spectacles.

"I thought to honor His Imperial Majesty with a sword," Destrian said, grabbing what Mellan held and sweeping the flag off of it. He revealed a golden great sword. Its hilt was filled with gems, each the center of the sun that served as Somme's sigil. It seemed more decoration than weapon, but the emperor's eyes were shining with excitement as he stepped down from the dais.

He took the weapon and inspected it, his smile widening. "My word, this is fine work! It is my honor to accept an Everett blade. An honor indeed!"

The emperor raised the blade to a smattering of applause throughout the chamber.

"I was sorry to hear about your father, though I didn't know him well. He didn't seem to pay as much deference to me as he did to my own dearly departed father." The emperor's eyes flicked toward me. Destrian didn't let his eyes follow. "I hope that, someday, the death of a loyal noble will be avenged."

"Morgania has been restless, it's true, but we've come to a peace, of sorts."

I wondered what he meant. Over the long weeks in his absence, I wondered if Destrian would take revenge for his father's death. I'd give anything to know his thoughts. To read his mind, as Agramon was doing on the other side of me, if his scowl was anything to read from.

"Now tell me, dear boy, what can I give you in return for your vows?"

"Your Eminence," Destrian said, bowing once more. At least from a distance, I could admire him. The way his hair seemed to glow in the candlelight. His dark eyes, so alive with spirit. Destrian pitched his voice louder. "I wish to call my lost Morganian brothers home. I request the return of the conscripted soldiers of Morgania. The war is over, so let those who called Morgania home return there if they wish, whether they still be in the army, farming the Fields of Forgotten Men, or fighting in the pits."

I sucked in my breath, my heart pounding in my ears at his words. I felt Sam stiffen next to me. Destrian had one gift he could've asked for, and he asked for that. The memory of us together, on the ship to Morgania, so long ago, flashed before my eyes.

"What if you were queen? What's the first thing you would do?"

"Well . . ." I said, trying to stall while I thought. "If I were queen, and therefore could have whatever I want, because both of us know that every whim of a queen is honored."

Destrian grinned. "Of course."

"Then, I would destroy the Fields of Forgotten Men and send them back to their homelands."

Tears pricked my eyes. The memory seemed so real, I could feel the rocking of the ship beneath my feet.

Still, Destrian wouldn't meet my eyes. I wanted him to look up. I wanted him to see how grateful I was that he would be so selfless. But he didn't. He only looked at the emperor, waiting for an answer as the emperor continued to grip the sword.

"Nobody has ever asked for the conscripted men to return," the emperor admitted, looking over his shoulder to Sage Bromwell, who shrugged.

It wasn't a no. I held my breath. Sage Bromwell muttered something I couldn't hear. The emperor nodded.

"The council will meet to decide," the emperor finally said, smiling at the room.

Destrian swung his head to Sam, to us.

I couldn't breathe. I couldn't think.

Agramon pulled me with him as the other council members followed the emperor and Sage Bromwell from the ballroom, which had erupted in a cacophony of noise.

Roaring filled my ears as we filed into a side chamber off from the ballroom. I glanced around at the men whose mouths were moving, but I didn't hear their words. Agramon was saying something to the emperor. Sam's arms were crossed, his brow furrowed as he spoke with Captain Diardo. I heard nothing of what they said. All I could think about was Destrian.

He was doing this for me.

He'd used up his oath's gift on a gift for me.

I registered the noise around me as the men's arguing grew heated.

"Do you really think it's a good idea to send an entire host of angry and seasoned warriors to Morgania? We know nothing of the boy's loyalties," Agramon spat. His eyes flicked to me. Destrian hadn't fooled Agramon. He knew the request was on my behalf.

Luc had followed Agramon and was practically radiating energy. His eyes followed each of the men, his mouth falling open as though to speak, then he thought better of it and shut his mouth once more. Destrian's request meant that even Luc could go home.

"Sage Bromwell says it's well within the cost of his oath's gift to request it," the emperor was saying. "He'll probably have mass riots on his hands at home, given the nature of some of these men. They're barely more than beasts, or so I'm told."

"Bromwell may be right that he can afford to make the request, but it also can't cause undue hardship on the empire." Sam grunted. "You would really beggar me by taking away men who farm my land?"

Captain Diardo nodded. "We called these men to Somme because of our war with Lu Shen. Granted, we're holding off the attack, for now, but who's to say there isn't another conflict looming on the horizon.

We'll need all our men," Captain Diardo said. "Just because you like your fancy sword doesn't mean we should abandon all sense of reason."

The emperor shot his captain a withering look. "Very well, I leave the decision to the person it would affect the most." The emperor turned to Sam. "Imperial Commander, it's your call."

"I don't think this is a good idea," Agramon said.

"I disagree," I began, but Agramon held up his hand, silencing me.

"He's doing this for her, you know," Agramon told Sam. "He thinks this will bring her back to him."

Sam's eyes darkened. He looked at me, and I couldn't help the heat flooding into my cheeks. "I cannot willingly give up a large portion of my armed force," Sam said, turning to the emperor.

"Very well," the emperor said with a sigh. "Perhaps we can come up with another, more suitable, arrangement."

Sam straightened. "It's settled then."

"Wait." I grabbed his arm. "I beg you to reconsider."

Sam turned to me. "How can you ask me to deliver the one thing that will send you scurrying back to him?"

It was then that I saw a way to outmaneuver Agramon. A way to escape from his grasp. A way to honor Destrian's gift. We had a dream of a united Morgania. I could give him that. If I gave him nothing else but heartache, I could give him the future we'd wanted for our land.

"Don't keep them here," I whispered to Sam. "Let it be a gift."

"I don't know why I should be inclined to gift anything to the lord of Helena," Sam grunted, grabbing a goblet filled with water and bringing it to his lips.

"Not to Des . . . the lord of Helena." I took a deep breath. There was only one way to convince him to do the right thing. Destrian opened the door to save those lost men of my clan, but the weight of the decision was left on my shoulders, and mine alone. I'd been powerless to help my people before. The entire clan had suffered under my gift, and for that they'd cast me out. Though their distrust and anger still hurt, Destrian had opened the door for me to make amends. No matter what had happened in the past, I couldn't deny the part of me that always dreamed of doing best by my people. "Let it be a wedding gift . . . to me."

Sam froze, the goblet trembling ever so slightly in his hands. "What are you saying?"

"Yes, Rowyn, what *are* you going on about?" Agramon demanded, eyes flashing in anger.

"You asked me to marry you," I said, trying to ignore the others in the room. "If you gift me this, I will accept."

A muscle in Sam's jaw flexed. "If I let your countrymen go, you would pledge yourself to me?"

I put my hand on his chest and looked him in the eye. "You need only name the date."

"Don't be foolish," Agramon snarled behind me. "You can't just let thousands of men free at the snap of your fingers, Rowyn."

Sam studied me. Finally, he turned to the emperor. "Send the men home," he said, his eyes shooting back to me, this time with a slow and steady burn.

"Now see here a moment," Agramon said, gripping his staff with white knuckles. "She is my ward. I am the one who decides who she will marry. There are other offers on the table that I'm still considering."

The emperor frowned. "I can't think of anyone more deserving of her hand than our Imperial Commander. Why should he not get his wish, especially if the girl is willing? Besides, Del has just finished the Crystal Temple. What a spectacle it would be to hold the wedding there on the last day of the quinquennial. We were going to bless the temple that day anyway. Why should we not bless a marriage as well?"

"The sooner the better," Sam said, his eyes on me as though I were liable to run out the door.

Agramon turned to Sam. "You know the Dragon is doing this for her, don't you?" he fumed. "You're playing right into their hands. Is that really what you want your marriage to be based on? Their pledges to each other?"

But Sam was looking into my eyes. "I don't care why she marries me, so long as she does."

"Thank you," I whispered, taking Sam's hand. The barest hint of a smile played on his lips. I kissed his trembling fingers.

We re-entered the hall and faced the courtiers. They stopped whispering and listened with bated breath. Destrian's eyes found mine. They were bright, full of hope, but the light dimmed, and his brow furrowed as he looked at Sam's hand clasped in mine.

Emperor Arthello, who strode to his dais, waved over a servant and raised a cup.

"Lord Destrian, we have discussed the terms of your gift and have come to an agreement." The emperor smiled as Destrian bowed stiffly. "Baron Samael, Imperial Commander of the Lyrican forces, has accepted your request."

The court erupted. Destrian's eyes widened, and a smile stretched over his face. Mellan slapped him on the shoulder and thrust a drink into his hand. Even Araceli was clapping with glee. But when Destrian met my eyes, his smile fell. His brow creased in worry.

Destrian continued watching me as the rest of the nobles delivered their vows. I tried to avoid his eye, afraid that I wouldn't be able to help my tears.

There would be no escape. There would be no finding a new life outside of Lyrica. What kind of person would I be if I freed my countrymen, then went back on my word? I'd told myself that I would never follow Agramon into villainy, and I still believed that, even if it meant sacrificing my future.

Destrian would make Morgania whole once more. He was far better equipped to protect my people than I was. Sam was my future now. I glanced up at him. The corner of his mouth was quirked up as he watched the remainder of the vows, his grip on my hand tight.

The empress was right, I'd made my bed, and now it was time to lie in it. Sam had only ever protected me. I couldn't deny that I'd enjoyed my time with him in Bruin. I could try to make him happy. I could try to be happy myself. It would be easier if the Morganites were gone from Bruin. I could see myself visiting Winnie's mending circles and seeing Nirah whenever I wanted, and exploring the forests of my ancestors. There would be nothing wrong with that life. The fear from the night before was unwarranted. I had no reason to be afraid of Sam.

"We have an announcement to make," the emperor said, rising when the last lord had spoken his vows and stepped away from the dais. "Rowyn the Morganite has accepted Baron Samael's hand in marriage. The wedding will be held on the last day of the quinquennial, so

I hope you all will join us in congratulating the two."

The court exploded with excitement. I fought back the tears, squared my shoulders, then looked up at Sam and smiled.

I couldn't meet Destrian's eyes. I could feel him watching me. I didn't want to see the expression on his face. I would lose courage if I did.

"I know she'll make you happy," the emperor was saying, clasping Sam's hand and bringing it to his chest while slapping him on the back. "You deserve a hero's retirement."

The emperor released him and called for more drinks to be served. Miyu beckoned to the musicians, and they struck up a celebratory tune.

"You won't regret this," Sam said next to me. I nodded, afraid to speak. "I won't fail to make you happy, Rowyn, I promise you that."

"I know," I said, then tried to smile. Sam leaned down and pulled me into a kiss, right there in the hall, his mouth soft on mine. My whole body was on fire, but all I could do was temper the flames.

Chapter 36

THE BALL AFTER THE VOWS was a raucous affair. It seemed like everyone wanted to offer Sam congratulations or grab my hand to feel my gem. He gripped my arm as though I would drift away if he let go.

But I'd meant what I said. I'd finally learned how to bargain, and I intended to go through with it. Sam led me to the tall military man I'd noticed in my dream.

He put his hand on my back. "Rowyn, might I introduce you to Admiral Abelard Valdis, Commander of the Lyrican Navy."

I put my hand in the admiral's and curtsied. I noticed a golden serpent embroidered around his cuffs. I then realized where I'd heard of him before. The empress's kind friend, lady Noemi, had married the man when he was just a mere captain. It seemed he'd risen fast during wartime.

"I suppose we've figured out a use for the navy," Admiral Valdis said, taking a sip from his glass as he looked around the room. "The Consul of Helena asked if we could transport the conscripted Morganians back to the western shore."

Sam frowned. "I thought you were going to stay to

patrol the coast."

Admiral Valdis shrugged. "I will keep a few ships, including my own, but since all of the conscripted are already here, it makes sense to send them home quickly, wouldn't you agree?"

Sam looked down at me. "Yes, we should send them home as soon as possible."

Mellan Lyon came up to my side. "Lady Rowyn," he said, then bowed to Sam and Admiral Valdis. "My lords, may I steal the great lady for a moment? There are others who would like to offer her congratulations."

A muscle jumped in Sam's jaw, but he eventually nodded and let my arm go. He turned back to Admiral Valdis, a worried look on his face.

I followed Mellan through the crowd of nobles to an alcove on the other side of the ballroom.

I found myself face to face with Destrian.

"Thank you for using your one gift for freeing them," I said. "I wouldn't have even thought it possible."

"If I'd known the cost, I would've asked for money and found some other way," Destrian said, shaking his head. "I'd no idea it would trap you further. Why do you always feel you have to sacrifice yourself?"

"They are my people, Destrian. It's what I've been raised to do since birth. My people have to come first. They may have sold me, they may have not truly seen my worth when they sent me to the capitol, but if there is a decision to be made between my happiness and bettering my people, I will choose them every time."

"Rowyn, soon you will have nothing left to give," Destrian murmured. He took my arm and pulled me to him in a hug.

I buried my face in his sleeve, the weight of missing him crushing me. "If it's for a good cause, what does it matter?"

"It matters to me," Destrian whispered. "How can you ask me to stand by and bear seeing you with him?"

A tear coursed down my cheek. I rested my head on his chest. "Why did you do it?" I asked. "What made you ask for that gift? You could've requested anything."

Destrian ran a hand down my hair. "I knew there would come a time when you had to choose." His voice dropped to a whisper. "And I wanted you to choose me."

Tears welled up behind my eyes, but I pushed them back. I couldn't believe such kindness could come from someone I'd grown up hating. I wished I realized sooner how lucky I was to have Destrian. Perhaps if I had, we would've had more time.

He leaned down, his lips finding mine, and I abandoned all sense of decorum. It only lasted a moment, but it was a moment I may never have again.

"I can't believe it's been so long since I've had you

in my arms." He gasped when I broke away.

But I'd made a promise to Sam. "I will marry in two days' time. You need to find another girl to love."

Destrian brushed his cheek against mine. "No matter how far you've gone, I will be the last to fall. I will always choose you."

I stepped back, brushed the tear from my eye, and strode past Mellan who'd been keeping watch. Instead of going back to Sam, I sped to the doors, ready to lay my head on the bed and have a good cry.

Before I reached my rooms, Agramon was there, lifting my hand and leading me through the corridor.

He was silent, but the fingers that held mine were stiff. I looked out of the window as we walked. Clouds gathered overhead. There was nothing else to do but face Agramon's anger. What move would he play next?

Agramon opened the door to our rooms and waited for me to enter. I strode inside and faced Agramon as the wind outside began to howl.

"You really mean to go through with it, don't you?" Agramon slowly shut the door. "You've always been more honorable than what was good for you. It's a fault, I think. Escaping one prison only to unlock a new one."

"I'm happy," I insisted. "I chose for myself."

"Tsk, tsk, tsk. All along the road, you kept allowing the Butcher to save you. Well, now it's my turn."

"What's that supposed to mean?"

"I told you that I would take care of you, and I meant it," Agramon said. He rested his hands on my shoulders. "We promised, remember? I will save you from this. Just continue to play your part." He chucked me under my chin before turning and locking himself in his bedroom.

I let myself breathe. The storm abated, turning to heavy rainfall as I backed into my bedroom, my heart sinking. Agramon would never listen to me. He would never let Sam or anyone else have me. I realized it would've always ended with him. I gritted my teeth. There was nowhere to run now.

"HOW COULD A MONSTER like you seriously expect her to love you back?" Destrian asked in my dreams that night. The air was hot from his fury.

"How can a boy like you know what love is?" Sam's eyes darkened. "How can someone like you seriously think you can protect her? You've already failed multiple times by my count. Me? I've never failed her. I *won't* fail her."

"But I've made myself better for her," Destrian said, palming Phyranox's hilt. The gesture did not go unnoticed by Sam's watchful eyes.

"Is that what you think she's wanted all this time? A better man?" Sam chuckled, crossing his arms. "This is why you will always lose her, Everett. She's only ever wanted to be understood and accepted as she is. You could never understand that—neither did Luc or Mordog or whoever the young pup who nearly wed her is called. I've looked into her heart and have seen the hate there. You would've hidden it away."

"You are wrong about her," Destrian said, standing tall. "There is good in her still. You cannot corrupt her completely. I've seen her fight for the good of man."

"You think I corrupt her?" Sam asked, his voice low. "Who abandoned her to the duke? Who turned on her the minute it became difficult? The only corruption in Rowyn was brought on when those who were supposed to love her the most, abandoned her to the wills of others. I didn't corrupt her. I pieced her back together into someone strong enough to defy an empire."

Sparks of fury began to alight from Destrian's fingertips.

Sam's nostrils flared as his voice lowered. "That's what you hate most, Everett. That it was I who saved her where you failed. You can tell yourself that you're angry with me, if it will make you feel better. But you and I know the truth of it. Deep down, it was you who failed her, and she will never forgive you for it. Even if she took you back, she would be waiting for you to abandon her again. You broke her trust, something I've never done, for I was never masquerading with her. I've only ever been honest about who I was."

"I want you to know that I will be waiting for her," Destrian said, his voice tense. "I will aid her escape from this prison that you all have built around her. She could never be happy with you—away from her people, even if she won't admit it to herself. She's always wanted to go home. You will only ever be a prison guard."

"But I will have her," Sam said, meeting Destrian's eye. "And that is all that matters to me."

Chapter 37

"YOU WERE RIGHT ABOUT HIM," I whispered into the early dawn light.

"I'm sorry the realization has come too late," Echo replied, the covers at the end of the bed giving way to her invisible form.

Arden cocked her head to the side, awoken by my voice.

"You should also know that nothing is to be done about it now." I sat up. "I don't want to see anymore."

"You are resolved in your choice?"

"I am," I assured her. "I could learn to love Sam. It is the only way."

"It is hard to watch."

"I can find a way to send you home if you want your freedom. Bruin is not so far from the Nightlands. I would understand if you didn't want to stay."

"There is nothing in the Nightlands for me," Echo said. I felt her icy fingers creep over my hand. "Close your eyes."

I did. An image of darkness swam into view. On either side of me, people were trudging through the dust. I recognized the man from before, who was friends with Echo, or Nirah as she was called then. He'd aged, his face hard in the moonlight. He clutched a bundle to his chest as I looked forward once more, weariness eating at my bones. From the bundle rose a feeble cry, but I had nothing left for the child. It took everything I could just to keep moving.

Then, the image grew dark. I waited, but nothing happened.

I opened my eyes.

"I will not show you the rest," Echo whispered. "You do not need to bear the same sorrows that I've had. My husband and child died in the Nightlands. There is nothing left for me in that dark world. I stay with you."

"What if something happens to you?" I asked. "There are some here who can see shadow-souls. Your kind is outlawed."

"If Pythia Golden-Eyes ends my existence, then I would rejoice. I've been seeking it out for centuries."

I frowned. "Why did Morius curse you like that?"

"Guilt," Echo murmured. "He wanted to save us at all costs. In the end, we would have rather perished."

"I am sorry," I said, wishing I could pat her hand as she did mine. I'd hug her if I could.

"You have given me a life after the curse," Echo replied. "I will be grateful for this, especially in the blessed end."

Arden squawked as the indentation on the bed smoothed.

AGRAMON INSISTED ON A GOWN of red silk for dinner that evening. It left nothing to the imagination, yet Agramon refused to honor my requests to don something different. My black hair was curled over one shoulder, completely down and loose. I wondered about the style. Sam always insisted I leave my hair down, which Gree tried to rebel against. What game was Agramon playing? I'd thought we were allies, but with Agramon, I knew I would never be a partner. An ally knows your plan. I was merely a willing pawn. My heart fell as I stared at myself, adjusting my breasts to ensure they stayed behind the thin fabric. I was not an ally to Agramon. He was using me.

When we entered the banquet hall, there were stares as everyone wore extravagant outfits to honor their sigils. Agramon had draped me in Sam's colors.

I didn't see my intended husband when we entered the room and wondered about his absence. Was there a council meeting? Surely Agramon would be there instead of by my side with a smug grin on his face. Luc had stayed behind to pack. He was ecstatic about it.

I sighed, meandering through the crowd as soon as Agramon let go of my arm. I passed Ingrid, who was shooting daggers at the low neckline of my dress. She probably wouldn't have been permitted to wear anything near so revealing. She could have my entire wardrobe for all I cared and Agramon with it.

"He wishes to speak with you," someone murmured in my ear. I turned to find Mellan eying the crowd. I searched for Sam. Agramon had immediately gone to stand by Elgar the Swift and Pythia Golden-Eyes, absorbed in whatever schemes he was conjuring.

"Who?"

"The Dragon," Mellan whispered, facing away from the crowd.

I shook my head. "I can't do this anymore. I told him that I wouldn't betray Sam."

"He has a way to save you—tomorrow night at two bells. One ship will lag and take you and Destrian to Morgania. You will be free. Your countrymen will be free."

"But I will have gone back on my word," I murmured. "I know how everyone feels about Sam, but he has always been a friend to me. I will not repay his kindness by stealing away the night before our wedding with another man. How cruel do you think I am?"

"I'm thinking of Aureliana," Mellan said. His fingers brushed mine, and I felt a piece of parchment slip into my hand. I clenched it tight, then switched my goblet over to cover the note. "I couldn't help her escape the fate of an unwilling marriage, but I can help you."

"I *chose* this," I insisted.

Mellan shook his head as he backed into the crowd. "I hope he may one day deserve you."

I looked over my shoulder. Sam was striding towards me, his eyes on the back of my dress. I shoved the piece of parchment into a welcome pocket.

"Did Agramon choose that gown?" he asked, coming up to my side and glaring at the opening where Mellan disappeared.

"Of course," I said, taking a sip of wine.

"I like the color," Sam said, turning his eyes back to me and traveling the length of my body. "I know the night is young, but I would be honored if you would come with me. There are things I wish to say."

I raised my brows. "Of course, my lord," I said, accepting his hand. As Sam began leading me away, I looked over my shoulder. Destrian stepped from an alcove, his eyes burning.

Sam led me into the corridors for the rooming quarters. I began to recognize the hall and shot Sam a questioning look. He stopped outside his doors and unlocked them.

"What is this?" I asked, stepping into his receiving room. Candles glowed on every available surface. Carpeted along the floor was a blanket of rose petals.

"I told you that one of these times, I would get it right." Sam sank to his knee. "Rowyn of Morgania, will you marry me?"

I tried to smile, shooing Destrian from my mind. "I already told you I would."

"I know," Sam said, his voice rough. He pulled something from his pocket and held it out to me. "But we need this if we are to start again." He grasped my hand and slipped a ring on my finger. I looked down. It was a signet ring of a bear rearing on a red field. I met Sam's eye.

"It is lovely," I said, my voice wooden, and lowered my hand. "Thank you for the gift."

A crease appeared on Sam's forehead. "You are not pleased."

"It isn't that." I bit my lip. "The problems between us, they remain."

"How?" Sam rose angrily. "The Morganites are gone from Bruin. That was the bargain. I refuse to be forever punished for doing my job."

"That's just it," I said. "It was the same with the war and the conscripted men running away and putting the weakest on the front lines."

"What would you have me do?" Sam asked, his hands outstretched. "What more can I do to get you to trust me again?"

"Relinquish command as general," I said, thinking back to Sam's conversation with Captain Diardo. The captain had warned as much.

"If that is what my emperor wishes, then I will gladly step down." Sam's voice had never been so guarded around me before. He was lying.

"The soldiers hate me, and war has already turned you into a villain once. I ask that it not turn you into a villain again."

"And what of your Lord Destrian? Would you ask this of him?"

"No," I said. "But I'm not marrying him."

Sam brushed a lock of hair off my cheek. "After the quinquennial, we will return to Bruin, and everything will return to normal, I promise."

I stepped towards the fireplace. Hidden among the candles was my miniature portrait, sent to the capitol at my keepers' request. "Where you hid my eyes from everything I would hate to see about what you do and how Bruin works?" I lifted the painting, running my fingers over the face. What would that girl have said if she could see me now?

Sam came up behind me, wrapping his arms around my waist and resting his chin on my shoulder. "I love you. At least give me a chance at making you happy."

"I am," I said honestly. "I will give you that chance, but I'm telling you what would make me happy."

"That's all I ask," Sam said, strengthening his grip. "Until that day comes," he whispered, "my love will be enough for the both of us."

I held him tight, feeling a small swell of hope at his words. It wasn't until I walked back to my room alone that the bubble of hope burst, shattering into a million pieces. Sam knew I loved another. He didn't care about my happiness at all.

Agramon was gone when I entered our rooms. "Keep watch," I asked Echo before pulling out the parchment that Mellan had slipped me. I unfurled it and recognized Destrian's measured hand immediately.

Two bells tomorrow night at the second pier.

The Avalon will wait until four.

I will always fight for you, my love, to the end.

I wiped the tears cascading down my cheeks. It was what I'd been dreaming of since that night almost a year ago in Darkport when I'd hoped Destrian would rescue me. He was finally fighting for me, but it was too late.

If I didn't have my word, I had nothing.

I carefully held the parchment to the candle and watched the flames consume my last means of escape.

Chapter 38

"YOU LOOK BEAUTIFUL," Gree said, setting a curl over my shoulder. The white dress I wore was cut low and made of lace. Duke Agramon had chosen the style and seen me through the multiple fittings. Gree had tucked white roses along the crown of my head. It clashed with my blue-black hair. My marking from Conal blazed on my pale chest, a stark reminder of what I was about to leave behind. My home, my forefathers—everything I held dear hung in the balance of what I was about to do.

But I'd given my word. Thinking back to my time in the Nightlands with Destrian, I nearly laughed at my naivety. Worrying about what my father and mother would say to my love for Destrian was nothing, nothing at all, compared to what they would say about what I was about to do now.

I would be the bride of the Butcher of Bruin. It felt as though the blood of those who he'd slaughtered in the emperor's wars was on my hands as well. But I'd given my word. There was nothing else to say except, I do.

I thought back to the day before—the conscripted Morganians filing onto the ships, overseen by all of the council, the commanders, and me.

I'd hugged Luc before he left the palace. He'd held me close and kissed the top of my head. "I hope you know what you're doing," he whispered.

I smiled up at him. "I'm just happy to see that you are going home. Say hello to Ferris for me."

Luc brushed a finger along my cheek and shouldered his pack. Arden squawked from her perch in the window. I walked over to the bird and shifted her to my arm. "Take her with you," I said, stroking Arden's head. "Why should she be trapped here too? She belongs at home."

Luc smiled and accepted Arden's claws. He moved them to his own shoulder guard and chucked me on the chin. "Good luck," he said, striding from the room to join the hundreds amassing outside the palace walls.

Agramon had taken me to watch at my request. Luc was down there somewhere, along with other boys I'd known from home. Espiria would have hope for tomorrow, and it wasn't because of me, it was because of Destrian. I looked at him out of the corner of my eye. He was watching the men board the ships, his hands in his pockets, his face somber. Destrian would know by morning that I was rejecting him once and for all.

Sam tightened his grip on my hand.

I would learn to love him. I'd nearly been there in Bruin before he butchered the conscripted men trying to flee the fields. Now that my brethren were gone from Bruin, I felt I could make a life there. Sam had said that he would consider stepping down as commander if the situation called for it. If he did that and the soldiers were moved from Bruin, then all the better.

I looked to the horizon. The first ships had already headed out to sea, their sails unfurled. I sent a light wind to hurry them on their journey.

In the distance, something was flying in the sky, growing larger. Arden was coming back to me. I held out my arm and she landed hard. Arden gave my ear a gentle peck, as though to scold me for sending her away.

I forced away the tears as I placed her on my shoulder so she would have a better view. We watched the men together, and I felt as though a weight was being lifted from my shoulders.

"Is she ready?" Duke Agramon's voice floated in.

"Yes, Your Grace," Gree said, bowing as she stepped away.

I rolled my eyes. If there any happiness to be found in my situation, it was that I would finally be able to send Gree away and hire my own lady's maid.

"I brought you something," Agramon said, stepping behind me.

I watched him in the looking glass as he held up a silver diadem with a crescent in the center, the face of

Imor.

"It's beautiful." The weight of the metal came to rest on my head.

"Come," Duke Agramon said, his hands on my shoulders. "It is important we are not late for the ceremony." Agramon looked out to the sky, but I wondered about his distraction. I controlled the weather, and I demanded a clear wedding day.

The duke held the door for me, and I stepped out to meet my fate. I hoped in the end my clan would forgive me for everything I'd done. What I wouldn't give to sit in our cavern hall once more, smelling the sweet scent of Morwood pine burning in the hearth while Ferris and Luc joked next to me. Grandmother weaving a plait in my hair while Pria stitched next to her, smiling and laughing at Luc's jokes.

The dream, or memory, drifted away, and I let it. I accepted my fate. It was my duty to be strong for them, whether they knew it or not. I would be a warrior till the end. Agramon hadn't spoken again about rescuing me, and Echo had sent another dream of him with Princess Willene. For two days I waited for him to do something, but he didn't interfere with any of the preparations. On the contrary, he'd helped plan the wedding down to the flower choices. I'd told him that I planned to go through with it, and perhaps, he was listening to my wishes.

542

I wondered what my life would be like as the baron's wife. At least he cared for me. Maybe, after some time, I could encourage him to disband the Fields of Forgotten Men altogether. We could send all the men back to their families and the lives they left behind. Even bringing the rain to the east didn't seem so bad. After all, it was the poor who were starving. We could travel the land together, bringing rain to those who needed it. Giving life to others, if not to myself. I could live with myself if that was the path we were on.

But then I looked up at Agramon's face, and my dreams came crashing down. He looked nearly gleeful, as if his wildest dreams were about to come true, and I couldn't help but shudder. No, the life I'd just dreamed for myself was not going to come true. There was no way Duke Agramon would let me off that easy. He had a plan for us. I would forever be under his thumb.

"Oh Rowyn," Agramon said, tilting his head to the side. "You wouldn't want to forget your sword."

I glared at him. Iranoct was a known gift from Destrian. How insulted would Sam feel if I wore it? Agramon was just trying to get into his head on his wedding day. Then I stopped and turned back to my room. Perhaps it was a warning. I returned inside and buckled the sword to my waist. My knives were already on my thigh. Agramon smiled and gripped my arm, ushering me down the corridor.

I took in a shuddering breath as we walked down the deserted hallway. It seemed the whole palace was absent, probably filling the Crystal Temple as we spoke.

"It is custom for the bride to ride to the altar," Duke Agramon was saying as we walked down the palace steps to the drive filled with guards from Solin, Bruin, and Somme. "It's tradition."

The emperor and his family rode in a carriage ahead of us. I mounted Starstruck, my eyes on the gilded back of the armored coach. Agramon mounted beside me, and the procession began slowly through the palace gates and into the city. Sam's mercenaries and other soldiers from all parts of the empire lined the road, pushing back the crowds from the city. I recognized the Sons of Sol, the suns etched into their foreheads, their shouts angry as they cursed me. Several threw food or other items and were quickly beaten by the soldiers there to keep the peace.

I took a deep breath and looked at the back of Starstruck's head instead, trying to ignore the hate-filled slurs flung at me from the mob.

I could love him. I could be happy with Sam. I *was* happy with Sam.

Slowly, we made our way to the Crystal Temple until, finally, I found myself at its steps. The demeanor of the lords and ladies was a far cry from how the commoners had felt for me, for their faces were wide with smiles and laughter. The ladies were throwing all manner of flowers onto the steps before me. The men shouted out crude comments about my gown and how much the baron would enjoy it on the floor.

I ignored them all as Duke Agramon appeared beside me.

"Come on, we've taken too long as it is," he murmured, turning me to face him. He lifted my hair and draped it over my shoulder before offering his arm. Beyond him I saw the empress standing with the little prince, holding his hand as she waited behind her husband.

The temple doors swung open, and I was marched inside. Those on the outside didn't even bother coming in, for it was hot, and they could see just as well through the glass that encased the temple and showed the eye of Sol above. The sky was cloudless.

I walked down the aisle as music played, announcing the emperor's and my arrival. Through the faces of nobility, I saw Mellan in the crowd. His arms were crossed, his face unreadable. Pedr and Araceli stood together, Pedr giving me a small wave. Araceli's eyes were somber. Destrian stood next to them.

Even though I knew he would be there, my heart dropped to the pit of my stomach. I wanted to cry out to him. To have him take me away.

Destrian's face was twisted in fury, his hair nearly

smoking.

How could I tell him that it was he that I wanted? To forget what I'd said before. That I would give anything to be with him once more. I missed his smell, his laughter, and how I felt in his arms. But those were memories now, never to be relived. Not if I wanted him safe. Not if I wanted my people saved.

I tore my eyes away from Destrian and looked up to the crystal altar. Sam had donned a richly embroidered coat of red, gold, and black. His hair had been trimmed. He wore his sword at his waist, like always, but he also wore a golden chain, his noble jewelry for the barony. When I met his eye, he smiled. I smiled shakily back.

The emperor and empress stepped up before us and sat behind the altar along with their guards. Mem paused in her scan of the room to grace me with a nod. Lesedi's eyes were more marked, her eyebrow raised as if evaluating me. I knew Lesedi pitied me, as I pitied her. In that, at least, we were equal. The princesses sitting next to the empress watched me, their eyes shining. They were too young to see the resignation in my eyes. They whispered excitedly to each other and waved flowers at me. I couldn't help but look away.

I looked down at my feet, walking on the petals that led up to the altar. Too soon, I was there, and Samael had taken my hands in his.

"Love," he said, squeezing my fingers, "look at me."

I saw hunger in Sam's eyes. There was no going back.

"Today is a glorious day in the eyes of Sol," Solston Gowther said, raising his arms. The crowd silenced, standing solemn.

"Sol is rising today—as he has risen with each and every day—to see the union of Rowyn the Morganite, Lady of the North, to Sol's son, Samael, Baron of Bruin. All of you who have come, bear witness to this union, and bless it as Sol blesses us each day."

The Solston nodded at Agramon, who dipped his hand in a basin filled with soil. "Repeat after me, Your Grace. By this earth, I bless this union before the eye of Sol. May the marriage be fruitful."

"By this earth, I bless this union before the eye of Sol. May the marriage be fruitful." Agramon met my eye as he traced a symbol on my forehead in dirt while the Solston did the same to Sam.

They stepped to the next pedestal, filled with water, and dipped their hands in.

"By this water, I bless this union before the eye of Sol. May the marriage flow around hardship and strife."

Again, Duke Agramon traced the blessing on my forehead, hopefully washing away the dirt he'd left before.

What was going through Destrian's mind? What I wouldn't give for Duke Agramon's power, to read his mind. Destrian owed me nothing, and yet . . . he was still here.

I was brought back to the present as Duke Agramon and the Solston raised small pieces of kindling with little flames flickering on the ends. By all the gods, they couldn't mean . . . But they did. Duke Agramon pressed the flame into my forehead, tracing another blessing, and I hissed in pain. Luckily the flame was small, but I wondered how many poor brides had put up with flames or sparks showering onto their dresses.

Finally, Duke Agramon and the Solston ended the blessings by blowing in our faces.

The Solston turned us to the crowd who shouted out blessings. The Solston let them go on for a moment before raising his hands again. He turned to me when the crowd fell silent. "Rowyn the Morganite, do you take Samael of Bruin as your husband, to serve in his home as a confidant, to bow to him and take refuge in his protection?"

I gritted my teeth at the vows. I looked to Sam, who'd taken my hand. There was no going back. I'd given Sam my word. "I do," I said, my voice strong and clear.

Solston Gowther turned to Sam. "Do you, Samael of Bruin, take Rowyn the Morganite as your wife, to defend her name and protect her as your own?"

"I do," Sam said, choking on the words. He cleared

his throat. "I do," he said louder.

The Solston nodded.

An excited murmur filled the halls.

Solston Gowther raised his hands.

The murmur turned into a roar. I frowned, looking toward the crowd. The Solston hadn't yet finished the ritual, but the nobles weren't watching the ceremony anymore. Their heads were pointed to the sky, their hands up.

The light filling the temple began to fade. I looked up through the crystal panes. The face of Imor was passing before Sol. The hackles on the back of my neck stood on end as I looked down at my gems.

My magic was gone.

Chapter 39

I MOR HAD OVERTAKEN the eye of Sol. I could see the light around the shadow that was my god, and I held my breath, even as those around me began to murmur. The sky darkened as though it were night.

"What does it mean?"

"Is it a curse?"

"Sol will forsake us!"

Something whistled past. I'd know that sound anywhere. I spun, looking past the altar to where the emperor slumped, an arrow pinning his neck to the throne behind him.

The emperor was dead.

Suddenly, a sound louder than anything I could imagine blasted through the crystal panes, shattering inward as two explosions rocked either side of the temple.

Sam lost his hold on my hand, and I was thrown to the ground. Shards blasted past me, raining on all the nobles below.

I scrambled to my feet as a pane of glass from the roof smashed beside me. I shielded my face from the fragments, then looked up and saw Agramon. He'd moved to the Solin soldiers who had been standing in the aisles to keep order. His eyes weren't on the sky; they were on the dead emperor and his family. The Solin soldiers began to move.

I looked down at my gems.

My magic wasn't working.

The emperor's protection spells hadn't saved him.

Agramon was vulnerable.

I pulled my sword from the sheath and climbed over a piece of the altar, trying to get to Agramon.

Solston Gowther grabbed me and held my hand aloft. "It's the Morganite!" he shouted, dragging me after him. "Sol will forsake us all for celebrating this infidel!"

I thrust Iranoct through the man's gut, then pulled the sword back out and turned back to the duke. The sky was already lightening, as though a new dawn had risen. I could feel the niggling of my magic at the back of my mind. If I were to kill Agramon, I would have to be faster.

A group of people ran past, presumably heading to an exit. I recognized Del. Her eyes were wide in fear, tears mixing with blood that coursed down her face from several cuts. Del's grand creation, a celebration of Sol's light, was now destroyed.

Someone grabbed my arm.

I was about to run my sword through him, but I hauled up short when I saw the shock of red hair.

"Come," Destrian shouted, covering his head as another rain of glass came down. The smoke from the explosions began to fill the sanctuary, choking us.

"No!" I yelled, pulling my hand from his grasp. "Now's my only chance to end this!"

"Rowyn, please!" Destrian urged, trying to pull me away.

"This is Agramon!" I shoved Destrian off. I couldn't let this chance slip through my fingers.

I strode toward Agramon once more, but it was already too late. I felt the roar of magic return.

Suddenly, the weight of small fingers pressed into mine. I looked down in surprise.

Prince Artian was clutching my hand, his face covered in tears, his eyes wide. "Mother said to come to you," he sobbed. "She said to come to you if I was scared."

I looked back at the empress. The Solin guards had surrounded her. She and Mem were arguing with them as they looked around themselves.

"Rowyn!" Sam was shouting on the other side of the altar, shoving noblemen aside as he tried to make his way to me over the rubble and flames. He reached toward me. "We need to get out of here!"

I clutched the little boy's hand, realizing that he wasn't Prince Artian anymore. He was the emperor. The most powerful person in the realm was a five-year-old child, clutching my hand in tears, completely vulnerable.

Agramon's face was filled with anger as he shouted orders over the chaos.

How long would the little emperor last against Agramon? Would he claim guardianship over the boy and use him as a puppet to his rule? Would the boy survive to adulthood? I realized then what the gods required of me. Artian couldn't stay in Somme if he were to live. Lesedi had no power to stop Agramon anymore.

I looked back to Sam.

"You are my wife!" he shouted angrily. He grabbed a soldier from Solin who'd stepped in front of him and threw him to the side. "He doesn't control you anymore!"

I faced Agramon once again, meeting his eyes. The guards from Solin had already spotted the child emperor and were running toward us.

I pulled the little boy into my arms and called a wind that swept us up into the smoke. I saw Sam's face as we passed into the cloud. He was shouting my name.

Sam's words filled my mind. *Do what they least expect.*

I was sure he'd never expected me to kidnap the child emperor.

I would need to conserve my magic. I didn't yet know my next move, and I would need to have full capabilities. What would Agramon expect me to do next?

I set us down not far from the temple. Chaos reigned in the streets as people ran from the blackened clouds caused by the explosions. I carried the prince into a doorway and stopped to think.

I needed more weapons. I needed time. I needed allies. I had nothing but the most powerful child in the empire and my powers. If Agramon didn't have the young prince, his claim to the throne would be tenuous. Rumors of missing royals meant that factions of loyal subjects would openly rebel against Agramon. He would never be able to cement his hold. I had to get away.

Agramon would expect me to fly.

Agramon would expect me to go straight to Destrian.

He'd first look for me in places I knew.

I looked to the west, toward the port. Agramon knew I hated sailing.

I picked up the prince and raced through the street. I chanced upon a saddled horse pulling at his reins in fear of the mob. I tossed the prince onto the saddle, slashed half my dress off with a knife, and jumped up behind him.

I needed to get out of the city. It would be impossible for me not to be noticed. I was wearing a wedding dress covered in blood and soot.

I rode hard, clutching the prince tightly as we wound

our way through the streets. I looked over my shoulder and saw a group of soldiers bearing down on us. They bore the white tunics and golden eagle of Solin.

Agramon's men.

They'd spotted me.

They urged their mounts forward, bearing down on me until I could see the whites of their eyes.

A screech echoed off the buildings around us. Arden stretched her claws toward one of the mounted soldiers. Suddenly, the falcon's figure grew hazy, and the talons morphed into fingers, the feathers into bare skin. A nude woman gripped the guard's tunic and threw him into the street, startling his horse. The animal reared, slamming into the other two riders beside it. Animals and men were flung into the street.

The woman rose, her unruly blonde hair whipping around her face. She turned. A turquoise gemstone was embedded in her brow. Her eyes met my shocked ones.

Recognition hit me like a bolt of lightning. "Fin!" I screamed, wheeling my horse around. Prince Artian scrabbled at the reins, holding on as tight as he could as the startled horse twisted beneath us.

Fin pulled a crossbow from one of the fallen horses, then turned toward the other guards who'd reined to a halt behind us.

"Go!" Fin shouted, turning away and leveraging the crossbow against her bare ribs to pepper the guards with arrow after arrow, reloading with practiced ease.

"Fin!" I called again, sending a bolt of lightning to the last guard who'd managed to get close to her. Fin raised her arms. Feathers sprouted from her skin, the blonde hair disappearing, and she rose into the air on Arden's wings, screeching her call above us. I watched her for a moment, shock freezing me into place, until Artian's fidgeting pulled me from my thoughts and I continued through the streets under Arden's shadow.

ARDEN WAS PERCHED ON MY SHOULDER as I looked out over the port, my eyes on a large battleship.

"I can't believe I've had you all this time, my friend," I murmured, stroking Arden's feathers.

Wind picked up the green flag bearing the golden snake of Iora. Admiral Abelard's personal command vessel.

I needed to find the prince a refuge. Someplace safe to keep him until I could figure out what to do.

Until I could make a deal.

A place that Agramon would least suspect. A place where not even Sam would find me.

I would need to hide where they least suspected.

I looked down at the prince. "Do you think you

could get us on that ship?"

The boy took a deep breath, his blue eyes wide, and nodded.

The End

The story concludes in Book 5

THE TEMPEST
QUEEN

Preorder today on Amazon.com.

Please be sure to leave an honest review
of
Empire of Dust
at Amazon.com or Goodreads.com.

Follow us online!

https://www.elliottvandruff.com

https://www.facebook.com/elliottvandruff/

https://twitter.com/EVandruff

Make sure to sign up for our newsletter
to receive communications on new re-
leases and special content!

Acknowledgements

I want to take the time to acknowledge the individuals who assisted in the creation of *Empire of Dust*. The first is my sister, Olivia, to whom this book is dedicated. I spent many evenings at her home while she helped me detail scenes and gave the characters life. Words cannot express how much I appreciate her patience and feedback.

An immense thanks to my husband who continues to champion my writing. It means so much to have someone believe in what you can do. My dreams are realized because of his unwavering support.

Lastly, my editor, Cayce Berryman from Kingsman Editing, has done a fantastic job again. Her outstanding work and feedback brought the manuscript to a polished product that I am immensely proud of.